To the King
a Daughter

Tor Books by Andre Norton

Tor Books by Sasha Miller

To the King
a Daughter

THE BOOK

OF THE OAK

Andre Norton &

Sasha Miller

TOR®

A TOM DOHERTY ASSOCIATES BOOK

NEW YORK

TO THE KING A DAUGHTER

Copyright © 2000 by Andre Norton, Ltd., & Sasha Miller

A Tor Book

Published by Tom Doherty Associates, LLC

175 Fifth Avenue

New York, NY 10010

Tor® is a registered trademark of Tom Doherty Associates, LLC.

Design by Lisa Pifher

Library of Congress Cataloging-in-Publication Data

ISBN 0-312-87336-0

Printed in the United States of America

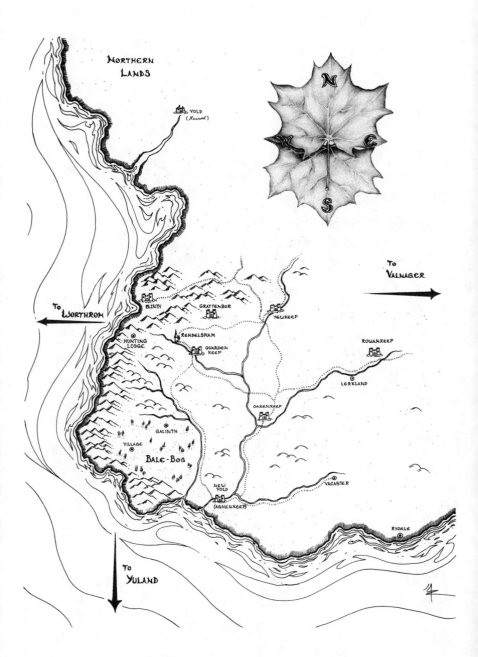

NORTHERN
LANDS

YOLD
(Ruined)

N

W   E

S

TO
VALMAGER

BLINTH

GRATTENBOR

YEWKEEP

ROWANKEEP

TO WORTHROM

HUNTING
LODGE

RENDELSHAM

GUARDEN
KEEP

LERKLAND

OAKENKEEP

GALINTH

VILLAGE

BALE-BOG

VACASTER

NEW
YOLD

ASHENKEEP

RYDALE

TO
YULAND

To the King a Daughter

Prologue

*J*t is only to be expected that all along the roads known to travelers there are shrines, some moss-grown and older than the last three dynasties of rulers. There are also the fanes—the cathedrals—and the lesser churches and chapels in every village and town. And does not the Great Fane of the Glowing overshine all of Rendel? These sanctuaries are in honor of that which cannot be seen or understood but under the rule of which, all life abides.

Yet the Almighty One remains in toils to the dark-handed Weavers, who know neither mercy nor concern for the lives they twist into their Web Everlasting. It is only needful that the pattern be not too greatly altered; so here a life-thread is broken, frayed, and left, and there one snapped is woven into another time and place, and sometimes even into a different square of Time's Web. The living may believe that they are free to make decisions, to act as they believe fit, but their thread goes through the fingers of a Weaver. Thus, some live, some die, Kingdoms rise and fall and are forgotten; yet still the Web shows no break. Does the Unknown ever view that weaving? If not, of what use are the petitions of lower life? Threads only, yet what a spread of color! What a net of history hangs ever on the Loom!

However, there are tales in plenty of those whose threads were entangled strangely and who came to ends far different from their beginnings.

Look at that part of the weaving which is the country of Rendel, great in its own eyes at least, for it is in the courtyard of the Fane of the Glowing that the Four Trees stand, and in a window of that Fane can be seen the reflection of the Dark Hands. On one night of autumn sleet and the courageous hold on life, there began in this reflection the weaving of a new thread, the snapping of an old one, and changes believed impossible years earlier.

Weave well now, you silent fingers, for the pattern is no longer twisted in the familiar way.

One

🌿

he chill gray mist of early morning had become a driving sword blade of sleet before noon when their last horse foundered. This was the Bale-Bog, or the edge of it, and no sane Outlander forced his way into that sludge of bottomless pools and unsteady islets unless the need was urgent.

The woman who had been plucked from the exhausted horse, escaping being borne down with it just in time, managed somehow to keep to her feet, but only because there was a hard, broad shoulder and a tough, war-trained body there to support her.

Instinctively, her hands pressed her swollen belly, and a grimace of pain twisted her once-beautiful, now gaunt features.

"How do you, Lady Alditha?"

The rumble of that voice came from the chest very close to her ear. She could feel under the sodden folds of a trooper's cloak a fineness of mail, which no common trooper could hope to wear. Forcing all sign of pain from her, she looked up into the weathered face of Hasard, the Marshal of the House of Ash. The icy wind drove the ends of a wide, gray mustache against his half-hidden lips.

"I do as well as I might, my lord." She brought out the words one by one, as if they were separately strung on a too-loose cord. Somehow, she summoned the pitiful shadow of a smile.

Two men wearing beggars' trappings over studded leather were stripping the bags from the downed horse. She could not see their faces. For a moment, her vision dimmed, overridden by the thrust of pain that swept through her. They were all who were left—just the two soldiers and the man who had once led the Ash host. And somehow she believed it was the fierce determination of the man now steadying her that had brought them also to this ending. She must strive to honor him with her strength, such as it was, and not betray his faithfulness by a display of female weakness.

Their greatest need was shelter. Without shelter, they would all be stark by morning. Ashenhold, where they might have been safe, was denied them. Again her hand supported her heavy belly.

Hasard—his appearance far different from what it had been in the days of his splendor as the Marshal of Ashenhold and the command he had led with keen wits and all the knowledge of one soldiering from boyhood—still sheltered her as best he could. He made his body a shield between her and as many of those icy blasts as he could wall away. There was not time now—

So many lives dashed out, ended by dagger in the dark, by sword during day, by poison offered with a sly smile that touched only one corner of the mouth. So many women dead, all of them Ash. She tried to shut it out of her memory but could not escape the fact that not only did she exist because of the child she bore—whom her pursuers would pluck from her living body if they could—but that the very child also brought her the greatest of danger. Once she had thought to deny; no more. In her womb she carried the heir not only to Ash, but to Oak as well, if the King's wishes would prevail when it came to heir-naming, for this was his only progeny, whether legal or not. Certainly her child was greater than she and her present companions combined. They had fled on this very night, bearing the Ash badge, trying to escape the Yew badge of the Queen who would reach beyond death itself for revenge, should that be necessary.

"Sir?" The men who had dealt with the horse awaited orders. She felt rather than saw Hasard's head lift. His hoarse voice broke through the screech of the storm. "The river—"

Ah, yes, the river; her wits were growing more murky. That waterway, part natural, part man-enhanced, had always been a merchant's path, but in fairer weather. Tonight it might not gain them safety in either direction, not from those who pursued, but there was no other road for them to follow.

One of the men pushed past her and her loyal protector. Could they indeed have reached a previously prepared point of safety in spite of the storm, despite her weakness?

With all the Ash Family pride she could muster, she kept to her feet when, a few moments later, Hasard urged her forward, step by faltering step. However, she could not go far on sheer nerve alone. She was near to fainting when she became dimly aware of being lifted, deposited on a damp pile of something that smelled like dead fish and things long rotten. It must have been a litter. She knew that it swung as they boarded a raftlike boat meant for the transport of heavy goods. Her teeth closed on the hand she raised to her mouth, and drew blood.

They needed—least of all, now—the travail that despite her inexperience, she was sure was near upon her. For as long as possible, she must keep silent.

Then it all became as if some dream had descended upon her, carrying her within it. She heard a shout, a muffled cry from near to hand, and knew not if it had been she who had raised the outcry or one of her companions. A boat. Yes, they were on a boat; she knew that much.

The twang of a bow—strong yew, given by the Will of the Above as a weapon—cut through the dream. Between pangs, she spoke, her head bent forward so that she might address the babe she carried within her.

"Oak and Yew, Ash and Rowan—truly yours, my son, my daughter, whomever I carry to the end."

Pain like none she had known before blotted out her world. The sounds of battle went almost unheeded. She was only faintly aware that men died beside her, that Hasard, even with an arrow through him, leaped into the water and with all the strength left in him, pushed the boat on into the dead gloom of the Bale-Bog, that core of danger. The craft lurched forward and immediately began dipping into the current, starting to spin. If she had had time, she might have become ill. Instead, she fainted.

A lifetime later, there came warmth, faint light, a shadow bending over her.

"Push, woman!" commanded that shadow. "Push as we must when we are in your case."

Weakly, she tried to obey, willing to answer any order that might put an end to her torment. Pressure. The slippery feeling of something departing her body. Then she felt herself likewise slipping away. Darkness began closing in, but not before she heard a voice, far off and very faint.

"A girl child—"

*

Zazar held the squalling baby aloft in the full light of the hearth fire. Healthy she was, with lusty cries that spoke well of the infant's chances for survival. Large, too—aye, one such as this would indeed have nigh torn apart her bearer. A fair fluff now dried on its head, and already it gazed upon the world, its cries temporarily stilled, looking as if for a moment it recognized, with knowledge beyond its age, where it was. And perhaps *why* it was.

"The woman be dead." The crooked-legged crone who served the Wysen-wyf looked at her mistress. With her thumb, she indicated the body. "She was quality folk, but we all come to the same end sooner or later. Do we give the babe also to the underwater-eaters? Joal will not take kindly to the sheltering of Outlander."

Zazar, proceeding after the fashion, which had been hers for years, washed the baby and wrapped it in the softest of her woven reed-fluff blankets. "We need a tit. Use the bottle on the second shelf," she said, as if she had not even heard Kazi's question.

Grumbling, Kazi obeyed; when the babe opened its mouth again to cry in hunger, the tit—heavy with the mixture Zazar employed to foster all manner of orphans—was ready for it.

"Joal be coming—" Kazi began again. With her good foot, she pushed at the limp, bloodied body of the woman. She sighed.

Zazar knew that Kazi had already managed, or so she hoped, to filch unseen from the dead one's cloak a shiny circle of a brooch set with a blue stone. It was undoubtedly the most beautiful piece of jewelry Kazi had ever had. In fact, it was the only piece of jewelry she had ever had. Zazar had taken some effort to instill in Kazi the certainty that her mistress had eyes not only in the back of her head, but all around it as well. Let Kazi think she had overlooked the brooch and because of that, wouldn't take it away from her. Actually, she didn't care one way or another.

"Yes, I agree. The woman is dead," Zazar said calmly. "Let Joal have what remains of her. The child, however . . ." She spoke slowly. The baby seemed satisfied, full-fed and sleepy. Zazar leaned closer to the lantern that lit up all the tools of her calling—bones, and seeds, dried leaves, the stiff, stark body of an orb snake.

With care, she drew aside the wrapping about the child. She had to be completely certain. Yes, the resemblance to both the mother and the father showed even now on the infant's unformed features. No mistaking the color of that hair-fluff or the future regal shape of nose, lips, face. She had seen the woman many times in the scrying-pot, and everyone in Rendel knew the man on sight. Further, she had confirmed her visions with the bones. Zazar's smile was gone; her lips tightened. Oh, yes, she had read the bones many times over in these past ten days, and every time they had told the same tale.

She held one who would be a *changer*, perhaps would even break the bonds of the Bog-land itself. Would it be for good or for ill? Zazar did not know; the bones refused to tell her. For a moment, she was tempted. It would be so very easy to put her hand over the small mouth and nose and let daughter follow mother, as any of the Bog-people would demand that she do.

But somehow, somehow there was that which forbade such action. She knew what she nursed. Before covering the little body again, she nodded. It was not to Kazi that she spoke, but to the Something that could ever command them all.

"To the King." She carefully chose the words of state that should rightfully have greeted the child after the trumpet blasts proclaiming its arrival: "To our most worthy Lord King, a daughter!"

Kazi huddled, curled protectively into a ball, and suddenly Zazar turned to look at her, as if remembering she had a listener. She loosed one forefinger from the hold she kept upon the babe and pointed at her servant. "Be silent!"

A thread of Power went out from that finger and enveloped Kazi. Zazar watched it vanish into the woman's skin. It might not be Kazi's will that would keep her silent now and in the future, but this would.

The Wysen-wyf did not rise but moved on her knees to the still body of the noblewoman. In the firelight, the woman's gaunt face looked old and pinched, with scarcely a trace remaining of the beauty that had once been the pride of her kindred. Zazar studied it carefully and laughed.

"So my little servants of the night cackle and squeak to a purpose, do they? Ashenkin, Ash-daughter, where is your man now? Perhaps in time you would have prevailed, but you never really had him save by the lusts of the body, and those quickly fade." She inclined her head a fraction. "Yet you bore the child reluctantly. I remember your servant who came to me searching for the medicine that I know you never touched. Was it because of one Power or another?" She paused, thinking. "Or was it because you bore a *changer* and it would not set you free?"

There could be no answer from the dead, and at this time, Zazar had no desire to cast the bones and see any farther than this room and this moment.

Kazi broke the silence timidly. "Is not named. The baby—"

That was true; a girl must be mother-named, for custom is strong. Yet those mother lips would never shape any sound again.

"Then I will name her," Zazar stated, almost as if she expected to be denied. "Ashenkin she is, and bane of she who bore her she was. She is named Ashen Deathdaughter!"

Kazi uttered a squeal of protest. "Say it not! Say it not!"

"She will be Ashen, and for the rest, forget it now, Kazi."

Mud and bramble-slash had dimmed the bravery of the royal surcoats the soldiers wore, but even in twilight, it was possible to see the tufts of feathers each man wore in his helm socket, and the design of the Yew badge—a circle of yew leaves surmounted by a bow—that each bore upon breast and back. Most strode away from the dead horse to cluster together, awaiting orders. One man, the best tracker among them, was half crouched reading sign on the muddied ground.

"They was headed there, m'lord." He nodded toward the bank of the canal-river. "Tracks still fresh. We be close behind them, right enough. I think they carried sommat. Their steps is heavier than they should be."

Lord Lackel of the House Troops of Her Gracious Ladyship the Queen, the man who stood a little apart, his hands curved into fists resting on his hips, moved now.

"Hasard, the old wolf, has run his last trail—or has he? Down to the bank with you," he told the tracker. "See what signs lie for the reading there. Hasard did not have much time." Now a bear's snarl showed beneath the shadow of his helm. "Yet with that twisty one, who can tell?"

It was plain that he spoke more to himself than to those he commanded, and there was a kind of wary admiration in his last tone.

Someone shouted from the waterside. The men fell into order, steel out. As driven as their prey might be, no man would go defenseless to this meeting. Their quarry might not be too exhausted to defend themselves.

The Yew soldiers passed by the deep gouge left by the prow of a boat to concentrate on something else, a limp body that lay face down, arms rising and falling with the swish of the current. An arrow jutted tall and deadly from between its shoulders. No arrow of theirs, they knew by the blue bandings of its fletching. Ash color. As one, they drew toward each other, eyes alert to any change in their surroundings. At least the wind had dropped so that the shrubs and tree branches had ceased their wild dance. The man who reached the body first hooked hands in the sword belt and with an effort, drew the corpse fully ashore. He did not turn it over at once, being far more interested in the arrow.

"Well?" demanded the officer. "Which other of the squads has outrun us?"

"None of ours, m'lord." The tracker flicked the stiff shaft of the arrow with his finger. "This fellow was unlucky. He missed the big fight." The man thought for a moment. "That, or else . . ."

"Do you know him?" Lord Lackel leaned closer now.

"Can't tell, m'lord."

It took the tracker and one of the soldiers to roll the body over and expose the muddied face to the light.

"Not known to me, m'lord. Tch. He was just a younker. But look you here." He used an end of water-heavy cloth to wipe away the concealing mud from a buckle that supported a quiver sling. The buckle bore a distinctive leaf inscribed upon it. "Now that there we has seen before."

"Ash!" Lackel pulled at his dripping beard. "But then, why dead from a comrade's hand?"

The tracker shrugged. "True, this be Ashen-branded. I understand it not. Maybe someone has stole Ash arrows, used 'em to throw us off." He and his fellow had ceased to keep a hold on the body, and now something hidden beneath the current seized upon the corpse with force enough to put both men into a panic and send them clawing their way back up the bank.

"Look you!" one of the other men called sharply. The dusk was growing thicker by the moment, but a shroud of mist parted and they could all see at a distance the boat, caught in a tangle of drifting vegetation. A body slid from the boat, into the water.

Lackel did not move toward this at once, for his thoughts were too bemused. An Ash arrow for an Ash kill! It was not just the personal guards of the one he served that had been a part of the hunt, but those of the woman's own Family as well. Rough justice indeed, unstoppable, brought even to this backwater. Brave Hasard, braver than any other he had ever known. He touched the edge of his helm as if he would salute an overlord, or at least a worthy enemy. Now he was chilled by more than the wind. She who had dispatched him on this wild mission was said to have her own methods of spying. And it was also whispered that some who served her did not wear human aspect. But such thoughts were best kept to one's self. . . .

Out in the stream, the boat dipped and dragged as if some weight had attached itself to its stern. Then the water about it was whipped to a frenzy of splashes, and those on the bank retreated. The reports of what might be encountered deep in the Bale-Bog were bloodily graphic. They saw a man's hand slip from the rough wood as a second body was dragged from the boat and under the water. Not all had fallen to arrows, Ash or otherwise.

"Lord! There by the bow!"

They had no torch lit, but the pale glow that hung above

Andre Norton & Sasha Miller

the boat, looking like some corpse-light of its own, revealed the scene clearly enough. Lackel did not see a woman's body, and reasoned that she, less strong than a man and weakened further by the child she bore, had already perished and been dragged away by the creature that was even now devouring the corpses of two soldiers who had accompanied her.

He laughed and raised his hand in mock salute to the other shore. "So, Bog-folk, you have served our purposes," he said softly. "Ready not yourself, for we are not warring on you, nor are we on the hunt today. Indeed, this night we have been on a mission that you seem to have finished for us. And for that, we give you thanks."

His men were retreating. Each walked backward, steel showing in hopes it could be seen by whatever might emerge from the deeps to drag them down. They were as white-eyed as horses forced into battle against their will.

He raised his voice. "Enough! It is plain that the trail has reached its end and that whoever wrought this has served our purpose."

Still, he could not rid his mind of that Ash arrow planted in Ash flesh. The Bog-folk were one thing, but the arrow another. He knew, if his men did not, that no commander from one House would countenance the use of another House's badge or distinctive arrows, not even to throw a pursuer off a scent.

They played deep games at court, and there had been enough rumors abroad these past few days about so-called hunting parties that were better armed for raiding. The Ashenkin might well have a reason for such a split in their forces. A King's son held in secret—whether born of a Queen or of a lesser mother—now that could be a rare prize, especially for a waning House.

If so, their plan had ended at the Bog border, as had that of his own troop. He could make this report in all truth, and he believed that she who was his liege-lady would find it to her liking.

To the King a Daughter

❧

Joal, headman of the Bog-folk, stood scowling barely inside the doorway of Zazar's dwelling. His face twisted with a grimace of distaste at the body that still lay on the floor. "Outlander! Send it to pools. Feed silent ones." He was a short, misshapen man whose wiry thicket of graying hair was knotted up with the finger-bones of at least five enemies. Others of the Bog-folk crowded behind him, but none wanted any more than he to cross that threshold.

"Well enough, Joal," Zazar said indifferently. "Follow custom."

Joal still lingered at the threshold. "There be smell of blood—birth blood. Did Outlander bear living child? Give it to us!"

Zazar's level gaze caught and held the chief's eyes. "I bide by my trade as you do by yours, Joal." She held up a bundle wrapped in a reed weaving. "This is my named daughter, Ashen. By my craft, I have the right to claim her."

"Already you have one to learn from you, Wysen-wyf." Joal jerked his grimy thumb in Kazi's direction. "That be custom also. Who says you need another?"

"Yes, I have one of your people," she returned calmly. "One whom you denied for her ill-healed, crooked leg and spared by me when no one wanted her and it was thought death would find her soon enough. But this child is my chosen daughter, born through my skills. Ashen she is to me, no matter what blood flows within her. And further, the Lady of Death herself witnessed the mother-naming!" She smiled grimly. "You can claim only what is allowed, and that you know well."

Joal drew back a step, crowding those behind him. Zazar knew she had won. The headman could judge the worth of an ordinary man, and of most women, but Zazar was alone, unique, and no one but she knew her full name or who had birthed her. It was never well to deal with the unknown, and this caution of theirs she depended upon when having converse with the Bog-folk.

"Take dead, leave squaller-brat," Joal said finally. Two of his followers stepped forward and bundled the dead woman's slight body in the stained mats and departed.

Zazar was well aware that Joal was scowling. She sniffed in disdain. Joal and his kind—she did not need any nudge of fear to be wary of them. But the tricks of Outlanders? Yes. She must send forth her messengers and learn what this unexpected turn of events might mean to her.

Two

Ashen's earliest memory, at the age of four, was of the same thing she was doing just now, as a big girl at the age of eight—stirring the kettle filled with mollusk glue, careful not to let the mixture come to a boil. It had to stay at a low simmer; otherwise it would separate and be ruined. Everyone, including the people in the village, used the noxious stuff to repair the thatched roofs of their huts. Their own roof—hers and Zazar's—had started to leak again, so they couldn't put off tending it any longer. And Kazi's roof, too, of course. She lived there as well. Ashen found it easy to forget Kazi, as Kazi found it easy to ignore Ashen. They just didn't like each other, though Ashen had no idea of why it was that way.

She gave the mixture another deep stir, bringing up the mollusk shells from the bottom and picking out those she could snag, using a twig lest she burn her fingers. She knew, from listening, that this had once been Kazi's job, but by now, the old woman had turned it over entirely to Ashen, at least when Zazar wasn't around, or when it was just dull routine. At critical points, Kazi took over and claimed full credit as well. Ashen wished she had someone else, smaller and easy for her to defeat, to whom she could give the task in turn, but there was nobody. Well, maybe there could have been, but the creatures she called the Squeakers seldom came around these days.

She had never been able to really *see* the Squeakers except with occasional sidelong glances, but she could certainly hear them when in the night they came to visit Zazar. They squeaked and chittered, and sometimes purred. Ashen thought they must be very nice little creatures, and she longed to be able to hold one and stroke it. Such a luxury, however, had been denied her so far. There was just too much work to do.

Also, since the thunder-star had streaked toward the north and landed with an impact that shook the earth even as far as the Bog and lit up the sky, the Squeakers' visits had become less frequent. All of the grown-ups now went around with worried expressions, especially when one of the fire-mountains awoke and streaked the sky with spark-filled dark clouds. All this had no great effect on Ashen, however, nor did it diminish in the slightest the number of ever-present chores that had to be done.

The roof eternally needed repair so they could at least sleep without being drenched by the frequent rains. Just getting in enough food to feed themselves for more than a day occupied much of the rest of their time. In this they were not any different from the people of the village located down the small hillside from Zazar's hut, close by one of the deep pools that made up most of the Bog-land. This pool was one of the rare ones, though, different from the others, because the water bubbled up from underneath, and was relatively fresh. Other pools held a stagnant, slime-covered, smelly liquid that people avoided as much as they could when they went out food-gathering. Because she had no freshwater pool near her dwelling, Zazar preferred to catch rainwater in her big pot for their use in drinking, cooking, and bathing. When she was using the pot for other things—such as boiling up the nasty glue, or making potions, or cooking a large mess of the stew that was their usual food—they had to rely on the village pool like everyone else did. Ashen was glad that this duty had not fallen to her. Even Kazi could not make her stir the pot and go down to the pool carrying water jars at the same time.

Ashen was always uncomfortable when she ventured into the village. She knew that she was different from the inhabitants and knew also that the villagers were uneasy with her presence. Why she was different from everybody else, she did not know or understand. It was a fact, however, and one she had to acknowledge.

For that matter, Zazar herself was different both from the villagers and from Ashen. She had told Ashen about it, a little, once in a rare mood when she had drunk a little too much of a certain potion Ashen was strictly forbidden to touch. Zazar claimed she had existed many more lifetimes than Bog-folk had and that she would be here long after they were gone. And further, she claimed that when she did get old and a young, vigorous Wysen-wyf was called, she would bring it forth from her own body, alone and without help. Impossibly, she claimed that the Bog-folk knew all about it. This, Ashen thought, should surely have turned the Bog-folk against Zazar forever if—and it was a big if—the stories were true. But somehow, the Bog-people accepted Zazar even as they rejected Ashen. Perhaps it was because of the brews Zazar could concoct, the healing mixtures, the herb-rich salves that kept away the worst of the stinging insects that tormented everyone in the Bog. Even Joal called Zazar "Wysen-wyf," and Ashen had heard the grudging respect in his voice.

"How goes it?" Kazi asked from behind her. Ashen jumped, startled.

"I think it is nearly done," she said. "You know that better than I do. It's at the point where you should tend it now." She smiled sweetly, knowing that the mixture needed at least another full hour of stirring but not willing to let this chance for release pass. "Zazar wouldn't be pleased if it got ruined."

Kazi scowled, but took the stirring-stick. Ashen was free now to go and occupy herself with more agreeable tasks.

First, she had to change her clothes. When she worked at the kettle, she wore an old tattered shift made of the remnants of a woven reed-fluff blanket so that any splashes would not harm her, or ruin the lupper-skin garments Zazar had painstakingly made for her.

These garments were, she knew, finer than those worn by the villagers, having been made only from hides taken from very young luppers, then tanned by Zazar's art to a suppleness that rivaled traders' cloth. She slipped out of the shift and wriggled into the leggings. Still bare to the waist, she fastened on the armor, made from small squares of turtle shell, that covered her legs from ankle to knee. It was scarred in several places by the fangs of serpents, thwarted in their attempts to sting her. Then she tied up her buskins and carefully cross-gaitered the entire arrangement so that it fit snugly and would not hamper her movements. She noted that the armor was almost too short to reach her knees; she had been growing again. She and Zazar would have to add another strip of shell pieces to the top very soon.

She slipped the lupper-skin tunic over her head, and then she was dressed. She debated on whether to add an over-tunic the way Zazar was always telling her to do, and decided against it. The days were not yet cool enough to make it necessary to wear the outer garment. She did, however, slip a shell-bladed knife into the top of her leg armor. From a shelf she took down a wooden jar filled with the salve that repelled the worst of the biting insects of the Bog and rubbed it into her skin. Once, she had forgotten and had been stung so severely that she had been sick for several days. She shook another jar, the one that held trade-pearls, and realized there was only a single pearl left in it. So that was where Zazar had gone. When she went to deal with the Traders, she always took all the pearls but one, left for luck and to bring more to the jar.

Ashen's errand was now plain. She picked up a woven basket

and escaped out the back way. Nobody could fault her for going pearl-hunting. Also, she might gather a few of whatever food-stuffs came to hand. Nobody had to know that she was, in reality, just getting away from the ever-present work, the chores, and especially Kazi.

Ashen had not been allowed to run wild. There were lessons, sometimes given painfully, which she had absorbed over the years. After all, Zazar had claimed her as an apprentice. And to that learning, Ashen had taken as those in a lean time welcome a feast.

Learning, however, had early awakened her curiosity. And above all, she wanted to know why Zazar went alone, and where, journeying over the wilder parts of the Bog as if she had some secret goal. Not all of her travels involved the Traders.

Ashen decided that perhaps, daringly, she would expand her borders today, go just a little way beyond the limits Zazar had set on where she could explore safely.

"There are places you may not yet approach," Zazar always told her. "When you are old enough, I will personally take you to them so that you may learn more of who you are, and what you are, and what you must be. Until then, be patient."

There was something about the Wysen-wyf's tone, and the way a spark sometimes came from her fingertip, that inclined Ashen to obedience. However, because of her own errand, Zazar had not been at the hut for several days now, and with the passage of this much time, her discipline had weakened. Ashen was more than ready to take as much advantage of the situation as she dared. And so with a light heart, she left Kazi behind and disappeared into the underbrush that marked the edges of the clearing where Zazar's hut stood.

※

In the capital city of Rendelsham stood the Great Fane of the Glowing, the largest and most important cathedral dedicated to the Ultimate Ruler of Sky and Land. A thing of conscious beauty as well as of reverence, it was the product of the best artisans in the land. Tall white columns held up the lofty roof, carved to represent the four Great Trees, which, in turn, were the badges of the four ruling Houses.

The Fane also boasted windows both great and small, decorated with pictures made of pieces of colored glass, set into the openings with great skill and artisanship. The largest of these windows surmounted the main doors. In the shape of a circle and designed with nothing in mind other than sheer decoration, this window glowed with the least amount of light. Flowers and leaves, picked out in jewel tones—ruby and garnet and rose quartz; sapphire and spinel and aquamarine; golden topaz and yellow quartz and citrine; emerald and chrysophase and tourmaline—representing the four Houses, shed rainbows upon any and all who ventured inside. There other windows, both small and large, depicted scenes of edifying content that represented the daily life such edification was supposed to improve. Not surprisingly, many of the tableaux featured artistic renderings with likenesses of the patrons who had commissioned the work.

Three of the smallest windows were virtually hidden from all but the most inquisitive, few of whom, after discovering them, would return again. Exquisite as these windows were, they nonetheless inspired vague feelings of dread, for they changed with time and no artisan's touch could account for the shifting. One of the panes depicted the Hands and Web of the Weavers. With the advent of the thunder-star and its impact when it struck the northern lands hard enough to make the entire earth quiver and certain fire-throated mountains to awaken, this window, which had changed only a little from the oldest man's memory, began to shift. Now the dark Hands of the Weavers moved more quickly, and the Web upon which they worked began to take on a different appearance.

The second window, the one showing a Bog-lupper, also began to change. The small lupper had moved away from the pool it had been sitting beside and vanished into the underbrush. Now the surface of the pool was starting to be disturbed, as if something dark and fell were trying to fight its way onto land.

But it was in the third window that the biggest peril was beginning to emerge, though the few who observed the change had no idea of what they were witnessing. This mysterious pane had ever shown a blank face, white and barely translucent. Its very lack of design made it uninteresting. Now, however, something was stirring in its depths, as if a creature more deadly, more horrifying even than the one still hidden beneath the surface of the Bog-pool, were emerging from a heavy snowstorm.

More agreeable to the inhabitants of the city of Rendelsham, and certainly better to look upon than colored-glass windows that refused to keep to their original design, were the four living trees that had long flourished in the Fane's forecourt. Oak, Ash, Yew, and Rowan, they, even more than the marble columns within, stood as tall symbols of the four ruling Houses of Rendel. And yet even these trees carried their own grim message that all was not well within the Kingdom. Oak leaves suffered blight, only a trace, but present and spreading. Ash drooped sadly, shedding leaves even during the period of growth, and no amount of care seemed able to reverse the tree's decline. Even Rowan looked ill with some unknown disease, a few green leaves still valiantly struggling to keep the tree alive. Yew, however, thrived. No trace of the ills that afflicted the other three touched this one, and people looked upon the Trees and wondered.

Queen Ysa could look upon the Trees in the Fane's forecourt from the window of her tower room. This was a place in the castle that was hers alone. More than thrice the height of any twisted tree of the Bog, the tower rose from the very heart of the castle. This tower, higher than any of the other lofty towers in Rendelsham, had long been deserted as too inaccessible before she took it for her own. At a distant time, it had been a place of farseeing, centered as it was in the main stronghold of the Kingdom. No spot was loftier, and only Ysa ever came here, by her own command. From this aerie she could see the entire city, and from here she frequently looked down upon the Four Trees in the courtyard of the Fane of the Glowing. Its very isolation was what she desired. Gazing down at the trees, she was not alarmed. Yew, symbol of her own Family, grew ever strong and healthy, and that had always been her aim, even if the other three faltered, even if they perished.

And when had the decline of Oak begun? She fingered the pendant about her neck, the shape of a yew leaf and set with a cabochon emerald, Yew's color. It had been about the time when Ash's sickness could no longer be ignored, when the Fane gardeners who were charged with the care of the Four Trees had begun to consult among themselves, trying to find the cause of Ash's ailing, and perhaps a cure. Eight years—

Ysa tried to cut off the thought before it could be fully articulated. Yes, eight years, but certainly the timing had to be merely coincidental with the unfortunate death of the last Ash rival to her power. Why King Boroth seemed drawn only to pale, wispy Ash-women, she had never been able to fathom. But drawn he was. She could overlook the serving-wenches and those from the common folk he was constantly taking to his bed, but highborn women connected to the great ruling Families she could not ignore. And so each of them had—she delicately rephrased it in her mind—met with an untimely end before Boroth could be tempted to bed them. Such folly would have led to civil war as Yew turned against Ash and, if encouraged, Rowan marched on Oak.

At one time early in Rendel history, Ash had been the wellspring of kings. As a consequence, the main branches of the House of Ash had always been quarrelsome among themselves as they sought precedence of place. It took just a little prodding to make Ash turn against Ash, each faction thinking that the other was plotting its downfall.

Alas, so many Ash-kin had died that the entire Family was now in danger of being extinguished. However, Boroth had only himself to blame for this. If he had had the sense to forgo flirtation with Ash-women, she would not have found it necessary to put the rivals aside. She could not risk the appearance of another heir to rival her son, Florian, born a year after the last highborn Ash-woman had perished so unfortunately in the Bog.

Her son. On a sudden impulse, she left the tower room and in a sweep of dark green velvet, trailing skirts, and spicy perfume, descended the winding stairs to pay a visit to the Prince's apartments.

Florian had arisen late and was still at his morning meal. She noted that he had merely pushed the oat porridge around in the bowl, though he had eaten the boiled bacon and a single bite of the fresh-baked bread. A covered dish, the kind that contained fruit, sat untouched.

"I want a pony," the young Prince said to his mother by way of greeting.

"Say 'good morning,' " Ragalis, his nurse, prompted him. "Even Princes must mind their manners."

Florian stuck his tongue out at Ragalis. "I want a pony," he repeated to Queen Ysa. "And I want it *now*."

"This morning?" she said, trying to find amusement in the boy. It was far from the first time he had shown such rudeness, and no nurse or tutor she had ever found had been able to teach him otherwise. He seemed more than healthily aware of his station in life, and even more willing to take full advantage of it.

His face darkened. "Now! Now, now, *now!*"

Ysa knew the signs. In a moment, Florian would begin throwing things. Then he would hurl himself to the floor and scream himself into a black-faced fit. "Eat your breakfast and do all your lessons, and then we will talk about a pony," she said hastily.

"I will eat the rest of my bread and do half of my lessons. And then I will ride the pony you promised me." He opened the covered dish. His face took on a horrified look and he wailed aloud as he slumped to one side, as if he had been mortally betrayed. Then he picked up the dish of preserved fruit and his porridge bowl and emptied both onto the floor.

"It is nobody's fault that there was no fresh fruit for you, young sir," Ragalis said. "It is yet too early in the season. Please. I will send for more, if only you will eat it."

"No!" But he did begin stuffing the bread into his mouth, for he knew that his mother would hold him to his own bargain.

Ysa sighed. She and Ragalis exchanged glances over the boy's head. She could read in the nurse's expression her disapproval of the way the boy was constantly spoiled and pampered, but she felt herself unable to do anything to avoid it. Florian had too much of his self-indulgent father in him, Ysa thought. He even looked like his father—dark of hair, without a trace of her own vibrant auburn tresses. She refused to consider how much her own actions, or lack of them, were contributing to her son's lack of discipline.

Upon making her return to her tower, she encountered Lord Lackel. As Commander of the House Troops of Her Gracious Ladyship the Queen, he had been entrusted with far more urgent errands than obtaining a pony for the Prince. However, he received her instructions with a bow and a salute and went off to find a suitable animal. The Powers help us all, Ysa thought wryly, if there were none of the mounts presently in the stable.

Then she forgot about the incident. A book awaited her, a volume of nearly forgotten lore. Though she had no measure of the Power as far as she knew, she felt that such lack could be compensated for by study, and in that book were many spells. Today she wanted to try one of them for summoning a creature out of invisibility, a creature that would be seen or unseen at her will, that could fly unmarked wherever she directed it to go and then return with what knowledge it had gained. Such a little servant, she knew, could prove very helpful indeed in the intrigues that were always cropping up both in the court and in the country itself. The visible supernatural entities she had once summoned had proved unsatisfactory for most errands, as they caused too much fright, and human spies could always be bought by the other side. One of these tiny, invisible creatures, however, could not.

❧

The lands to the north had fared ill when the thunder-star struck. The earth for a dozen days' ride in every direction rang like a gong, and in the cities, buildings fell as if victims to a giant scythe. Out on the tundra, the story was much the same as felt yurts collapsed upon their inhabitants and great rents opened in the ground. There, too, as with other countries, fire-mountains awoke and began sending plumes of foul-smelling smoke into the sky. Streams of burning rock cut paths through ice fields, and steam mixed with the smoke to shroud the land in a well-nigh impenetrable fog.

At the southern shore of this far-north land, two enormous waves had come and worked devastation on the cities of the Sea-Rovers. Only those of their ships that happened to be out of port had had any chance of surviving, and of those, more than half perished. And so the sea-people went to the court of the NordornKing.

"We'll not stay here, by the King's grace," declared Snolli, now High Chief and leader of the Sea-Rovers after so many of his kindred had died. "We are a restless people at the best of times, and these border on the worst of times. Our one city is gone. Like our people in times past, we will take our women, our children, our goods, and live on our ships if need be and if we cannot find a more hospitable spot upon which to build a new city." He put his hand on the shoulder of his son Obern. Barely a man as the Sea-Rovers reckoned manhood, Obern none-theless showed much promise as the eventual worthy successor to his stalwart father.

Cyornas NordornKing nodded his snowy head. "If you wish to leave, we will not detain you," he said. "Were it not for the grave burden we bear as guardians of the Palace of Fire and Ice, we also might be tempted to seek a happier clime. But our choice was made for us long years past. Now we must make the best of the disaster that has befallen us and survive it as we will. However, I know that some of our people have not the heart to remain in the face of the very heavens turning against us. For those who wish to inquire elsewhere if they will be welcomed, I will send as emissary Count Bjauden."

A slender man with hair the color of honey stepped forward from those who stood respectfully, attending on the meeting between Cyornas NordornKing and Snolli Sea-Rover. He bowed. "Thank you, my King, for entrusting this grave mission to me. I ask only that you take my son Gaurin as your ward, to foster and protect the lad while I am gone, and to rear him as your own if I do not come back."

"Gladly, Bjauden," Cyornas said. "He shall be to me as my son Hynnel, neither holding precedence over the other." He turned to Snolli. "Will you agree to having Bjauden with you, on your own ship, where he will be safest?"

"I will," Snolli said. "And if he meets with welcome news, I further promise to send him back on as swift a ship as we have, to bring you his report."

"Then we both are satisfied," said Cyornas. "Come, drink a horn of fair ale with me, and let us exchange a drop of blood to seal the bargain."

According to custom, Cyornas and Snolli pricked their forefingers and touched them so that their blood mingled. Then they locked arms, and with their heads so close that each could count the eyelashes of the other, they emptied horns of ale at a single draught. Snolli looked rather more at ease in this activity than he did in courtly courtesy, which he had obviously found to be a strain.

Nevertheless, Cyornas NordornKing discouraged any great rejoicing over the good bargain struck between the Sea-Rovers and the Nordors. He knew what he had not yet divulged—not even to his most trusted advisers—what was only whispered about by the frightened workmen who had seen. The Palace of Fire and Ice had suffered great harm from the thunder-star's impact. One wall—that adjacent to the tomb that held the sleeping body of the entity that was known with unspeakable trepidation as the Great Foulness—had cracked. Inside the tomb, unseen but felt by those whose task it was to guard it, the Foulness had begun to stir, and perhaps to awaken. . . .

Three

A *shen knelt on a* small hillock of island where she had
found a goodly stand of the best kind of weave-reeds.
She tensed within, but now, at age sixteen, she had learned to
disguise her awareness of danger until the last possible moment.
Through the many odors that were thick in this place, she had
caught a trace of one particular scent that might mean trouble.
However, she did not yet raise her head but, rather, she kept on
sawing at one of the reeds whose milky fluff could be collected,
spun, and woven into a kind of cloth. Her shell blade was almost
unequal to the task. Weave-reeds were tough, this one especially
so. She pursued her task energetically enough to raise droplets
of sweat on her forehead.

With a rasping croak, one of the Bog-luppers soared over the
edge of the hillock only a hand's reach away. It splashed into the
dank water ringing her perch and disappeared. Now she allowed
herself to turn partway around. She touched the circular disk of
smooth stone, holed in the center, that hung about her neck by
a twisted cord. When first she had discovered the amulet lying
dusty and forgotten on one of Zazar's shelves, she had innocently

mistaken it for an ornament. So thinking, she had threaded it on the cord, one woven of fibers through which shifted muted shades of blue and green, and put it around her neck.

The only other ornament she had ever owned was a pair of earrings, gold wires with brownish stone dangles. They had come from a Trader, Zazar said. Ashen had lost them when, unthinking, she had laid them aside while she bathed and someone had stolen them. When she started wearing the disk, Zazar had corrected her and taught her the true use of the stone. She had also given Ashen a bit of wood, which she called a hearth-guide. She claimed that it would point the way home should Ashen become lost. The disk, which Zazar told her was called the power-stone, interested her more, though. Now she wore it knowing it to be greater than a mere ornament.

Though there was as yet not the faintest of movement behind her, that warning odor was stronger. She recognized the stinking grease that any roving Bog-hunter used as a shield against the continuous assaults of insects in these raw pockets. Ashen dropped the last half-shredded reed into her carry-basket.

There were at least two, possibly three of the intruders; of that she was now sure. They might bear spears and shoulder turtle-shell shields as if they were engaged in a regular hunt, but she was certain—as if some light breeze carried guttural half whispers—that she was their quarry. If she was right, she knew them, and had known them from the time they all toddled.

Having made sure of her harvest, she did not look up but suddenly spoke clear-voiced, her words lacking the heavy accent of the Bog-folk. "How goes your luck, Tusser?"

She might have been seated by Zazar's fire-hole, casually addressing one who passed by the Wysen-wyf's home place. Hopefully, she trusted her tone did not convey anything but confidence.

Yes, there were at least three of them out there, and their

purpose was one of ill will, for they had not shown themselves. If it were Tusser playing leader, then his fawning liegemen, Sumase and Todo, would be his aides.

Ashen knew very well that her difference from the Bog-born was a matter for hatred. At one time or another, almost every one of the villagers had made it plain to her that only her having been claimed within the very hour of her birth by the Wysen-wyf had kept her from being tossed into one of the sluggish streams as food for the bottom-dwellers. She was Outlander through and through, her breed clear to read in her slender height, her finely marked features, the pallid strands of her hair.

No, there were none among the Bog-folk who would ever welcome her. They loathed her kind, but even more, they feared Zazar, by whose quirky favor she was allowed to live.

Only a few moon-turnings ago, when she reached womanhood by Bog-folk standards, Ashen had begun to realize a shift in the way she was regarded not only by Tusser, but also by some others of those only recently promoted to manhood and allowed to attend the talk-fires of their kindred. Perhaps it was her very oddity that led to this waking interest in her as a person, no longer seen as an outcast. But perhaps not. Of the way matters stood between men and women, whether of Bog-kind or Out-lander, Zazar had told her only enough to make her wary.

She could almost taste the bile rising in her throat when she suspected what might be the reason Tusser and some of the others stared at her. She gave thanks again that Zazar's dwelling was set apart from the settlement and that the reputation of the Wysen-wyf raised enough awe that her quarters were shunned. Ashen knew she could not depend upon the Wysen-wyf to come to her aid now. It was impossible.

She had come this deeply into the Bog trying to follow the Wysen-wyf on one of her mysterious errands. Zazar, as usual, had eluded her—whether accidentally or by design, Ashen could not determine. Under other circumstances, she was able to follow even faint trails. When tracking Zazar, however, at some point she was always baffled; it was as if Zazar had suddenly grown wings and taken to the air. Sometimes she wondered if the Wysen-wyf was testing her in some fashion, a testing that so far she had failed.

And so, once more Ashen had turned aside to find another errand. She often went out alone even when not following Zazar, the way she had done since she was eight years old. Today, her harvest of superior weave-reeds would be her excuse upon her return, and Zazar might even forget to interrogate her. She was well aware that Zazar could read minds—or at least past actions—by a mere survey of one's person.

This day, however, Ashen must have been careless, thinking more of what she wished than of what might happen. She had found herself on one of the lesser-known ways, where even hunters did not ordinarily go. Because of her thoughtlessness, now she was to be prey—or so the trackers intended.

The bushes shook and three of the squat, sallow-skinned, ill-smelling youths emerged into plain sight. But they took only a step or so and then halted abruptly.

Acutely aware, she knew what they saw. An Outlander, crouching and apparently vulnerable, on a tiny dot of island. Between the hunters and the one they hunted, there lay like a moat, a sullenly dark pool. No Bog-man except one totally lacking in proper wit would ever attempt to wade through that. She could see the puzzlement spread from face to face and could almost read their thoughts. There she was, safe on the only good footing for some distance around—how had she gotten there? A flicker of something like fear crossed first one countenance, and then another and another.

There was, of course, a rational answer, but Ashen preferred to keep them in awe for as long as possible. Tusser snarled. He was never one to take opposition lightly.

"Are you lost, shield-men?" The girl inquired as one who had been asked for directions and was able to give them. "You must retrace your steps—"

Tusser merely laughed unpleasantly. "C'mon over here and let's all play. We knows nice games." He wriggled his body in a suggestive manner, and Ashen knew that her worst suspicions had been correct.

She tightened her grip on the cord around her neck that held the stone. They were watching her closely, yes. But—

She leaped to her feet. In one hand she clutched the carry-basket containing her reed harvest, and with her other, she sent the power-stone whirling in a circle over her head at the end of the woven string.

A thunderous roar filled the little clearing. Then, after the first burst of sound that sent her pursuers, frightened, back a few steps, it dropped to a droning hum. From the power-stone there spread a growing shadow; it descended to encase and befog her whole body. This trick, one that Zazar had told her about and that she had practiced against just such an occasion as this, was working. By the open astonishment on their flat-nosed, wide-mouthed faces, she knew they could scarcely see her, though she could make them out clearly enough.

She had to pick her path very carefully now, so that she would not come too close to them once she crossed the water onto the firm land. They were drawing in, bringing their shields up, one throwing-spear at the ready and the other in reserve.

Ashen touched one foot to the murky water. The opaque surface shivered about her ankle as she put her full weight upon it. She was sure of her earlier explorations. Well-hidden under the discolored surface she had discovered broad stepping-stones, certainly arranged by intelligent purpose in the past.

Though Tusser was now stubbornly holding his ground, his two companions had retreated a few more steps again. Some of Ashen's own confidence was shaken. If she held to the path of the stones hidden beneath the water, she would emerge on the high land almost directly in front of Tusser. She kept the power-stone on the blue-and-green cord buzzing in a constant circle above her head, and she was sure that she remained unseen.

Now, however, Tusser was raising his spear. His desire to get at his quarry was beginning to overpower his first startled awe. She had never tested it, but thought that the shadow was no real protection. It would provide no barrier, no shield against a weapon, for it was meant only to guard her by confusing another's sight.

Ashen had reached the final step. With a sinking heart, she felt that she had dared too much—had believed they would falter before the unknown. As Zazar had pointed out on several occasions, Ashen was inclined to act too soon after gaining any new knowledge. Silently, she vowed to listen more carefully the next time, if there were a next time.

Now she pursed her lips and whistled. This trick she had never tried. She had read it only as a faint line on the graven tablet from which Zazar had shown her the use of the power-stone.

It might not have been pitched as well as it should have been, but the throaty half-whistle was picked up instantly by the hum of the stone. And, to her relief and amazement, it was answered! The layer of protective mist around her deepened, and from within it, she could tell that the sound of the stone held its listeners so they could not move, at least not for a while.

Ashen prepared to step off the last submerged stone and past Tusser. His gaze was now fixed not on the shadow enveloping her, but on something else, something she sensed behind her. She needed all her courage not to look. But the stark fear that masked Tusser's face was a fierce warning. The water about her ankles washed higher, not from her movements, and with a paralyzing chill, she knew that something was stirring in the depths of the pool.

His fear overcoming the effect of the humming of the stone, Tusser threw his spear. Todo shrieked as he hurled himself back into the brush curtain. Sumase had already disappeared.

Though Ashen had stopped whistling, the sound continued to echo at each swing of the stone. Whatever it was behind her, it uttered a horrible, croaking bellow. Tusser half crouched, his second spear ready.

Then his shout rang out, challenging both Ashen and the creature that had made the bellow. "The deep one! Boggit! Be you his feast, Outland witch, and not me!"

And she might well be just that if she could not get past that last stepping-stone and reach safe footing—which was too near to Tusser, much too near!

Water swirled higher. Desperate, she kept the power-stone humming. She would much rather take her chance with the enemy in front, one she knew, than with that which was rising, almost lazily, behind her.

Ashen steadied herself to take the last step. The croaking grew louder, higher-pitched, and became a sound that was like a thrust of sharp light through her temples.

Tusser dropped his spear and clutched at his head. His wide mouth opened and a scream of sheer terror overrode the droning hum of the stone.

He did not retreat backward; rather, he made a sidewise leap away and landed in the brush. The branches broke under his weight. Not even trying to regain his feet, he scrambled on all fours, hindered by his shield, which caught between two of the thicker branches until he shrugged it off and left it behind. The broken spikes of the greenery arose to conceal him.

Ashen had wit enough left to make a try for the solid land while the creature's attention was presumably still focused on Tusser. She stumbled and fell to her knees. The power-stone on the cord faltered in its swing and hit her shoulder, hard.

The echo of its last round was swallowed by a thick bellow. Against her will, she turned and looked back.

The horrors that dwelt in the lowest portion of the Bog-pools and dark streams were well known to all by story, by legend, by drawings in mud and on walls. In a way, the Bog-folk were grateful to these creatures and considered them an additional barrier to penetration from the outer world. But few, a very few, of the boggits had ever been seen in the open day.

The monstrous shape showed only its forequarters clearly; the rest of it was still hidden under the churning surface of the pond. Ashen knew well the small swamp-luppers, for it was part of her duties to hunt them for the pot and for their leather. But even the drawings had not conveyed the immensity of the ones Zazar named "boggarts" and the people called "boggits." This wide mouth—a yellow-green cavern, a tooth-walled cave—could belong only to a lupper of more mass than the hillock Ashen had recently left. The baleful yellow eyes, set high on its head, swiveled independently, searching for . . . for what?

Frantically, she scrambled forward on the firm land, even though she sensed that this boggart was one that could exist in the open air as well as in water. She dared to glance backward. It floated at ease, eyeing her as if it were supremely confident that it could finish its hunt at leisure.

The Bog-lands were ever treacherous, sometimes only a quivering surface over the peril beneath. Though Ashen was again on ground able to support her weight, with that thing lurking behind her, she must move, and her choice of direction meant perhaps the difference between life and death.

Her arm was now wearied to the point that she could no longer swing the stone; even that small defense was useless now.

Ashen struggled to her feet. In addition to ruining her covering spell, she had lost her basket, though she still had her stone, as well as her shell knife. This was small comfort; she doubted that any weapon known in the Bogs would serve her now. Before her, broken branches marked Tusser's retreat.

She plunged forward even as a mighty croak sounded from behind. She did not look back. In spite of the thorn scratches and whip-stripes the brush left upon her, she thrashed her way through it with all the speed she could summon.

The brush was like a miniature forest, raising tips of growth well above her head to swallow her from any ordinary danger. However, that would be no barrier to the creature behind if it chose to follow. She must not fall. There were always slick patches of footing on even the largest and most stable of the landmasses, quick to bring the unwary down.

She still had the stone. It swung against her knee and struck flesh bared and bloody from the rents that thorns had torn in her lupper-skin garments. Her knee hurt as if a brand from a cook fire had seared it, and she took a reckless forward leap, which landed her face down. Under her, the earth quivered, as if from huge footsteps. The thing from the pool must have picked this moment to hunt, and its huge body now shared with her this scrap of firm land.

As Ashen tried to crawl on, another bellow erupted from the creature pursuing her. It was not a hunting call, but a sound of pure rage and pain. The beast must have met with some un-known mishap, perhaps from the thorns that had tormented her. Whatever had happened, it was a fortune for which she would be forever thankful. As she tore her way deeper into the brush, her every movement released from the spongy carpet beneath her the fetid breath of long-dead vegetation. She panted for lack of clear air. At last she broke out, gasping into an open space. As she ripped flesh and garment on the last sharp-thorned branch, she dared to look back again.

The taller growth, through which her last plunge had taken her, was moving. There was another cry of rage, but different this time, not that of a boggit. Then a spear-shaft skimmed across her shoulder; it would almost certainly have brought her down had she not turned when she did.

"She-demon!"

Tusser! He was almost close enough to touch her.

Ashen threw herself to the left. He would have to turn aside to retrieve his spear, now lodged in the brush. She knew he was still armed with one of those deadly bone-knives that Bog-folk used with ease.

He made a mad rush in her direction before she could gather her feet under her. Then he stopped as suddenly as if he had slammed into an invisible barrier. She could see his features actually mash out of shape. He cried out; the knife fell from his hold, and then he was down, scrabbling it into his grasp again.

With all the quick skill of a Bog-hunter, he threw the knife her way. However, just as his leap for her had come to such an abrupt halt, so did his weapon halt. It struck *nothingness*—a nothing that echoed—and fell to the ground.

Tusser's cry of rage was nearly as loud as that of the horror from the pool. Flecks of white appeared at the corners of his thick lips. "Call off boggit! Call off Gulper! It—"

At the shoreline, past her enemy, Ashen could still see motion in the brush. Whatever the invisible protection might be that had risen to save her, she could not guess, but she found her energy renewed. On her feet once more, she edged toward the left. Now Tusser had retrieved both spear and knife. One spear; he had not retrieved the other that he had surely thrown at the creature from the Bog.

Suddenly Ashen knew what had caused the creature's cry of pain and why Tusser had been frantic to get away. Fear of the monster he had wounded and lust for her had to be warring within him. His burst of boldness told her he must think that his companions were nearby. Indeed, if Sumase and Todo were now to appear on the path she had been forced to choose, she would truly be trapped.

An earsplitting cry erupted from the brush wall. Tusser whirled, and with a leap nearly as long as any water-creature could make, he was gone.

The last cry of pain and fear still ringing in her ears, Ashen fled also, in the opposite direction Tusser had taken. Had Sumase or Todo fallen prey to the water-dweller? Surely that cry had come from a human throat! Could she dare hope that whatever invisible Power had saved her from Tusser's attack could also shield her from the monster?

Her lungs were laboring as she ran. Then, faced once more
by a wall of growth, she fell to a frenzy of pushing and breaking
apart the branches, hoping that there would be free space beyond. She could no longer think or plan, but only keep on with
such strength as she could summon.

❦

In the stables attached to the royal residence at Rendelsham,
fifteen-year-old Prince Florian was beating one of the grooms.

"You left a tangle in my horse's mane!" he cried, his voice
shrill. "I ought to beat you until you die, die, die."

"Have pity, Master," the groom pleaded, trying to shield himself from the blows.

"I could, you know. Beat you until you died. I wonder how
long it would take."

"Florian!"

The Prince turned with a guilty start. "We were only playing,
Mother," he said. "It was just a game."

"Dinas?"

"It is as Prince Florian said, Lady," the groom replied. He
tried to hide the bloody stripe the Prince's riding whip had made
across his cheek. "We'm, played a little rough. Please forgive."

"I am not certain that I believe any of this," the Queen said,
the corners of her mouth turned down sourly. "But no great
harm done if the—the *game* stops now."

"Oh, we're tired of it anyway," Florian said. He strolled toward his mother. "How is Father today?"

"That is why I came looking for you. He seems a little better.
He wants to see you."

"Oh." The Prince appeared downcast. "If I go and am very,
very good, will there be plum pudding for dessert?"

"You should visit your father's sickroom with a pleasant
heart, not angle for a bribe," Queen Ysa told him.

"Yes, but will there be plum pudding?"

"Very well. I'll give orders to the cook. And you must be on your best behavior at the midday meal. We have an ambassador at court this day."

Florian made a face. Having ambassadors at court and having to entertain them was always a trial to him. "I won't sing."

"Nobody has asked you to."

"And you can't either."

"It is manners for the hosts to entertain their guests. You are excused only because you can't carry a tune."

"I don't want you to sing for anybody but me." He pouted for a moment, and then he shrugged. "Actually, I don't care, as long as there are jugglers and dancing girls."

So much like his father, Queen Ysa thought, shaking her head sadly. Well, he was still very young. There was plenty of time to train him to loftier pursuits, to make him worthy to succeed to the throne. Boroth was ill, certainly, but in no danger. And he was definitely better this morning. Perhaps he would even recover sufficiently that he could begin to take over his son's instruction himself.

So thinking, she led Florian away from the stables, toward the lightly fortified residence, in all but defensibility a castle, where the royal apartments were kept. Her mind was already on the errand the man from the northern lands had come seeking.

※

Count Bjauden was as bored as Prince Florian was, but he knew better than to show it. Nevertheless, he found himself fiddling with his armlet, a band carved of iridescent, milky stone. It was an heirloom of his House. He twisted it firmly into place and told himself to pay attention.

He sat in the place of honor at the high table set up in front of a chair upholstered in red velvet. Over this was draped a cloth of state. Had the King been present, he would have occupied this seat, with his favored companions on either side. The Queen, as his deputy, sat in this spot, but not in his chair. Down the Hall, at right angles to the high table, there were tables seating others of the court. The din of their conversation was nearly deafening.

The Prince twisted in his seat and yawned openly while the feast in Bjauden's honor toiled on. A whole roasted swan, prepared in its feathers, lay demolished on a platter, and several bowls of sweetmeats had disappeared into Florian's mouth after he had devoured more than half of a plum pudding. No wonder he was yawning, and no wonder also that he was more than a little plump, and despite his obvious youth, his face was beginning to break out in spots. Bjauden thought of his own son Gaurin, safe in the court of Cyornas NordornKing. Cyornas would not have allowed such behavior from Gaurin, even though he was but a royal ward, for the length of time it took to pinch out a smoking candle. Bjauden hid his disapproval, however, for the boy's mother doted on her son, and it was from this royal lady that he must beg permission for his people to come and live—those who preferred to escape the turmoil that now gripped the northernmost lands.

Somewhat to his dismay, the entertainment was not, as he was accustomed to, soft music and brilliant, polished conversation. First, Queen Ysa had sung a song, her husky contralto not entirely sure on some of the notes. Then came the antics of rude acrobats who juggled fire and live puppies in the space between the high table and the rest of the company, followed by the loud, only sometimes harmonious, singing of strolling players—he could not call them musicians. His head was beginning to hurt.

He did not feel that his errand would be successful. This lady obviously liked very much to be in command. Her lord still lived, though ill and weak, and she had her way in everything but the discipline of her son, the heir to the throne. The very shape of her face told him so, with its square, determined jaw and its beauty that was owed somewhat, he suspected, to the cosmetics jar. He found himself noting irrelevant details just to fill the time. She had turned herself out well; she wore a splendid, deep-green dress powdered with tiny golden oak leaves. The Oak badge was represented in paintings throughout the Hall—one of a bear standing erect against a background of oak leaves, and in a circle, the motto, "Strength prevails."

With her dress, the Queen wore an elaborate coif, to which was pinned a brooch representing her own badge. It was a circle of yew leaves, surmounted by a crown. Over the leaf circle was a bow, and the handgrip was set with green stones over which was laid a ribbon bearing the motto, "This ever I defend."

The Queen might or might not be truly past her prime; it was difficult to tell in the dim light of a few carefully placed candles. Bjauden had a feeling that the lighting at the Queen's table was no accident. The Hall itself was dim, for the windows were still curtained to keep out the early spring chill, and candelabra were set everywhere. Overhead, vast chandeliers hung, adding their own pale and flickering glow.

Did he really want to bring his people to this land? Would he not serve them better if he sought sanctuary elsewhere?

His musings were interrupted by a question from the Queen, a question he had not heard. "Forgive me, fair lady," he said. "I was momentarily distracted by your beauty, and by your great hospitality. I can truly say that this has been a unique experience for me."

"I was inquiring after your lady, and why she does not grace our gathering."

"I am widowed, alas—"

Something splatted on Bjauden's plum-colored surcoat, the best garment he had with him. He turned only to have an entire mouthful of wet, chewed sweetmeats strike his face. His hand went automatically to his dagger, a gesture he could not call back. Prince Florian laughed openly.

"That's for you and your stupid old northerners," the Prince said. "I wish you'd go away."

Bjauden could feel the blood draining from his face. Carefully, he wiped his cheek with a napkin. "Your manners are worse than those of the lowest churl," he said, keeping his voice low and pleasant, "and if I had but an hour and a little privacy, I would mend you of them to your mother's rejoicing."

Queen Ysa's face reflected no official notice of the shocking breach in her son's manners, nor of the way Bjauden had answered. She got to her feet, signaling that the festive activities were finished.

"Go to your room at once, Florian," she said in a quiet, dangerous voice. "I will deal with you later. Really, you have gone too far." She turned to her guest. "My apologies. It is true that the Prince is a little spoiled, but he is young. You had no call to reach for a weapon."

"Your apologies are unnecessary beside the one I owe you for my unacceptable reaction. I moved before I could think. I am not accustomed to being spat upon," Bjauden said, his voice strained. "I fear that this puts my petition in full jeopardy."

Queen Ysa smiled, not pleasantly. "It would have, if your petition had ever had a chance of being granted. I will not permit you any land from any of the four provinces for you to build a city on." It was as flat and insulting a refusal as the Queen could proffer and still remain within the bounds of courtesy.

"I see. Forgive my intrusion. Indeed, Madam," Bjauden added through gritted teeth, "I will take my leave now and not impose on you further, not even for as much as a night's lodging." He bowed, turned his back—for all he knew or cared, a sign of disrespect—and left the royal Hall.

❦

Later that evening, the Prince's whipping-boy received a thorough flogging, and even Florian, to his surprise, endured a tongue-lashing from his mother, the likes of which he had never before known.

Still smarting from it, Florian sent for one of the house servants, a man called Rawl, who had the reputation of being an assassin. Indeed, as Florian stared at him by the one candle he dared keep alight, Rawl did have the very look of a ruffian.

"You know the nasty Count Bjauden, who dined with us tonight?"

"Aye, m'lord. I was servin' th' bread. I marked him well."

"Good, for I want you to mark him again. He tried to pull his dagger on me, and all for nothing. Just a little prank."

"How hard a mark, m'lord?"

"I'll leave it to you, but if he never comes back, I won't be sorry."

The man stood silent. Then he rubbed thumb and fingers together, and Florian realized he wanted to be paid. The Prince rummaged in a chest, took out a pouch heavy with gold coins, and handed it to him.

Rawl hefted the pouch and nodded, satisfied with its weight. "This will buy quite a mark that won't rub out. He wanted land, didn't he? Let me give him land not to his liking."

"Yes?" The Prince tilted his head, interested. "What do you mean?"

"There be in the Bog-lands an ancient town, once fair and now all to ruin. There's many a one who has wound up there, where creatures in the night quickly eat their flesh, and in time, even their bones disappear so there's no trace they ever lived."

"Really? How do you come to know of this?"

"Sometimes we goes a-hunting Boggies. It's good sport but not a trophy to parade through Rendelsham streets, so we leaves our kill there where others doesn't go. When we come back, all is as I said. No body, no bones, nothing left behind."

Florian grinned. "That sounds very nice. Very nice indeed. This fellow should be taken out and left there, by all means." The Prince had no real idea of life or death, or even of pain that was his own. He might as well have been discussing getting rid of a toy he had tired of. "But be careful, because Mother mustn't learn of this. And beware of that big dagger of his."

Rawl grinned in return, showing dark, snaggled teeth. "Never fear, m'lord. I've been in and out many times with no worse to show for it but a few insect bites, and I know how to keep my mouth shut when need be."

"Then go, and follow the nasty Count, for he has gone out of our home all unmannerly—he who would teach manners to me, the Prince!"

"It shall be as it shall be," the man replied. Then he glided into the shadows, and as far as Prince Florian could tell, vanished.

Four

*T*hough *Ashen's constant explorations* in the Bale-Bog, always aimed to follow Zazar, provided her with some faint idea of direction, she clung to a tangle of small brush limbs. Such support was, she told herself, to help her keep her balance. Striving to regain control, the girl looked around for possible landmarks to point her a safe way from the creature she was sure was behind her, whose unhurried leaps forward propelled it faster than a man could walk in the open.

Again she became aware of the buzzing of insects. There were no more cries—only the general Bog sounds could be heard. She drew a deep breath; she could not yet abandon caution. At least for the moment, there was no sound of pursuit. Unfortunately, to seek out a path other than that which had led her here might angle her once more in Tusser's direction.

Moving with care, the girl rounded the side of a high-reaching bush the small ones had led her to and came out into an open space. The partial gloom produced by the interlaced vegetation was lightened here. And she confronted a scene she had not expected.

The Bog was composed largely of stretches of islands and

marsh linked together. Bog-folk lived on the largest areas of firm land they could find. There they anchored their huddles of clan villages, each a part of that land itself, not buildings able to stand for long against winter storms. The straggly huts were mud-and-brush walled; moored close to each was a clumsy craft with which the inhabitants could reach possible safety if the waters and wind scoured over the land they knew.

What Ashen had found here was far different. Ragged and saw-edged grass grew in clumps, rooted apart from each other in crevices between stones, which floored the open. At the far end there reared—

The giant lupper! It had circled around to wait in ambush for her! She pushed back against the tall brush, her hand to her mouth as she sighted the thing. But even as she drew in a shuddering breath, she realized that it was made of stone and, like the pavement, possessed no life.

It must have been here for many, many years, but now it was only a time-worn image of the thing she had half seen at the pool.

Ashen squatted down on her heels, her mud-splashed legs trembling, unable to look away from that carven monstrosity. It was indeed akin to the Bog-luppers, yet it did not stand here on all four feet. Rather, it reared up on the more powerful hind ones, while the forelimbs rested on the huge swell of its belly.

That gigantic mouth, which on the living creature had been ready to engulf anything it caught, was closed. A green growth like pond scum half veiled it. But it was the eyes—large, bulbous, situated well up on the skull—that made her shiver.

Yes, she knew that this was stone—no living organism, but something wrought for a purpose. Nevertheless, those eyes, so large she did not think she could cover them, even one at a time with her hand, gleamed brightly yellow. In each was a pupil the shade of welling blood. Ashen could not believe that they were not real and meant to be used for some threatening purpose.

She clung desperately to vestiges of sense, yet certain that those eyes had marked her arrival. It was only rock—rock! Indeed, it had been planted there for so long that the scanty grass around it had fringed the body with yellow-green spears that rose high to curtain the powerful hind limbs.

Scolding herself for being so gullible, Ashen forced herself to her feet once more. She held the power-stone on the cord tightly in one fist. Very slowly she began to relax, realizing that the longer she stared at the figure, the more she was sure that the life of the eyes had to be a trick. This, this *artifact*, could not have life, no matter how knowingly it seemed to regard her.

However, in all her years as Zazar's pupil, in all her journeys made both with her mistress and alone, Ashen had never visited such a place fashioned of stone. Bog-folk made pots and bowls of clay, fired hard for use. She had never heard of any tool being applied to the working of stone. Then she remembered. There were those stepping-stones, so conveniently laid—those were not natural, either. Perhaps they had been placed by the same folk who had wrought the giant lupper.

Stone could not leap, rend, or tear. Slowly the girl advanced step by cautious step. As she grew closer, she became more certain that this was a thing of the far past. Who had fashioned it, and for what purpose, was a mystery. But perhaps this discovery would please Zazar better than any bundle of reeds would. Besides, the reeds were lost, dropped in her flight.

As she stepped from the mire out onto the stone pavement, her hand jerked up by no will of hers and in answer to no purpose of her own. The fist holding the power-stone rose in half salute to the figure.

From between her fingers there flickered a series of sparks, and she could feel growing heat from her odd weapon. Nevertheless, she made no attempt to once more swing the stone overhead. Somehow, she was certain that its warning—or protection—was not necessary here.

Emboldened, Ashen came to a halt before the looming stone figure. The eyes—had there been some subtle change in the eyes? Had they glowed more brightly as the stone warmed in her hand? Again she felt as if she were being viewed, but from a long distance. Ashen opened her fist, to find that the stone she held was also glowing. It was almost too hot to wrap her fingers around, as if she had picked up a blazing coal from a fire-pit.

It could have been her imagination, but a tenuous flame seemed to rise from it. The flame flickered once, twice, and was gone. With it vanished the feeling of being under observation, and all the mysterious aura of this strange carved creature disappeared as well. Now she faced only a piece of worked rock, which had never held life. Save for the buzzing of the insects, there were no more sounds, no cries or croaks; nor did the ground shake beneath the shifting of any great weight, as she had half expected.

One step at a time, Ashen circled the monstrous statue, viewing it from head to foot. Vines of bindweeds had looped themselves about its hindquarters, as if such fragile ties had grown to hold it prisoner. When she returned to stand directly before it, she saw that the forepaws, even though placed across the rounded belly, did not hide a series of markings incised there.

Bog-folk were not scholars. In every generation there was a Wysen-wyf such as Zazar, among but not of the Bog-folk. Each Wysen-wyf, it was claimed, had lived twice or more the length of an ordinary life. All of their strange kind had always kept in trust strange records, as Zazar did now, and from these, Zazar had taught Ashen to read. Ashen had spent long hours mastering markings that recorded events the various guardians had thought necessary to be remembered. She could make these signs as clearly as her mistress, and she had even read notes on what Zazar decided would be added when the time came. But never before had the girl seen such columns of dots, straight marks, and wriggling lines as existed here.

She hunkered down, her power-stone clasped in both of her hands. It had cooled, but nevertheless Ashen was sure that it would give her warning of any peril to come. She might not be able to truly read the inscription she examined, but she could at least memorize it.

☙

Queen Ysa was dissatisfied with the way her plans were progressing—or more accurately, the way her plans had ground to a halt. Over the years, she had repeatedly tried summoning the little invisible servant, and each time, she had failed utterly. After the first few attempts, her efforts grew farther spaced. She discovered that each trial had drawn heavily upon her store of beauty. Always pale, with the fox-eyed look so many with auburn hair endured, she had become expert in the application of cosmetics.

The last time, half a year ago, had been the worst.

Spell-making had to be done with the person in as natural a state as possible, artifice removed, garments plain. After that last terrible attempt, when she went to repair her appearance, she was shocked. Without any of the cosmetics she ordinarily wore, hers was a face that would not keep any woman long before her mirror. The eyebrows, untouched by the pencil, were threaded with silver hairs. They loomed over deep-set eyes not a warm brown, as might be expected, but the cold color of a sword blade.

Her unpainted mouth had become a thin slit, the lips tightly pressed together, seeming to echo the ever-present anger that was carving wrinkles across her high forehead. Bracketed with more wrinkles, her jaw was square and heavy, more like one to be seen under a war-helm frame than a lady's coif.

She couldn't bear looking at herself. She had married at fifteen, borne Florian at seventeen. Only now a little past thirty, she looked fully two-score years older. Shuddering, she reached for the jars and bottles, and with their help, managed to concoct a mask that hid the worst of the ravages. Or so she hoped.

With the depredations of chronic ill health, King Boroth had begun a steady decline. At first, she was inclined to put it down to the drink with which he plied himself night and day. But gradually she began to see that it was more than that. It was as if some kind of strength upon which he had long relied was being withdrawn.

Not knowing what else to do, Ysa hid this ongoing weakening of the King as much as possible, putting it down to a slight infirmity, a chest cold, a touch of joint-ache. But she couldn't expect to hide his growing helplessness forever.

When the mountains began to awake and belch forth fire, shaking the very ground beneath the city, Boroth's condition deteriorated even more rapidly. At last he took to his bed, and only the most deluded maintained that he would ever leave it again.

This produced mixed feelings in Ysa. She welcomed the finality of the King's withdrawal from the day-to-day matters of the Kingdom, for it put even more power into her own hands. And yes, she even welcomed the fact that Boroth no longer dallied with the palace maids, despite her own lack of any real affection for him. She was well past jealousy these days. However, she did not wish him ill. Rather, she hoped that he could last long enough for Florian to come into his own without her having to battle for the Regency. Ysa knew that her greatest strength lay in being influential behind the throne, rather than openly wielding the power that had become hers by default. This, however, would take time, as Florian was still too immature to be trusted to rule without a panel of regents.

Thus she tended Boroth with her own hands, trying to instill in him a measure of her strength, of her determination. It was as if by trying very hard, she could *will* him, if not back into health, at least into a condition that did not smack so much of decrepitude.

She felt as if she were holding her own, but then a firemountain erupted just a few leagues distant where there had been none before. It shook the city so severely that the bells rang in all the church towers. The upheaval threw Boroth into a fit, and she hurried to tend him.

"Have courage, husband," she said. "The city is sound and whole, for all the commotion, and you have nothing to fear."

"Wine," the King said. "Bring it to me now."

Of course his reaction would be to drink himself into a stupor. Nevertheless, Ysa gestured to Rugen, the King's body-servant, to obey his master's wishes. The man had no sooner placed the tray on the table beside the King's bed than another tremor, the greatest yet, nearly upset the wine flask.

"The land is dying!" Boroth exclaimed. "And with it, I die as well!"

He fell back on the pillows in a swoon. Ysa quickly filled a cup of the neat wine and held it to his lips, but Boroth did not react. She poured a little into her palm and began to chafe the King's hands with it, trying to revive him.

Then something happened that she was still trying to understand completely. With that contact, the four great Rings on the King's hands—the mysterious Rings that he had worn so long on thumbs and forefingers that the circles of metal seemed to be a part of his very flesh—transferred themselves from his hands to hers. Impossibly, mysteriously, they slipped past the swollen flesh on the King's fingers and passed over the two rings that she had been wearing—one on the forefinger of her right hand, the other on the thumb of her left.

Nor would the Rings be removed. Shocked, she had immediately begun trying to twist them off, to return them to their rightful place. To no avail—the Rings refused to yield.

After a few moments, the King roused enough to drink the contents of the wine flask. Shortly thereafter, he fell into a slumber that was more stupor than natural sleep.

Ysa arose from Boroth's bedside. Rugen still stood nearby, his expression carefully neutral. If he had noticed the amazing movement of the Rings, she knew he would keep this knowledge to himself. Undoubtedly he had held much greater secrets during the past years.

"Bring the King as much wine as he desires," she told the servant. "Keep him comfortable. Let him sleep."

Indeed, as she gazed back on Boroth, it seemed that he had settled into a real sleep. Could that have been by her own strong desire?

Once the door of the King's chamber had closed behind her, Ysa had time and privacy to study the Rings that now, apparently of their own volition, had come to her. She pulled off her own circlets, over which they had passed, slipping these onto other fingers.

The Rings were unlike ordinary gemmed trifles. Rather, they were massive, heavy, and plain, with no lighting of gem-fire. Each was formed of a broad band of a metal so rare that its like had never since been found in this country. In color, each had a touch of green shimmering across gold here, while there a hint of red flickered against light traces of blue and purple. In place of a gem-setting, each Ring bore an inlaid band of wood, each band on each Ring distinctly different. The only ornamentation the Rings bore was a small golden leaf, each representative of the wood, the tree, the badge of the House.

Oak. Ysa murmured the word and folded the forefinger of her right hand against her palm. Yew. Now thumb in turn moved under that forefinger, hiding its burden. Ash. The forefinger on her left hand quivered, but it did not fold under.

The Queen tensed, staring at the finger that had not obeyed her. She moistened her lips with the tip of her tongue. Rowan— the last command. Her thumb jerked, not entirely because of her will, but it did not disappear.

This would bear thinking on. And study. It was true then, what she had learned by hidden burrowing in the old records. The Rings chose the one to carry them. Suddenly she was aware that she felt lighter, less burdened, than she had in weeks. All her senses seemed heightened. Almost, she thought, if she tried, she could reach out tendrils of thought into every section of the palace—perhaps into the city, yes, perhaps even into the entire country—and know what any given inhabitant was thinking and feeling.

A surge of energy filled her. *Now*, she thought. Now I can complete the summoning! The King was safe enough for the moment, and she was all impatience to try out the hint of growing power and learn if indeed the Rings would be a help to her in her undertaking.

She hurried in the direction of the tower room, her refuge, where all of her magic paraphernalia was kept. Her route took her by the door to Prince Florian's apartment. Now she did discover that her heightened senses were not a product of overheated imagination. There was no need to open the door a crack and peer in; hearing sufficed. Two bare bodies rolled and panted together like common beasts. Florian, Crown Prince, was engaged in his favored occupation. The harlot who shared that embrace this night was one of the castle maids. A bubble of laughter rose to Ysa's lips, as quickly stifled at the thought that these women didn't have to do without, not as long as a male of Boroth's line lived.

Well, at least it wasn't that girl whose name she hadn't caught, the house daughter to Jaddeen, a petty border Baron with only tenuous ties to any of the ruling Houses. He had obviously brought her to the city with an eye to setting her about just this sort of activity, thinking that some advantage might come his way because of it.

How fortunate, she thought, that Florian's tastes ran much in the same direction as his father's. And that he had sense enough not to dare entanglement with someone of another rank whom he would not, or could not, marry.

She climbed the stairs to the tower room, entered, and locked the door behind her. Four great windows looking east, west, north, and south were covered with a transparent stuff across which flickered now and then a faint sheen of rainbow when a stray breeze caused the curtains to move.

In the center of that round chamber stood a single massive

chair, carved from a precious wood that was not only the color of blood, but of such density that to work it had required unusual tools and great strength. Beside it, on a small table fashioned of the same wood, lay the book of magic, still open to the page with the summoning-spell, as she had left it.

Off to one side were another, smaller table and another chair, much less ornate; there she sat to take off her coif and remove her mask of cosmetics. She lit a candle and set it beside her mirror. Her hair, still barely touched by the ravages that showed on her features, was of a ruddiness to rival the hue of the wood of the great chair. It tumbled down her back when she took the pins out, a glorious riot of color.

Then she donned a simple robe of red velvet, one that had a hood because of the chill of the season. She pulled this protection up over her head, moved to the great chair, picked up the book, and began the ritual.

With an ease she had never known before, the words rolled out, reverberating from the stone walls and creating a nexus of energy that hung in the air. Before her eyes, it coalesced into a creature that, startled, seemed to forget that it was winged. Lest it fall, she reached out, took it from the air, and set it on her lap.

Savoring the moment—and reluctant to witness in her mirror what this latest foray into magic might have done to her features—she stroked the creature until it stopped trembling. It gripped the fabric of her robe with its tiny paws, but did not look at her.

She took the little body by the nape of the neck. It struggled in her hands, kicking and flapping its leathery wings, but she held it up on a level with her eyes, imposing her will upon it, dominating it.

The creature's mouth opened, revealing sharp teeth. Its tongue was purplish red, and curved up at the tip. It chittered and then uttered a thin, high shriek of protest. Ysa continued to hold it until she was certain it had become entirely hers.

"Go, and seek," she said. Then she tossed it up and out into the air. Its wings spread and beat as it headed toward the window directly facing its mistress. As it went, its outlines seemed to grow hazy, and then it vanished abruptly.

Ysa's mouth turned down at the corners as she stared intently at where the flyer had been seen last. Then she clasped both hands quietly on her lap, waiting. While she waited, she allowed herself the luxury of remembering.

More than sixteen years had passed since her powers had been tried successfully. That had brought a full victory. Oh, the wretched woman had hidden her shameful condition long enough, thanks to the fashion—snug bodice ending just under the bosom, with a full-flowing skirt. There were those who had not known Alditha was carrying until she was practically in labor. But the slut had been found out eventually. She, together with that ill-planted seed she carried, had died. Bog-death was merciless. And there had been no wergild death-claim for her, for the Ashenkin would not air their disgrace.

She laughed aloud, to her ears a sound like the cackle of a vorse hen, and as deadly as that alarm could be.

In the great bed of the high chamber below lay—what? A man? To others it might seem so, but she knew it was a husk that lived only because it had not yet stopped breathing. The task of keeping him alive would be lighter now that the unthinkable had happened.

She stared again at the Rings—*her* Rings—their weight still new enough that they felt foreign on her hands. But that, she knew, would pass quickly.

After all, she had ruled for years, long before he had taken to his bed permanently. She had worked hard, sacrificing her youth and her fresh beauty to maintain the illusion that the King was whole and well. So it must remain, at least for a time.

With the Rings on her hands, she would know if there was any meddling in the direction of the King's life. With the Rings on her hands, she had successfully summoned the flying creature,

Andre Norton & Sasha Miller

and done it easily, after the disastrous attempts before. With the Rings on her hands, she could feel her power growing.

Boroth and Florian both rested snug under her command, and had done so long before the Rings had transferred themselves to her. They would be even more dominated by her now. She wondered only why the Rings had waited so long to recognize what was fact. Dismissing husband and son from her concern, she mentally listed those who might be a future danger.

Ashenhold was empty, half of its territory vanished, drowned in the Bale-Bog, the name one to spit upon. Of affiliated Families, there were Vacaster, Mimon, Lerkand, perhaps others of whom she was not sure. But she had her own ways of keeping in touch with their comings and goings; hired eyes ever watched them. Trouble in the north—yes, there had been reports of such, verified by that foreign noble, Count Bjauden, who had visited recently and then departed, never to be seen again. However, a war against invaders, well handled, would unite even feud-foes to fight under the same banner. She felt secure in the north.

The messenger she had sent forth this night would assure her of what chanced beyond the northern border. Still, that sense of unease did not lighten; there were things she could do if it came to strict need, but such acts would suck energy from her in turn, and she was cautious. If she had not been ever on her guard, she would not have had the leisure to sit here this night able to watch and plan.

It occurred to her that her messenger would not return for many hours. She got up, surprisingly unwearied, and went to the table against the wall. With a certain amount of dread, she picked up the hand mirror to survey the damage this time. To her astonishment, she discovered that far from her haggard appearance previously, now her complexion had assumed a touch of the bloom of youth. Her mouth was plumper, fuller, the silver strands in her eyebrows had vanished, and the deep wrinkles at brow and mouth were definitely lessened.

"Yes," she said. "Oh, yes." Now, in a blinding flash, she realized the situation fully. It had been the Rings all along—not *her* will, not *her* efforts—that had kept Boroth propped up, functional. Now, when he failed nonetheless, they had chosen to come to her. Well, even though Boroth had become an empty husk, she had the resources to maintain him for as long as necessary. And not suffer because of it.

With an effort of will, she finished renewing her lost beauty, removing age lines and restoring the bloom to her skin, until she was even more dazzling than she had been on the day she had married the King. In love with what the mirror showed her, she stared into it, singing softly to herself.

And, in rhythm to her song and almost unaware of what she was doing, she began to stroke the Rings.

🌿

Vold burned, as had the cities of Shater, Dosa, and Juptue earlier. From the packed decks of ships, children wailed, and there was also the brokenhearted sobbing of women who had seen their world fall into ruin under the onslaught of the armies of the far north. Though the Sea-Rovers still held to their courage, seamanship being their way of life, it did not take the boldness of omens to let even the most slow-witted of those milling about the deck here to understand that they must head out with what speed they could summon.

Snolli Sea-Rover of Vold was not slow of wit. A trickle of blood still oozing from his mail-coated arm, his face a set mask forbidding emotion, he planted his kin sword point-down into a plank before him, gazing sternward to that fire in the night.

Whatever else of note they might be able to accomplish, the Sea-Rovers knew best the building of ships. As a result, a world of many shores and countless lands had become as familiar to them as their own homecoming halls. Had been—but this was a world gone awry. There was near chaos on the mid-deck of the sturdy wave-splitter. Despite Snolli's defiance, behind them a crimson and yellow glow smeared a stain across the inland sky.

Those whose task it was to guide the *GorGull* to sea were busy at their work, but around Snolli stood his sworn war-band— those who were not too maimed to drag themselves to this saying of farewell. His son Obern, flanked by the wave-reader Harvas, joined the group. Both held large skin bags. The ship Harvas once served was no more, and he was still searching for some way to be useful until he could attach himself to another ship and again take up what he had been born to do.

The three survivors among the women who had fought beside the warriors, their bows punishing the enemy in these past days of defeat, stood nearby as well. Harvas gave each of the men and women one of the Farewell Horns from the bag he hugged close to his side. Then Obern poured a measure into each horn.

His task done, Obern took his battle place as back-guard to his father. The clamor from the deck did not lessen and yet it was easy for all who stood there to hear Snolli's words—words as old as their people.

"Stand by, your steel steady." There was no catch in Snolli's voice, no hesitation in repeating the ancient injunction. "What the kin could do, we have done. All hail to those dead already." He raised his horn in the salute of a toast. "Here's honor to the next to die!"

He emptied his horn in a single gulp and hurled the empty vessel out over the stern. Those in his war-band followed his gesture. With the Farewell Horns went the signal to Wind and Wave that they foresaw their fate, but to it they would not easily yield.

Obern had to control himself to keep from ruining the moment by spitting out his mouthful. The wine had a sour taste, for it was not a brew intended for feasting. Rather, it signified the bitterness of farewell, its dour meaning known as soon as it met the tongue. Determinedly, Obern swallowed. He wanted to spew it out; inwardly, he raged against the portent of that he had nearly choked upon.

They had fought, oh yes, how they had fought! Near three years of battles, of doomed skirmishes, of dogged standing up to defeat after defeat lay behind this night. They were not the first of the kin to make this choice, to labor in a frenzy of determination to lade the six ships that had already been shifted out of port for safety, to bring the last people who had retreated from the buildings behind. Rear guard they were, and there was little hope that Wind and Wave would come to their aid now.

Where had they come from, these invaders led by sinister riders mounted on beasts out of nightmares, armed with rods blasting the mist that burned out a man's lungs? None of Snolli's spies had been able to learn what had dragged this horror out of the northern ice regions to stamp a way into the fair land that the Sea-Rovers had held for time out of mind. The enemy could be killed, yes, but any captured seemed to die by will alone before information could be extracted from them. And they took no prisoners; man, woman, and child coughed under the cloud of poison mist and quickly died.

Now the enemy had taken the last of the defense keeps, or the fire-wrapped ruins of it. And only the open sea was left to those aboard this unwieldy, overloaded fleet.

The band on the stern deck stood still together, watching the fire reflected against the clouds behind.

"Flyer!"

A lookout's hand swung up to point in the air. Something did swoop there, coming down toward the ship. Obern's eyes were scout-keen.

There were two flyers, one a minute speck against the night sky, a much larger one following. As he watched, the small one seemed to wink out of sight. He rubbed his eyes, certain that the larger flyer had merely swallowed the small one.

The dark thing following them was no common sea bird, nor had he ever seen its like even in foreign lands. Of all that had happened this night, it was strange and apart from anything they had known before, and a sense of dread and foreboding enveloped him.

Apparently he was not alone in this. A bow cord twanged from behind him. The arrow hit, but did not bring down the flyer. Instead, the mysterious apparition soared even as a landeer would leap a stream. Then it veered off and was gone, swallowed by the darkness. Even so, Obern felt a chill of more than the sea breeze. It was a sending, of that he was sure, but why and by whom, he could not guess.

Five

Ashen leaned closer to the carved giant lupper, her original dread of it forgotten in her interest in the inscription embedded on it. She was finding it increasingly difficult to see the incised lines on the torso. Then, with a start, the girl recognized that time had fled and night was drawing in. With the shadows would come such dangers as sent all Bog-folk into shelter. She straightened up, looked around, and then concentrated all her attention on listening. Though she had been heedless, she had also been lucky; there were no more cries or croaks, no more thuddings on the ground behind. One of three likely possibilities had occurred. Either the lupper that had been chasing her had grown weary and returned to its underwater dwelling place; it had succumbed to the spears of the huntsmen; or it had eaten them and was now sleeping off its meal. Of these, she thought the third was the least likely.

She knew where the proper trail lay, but she was also well aware that Tusser might have recovered from his initial terror and, in his wrath, could already have set up ambushes along that thread of solid ground. She had no weapon but the curved stone knife with which she had harvested the reeds, and which had, by some accident, stayed with her in her flight.

This was not a safe area of the Bog. She knew that every moment she lingered where she was, she invited danger, if not from the deeps of the pools, then from the malice of those who had thought to take her this day.

Cautiously, Ashen got to her feet. At one time, some people—or things—had made a sanctuary here. Even as those stepping-stones had long endured just under the surface of the water, there could be another ancient path to this place.

The girl turned out again to the left and began a renewed inspection of the stone monster. This time her attention was not so much directed toward the image itself but rather, toward that walling brush, thick and menacing enough to drag her trail garments into tatters. Here and there in the stunted and twisted greenery, she could see monstrous thorns as long as her finger, glistening with a threatening, yellowish sheen. Those she knew, and they were deadly to humankind.

When Ashen reached a point where the lengthening shadow of the stone figure laid darkness across her, she noted that there was a thinning of the surrounding growth. It might be a path laid to entrap, but she realized that unless she wanted to risk running into Tusser again, this path was probably her best chance for safety. Surely Tusser would steer well clear of a place such as this.

By instinct, she whirled aloft again the power-stone that had served her so well before. Though she did not utter the call that had summoned its power earlier, there came an answer. Ahead of her, a glow of verdant brilliance lit up what she saw now was definitely a path—or at least the beginning of one. Ashen straightened her shoulders and deliberately approached it.

Though she had left the vicinity of the statue, she could sense by the firmness underfoot that she was still following an outreach of the pavement, overgrown though it was with vegetation. The glowing plant-life led her onward. After a moment or so, she began to understand that she was on a narrow trail—paved, although here the stones were smaller—almost completely hidden by a slime of moss and clods of grass. The only difficulty was that it headed in the opposite direction from that she wished to take. Still, there was no side way open to her, and in the growing darkness outside, the light guided her. So she was reluctant to push through the surrounding bushes and head out blindly across the mire.

Twice Ashen glanced back and knew a cold trickle of fear, for it seemed in this greater gloom of the brush that the trail she had come along was now being swallowed up from behind her as she went.

She came out into a second space. Here there was no more sign of pavement, and the footing was soggy. Now she knew she must have help to pick her way along. She turned toward the last bush she had passed on her way into the clearing. Though there were more and heavier shadows here, her trained trail-sight showed her several branches that did not bear thorns, only twigs to which withered leaves still clung. Across one of those branches an insect scurried, and for the first time, Ashen knew a lift of triumph. She was as well Bog-trained as any warrior, and here she had found what was wanted—something that was not the enemy of all animal life.

Still, it paid to be prudent. Reaching out with care lest her flesh touch the leaves of other, less friendly growth, she brought her stone knife down hard on the surface of a large, sturdy branch. A second blow, as carefully aimed, broke through the portion of wood where the insects had trod, and a length of the branch fell. Ashen struck again and then jumped back swiftly, before any prickly leaves could rake her.

The outer part of the branch had broken entirely free, showing under its bark a pitted passage from which were now boiling a number of disturbed burrowing insects. Ashen shook them loose, freeing them to make their way by determined leaps to other branches. Then she groped in her belt pouch and brought out a little packet. She slung the cord of the guardian-stone about her neck, leaving her hands free to untie the grass lacing of the pouch until it lay flat on one palm. Within was perhaps a spoonful of a reddish dust. Carefully, she blew so that a puff of the dust struck and clung to the branch she had chosen.

In moments, those mites that still remained inside the branch began to fall like dark rain. Taking up the branch, holding it well away from her, she shook it vigorously until she was sure that all the pith-eaters were gone and only a walking staff remained. Then, feeling a little more secure with the weight of the branch in one hand, frail and insect-chewed though it was, Ashen turned to survey the land ahead over which those spark wisps that hunted by night had begun to hover. She must concentrate on searching out the best places to go on the ground ahead. Yet she could also hear the warnings that had been dinned into her ears since childhood. The Bog came to life at night, showing a greater and more dangerous population as darkness closed in.

To her relief, when she poked at the surface just ahead of her, she discovered that she had been fortunate. Less than a finger's length below the mire, she found a solid base. Patiently, she followed this hidden trail. Twice it made a turning and she was afraid that it had ended. However, by probing to both sides, she discovered the next step, though the direction varied according to no plan that she could ascertain.

This space of the open was too wide for her liking. The dark was not deep enough yet to form a cover against any lurker watching, and even worse, she discovered that the power-stone swinging about her throat now shone with a pale, greenish gleam. Nevertheless, she did not tuck it away inside her tunic or put it into her belt pouch again. Though it revealed her plainly to anybody who might be observing, there was something reassuring about that light.

The wall of taller growth toward which she was heading now curved to bring her out on the bank of one of the sluggish Bog streams. There again she literally stumbled upon something that proved this had once been a traveled way. She rubbed her shin and studied a stone block balanced on two fellows to form a kind of bridge. Not only that, but there were also signs of more stones ahead, promising safe footing.

Ashen stepped up on the first of these and stood for a moment to rest. The rigid attention she had had to give to the last part of her journey had wearied her. Suddenly remembering the hearth-guide, Zazar had given her, she settled her staff in the crook of her arm so she could open her belt pouch again. From it she took out the small square of wood so well-handled through years that its surface was as sleek as a lupper's skin. She could think of no better opportunity to find out if the hearth-guide worked as promised.

"Zazar." She raised the bit of wood to her lips, though she did not allow it to touch her skin. A spicy scent wafted from it. "Zazar," she repeated, wondering if she was merely wasting time. Perhaps she was too far away for the hearth-guide to be effective.

But then the wood began to glow faintly. Across its surface there wove a line of yellow as faded as the thick grass that grew around the stones on which she stood.

Perhaps it was true, and perhaps not. Ashen had never tested the power of this guide, and she knew that she was well beyond the boundaries for her certain knowledge of the Bog. Out of the fast-deepening dusk, she heard a thick cry that might have been uttered by one of the creatures from the depths. Luckily, it did not come from the direction she would be taking.

The girl strode ahead at what speed she dared use. From the shape of the land, she knew that she was indeed now on another of the isles that dotted the area—perhaps a large one, sturdy enough for a Bog-folk settlement.

Then she smelled fire and the roasting flesh of a fallowbeeste. But she did not turn in that direction. No one Bog-born or bred approached the hearth of another without the proper identification whistle, and this hearth was entirely foreign to her. She had been taught not to trust the unknown.

In a moment, she knew the soundness of this teaching. There came the throb of a skin drum, the common means of far-speaking, but those fingers on the talking-drum, flitting in proper pattern, produced sounds she did not recognize.

Suddenly she knew where she was—close by the holding of one of Joal's rivals. It was less than a league from her own village. It housed neither friend nor enemy—the two settlements cooperated at need—but it might as well have been in another land. Zazar could walk the entire Bale-Bog with impunity, but without the Wysen-Wyf's company, Ashen had no reason to believe that she would be welcome.

She left what was now a plain path and traveled eastward with slightly more confidence than she had known earlier. By using the staff with every step, she was assured that she would not go dangerously astray. Yet she shivered as if the drumbeats formed an invisible cord striving to jerk her in another direction. The guardian-stone on her breast began once more to warm. Its glow deepened, but she did not need that warning to keep her away from strangers.

Twice she crouched, her whole body shaking to the drumbeat, watching as shadows moved into moonlight, revealing armed Bog-folk. They must have sent their keenest hunters out, yet it would seem that none of their attention shifted in her direction.

Still, Ashen drew on every bit of trail-craft she knew until she gained sight of a landmark. Only then did she dare put on speed to reach the door poles of Zazar's sprawling hut. She stopped in her tracks as Kazi arose from a crouch. The serving woman might have purposefully placed herself there on guard.

"Flit-flit." The stoop-shouldered woman stood as if she did not mean for Ashen to get past her.

Ashen was sure that Zazar had not yet returned. Otherwise, Kazi would not have ventured to face her in this fashion. The Wysen-wyf's continued absence made her bold.

The girl walked directly forward until the woman had to give way, dragging her crooked foot. Inside, there was the familiar warmth, the mingled smells of Zazar's plant harvests.

"*She* will know what you do—"

Ashen turned her back to Kazi and put the power-stone and the wooden hearth-guide in her pouch. Then she turned to face the crone. The coals in the fire-pit did not give much light, but an oil lamp flickered on the low table by Zazar's chosen pile of cushions. A gleam of that light caught an answering glitter from among the folds of Kazi's reed-weave shawl.

As if aware that Ashen had seen, Kazi instantly put her hand to her breast, and the small spark disappeared. Ashen knew what the other had hidden, however. She had never seen it closely, but she knew that it was an object made of metal. She also knew that Kazi kept it hidden from Zazar as well. Well, sooner or later she would solve this little mystery. When she discovered what Kazi wished kept to herself, she would have gained a fraction more of power. She knew that Kazi hated her and always had. Ashen did not doubt that the woman was a tale-bearer and had a malicious tongue. Undoubtedly she had served to keep alive the barrier between Ashen and the Bog-folk.

"*She* will know," Kazi repeated ominously. "Know what you do, *she* will."

Ashen paid no attention to Kazi's implied threat. "What happens? Are the clan guards out?"

Kazi scowled and hesitated for a moment before answering. "Outlanders—your kin—come take you. You be Bog now. When they in Bog, they kill, burn. Feed to their hounds."

Ashen grinned. "A very cheerful prospect," she returned. "So all the guards would deliver me to these invaders? I think that Zazar will have something to say about that."

Deliberately, Ashen took a bowl from the shelf, reached for a dip ladle lying across the table, and filled the bowl from the pot of soup thick with noodles that always hung over the fire.

Ysa, Queen of Rendel, First Priestess of Santize, sat wrapped in shadow now. Night had fallen in earnest and still her little messenger had not returned. To pass the time now that her physical appearance was one that suited her, she decided to test the powers of her knowledge of the Great Houses, by the Rings that represented each.

She brought the Ring on the thumb of her right hand to her mouth and touched its golden leaf with the tip of her tongue. "Oak," she said.

Her perception altered, and it was as if an invisible part of herself swept through the castle, seeking to know the well-being of the head of the House of Oak. Down in the maze of corridors and rooms, small towers, even to the rock depths of the dungeons, all was quiet. Boroth still slept in a swine's snorting slumber, unaware as yet that he was no longer master of the Rings.

"Yew." She touched her tongue to the Ring on the forefinger of her right hand. It was her own House-mark, and by right of her heritage, the head of the House of Yew was Florian, the whelp she had seen as a failure from the hour of his birth. Boroth's attention, of course, had been elsewhere long before that time. A sire with an eye for the stoutness of his line would have put an end to such a disappointment within its first hour of life. Now, with the Rings securely in her possession, Florian was even more of a tool than he had been before. However, she must never forget that this was one which she could never be sure would not turn in her hand, just at the moment when she must strike swift and sure.

He was alone now, and sleeping. Replete. One could find it easy to think him of no account. He had a following, though. There was a cadre of fribbets that fawned upon Florian, shoved and scrambled for the right to support him. But there was none among the High Lords who had done more than express a very circumspect contempt for his person.

She hesitated for a moment before she touched the Ring encircling the thumb of her left hand. "Ash."

There would be little—which, she told herself fiercely, was as it should be. Blown away like last year's leaves was that tenuous Family claim to the throne of Rendel, a claim reaching back for so many years it had become a legend. No, wait, there was—

Once again she touched the tiny golden ash-leaf with the tip of her tongue. A ruined city, far to the south. Had she sensed a kind of stirring in those ruins? No, there was nothing, certainly nothing. Yet . . . why did her head turn a fraction in that direction, toward but not facing the ever-deepening gray outside the south window? Ashen—Ash. For the third time, she sent the call, to have it return unanswered clearly. Nothing, and surely nothing. But still her frown lingered and she hurried on to taste the last Ring—Rowan, ever the weakest of the Houses, the one whose traditional ally was Ash, even as Oak and Yew were allied.

Yes, there was an answer, far away and faint. What were they now? Erft, the titular head, a man too old to mount a warhorse. He had not been seen outside the wall of his major keep for near a full year. She sought him again, specifically, and had only a weak return for her efforts. Yes, Erft was undoubtedly now as much a nothing as was his King. Yet— She tried again, for there was a hint of more. Erft had had no blood son since the fall of the Ashenkeep . . . when? Seven, eight years past? She caught the whisper of a young and scarce-formed girl. Only a female. . . .

The Queen grimaced. She had little liking for those of her own sex. There had been an incident, years ago, a chance touching from which she had withdrawn in a hurry. Power could be drawn when greater met lesser, and that touch had been a warning. Did she sense another of this ilk? Growing bolder, she summoned memory as one might run down a corridor jerking open door after door to see what might skulk within.

She cast her perception wider, found what she sought. Yes, here it was. She could see clearly now. Erft had an heir—a granddaughter, supposedly a frail wraith of a child. But seasons pass quickly enough, and since the girl had struggled through the first threatening years of life and survived . . . well, she must have strength of a sort. Her name—Ysa sought again, ignoring the headache that was starting in her temples.

Laherne! Her questing ended abruptly and she opened her eyes wide, thrown off guard for a moment. How could she have forgotten? Not surprisingly, this girl was not only Rowan, she was also Ashenkin, the result generations back of a mating to enmesh the strength of two lordships. And all concentrated in this single girl, as delicate as the yellow rose on the Rowan badge, and as unsullied as its motto, "Here find all peace."

Ysa settled back in her chair, her hands dropping again to her lap. Yes, though young and not yet aware of who or what she was, this Rowan-Ash creature was of marriageable age. Now Ysa smiled, a small, tight movement of lips. Why, it worked out to her purpose. Ash was gone, Rowan nearly so. Still, there could be a mating of power once again, bringing all the remnants of the four Great Families into one place, distilling them into one heir. The Prince, Oak and Yew, was yet unwed. As for his fumbling in bed and chasing anything in skirts, his wife would have to learn to cope the way her betters had. The way Ysa herself had.

The Queen rubbed her forehead to ease the ache. Certainly she had no hope of trying to seek a bride for the Prince from abroad. Those eyes and ears that reported to certain ones she controlled had made it plain that Rendel need not bother to look elsewhere for new blood to shore up their failing lord-lines. This was a time for bargaining, for shadow-seeking, not a time for delegations to neighbors with the offer of a possible crown for a stray daughter of a solidly founded House.

Ash and Rowan. Her right hand slipped across the left, covering them with the Oak and Yew Rings. There was symbolism for you, she thought. Then her small moment of satisfaction was interrupted by a commotion at the window just in front of her. Through its arch the little flyer darted, and she raised her hands quickly to catch it. To her surprise, the tiny creature trembled, and she stroked it with an unaccustomed gentleness, crooning to it. In a few moments, it settled down. Then the Queen raised her servant to eye level. The sparks in its head were vivid with knowledge ready to be given her.

There was a moment of vertigo as her sight passed, it would seem, from one set of eyes to another. Now she hung aloft, while down below raged fire enough to turn an ice-bordered night into day. This must be the northern lands, home of uncouth wanderers. Here burned a keep the might of which shook her somewhat. There was little barbaric about these flame-scorched walls. For a moment, she saw destruction, and those who rode strange, monstrous white beasts and circled the site.

Vertigo assaulted her again as she swung out over water, where the rise of the moon gave light to see the vessels that parted the waves there. Ships of that kind could cause terror along the coast, as she herself knew. Northern people were in flight, having managed to escape destruction in their stronghold. They would beat a way south eventually. She must raise defenses at once.

Then, behind her, a shadow. She turned and glimpsed the ravenous mouth of a huge flying creature, not a bird, and knew at once that it was ready to scoop her up and swallow her. She knew also that anyone so caught would be less than a morsel served at her table as an aperitif, and that the creature's real seeking was not for her, but for those on board the northern ships. . . .

Then she blinked out. With a rush, she returned to herself once more whole and separated again. She set the little flyer on her shoulder, and she could feel the heavy beat of its heart against her cheek. It had indeed served her well. It deserved a name.

"Visp," she said. "I'll call you Visp." It began to purr, as if pleased. If only she could find those among her own kind who would serve her even half as well as Visp.

Six

🍂

oroth had been dreaming again, thrashing the covers about on the bed in his struggles against some dark assailant. He lay staring upward into the black rise of bed canopy above him. His heart was thumping fiercely; there was a taste like barnyard mud in his mouth, and an aching that might have come from a grievous wound behind his eyes. They burned, and he knew from long experience that if he looked at himself in the mirror, he would see they were deeply bloodshot.

As always, the waking was worse than the dreams, a truth haunting him these days. Slowly he levered his flabby body up into a sitting position. He was dry, near perishing with thirst. With one hand, he fumbled on the table next to his bed while he uttered a guttural growl.

The night lamp, which was always to be kept alight, had failed. Nevertheless there was moon enough to show that the trundle bed of his body-squire was empty.

He strove to lift his voice above a croak. "Rugen!"

He was alone in the huge bed on the dais. Not only had the curtains to his right been left open to the dark and the night, but those at the foot were also undrawn. Boroth squinted. There was something there, faint sparks of light. Shifting all his weight to one elbow, he made a grab at those sparks and slid toward the edge of the rumpled bed.

"Staffhard!" Even his guard— Had they all deserted him? Had he been true-dreaming? Had he really been left alone, to face whatever might prowl the dark?

He could smell the thick odor of wine. Saliva flooded his mouth and he swallowed convulsively. He wanted—must have—drink. Only give him a full goblet of wine and his world would come right again.

Those points of light—eyes, surely they were eyes!

Spying upon him. In a hidden curtain sheath, not far from him, hung his pillow-sword. Not daring to look away from the eyes, he flailed out in panic and tore at the heavy tapestry with his fingernails until he found the weapon and closed his hand on the hilt.

"By the Wraith of Kambar, who are you?" He licked his parched lips. The Power he called upon was one long forgotten in these days. He hoped it still protected him.

Except, except . . . his own eyes had been captured by those that glowed out there. His breath began to come in gasps as he found it more and more difficult to fill his lungs. He saw the eyes, he saw beyond them. . . .

There was a darkness that hung like one of the deep red curtains of the bed. And then there was a grayish gleam. It slowly swam into focus and took the shape of a leaf. His befuddled wits were clearing. Yes, truly there was a leaf, man-tall, standing straight as a guardsman on duty.

A leaf. What leaf? Memory stirred. His brain felt sluggish and even more in need of a drink. Then he recognized it. Ash! The leaf—it was Ash! Before his eyes it shifted, melted, turned into a woman, she whose face he had thought never to see again.

"Alditha—"

"Boroth," she whispered, the word as faint as a sigh. She gestured with both hands, and then faded from view.

Something about the grip on the pillow-sword was different. The weapon fell from his hand, and he felt frantically over his fingers for what was missing—there were no metal bands half sunk in his puffy flesh. No tightness of metal-and-wood bands. Unbelieving, he touched the deep dents where the Rings had lately been—thumb, forefinger, thumb, forefinger. Anger, fueled by fear, found outlet in a bellow of rage.

Someone answered. "Sire! Lord King!"

There was light enough now, and not that of the eyes. A candle, unbearably bright. Boroth was shaken, dazzled, so that he blinked several times.

"Rugen?"

"Yes, sire. I am here. What do you desire?"

Old habits die hard. Boroth was aroused enough to attempt to be what fate had made him—a ruler and a leader.

"Bring me wine!" he said hoarsely. "Where have you been, you sneaking whoreson? Do you go about at night trifling with some loose wench, forgetting your duties? I'll have the skin off your back come morning—"

By now, Rugen had come around the end of the bed. He set down the double candlestick so that the light showed him busy pouring from a tall pitcher into a goblet. Boroth fairly snatched the vessel from Rugen's hand, dribbling some drops onto the bed. He drank like a man dying of thirst. He lowered the goblet and breathed deeply, eyes closed, waiting for the familiar ease. It did not come.

Surely it had been only a dream. Why, he couldn't summon even a clear memory. Nothing but a dream. Yet there had been a time when some dreams had been sent as warnings. He raised the goblet again and saw his hand plain once more. He had not imagined it.

The Rings were gone!

His old power had not deserted him. Alditha had come to warn him, to tell him.

He hurled the goblet into the darkness and lunged across the bed toward Rugen. Though the servant stepped back, startled, the King caught him by the shirt and dragged him over the edge of the bed. Rugen lost his balance and went down on his knees, clutching at the bedclothes to keep from falling entirely.

Boroth thrust his face close to the servant's. "Where are the Rings?" He shook Rugen with some of his former strength. "You are a dead man if you don't tell me at once! Where are my Rings?"

"Sire—sire—I have them not!" Rugen clutched at the bed, striving to free himself from the grip without raising his hand against his master.

"Then who does?"

Boroth was no longer befuddled with drink. He might have dreamed away many memories, but this had sobered him completely and, perhaps, permanently. He well knew on whose fingers those Rings belonged.

"Her Majesty, sire, the Queen."

Rugen near tumbled to the floor as Boroth released him as quickly as he had seized him.

But Boroth was no longer paying him attention. The King was spreading his hands into the light and staring down. There were marks in the flesh there, mocking him. It was as if the Rings had bit into skin, and perhaps been forcibly taken from him.

So that was the way of it! Though his head throbbed and he was fighting down nausea, it was as if he had opened a door and brought in more light upon himself and his state than he had been aware of for years.

He touched thumbs and fingers in turn, whispering the words aloud, but only to himself. "Oak." He rubbed the thumb as if he could still caress a metal band. "Yew." Now he grimaced. "Ash." What was there about Ash? He could not remember, but he would once the last of the wine fumes was out of his head. Oh, yes, he *would* remember! "Rowan!"

Never again, he vowed. Never again would he allow himself to become so besotted with wine that such a monstrous indignity could be lodged against him. The Rings were his, to answer him since his crowning, and he was not to be despoiled. He would have them back even though he could never again have the one whose memory had come to him to tell him of the theft.

As would be discovered.

🌿

Thus far had Wind and Wave favored the precipitate flight of the Sea-Rovers. But as the far overloaded ships wallowed into the heavy dark of the night sea, none aboard were released entirely from fear. However, the north-bred demons could not put their monster steeds to treading waves behind the fleeing ships. Of that much, they could be certain. Nor could their foes send great ice blocks after them; the time of year was wrong for it. This was the season for winter's-end storms. But despite all their frenzied efforts at the last, the fugitives had not been able to gather much in the way of food and other supplies, and as yet they had no plan for a near landing.

Those war captains who were still hale and on their feet gathered in a conference on deck. Three wind-shielded sea lanterns centered the small circle where they knelt or crouched, intent on what the ship's captain was pointing out on a salt-stained map.

Their way of approaching any unknown land had always been to prepare to fight, raid, and then return as speedily as they could to their ships. Most of these expeditions had been carried out by one or two ships alone. But now there were no longer home ports in which to lie safely and refit.

The captain indicated a spot on the map. "Not Volen—the voyage is too long, and we would be starving before we were halfway there. The storm season hangs ready to strike within days."

One of the men moved and Obern glanced up. It was Grabler, one whose advice his father often heeded.

"South and shore creep." Grabler's words came almost with the snap of an order.

"South is swampland save for Idim, and that is but a pocket of ruin. We could not even land all our people safely there. And the Bale-Bog—well, we all know about it."

The Sea-Rovers were not masters of the sea; no man could claim to be that. But they had had generations of learning its ways to mold them. They must establish a temporary port and find shelter for those who kept the home hearths while the raiders were out. There were enough tales of the Bog-land to warn anyone off those reef-edged and cliff-lined shores, shores even seamen less careful than they themselves had for generations avoided.

"There is this." Another hand swept into the dim circle of light around the lanterns. Even if Obern had not known his father's hand, he would have recognized the broad thumb ring of High Chief, its red stone seeming to take fire from even that limited glow. His father was well at home with maps. In the keep, whose burning still cast a red glow against the sky behind them, there had been a repository for a large map collection, and the High Chief paid good prices to any Rover who had voyaged off the known lanes and brought back a record of his travels.

"The south," Snolli said. "Beyond the Bog, across the boundary river. There have been many reports of what may be in progress there. Five, maybe six or seven years ago, no one of us with a thought in his head would have ranged far into the waters that the Ashenkin controlled from their watch-hold. They were seamen, regardless of what name be laid upon them by others. But the entire land, the Ashenhold, is vacant, and the great Ashenkeep now lies as empty as Vold, swept away by fire and sword, deserted. These southern warlords are ever at each other's throats, and among them, only Ashenkin sought sea roads. There has been no word from the Year Traders that any have come to hold what Rendel men themselves destroyed."

Around him, his chieftains murmured. To most, this might have been news, but some were well aware of the story. Snolli spoke to those who did not know.

"You heard at last midwinter feasting that speaker for the Year Traders report that the whole of that land is bubbling like a tar-pot left too high on a flame. Their King wallows in strong drink, and his son is a wastrel. The lords of the Council sit and watch each other lest one be on the move to take what his fellows also see as theirs. Who rules?"

"Aye," one of the lesser chieftains echoed. "If not the King, then who?"

"The Queen Ysa is a woman of some powers and all the strengths she can gather to herself. She plays one lord against another, using dark ways to make certain of the support she needs."

Snolli stabbed his forefinger at the map, just where it showed a curve of inlet.

"Ashenkeep?" His gesture was answered by cries from two of that company.

"Aye, that it be," Grabler said. "The harbor there is a good one. The river feeding into it runs from a fertile land that is now sparse of any dwellers. It's said that a small ship can sail right up and anchor outside the very gate. And as great was the fury of those who strove to level it, stone walls such as held there are not easily toppled. We may need but a temporary landfall and then we can send out scouts to learn what faces us."

"They say that the place lies under a Red Saying." That was Hengrid, who was always ready to see danger and ill in any offered project.

"Are we Ashenkin?" Grabler asked, a challenge in his voice. "A Red Saying holds only for the bloodline it is put upon. We are not of these queasy southern kind who would fight with a cursing instead of sword in hand. I say our High Chief has spoken wisely. We must have a port before the storm season. If others of our kin-lines have fought to freedom, the Traders' messengers will carry the word and they can join us."

"So be it said and heard." Snolli looked at each man in turn. The verdict was repeated around the circle.

The captain set about folding his map. He rose to his feet. "Signals up, and south it shall be."

Obern slipped back from his position at his father's shoulder. He was a true Wave Rider and had been for these ten years and more. However, all his forays had been westward to the strings of islands, large and small, overseas. By the luck of the Sea-Rovers, he had never before been on the run from any foe, nor unsure of a safe port ahead.

The Traders refrained from venturing far from the safety of shores. They came to barter for foray loot at the beginning of autumn, or at the Winter Feast, when more than one clan met in friendship. Obern had always been interested in their stories, and his interest had been encouraged by Snolli, who set him to record such tales as seemed to have an element of truth in them.

Now the survivors of the burning of Vold were heading south, making their way into the very waters that had once been held so firmly against them. Obern knew as well as any that they would have to stop and gather food along the way. But between that desolate port they sought and here, where they battled an uneasy sea, lay the Bog, and of this, Outlanders knew little and had never striven to learn more. It was as if a blackness that was not a common dark curtained that waterlogged land from the clean world without.

He thought again about that winged thing that had been a shadow visible against the fire-painted sky. Why had it not pursued them when it had a clear opening? Had it been that other, smaller, flying thing, the one that had vanished so abruptly that the lookouts swore it had never been there at all? Whatever the reason, it had not attacked. Not then. Nobody yet knew what it was, except that it had to be a sending from their enemies. He had asked Fritji about it.

Some of the sea clans had wave-readers; they did themselves. Some men, and women too, were born with special talents; all knew that. One could not turn away, scoffing, from the idea that there was much in the world that humankind did not yet understand. And though such with special gifts were few, they were encouraged to use what they had brought with them from the womb for the good of kin and clan. All wave-readers could set courses well enough for an expert mariner to follow in turn. Some could even foretell the coming of storms. Fritji, wave-reader to Snolli, was one of these. And he had confirmed Obern's suspicions.

That shadowy thing—had it been some servant of the monster riders, or had it come from another source? One could only wait and see.

"No good."

Obern jumped a little, startled. Hengrid might have been answering his silent query. Characteristically, the armsman had spoken as in a riddle. "Eh? Finish your thought, Hengrid."

"No good ever came to them as wanted to try that coast. The pull lights would be out in a hurry any night, were we sighted close enough."

Nerves made Obern more than a little edgy. "So? And where would you have us dump ourselves and our goods then? Those before us have headed for the Fringe Isles. Do you think there will be peace when a new hand-count of ships wants anchorage where two might hardly squeeze?"

Hengrid was well known to be a storm-screecher, one who always predicted doom. At the same time, he was an axeman of note and had left plenty of the foe to board the Ship of Death behind them. Obern could not afford to dismiss him out of hand.

"There's the pull lights," Hengrid repeated vigorously, as one who would not accept anything but the worst.

Pull lights? Obern tried to remember. In his time of roving, he had never ventured into these southern waters. The many reefs and sandbank traps where sea and the great river emptying

from the Bog made a muddled stir of meeting were wisely
avoided. Yet, to reach the Ashenkeep, they would have to risk
near a surf-wet course.

Then he remembered about the pull lights. Those stories
were little more than ghost tales these days.

Pull lights were what was meant by lights ashore that caught
the eyes of the helmsman, somehow entrapping him and any
others sighting them, so that the ship was swung directly into
the death-path they marked.

Well, it should be easy to avoid such simple traps. The Bog-
folk might be another matter. The Bog-folk had weapons wholly
of their own. Yes, the Bale-Bog was a stink to spread o'er half
the world at times. Obern took a deep breath of fresh sea wind
to clear his thoughts away from unseen dangers. There were
enough present perils to be watched for.

🌿

"Zazar hearth!" a voice called from outside.

Ashen took another mouthful of noodles. Let Kazi answer
the call; the old woman liked feeling important.

Sure enough, Kazi was quick to reply. "Two within, one
gone. The curtain be unlaced, Chief Kin."

Ashen stirred. Had Kazi gone entirely dimwitted? If Joal had
been somehow moved to take the night count in person, he need
only be answered.

"Hearth in ember."

Ashen relaxed a little. It was the Bog-folk's way of saying
"All is well." Joal knew better than to question Zazar's household
about their comings and goings.

She dropped the ladle into the soup pot and watched the
curtain as it was shrugged aside by the headman's thick shoulder.
Joal was no youngster who had not long carried his turtle shield,
and all knew that he had little liking for the Wysen-wyf. Too
many times had she defeated some cherished plan of his.

Now he was glaring straight at Ashen. "You took trails," he

said, scowling, "for almost full sun length. Where went, and why?"

She nodded in a bare salute to his office, and her voice was clear and concise as she answered. "I do my mistress's bidding, Joal." It was a lie this time, but one he could not disprove.

"Zazar be not here to answer for you. You been seen near the way of Gulper. That land be closed to all kin. You go there, Old Ones know. Very bad."

Ashen heard a gasp from Kazi. It covered her own. She knew exactly where this story had come from. Tusser had used the same word, Gulper, as if it were the fell creature's name. Joal could not know about Gulper from any other source. Tusser was alive.

Beyond that, even if Kazi did not believe in the Old Ones, who had not been observed in that section of the Bog supposedly theirs, she had a multitude of stories to embellish their dread acts. From her earliest childhood, Ashen had heard most of the tales. She realized that in her exploring, she must have strayed into one of the Old Ones' secret, perhaps sacred, places.

"I tell truth to my mistress, Kin Chief." Kazi seemed almost defiant.

"And where be Zazar?" Joal dug the point of his spear into the well-pounded earth and matted dried herbs, which served them for a flooring.

"Behind you, Joal!" Zazar's voice was waspish. "Striving to enter my own hearth past a lump without the manners of a slithcreep."

He shifted his weight quickly but she did not push past, waiting in obvious impatience for him to show proper respect.

Joal was disturbed enough to indeed forget formalities. "Where be you, Wysen-wyf—fishing for Outlanders?"

She laughed. "So that old cry has been raised again, has it? And where do these Outlanders come from? Eh? The few ways they can hope to come are well guarded, are they not?"

"They come!" He near spat out those words as he turned and

blundered through the curtain folds. Zazar waited for a long moment.

Ashen scrambled to her feet hastily as Zazar turned toward her. She knew well that particular look.

She had been a fool, she knew it at once, to try to avert Zazar's wrath. Her head near snapped back as the Wysen-wyf slapped her cheek full force.

"You are totally empty-skulled." Zazar stood with both balled fists on her hips, looking the girl down and then up again. "Now listen, and listen well, you Outland whelp. It will take very little, now that you are older, for Joal to order you to the feeding pool for the good of the kin. It is the oldest of all the First Laws— Bog-folk must not take Outlander women. If they do, it means death. I have seen Tusser and his foot-kissers talking behind their hands while they watched you. To some men, that which is different is desirable—for a little while."

"They—they would be punished." Ashen said. She licked the corner of her mouth and tasted blood.

"Punished? Perhaps. Such actions have been known before. There are stories of Outlander women who came looking for adventure in the Bog and found more than they could conveniently manage. And since such females were not seen again, they were just as conveniently forgotten. Outlander men, too." She spat. "You—where did you go this day?"

Ashen straightened her shoulders. This was, she knew, the time for truth-telling. But would the strange tale she had to tell be enough to divert the fullness of Zazar's rage?

With Zazar in this present mood, how much dare Ashen admit to? She gave a quick glance to where Kazi sat grinning, enjoying the girl's fall from the Wysen-wyf's good graces.

Seven

O nce more, it was confirmed for Ashen that the Wysen-wyf could read minds. Quick as thought, Zazar turned on Kazi and pointed both forefingers. "Hold your tongue!" she said sharply.

This was one of her powers. When she set that order upon one, there was no hope of retelling anything heard. Ashen had known such gagging herself at times when Zazar had welcomed cloaked and shadowed figures to the night hearth-fires. Those pointing forefingers stopped any speech thereafter. They almost stopped even the remembering of it.

However much the Bog-folk might hate and seek to destroy any Outlander venturing into their murky territory, there were those who came by stealth to Zazar. Some came through bravery or bravado. Some came through desperation. Some looked to be human kind, though Ashen never saw their faces. They were always muffled in the folds of large cowls or the hoods of their cloaks. And as for other things—some were not human at all, and these came not always of their own volition; rather, they were called.

The least frightening were the four-footed creatures that

would appear at times through holes in the ground and squat before Zazar. Whatever communication passed between them and the woman who had summoned them was not to be heard, at least not by human ears, but that they reported, Ashen had no doubt.

Though she could never afterward speak of it, by listening quietly in the shadows, she heard the rumors and gossip of the outside world that the other visitors, those of humankind, brought with them. Their news seemed part of the price for Zazar's services. Thus Ashen's knowledge of the Outland was greater than that of most Bog-folk, although she could not share it with anyone because of Zazar's spell.

Now, she learned, the spell could work the other way as well.

"Speak!" She might have been fastened to the wall by those forefingers Zazar was pointing at her. Even as Kazi had been silenced, so did Ashen now need to answer. Swiftly she spilled out the adventures of the day.

Zazar waved her to sit down as she herself pulled forward a thick mat and settled cross-legged within the full warmth of the hearth. There she listened without comment or interruption to all Ashen had to tell.

The adventure on the hillock tumbled out quickly—the arrival of Tusser and his tagalongs, the rising of the giant lupper, the one they called Gulper. She left out nothing, neither the plans she knew Tusser had for her nor the wounding of Gulper, nor the mad flight to get away. There was so much, and the girl told it swiftly. Then came the finding of the great stone monster and she began describing the writing on its mossy belly.

Zazar stopped her with an upheld hand. She reached behind her mat to one of the storage baskets and brought out a smooth strip of writing bark, clean of any previous note-taking. She tossed it to the girl. Knowing without any voiced order what Zazar wanted, Ashen took up a charred stick from the fire's edge and began with great care to inscribe the symbols she had set to memory. Twice she had to pause, thinking, until she was sure. Sometimes it seemed to her that for an instant or two, she was still in that clearing, the inscribed stone figure before her. When she had finished, she was certain that she had indeed emptied her memory as thoroughly as she could.

Zazar jerked the bark strip from her then. Reaching within the laced jerkin she wore, the Wysen-wyf brought out a stone somewhat similar to the guardian-stone Ashen had depended upon this day, only this one was triangular in shape. She unfastened it from the cord, and using it pinched between thumb and forefinger, drew one point across each symbol on the writing bark. Somehow, Ashen was not surprised when the marks she had worked so hard to reproduce gleamed as if sparks followed the passage of the stone. When she had finished, the Wysen-wyf sat for a long time, or so it seemed to Ashen, looking at the now-bright marks. Perhaps Zazar was also engaged in seeking some memory. Ashen dared not ask.

At length, Zazar tossed the bark into the fire and it blazed up. With narrowed eyes, she regarded Ashen, and the girl tensed. In the past, Zazar had looked at her in that way just before she brought a switch down on Ashen's shoulders.

At last, Zazar broke the silence. "What is done, is done. You, Outland whelp, are more than I have thought. Look you." She raised her forefinger in the air between them, moving it smoothly, and leaving on the air itself the faint but discernible outline of what was certainly a leaf. To Ashen's wonderment, this continued to hold a shadowy form as Zazar added another of a different shape, and yet another, until four such leaves hung there, dim but still visible enough to be named.

Ashen found herself naming them, aloud and with the certainty that she was right, not merely guessing. "Oak, Yew, Ash, and Rowan."

"No such trees ever grew in the Bog." Zazar snapped her fingers and the ghost leaves were gone. "You are of the Blood or you could not have seen them, nor known them without having

seen them before. The old talent runs strong in you. Never speak
of it, not outside these walls. Knowledge of what you have done
would set not only the Bog against you, but indeed, it would also
bring outside hunters, keen for the kill among us."

"I have no wish—" Ashen began shakily.

"We may not *wish* at the hour the Weavers take up our
threads, by chance or by intent." Zazar stared into the fire. The
light, playing over her features, revealed the toll of age that had
not been there before. "I have seen signs but until now, could
not discover what they meant. Now I think I know. Heed you
this. We are in a time of great change, when old Houses will fall
and be forgotten and new ones shall arise. Heed this also, girl—
you come from high blood. It could bring you to a throne. But
if you are wise, you will not walk that way. You must, however,
find a path out of the Bog lest you be discovered and die. And
what can be given to you as a journey aid, that I shall find."

"Bog-folk—" Ashen's mouth suddenly felt dry. She knew
that Joal, for one, would be cheered to see her bound and flung
into the eating-pool.

"To each kind their own. Yet as the world changes, by the
Weavers' patterning, we cannot know how or why. There is this,
Ashen Deathdaughter, and it you must believe; you already walk
under a shadow. Go carefully, lest you bring it down upon you."

In a far corner of the room, Ashen heard a faint scrabbling
noise, of a kind she had heard before. Zazar looked in that direction. "Get you to sleep," she told Ashen. "One of my little
ones is on the way, and with it, you are to have no dealings."

🌿

Ysa was midway down the steep tower stairway when she heard
her husband's furious shout, followed by the blast of what could
only be one of the large chamber doors sent open with a force
so great it struck against the corridor wall. She stood very still
for a moment, letting her newfound senses go free, seeking—

He had discovered that the Rings were missing from his fin-

gers. Her hands flew to her breast and clasped tightly together.
She composed herself and erased all signs of fear from her face
as she deliberately descended the next few steps. The oil in the
crescent lamps along the walls was low, some of the flames gut-
tering; she hoped that in their dim light, the uneasiness she felt
could not be noted.

"Siebert!" That roar of a call echoed down the corridor.
Surely it was enough to rouse half the castle.

There was the sound of running feet, and shadows came hur-
rying into the corridor from the other end of the hall. The low
light glinted on the steel of unsheathed blades.

She waited until the foremost of those runners came into full
view. Siebert, the Marshal of the Guard, a man sparing of words
but always correct in action when she chanced to meet him,
caught sight of her now as she deliberately moved forward toward the door that stood wide open. He stopped, the point of
his blade wavering downward.

A man uttered a sharp cry of pain as he crawled out into the
corridor like a badly beaten animal. Rugen, the King's body-
squire, was followed by the burly figure of his master, who
kicked viciously at his unfortunate servant.

The King's night robe had a large rent in it, showing the
obese upper part of his body, as if he had tried to tear free from
its silken folds. His puffy features were hardly those of humankind but more those of some farm beast run amok. He had put
on one boot, the better to kick his servant.

Now he lifted his head a little and brayed forth jangling
laughter, drawing his foot back to kick Rugen again. Only then
did he appear to become aware that there were others watching.
His head, thatched with a bristle of graying black hair, turned a
fraction so he could address the audience of his rage the better.

"This filth—" Spittle flaked the corners of his mouth. "Take—
take—" Then his head turned a fraction more and it was plain
that he was looking straight at the Queen.

"So." It was not a roar this time, but far from the speech of a sane man. "My very dear wife, my sweetling, sworn to me by all the Powers." His voice had turned unnervingly gentle. At the same time, the cruel rage that had galvanized him before shifted and became something darker, something worse. "How well you look, in your Oak crimson. Have you found a new woman to paint your face? I have not seen you so beautiful in years. Come you hither, my love's own heart, for we have great matters to talk about." He gave a last kick to the moaning squire and held out his hand to Queen Ysa in a grotesque parody of one about to lead a partner into a formal dance.

She did not falter, only held her hands in fists now pressed tightly against her, hidden in the folds of her skirts, finding consolation in the warmth of the Rings. They had accepted her, but what use she could make of them in this coil, she had no idea—yet. He was now standing aside, in absurd mimicry of a mannered gentleman, and she must proceed him into his chamber. She ached with the tension of her body as she fought against any sign of fear. She passed him silently with her head high.

As she swept past, the odor of sweat and wine fumes nearly made her sick. Calmly, she went to the long table at the foot of the bed, where two six-branched candlesticks sat along with a goblet and the wine flask. Willing her hand not to tremble, she picked up a candlestick on which two candles were crowned with flame and proceeded to light the others. To face this meeting, she felt that she must have light. Only—only the confrontation had come so soon! Too soon? She dared not allow herself to think of that.

The door slammed shut behind her almost as violently as it had crashed open, and she turned to face Boroth. It was better, she knew from bitter experience, to wait for him to speak first, for her to remain passive. Sometimes that could calm him down. In his present state, he might even strike out at her—or try to do so.

He had come closer than she anticipated, and his flushed, sweating face was too near. How could he have padded across the room without sound? Then she saw the one boot lying near the closed door, and knew.

Now he was licking his lips, his gaze sliding down from meeting hers to fasten on her hands, which she discovered were now open and displaying the Rings, almost unnaturally so, as if the light somehow was drawn to center on them. She had not willed this; it had to be the Rings' doing.

"You do not whore. This is the way of one who would gain power." He appeared to have his violent anger under tight control. "Instead, you thieve. And the price for theft, as you well know—"

He was on her, as a cat might pounce upon some small prey, clutching her right hand with a painful grip, dragging it and her toward the nearest candle.

"Burn, dear wife, the one I lifted to share a throne, while another— Burn and have a taste of how the law is set!"

His fingers had closed as tight as a torturer's irons about her wrist. However, he came only so far toward the candle and no farther. Hard as he tried to force her hand into the flame, he could not move her.

The relief was enough to bring a sob from her throat, one she quickly stifled. So heartened, she freed herself from his hold. His face lost that darkened hue and began to grow pale as he stared at her, comprehension dawning.

"Oak," she said, beginning the tale of the thumbs and fingers. "Yew, Ash, and Rowan." She held out both hands, the fingers widespread. "There is no need for force. I did not steal them. Take them back freely if they are truly yours. Come, Boroth, I implore you. Take them and do with me what you will."

But he was pushing back, away from her. His hand rose as if he would answer her challenge, and then fell again.

"What—" His voice was a shaken whisper. "What witchery have you wrought, you evil creature in woman's shape?"

"I have done nothing, Boroth. Ask yourself what you have done that they left you. They choose. We have read it, both of us." She looked full at him and spoke slowly, with a thread of pause between each word to accent her question the more. "Do you think that that which is the very heart of our land will serve a drunken sot, a creature of some dark choice?"

He found his full voice, but this time his bellow was an outcry of rage and anguish. He reached out and grabbed one of the candelabra, the flames flaring high as he drew back and hurled it straight at her face.

The flames winked out, and the golden holder crashed to the floor at her feet.

It was she who moved now, reaching for the goblet. She filled it to the brim. Though tempted, she did not fling it at him, though he moved as if to dodge such an attack. Rather, she slid it along the table as she gave him a tight smile.

"Boroth, you have aroused yourself. Men of your kind can die, killed by rage. Drink, husband, drink once more and forget. This I promise you—life, and among your people, the semblance of what you were. Drink and be satisfied."

His hand twitched toward the goblet. "I swore never again to touch it—"

"It was an oath ill considered. Mine is not. Your body is accustomed to wine, and indeed, it craves wine. Wine is its medicine, the sustenance of its life. To deny it is to order your own death. And hear me further. This I also promise, that this Kingdom and your line I shall serve as best I may. None shall know from me the extent of my rule, for I shall say all decisions come willingly from you, through me, for your steps are lagging and your body must not be put to stress."

He stumbled, demonstrating the truth of her words, but he did not try to pick up the goblet. Rather, he drew himself by handholds around the edge of the bed, as if unable any longer to walk unsupported. Then he fell forward, head down, his legs buckled so that he knelt as one who seeks comfort from the Unknown.

Andre Norton & Sasha Miller

The cramped quarters on board the ship led to difficulties for the sailors going about their duties. But the continuation of the sea as calm as it might ever be, and winds mild and fair, favored them. Those not needed for manning the vessel rolled up in their cloaks, in any corner they could find, to sleep.

All were weary of the days of skirmishing, followed by the one great battle. There were many kin whom one would not see in the sword ring again. And then the final humiliation—the destruction of what had been their proudly held keep, and that by their own hands. It was not strange that sleep this night was fitful.

Obern rose at last to wend a way among the sleepers to the prow. No longer would he look back, but forward. A man of courage cut his losses to try again, sharp and wounding as those losses might have been. The moon had risen and now sent a silver path across which their small, battered fleet cut passage.

There were always noises aboard ship, most of them familiar. Timbers creaked under the push of the waves; ropes and canvas sometimes snapped and boomed overhead. This night and on this crowded deck there were also the sounds of sleepers touched by dark dreams, the soft sobbing of a woman, or the slightly louder lulling of a crying child.

For the first time, Obern was glad of the order that had separated families, except for warrior-kin, on this voyage. His hand-fasted beloved, Neave, and their young son were aboard another ship. He missed Neave, yearned for her warmth at night, but knew that he could not have withstood having to endure his family's misery.

Now another sound began, so close to where Obern had positioned himself that he was startled out of his painful memories. He felt his tight hold on the rail relax slowly. It seemed to him that that small throb of drumbeat matched the flow of his blood, shutting failure from his mind, awakening in him a desire to go forward with all his strength.

The few lanterns gave little light, but these, along with the moon, were enough for him to make his way to where he expected to find their wave-reader, Fritji, hunched over his small rhythm drum. To his surprise, he discovered Kasai, the Spirit Drummer, instead. Kasai was rubbing his hand across the drum's surface in a pattern that matched the slight rise and fall of the deck on which he crouched. Spirit Drummers were different from wave-readers. Their powers lay in other directions.

Obern approached the drummer and dropped down beside him, knowing that Kasai was aware of his coming, yet did not warn him off. So, this was not one of the great secrets.

"Obern!" It was a whisper, coming out of nowhere, but one that cut through even the drum sound.

He tensed again. That word had been more than recognition; it was a hail such as might summon a scout to a meeting of war chiefs.

"I hear; I come," he found himself repeating, in the formal answer to such a hail.

"Take the hard path; travel it well. It is your task to be eyes and ears—and to give us a harbor once again!"

With a start, Obern realized that Kasai had been the speaker, though the drummer's eyes were shut and he seemed unaware of what he was doing. That meant Kasai was reading! Obern's hand tightened on the hilt of his long knife. He had never known for himself a reading—had only heard of such. They were few, and those for whom these came were indeed thereafter set apart until some task given them was accomplished. But why him, Obern? He was only backshield to a war chief, and of the blood of that same chief to be sure, but that was all! By the charging of the Steeds of the Great Surf, he was no Battlesworn!

"Follow the way as you see it open. . . ." Kasai's voice trailed into silence. His hand ceased its sweep across the drumhead and he curled himself around his instrument as if sleep had overcome him. Obern knew that there was nothing more to be learned from him now. Perhaps he could ask later, but those who were in the reading trance seldom remembered what had been said.

He pulled Kasai's cloak over him and his precious drum, and then settled his own cloak tighter about himself. He felt cold, cold as if they had taken to a sea where vast ice towers drifted at their will.

Eventually, toward morning, he slept.

Eight

🍂

"*Ashen!*" *Zazar's voice cut* through her dream.

Perhaps she had only been dozing. At least she was already sitting up in her bedplace to answer. Zazar's hand moved. She must have tossed oil on the low flicker of flames; it brought them leaping high. But there was other light, too, one that Zazar summoned on occasions for her own purpose.

Two light-balls bobbed above Zazar's head as she sat on a mat cushion, a mass of tangled cords in her lap and her hands busy sorting out curling ends from a loose ball.

Similar small balls of pallid light might often be sighted in the Bog. Usually they signified danger to any of the folk who had dared the night. It was well known that such led Outlanders astray into the worst of the miry land when they were lost on the fringe of the Bog and took such for a traveler's lantern.

Intrigued, Ashen watched Zazar at her work. There was more than one way of keeping records, as Ashen had learned long before. Squares of stone no thicker than a knife blade were stacked in piles on one of the crowded shelves. When they were washed with a rag dipped in a brew Zazar alone held the secret to, they displayed lines and curves, until the wetness dried. There were four of these blocks beside Zazar's knee, but she was more intent on the ball of entwined strings and the cords she had plucked from it.

Those were of different colors, muted in this limited light, but each carried twists of knots along its length. The sequence of those knots had meaning to one trained in their use. Once, she had heard Zazar refer to them as trimmings from the Loom of the Weavers.

As Ashen stumbled toward the fire-pit, yawning and rubbing her eyes, she could see Zazar's fingers passing the knotted strings the faster, discarding some to one side or laying one across a stone square. There were only a few so singled out.

"Come close. Sit." The Wysen-wyf jerked her head toward a space beside her. The various balls of the unsorted and untangled had diminished quickly and she was handling one of the few remaining now.

Then she was done. Quickly, she re-rolled the discarded cords and put them aside in a box carved from the lumpy root of a Bog willow. But the others—there were six of them—remained on the square.

Two—no, three held a glint of gold, one brighter than its companions. Another was of a blue that appeared to grow more brilliant as Ashen studied it. The fifth was the glowing green of new spring leaves, and the last, which lay apart from the others as if deliberately placed so, was as black as the surface of the killing pool, its knots touched with gray as if rimed by winter frost.

Zazar sat regarding the cords, acting as if she was no longer aware of the girl. Still, she spoke, and with the emphasis that meant her mind was fully engaged with the message the knots would deliver.

"Queen," she said, indicating the brightest of the three gold cords. "King." She pointed to the dullest. "Prince." That was the thinnest of them all, lacking many knots and none evidently intricate. From that rather sorry thread, she went to the green length. "Kin unknown."

Now she looked at Ashen again. "The times swing us along more swiftly. It is not your clan color, but you are green, yes. Untaught in much, yes." She had picked up the green cord and was running it along between thumb and forefinger. It was slender, hardly thicker than the one she had named Prince, and the knots on it were also few. But of those, several were doubled and redoubled.

As Zazar held each of those knots for an instant, Ashen thought she felt pressure at the nape of her neck, as if those strong old fingers had gripped her instead. A tingle of excitement, faint but definite, spread through her whole body.

"Let it be so." Zazar did not seem pleased, but rather that she had been out-argued by some power unseen. "Listen well, Ashen Deathdaughter. Every kin, people, and land knows birth, a rise to strength, a decline, and, at length—an ending. For some, it comes swiftly, and for others, it covers a tale of years upon years."

Ashen stirred slightly but did not speak.

"You have been born in the Bog, and have never ventured beyond it. Now comes the time when you must awaken, shed your long innocence, and learn something of the world. Most of those we call Outlanders are from the south, as the greater world is reckoned, but north to those walled as we are by the Bog. Outlanders come mainly from the Kingdom of Rendel, once a paramount and powerful state, though now rot eats at its heart. There the way of life is not that which you have known. However, it is one you must learn with all the caution and care you can bring to that task."

Zazar took the threads into her hands again, speaking more to them than to Ashen.

"To the far north lies another land, one of mountains and valleys, knowing far more chill than we face in our worst winter time. Now a measure of their end has come to them, though they are still of vigor and strength, and they look afar for a new rooting. What sweeps upon them is not inner rot but outer darkness, from a source none of us have yet been given to understand, save that it means death, not only of the body, but of the spirit also. It massed in attack and has taken the mountainland. There is no indication of what it seeks, only that it comes forward. Whether the Bog will halt it for a while, we cannot tell."

Now she glanced keenly at Ashen.

"One thing, however, is certain; Rendel cannot stand. It is a country of great lords who look to their own gain, and among them there is an ever-hidden struggle to garner more power and bring down a neighbor one envies. The present King is a weakling, a mask from behind whom acts one who has meddled to some purpose with strange learning. You must know this also— our world has seen many changes, not only in people, but in reaches of land and sea as well. At times, great Kingdoms have been wiped away by the fury of the very earth in which they are rooted. There are remains of earlier knowledge to be found, and this Queen Ysa has discovered such, conveniently bringing to herself more power and the ability to control others."

Ashen was bubbling with questions by now, but Zazar silenced her with a look.

"There is a single heir to the throne, a Prince. He is of tainted blood from both sides of his kin-lines. He can cause harm such as leads only to utter chaos. Meanwhile, the Queen plots to ensure that her line will remain the ruling one. As she controls the father, so does she mean to make a tool of the son. Now"— Zazar's dark eyes seemed somehow to grow larger as she stared at the girl—"we, too, must see to our defenses." She fell silent and Ashen dared a question.

"Does this Queen then threaten the Bog?"

To her surprise, Zazar smiled slowly. "Have you not listened, girl? The Bog is only a small part of the whole of this land. Yet now, once again, it will have a role to play. Yesterday you found a place older than the records, where those before us walked a country far less a plaything for the streams than what we know today." She tapped her finger against the square of stone across which lay the knotted cords.

"Soon," she continued, "you shall begin another journey. There is an uneasiness growing to possess this small world of mud and water; it is better that you are out of reach of such as Joal and his kind. For when a man fears, he will turn upon that which he can control and vent his rage."

Zazar laid the threads upon the stone again. To Ashen's astonishment, all were woven together now—hers, that of the King, the Queen, the Prince—and the two others, as yet unknown.

She stared at them, comprehending as if from a distance that with this gesture of Zazar's, the thread of Ashen Deathdaughter had been drawn into a new pattern of the Web Everlasting.

🍂

The small Sea-Rover fleet did not sail out of sight of the land, according to custom, but kept to the water road known through generations. The last of the towering heights to the north dwindled, though the shoreline was still a wall of cliffs, one locked upon another. And with the flow of tides, a lookout could sight the cruel fangs of reef rocks waiting for what fate and the sea might bring them.

The majority of those on board were accustomed to the sparing use of food during voyages. Never before, however, had all their old men, their womankind, their children, been mouths to fill. Already, children were crying with hunger.

Obern manned one of the sturdy fishing lines trailing from the sternways. There was life enough in the sea; it only remained to be caught. Something struck, hard, taking the bait. He had given the line a turn around a railing cleat—luckily, or the strike would have stripped the flesh from any hand holding it.

Obern's shout brought one of the sailors and one of the sea-

—110—

Andre Norton & Sasha Miller

guards on the run. They had no more reached his side, ready to aid him in the fight, when there was a thrashing of the water and a thing, unlike any creature he had seen or heard tale of, broke the surface.

It was no fish—rather, the thing possessed what appeared to be legs of a sort, covered with warty skin. One of the legs was stretched to the limit, dragging at the line, striving to jerk it from a gaping mouth whence the cord disappeared.

Both forefeet now grasped at the line, so taut that Obern feared it would break at any moment, if it didn't bring part of the railing with it instead. Then, suddenly, the line fell slack as the water-thing plunged toward, not away from, the ship.

In an instant, it had reached the rudder. Then, using that as a platform, the creature leaped upward, the pads of its forefeet slapping against the side of the boat. Suckers on those forefeet held it fast. Waves washed over the massive body, now stretched out on the surface of the water.

One of the seamen, sea-spear in hand, crowded against Obern.

"Give room!" he shouted. It didn't seem likely that launching this weapon against the target so available would hit a vital spot, but no better opportunity presented itself.

And, indeed, he succeeded only in wounding the thing. Now the creature uttered a deep roar and was answered by screams and cries from the deck. Those non-fighters who had gathered to watch scrambled to give way to armsmen and seamen alike.

Obern drew his long boarding knife. He had given way as required, but now he pushed back until he stood almost directly above the creature. Bulbous eyes looked up at him. Eyes of *what?* In the shock of meeting that gaze, he could not believe that this was any normal denizen of the sea. There was hot rage and knowledge of a sort in the yellowish orbs raised toward him.

More spears flew through the air. A few caught in the skin of the thing, and it shook its body vigorously to rid itself of them. It was as if that skin bore a strange kind of armor. The creature was beginning to climb, releasing one suckered forefoot and then the other, planting them ever higher against the hull of the ship. Unlike any fish, it seemed as able to move in air as in water and showed no distress for it.

Obern drew back his arm. Boarding knives more closely resembled shortswords than throwing weapons. Where spears had done little damage, would this length of steel succeed? None was better trained at this weapon than he, and—

The attacker opened its huge mouth. Obern, calling on the hope of luck, threw. The weapon flashed down and into the gaping cavern of the mouth, lodging upright in the bottom jaw. The creature snapped its mouth shut just a moment too late, driving the knife more deeply into the tender flesh. One of the sucker forefeet jerked loose from the hull and clawed at the long, hideous jaw. A thin line of blood oozed from between bulbous lips.

The beast wrestled with its own pain, seeming unable to realize that if it opened its mouth, it could pluck out the source of its torment. It clutched at its jaw with both of its forefeet, and its hold on the ship gave way. Dropping back into the waves, it furiously began ramming its head against the hull. Twice it struck before abandoning this useless form of attack.

All aboard could feel the shudder of those blows, but the monster had now turned and was floating on the surface of the water, waves washing over it. Its hind legs kicked slowly, but the head faced up toward the sky. And around that head there was spreading in the water a swirl of dark clouds.

Obern could see no outward sign, but that the thing was badly wounded, he was almost sure. How the knife alone could have caused this, he could not have told. Certainly he had not knowingly centered it on any target save that gaping mouth. Perhaps, by accident, he had severed a blood vessel, with the result that the thing was drowning in its own blood.

The creature was still moving, after a fashion. Now, with a visible effort, it was turning over, all four limbs outspread.

Twitching them feebly, it drew away from the side of the ship. Obern quickly cut the line free, not wishing to engage the creature again, even in its weakened state.

As the space between vessel and beast widened, the wounded thing did not dive, as a great fish might, nor did it head out to sea. Rather, its painful progress, growing ever slower, was aiming it for the distant barrier cliffs.

Obern studied his empty hand as the ship separated from that floundering creature in the water.

"A goodly stroke." His father caught his shoulder in a firm grip.

He looked around at Snolli. "But it was not my planned doing. I do not know how a thrown weapon could—" He took a deep breath. "It was an accident."

His father gave him a gentle shake. "But if chance favors you so, do not deny it. Look you—the thing still lives, yes, and you may not have given it a deathblow, but it flees and I do not think it will come again. A boarding knife, or even a sword, is a light price to pay for that."

Snolli lifted a scabbard he held, and Obern recognized what it contained. He smiled in turn but shook his head. He knew what Snolli was about to do. Ordinarily, he would have been ecstatic. Now, however, he only felt empty. "My man-sword, is it, Father? A sword from the forge of Laxes? That is a treasure." Again he shook his head. "Perhaps I should truly earn it first."

His father's hand dropped from his shoulder and moved to the weapon at his own belt. "No shield-mate must go swordless. It speaks well that you feel unworthy of a worthy deed." He pulled his own personal sword, one given him years past as he stood among armsmen, a recognized equal. "Sheathe this. It is of Rinbell's forging."

"But—" Words deserted Obern as he held his father's sword. Laxes' work was good, given to a favored son when he reached the proper age and had performed some deed of arms, but Rinbell's work was the finest. A Rinbell sword was a gift beyond price—an honor seldom given, this one even more so.

"Sheathe it, sheathe it!" ordered his father. "I have that in me which says you will meet with such as that monster again and you will need to be properly armed. The thing was not truly of the sea, though I have never heard of its like and the sea holds tightly many secrets. But did you not see that when it would flee further harm, it headed shoreward?"

The captain had come up beside them. "True, Chieftain," he said. He turned toward those tall cliffs. "Look there—" He was pointing at the water instead of at the land barriers.

The water bore a stain oozing out over the once-clear waves. It was far too great a stain, Obern believed, than could have come from the body of the thing unless it were, truly, most of its life blood. It trailed, as far as the eye could distinguish, straight for the land.

"There are rivers hidden in those rocks," the captain continued. "Some cut deep ravines, and some drop in great falls. All feed seaward through a strange land. Better never be washed ashore here, for the water that flows from such outlets is death— in more ways than one."

"We coast the Bog now?" Snolli asked.

"Aye, and well out from its filth." The captain nodded vigorously. "And so it shall be for a night, a day, and another night. That country is no small one, and it has always been damnation for any Outlander."

"May the Ruler of Waves set us a right course."

Obern had seldom heard just that note in his father's voice. He began to search his mind for all he had ever heard concerning that distant stretch of country.

❧

Queen Ysa looked down at the metal tray, lavishly bordered with jewels, that the foot-squire had so carefully placed on the table in her chamber. There were two covered dishes that matched the tray in splendor, a small goblet and matching flask, and an open dish cradling two red rounds of fruit, early for the season and forced to ripeness. She nodded, and the squire left at this signal that she wished no further service. Her stomach growled but she did not yet lift the nearest cover or pick up the spoon resting beside it.

She was unaccountably pushed by hunger now. She wanted to fall upon the food and devour it at once, yet she refrained. She had no desire to grow as gross as Boroth. Nevertheless, eat she must, for despite the unworldly aid she commanded—or, perhaps, the thought came unbidden, *because* of it—she found it necessary to strengthen her body. What had happened in the night just past— She noted the hand she slowly lifted. It was shaking, and she fought to control the unwelcome tremor. But with the reassurance of the two Rings that adorned that hand, she straightened even more in her chair and put forth the other hand to uncover the porridge within the bowl. Honey-scented oat grain, thickened with certain herbs. Yes. Eagerly, she took up a spoonful of the breakfast assembled to her desire.

Let the stories spread. No one could rein in rumor. There would be many guesses about the night past, and whisperings among the people in the castle, before the coming of midday. And from the castle, such threads of storytelling would weave throughout the city.

Her lips tightened. Then she looked again at the Rings. At least this much was acknowledged—that the Rings in their fashion chose, and their choosing was the best for the land. Boroth was still the King, and the lords would turn first to the King, rather than to any woman born. She could manage that.

She could also deal with Boroth now; what remained was to draw together those very jealous and intriguing Houses with their arrogant and vengeful rulers. Four she could count on, mainly because she had earlier subtly led them to believe she favored their own plans. Three others she doubted would ever recognize her, so they must be removed. Removed. She ate steadily and tasted none of what passed her lips, for her thoughts walled her in from the outer world.

❦

Boroth likewise was at breakfast, his thoughts still upon the dream that had come upon him the preceding night. He only toyed with his food, though he drank thirstily of the wine.

Alditha. Once more she had come to him, and this time she had stayed for a while.

As before, he had seen the Ash leaf, and it had melted into the beloved form. She had moved toward him, smiling, and kissed him. "Boroth," she said. "My love." She shone in the darkness.

"Stay with me. I am betrayed on all sides."

"I will stay as long as I may. I am always with you, even when you cannot see me."

"Will you come again?"

"As often as I am allowed."

"My wife despises me, and my son is eager for my death. And I—my greatest wish is to be with you."

"And so you shall be, in time. Be patient."

"But you are departed. They told me of your death."

"Yes, that is true. And yet I am here with you."

"Will you advise me when there is danger?"

"There is always danger."

"Aye, but where? I can no longer be about my business, and they do not tell me anything."

"There is naught that you can do, my beloved. All that is left is to wait."

"Wait for what?" Boroth shifted and raised himself on one elbow. "What is the purpose?"

"That will become clear, in time."

"My Rings are gone."

"I know. It is their way. Your time has passed, my beloved."

"I am weary of this, of the Queen, of Florian. Of the people who crowd into my chamber, waiting for me to take my last breath. All I want is you."

"As I said, beloved, we will be together . . . eventually."

"But when?"

"There is one last thing remaining for you to do, but the time is not yet ripe for it. Then you will join me, and we will go into Eternity hand in hand."

"What thing must I do?"

"You will know."

"When will you come to me again?"

But all she would say, soft as a sigh, was to repeat her words. "You will know." And then she had kissed him again and faded away into the darkness.

Now Boroth concentrated on the food. If there was a thing he must do, he must be strong enough to live until that moment. He surveyed his tray with distaste. Bread, wine too watered, and a soft, sweetened porridge. A meal for an invalid. Grimacing, nevertheless he ate.

Nine

Zarar was moving about the hut more swiftly than usual, but apparently well aware of what she was doing. The largest of their traveling backpacks lay unfolded on the floor, and into its many inner pockets and loops the Wysen-wyf was fitting what she gathered from shelves and chests, boxes, and two cupboards in the darkest corner of the room. Kazi's snore became a succession of snorts. The crone drew herself up on the sleep-mat and rubbed her eyes as if to banish the last of the deep sleep Zazar had willed upon her.

But the Wysen-wyf paid no heed to her. For the most part, she remained silent in her packing except for occasionally identifying some packet or object as she stowed it with a few firm words, muttered under her breath, as to its use. Meanwhile, Ashen hunkered down by the fire-pit, having drawn out the flat baking-stone, which she set at an angle within the newly fed flames. She had already pounded the root meal into flour and mingled herbs with it. Then she moistened the mixture with special water from a flask to make a paste, which she spread with flying fingers into a cake on the stone. The odor of the baking trail biscuit banished some of the other smells from the assorted herbs, newly opened boxes, and the pack goods.

Zazar stood still at last, regarding the spread-out shoulder pack, and then nodded. "This must do. Remember, you shall not again harvest such outside this home hearth."

Ashen nodded and flipped over another hot, firm trail biscuit on the stone. Kazi had risen from her bed, her eyes upon the both of them. Her mouth drew into a sour pucker. Because of her crippled leg, she seldom went beyond the cluster of huts that served Joal's clan. Here, however, was proof that someone, or ones, were about to leave.

There was a call from outside. "Ho, Zazar-hearth!"

In an instant, Zazar stooped and caught the end of one of the mat covers from Ashen's sleeping place, tossing it over the pack. "Ho, the kin," she replied.

The double night-curtain was shoved aside and a woman of the Bog entered. It was Joal's second wife, Pulta. Her dark hair was frosted at her temples, and her back was stooped from hours of labor at loom and fire-pit. She was near as lean as a reed, and a dark bruise painted one puffy cheek. She looked around the room, not missing the stack of biscuits at Ashen's knee. She was clearly spying.

"Someone travels?" she asked in a raspy voice.

Zazar moved a step between her and the girl, who still balanced a lump of coarse dough in one hand.

"There is a reason to ask?" Zazar returned.

Pulta leaned to one side so she could see Ashen beyond the figure of the Wysen-wyf. "Trouble be coming. Better keep to hearthside unless all comes different at talk-fires." Then what could have been a friendly warning changed. She shot a challenge, along with a fierce frown, at Ashen. "Three left village." A speck of spittle gathered in the corner of her lips. "Two came back, and with a tale. Todo lost, lost. Now they summon this Outlander slug to answer—"

"Your tongue is sharp, Pulta. Such tongues have been trimmed beforetimes. If there needs be any talk by the fire concerning my household, then let it be said by the heads of hearths, and publicly. They do not need to send you as messenger. There are duties that are mine, even as you weave and do tasks about your own hearth." She stared down from her greater height at the woman. "Do you question when aid is summoned? Shall I believe that the kin gathered here wishes me to go forth, to call in—" And her voice changed. No recognizable words came from her—rather, a grunting sound that startled Ashen, for in part, it caused the memory of the under-thing, Gulper, on its hunt, to flash into her mind.

Pulta took a step back. "You have many mysteries. How many for Bog-folk, Zazar? You took Kazi, she been promised to feed the under-ones. Then you have abomination indeed. *Her.* Outlander demon spawn. We know trouble coming. You stand to our defense, or you let us all go to darkness?" She gathered her reed shawl closer about her shoulders.

"So." Zazar appeared in no way ruffled. "Yes, you are correct. Trouble comes. Do you not understand that such as I would sense that long before your kin could mouth a warning shout? Remember this, Pulta. I have at my command powers of a sort that Joal and his blood can never hope to summon. You came pretending to give a warning, but your errand was otherwise. Therefore, you may tell him, since you have come to seek knowledge, that I do not command spears and bone-knives, but I am not to be reckoned the less because of that. There are weapons, and weapons—and this much you may also say. This day I will do what I must. Now go. It will begin to rain in earnest before you reach your own hearth."

Pulta's mouth worked as if she would make a retort as soon as she could think of one, but Zazar stared her down. The woman grunted and made her way to the curtain, passing into the daylight. Dull gray that was, and they could now hear both rising wind and the first slaps of heavy raindrops against the roof. Zazar closed the door-curtain behind her. Then she threw aside the covering over the pack and busied herself with its straps and fastenings.

Ashen stowed the trail biscuits into a thickly woven box lined with lupper-skin, so tight that no rain could find its way in to spoil them. On top of these she placed packets of dried briar fruit, trail mixture, and boiled luppers' eggs.

"Now," Zazar said, giving her a peculiar look. "Since the rain favors us, we do not wait, Ashen Deathdaughter. I shall see you on your way, one that only you will walk as of this day." She went to a rack on the wall and brought down a supple belt of snakeskin from which hung a bone blade, discolored by age, but Ashen recognized it as one of Zazar's treasures.

The Wysen-wyf passed this to Ashen. As the girl fastened the belt about her slender waist, Zazar gestured and crooned aloud in a singsong fashion that hinted of speech, one that Ashen could not understand.

Then the Wysen-wyf picked up her own cloak while Ashen strapped on the pack. Zazar smiled faintly again as she waved the girl toward the door-curtain. "You have wondered, now maybe you shall know."

The rain was coming down with full fury. It beat at them as they left the shelter of the cottage, and for a moment, Ashen was greatly tempted to go back inside. This was such a day that all prudent ones kept to the hearthside. Yet Ashen did not flinch. They could not have done better, even under cover of night, to go unmarked. If their departure was noted by any in the cluster of crude huts, there was no sign of it. The path Zazar followed was not the one she had taken three days earlier, when Ashen had made her most recent, disastrous attempt to track the Wysen-wyf. This time they were heading, as far as the girl could determine, north rather than west.

As they traveled, the rain continued to beat steadily, and time and time again, they had to change course to skirt rising pools of water, fed from many streams. When they reached the far northern side of the isle on which the settlement was situated, Ashen saw what she would have accepted as an unpassable barrier. Athwart their track lay a vast stretch of rain-dappled water.

There seemed no hope of crossing. Somewhere under this swollen surface was one of the feared dark pools wherein lurked certain death—a death courted by the Bog-folk, who fed into it not only captives and the refuse from their meals, but also any child of their own bearing who was defective in their judgment.

To the west, a tall tangle of willows fringed this pool, and it was toward this that Zazar headed. She walked with the constant care of the Bog-folk, but she did so at a good pace. Ashen matched her, close on her heels, marking just where the Wysen-wyf trod, for the pack weighed heavily on her. She feared that a misstep could send her into a treacherous spot that would suck her down before Zazar was even aware of any danger.

Zazar hand-signaled and Ashen stopped abruptly, waiting for further orders. She noted that Zazar made no attempt to hack away any of the rank growth; rather, it appeared to part before her, almost as if on some unheard demand. Now Ashen could see a narrow tunnel where branches met raggedly overhead and, a short space away, the open water again. Zazar groped until she located a partially hidden rope. She heaved vigorously and out from the willow branches there lurched with some force one of the common, shallow Bog-craft.

The vegetation that concealed it had kept the rain from gathering in its hull, at least not to any dangerous extent. Zazar gestured and Ashen sidled past her, clambering into the boat awkwardly, the pack overbalanced her. She sat facing Zazar.

The Wysen-wyf settled herself in the stern and shrugged her cloak up about her shoulders. From the side of their transport, she freed a pole and a paddle.

The latter she used to push out into the open and then, with expert skill, sent them angling across the water, still to the northwest. Bog-folk grew up with their boats, and the tricks to gain passage across the larger stretches of water were lessons early learned. And Zazar—whose age Ashen still had never been able to guess—had the expertise of the finest of hunters.

By now, the rain had lessened a little. Their clothing was

soggy, and a mist seemed to form about them as they moved. However, the journey was not a long one, for Zazar soon sent the craft toward what looked like another break in the overgrown edge of the pool, nearly across from the point where they had entered.

Once more it seemed to Ashen that this waterway opened strangely as they continued. This new way was also like a trough from which water ran back into the very land itself, and the edges of the cut were banked in rank growth that half veiled the way ahead. Ashen turned her head, as far as the bulk of the pack would permit, to see what lay beyond.

Zazar put aside the paddle, rose to her feet, and took up the pole. They were well within the sides of the cut now, and yet the overgrown vegetation continued to open before them, a watery trail.

Zazar wielded the pole with practiced vigor and their progress continued. Then Ashen noted a change in the banks beside them. The thick tangle of growth was here and there pierced by what could only be standing stones, tilted at angles, and yet not unlike those she had seen in the place of the water monster. Walls? Yes, certainly, but what to wall in—or what to keep out?

Her hands went to her belt, and she grasped the hilt of the knife Zazar had given her. Though those walls certainly had been there for a long time, they had been placed with a purpose, and after her encounter at the pool of the hillock, she wanted no more attention from what might dwell behind them or under the boat.

They came at last to another wonder, or so it seemed to Ashen. Here the walls ended abruptly with a large stone on either side like the frames of a doorway, and before them again lay a stretch of open water.

Another pool, the girl thought with some dismay. One could think much during such a journey, with no assurance from her companion of where they were going and why, for Zazar had not spoken since leaving the village.

What faced them across that stretch of open water, however,

was a huge hillock, made not of land once water-soaked, but rather, entirely of stones. This was nothing of nature's building, Ashen was sure, even as she had been sure in the place of the stone monster. Here, as there, for all its tumbled aspect, there was a certain conformity to the setting of the stones.

They rose high enough that those in the boat could see only the uneven line of the top, but not what lay beyond. Zazar's poling became slower and she caught her breath between each push. Ashen half expected the pole to be caught in the thick mud of the bottom level, but it was not.

For the first time since the start of their journey, the Wysen-wyf broke her silence. "Ready yourself!" She indicated an out-thrust of rock, one that presented a reasonably smooth surface. "Loose the pack and when I say, toss it with all your might onto those stones."

Ashen unlatched and dropped her cloak, then hurriedly pulled at buckles and thongs, drawing the pack around until it lay on her knees.

"Now!"

Zazar had managed to bring them very close to the stones. Ashen was in an awkward position for throwing, but she heaved and swung the heavy pack. More by luck than by design, it came to rest on the very edge of the rocky platform.

Zazar gave a last vigorous shove with the pole, and the craft swung sidewise to grate against the rocks. Ashen needed no instructions this time. She scrambled up and crawled awkwardly from the boat to the nearest even-surfaced rock.

"Hold!"

Ashen was still on her hands and knees. She seized the loop of heavy line the Wysen-wyf threw, then braced herself to keep the boat from drifting away as Zazar clambered ashore in turn. Then Zazar thrust the pole with practiced ease into a crevice between two of the rocks and looped the rope tightly around it, providing safe anchorage.

"Up!"

Zazar, who had always been talkative before, seemed unwilling to use many words. She jerked her thumb to indicate they must climb to the top of the ragged barrier. In one spot, these time-battered blocks were stacked in such a pattern that someone could easily enough step from one to the next higher.

"Stairs."

It was a word unknown to Ashen. Balancing the pack she had not stopped to strap on, she toiled along in Zazar's wake until she reached the top. She turned and faced landward, eager to see what she could of the place. Surprise turned to awe. Here was an old world, but new to one who had spent all her days in one of the crude Bog huts. Here there had plainly been buildings, though roofs had long since vanished and piles of rubble-filled passageways between the structures. There was indeed a pattern such as spoke purpose. The ruins extended for some distance until she could just see the rise of what had to be the rest of the wall, the curling length of which was concealed beyond the place where she now stood.

Zazar gestured toward the mass of rubble below. "Galinth."

"Galinth?" Ashen repeated. Another word she had never heard before. Zazar did not elaborate.

Instead, she had raised both her hands palm out, and the words she spoke in a sonorous singsong were as before, unintelligible. It was, Ashen thought, as if the Wysen-wyf were announcing something of importance. Or was she asking for refuge here? If so, asking whom?

This improbable stone place—she did not know the word for it—that certainly had no likeness to any Bog dwellings was, as far as Ashen could see, deserted. Nevertheless, she considered the many rock piles uneasily. There were a number of scaled things that might seek out lodging here, and most of them it was better to avoid.

Zazar had ended her chant. Now she stood staring out over the gray jumble below. Ashen stared out also, but she could see nothing stirring.

No, but she could hear! From somewhere, Zazar's chant was being answered.

This was no croaking roar such as the monster had bellowed by the other lake. Rather, the sound was like a song, but one far removed in rhythm and tune from any of the coarse chants that might arise from a fire-talk in the village.

Who sang? And what was the meaning of that song? Ashen shivered. This was all far from any experience she had known before, and for one brought up in the Bog, the unknown was never to be wholly trusted.

The swing and rise of notes—no, she could not believe that they were in any way a threat. An invitation? She reached for the backpack and fastened its many clasps. Zazar seemed to have forgotten her. Saying nothing, the Wysen-wyf stepped out on the broken surface of the wall. Several strides away there were more of those stones—stairs—arranged one above the other, which had made it so easy for them to climb. Now they could as easily descend.

Nor did Zazar look in her direction as they again reached ground level, but set out as if she knew perfectly well where she was going. Ashen hurried after her, taking heed of the uncertain footing. More walls loomed on either side, but these were not high and Ashen took them for the supports of what had once been individual hearths.

At last they came to an open space, wider than the half-filled paths between the buildings. But here also there had been destruction. A figure, carved of stone and now broken into thirds, lay facedown before them. But that was no monster body such as Ashen had discovered during her own adventuring. It was plain that this was meant to represent a being like herself. The cracked and broken body and limbs matched hers except in size, for this had been far taller.

Also the proportions she could trace were not those of any squat and thick-bodied Bog-folk. She felt choked with the questions she wanted to ask, but Zazar was edging past the figure and plainly silent by her own desire.

The feet of the figure were still on a wide stone base from which the rest of it had fallen, or been cast. And that base stood just before the entrance of a much larger building, one that differed from its fellows. Here the rubble had been pushed aside, leaving a short set of stairs. These were not as steep as those on the wall. Four steps brought them to a wide, open space before the rise of the wall. Ashen could see, centered in the wall, an archway giving on shadows beyond. But across that doorway stretched what Ashen did not expect to see, a curtain thick and sturdy enough to have been but recently hung. It was just such a curtain as would serve as door to a Bog hut.

She followed Zazar, but when they stepped on the ledge by the curtain, the Wysen-wyf swung around. Her eyes were set now on Ashen and she found the voice she had not used for hours.

"Ashen Deathdaughter, this is the heart of very ancient knowledge. Most of that has seeped away through the years. But those born with the Gift of Learning, Knowing, and Holding, have made it their own. You have been welcomed by the Blood Spirit, and therefore you are believed to be talented, as I have thought."

She gestured at the ruins about them. "This was once a great city such as Bog-folk never knew. When it stood strong, there was no Bale-Bog and the water had not come to eat away the land. I told you that there have been many, many peoples who ruled this land before us. This was one of the heart places of such a long-lost race, but, as I said, the Wheel turns and this is a change time. I give you this secret freely, since there is a far-knowing that it is time to serve again to awaken new powers. And you have before you a part in that."

Ten

The Queen kept her face serene, aloof, as she tried to assess the expressions of the three men, each a member of the Council, who had been bowed into her presence. She occupied a chair in the center of the room—not on a dais; that would have looked too much like a throne. Now she lifted one hand in a barely perceptible movement and the page on duty hurriedly pushed forward three of the chairs awarded to nobility whose rank entitled them to be allowed to sit in the royal presence. With a second small gesture, she then emptied the room of all but herself and those who sought audience. She enjoyed showing off how well-trained her servants were—not that it would matter to any of these men.

Care and caution, prudence, patience. The words strung together in her mind as she held to her remote expression, meeting one set of eyes after another. Her hands lay clasped on her lap and she could feel the four Rings as if their power gathered weight enough to press heavily upon her flesh.

Royance of Grattenbor, head of the Council. His family was ally to the House of Oak, and in his youth, he had been a close comrade to Boroth. Royance, however, had not allowed any appetites to rule him. He was a fighting man by choice. Twice within the last ten years he had defended his property, or what he deemed his, in full siege from neighbors too ambitious. His face resembled that of a roving burhawk and, perhaps knowing this, he had taken the bird as his personal badge. Ysa knew that some of the fierce nature of that bird was also in him.

Gattor of Bilth. He sided sometimes with Yew, sometimes with Rowan, and made no permanent alliances. He was no open fighter, looking upon the clash of arms as the improper way to settle a quarrel. No, not he. Gattor's thick body, that round face with sleepy eyes, belonged to one who was indolent, slow to act. Openly, that was. Gattor's warring was always conducted in the shadows, and few were the times men could more than speculate on his part in the sudden collapse of an ally of a House rumored to be encroaching upon his own holdings.

Then Harous of Cragden, youngest of the three, and perhaps the most dangerous. The others were clad in deepest midnight-blue, the proper court color, but he wore a russet surcoat that fairly glowed in the dim light of the room. He had never, as far as Ysa knew, allied with any of the four Great Houses and so had avoided their quarrels with each other as well. This was entirely prudent, because of his hereditary position as master of Cragden Keep, the castle that was Rendelsham's primary defense. Thus he could raise a skillful sword upon occasion, and he had done some intricate weaving of political webs. Also, he was somewhat of a scholar, though he had never allowed his interest in learning of the past to cloud his actions in the present.

Ysa inclined her head slightly. "My lords," she said to them in greeting, well aware that enticing these three to follow her would be one of the hardest tasks she had ever undertaken. They must be made to see that now was a time when all must stand together or, apart, crumble into nothing, one by one.

The three bowed to her and then seated themselves. "Your Majesty." Despite Harous's youthful years, she was in no way surprised at his being their spokesman.

"I shall be plain with you," she returned in an even voice, lifting her hands to the arms of her chair so that the Rings were well in sight. "Good my lords, this is a time of rising troubles and not for covert dealings. I promised plain words, and so they shall be, though it would be well that such words do not pass beyond this chamber. My husband, the King, is not as he once was; we can no longer overlook this fact among ourselves. Nor is the Prince one who shows at present any interest in state affairs."

She noted how Harous stirred, Royance drew himself more upright, and Gattor's expression became even sleepier.

"It has been given me as certain knowledge that Rendel stands in the way of peril such as this land has not faced these twenty generations or more," she continued. "There is a boiling in the lands to the north. Those Sea-Rovers, who have ever been a threat to our peace, are now on the move—and not of their free will. One by one, their strongholds have fallen to a growing threat from far, far beyond into the Country of Ever Snow. There an army has risen and is on the march to seize land more fruitful than their own. Who they are and whence they have come is not yet known." She paused, for with this statement, Harous had stirred again on his low chair. He was leaning forward a little.

She turned to address him directly. "My lord, it is said that your knowledge of the past can outreach that of most of our scholars. What know you of the north?"

Royance glanced at Harous in some surprise, and even Gattor raised one brow enough so that his eyes caught a gleam of light, though he did not turn his head.

Harous answered promptly and without hesitation. "There are legends, Your Majesty, very old, telling that once all the land of which we are now aware was a mighty Kingdom and the four Great Houses flourished in peace one with the other. Then a foul fate turned brother against brother, son against father, until there was utter chaos. Even nature itself took a part in this evil struggle, and the sea assaulted the land. The stories say that the

Bog came into being then. Even mountains arose and blasted fire into the skies. Those of our kind could only cower and live on in shreds of hope. But then there came Jarnel out of Karn—"

"That is a tale to be told beside a winter hearth simply to make the listeners shiver," Royance said with a frown. "There has never been a shred of evidence save the mouthing of story-tellers that Jarnel ever lived."

Harous shrugged. "Be it so, or be it not so, that tale ends with the claim that Jarnel and his host drove the remnants of the evil force into the far north and locked there some Power to hold them imprisoned. Afterward, the Great Houses were main-tained, but far reduced from their former sway. Can any deny that there are those among us, man or woman, born with some traces of an inner strength they cannot understand? Such gifts might have been much stronger in an earlier time."

The Queen nodded. "My lords, these words are not simply speculations. Ancient records reveal that from time to time, even in our own memory, there have been happenings that defy ex-planation."

Royance eyed her intently now, his face showing his keen intelligence. The silver trimming of his court dress was no more austere than the gray of his eyes. "Ashenkin is gone," he said flatly. "Legends say Ashenhold was once mighty and stretched across our southern coast . . . until a shadow came."

It was as if he had thrown a smoldering brand into their midst. The other two men drew away from him a fraction, and even the Queen's composure faltered. Her lips twitched as if she would shout forth some word unbidden and unwanted. Then she regained command over herself.

"Ashenhold and whatever shadow grew there," she said in a carefully measured voice, "are no longer any danger to us. The House has vanished. But you are right, my Lord of Grattenbor, we have kept some unexplainable memories to this present day." She returned deftly to her intended topic. "That is in the past. Now, whatever lies in the north, it is no longer under any restraint, and once again mountains awaken and belch out fire. An army has spilled down upon the lands of the sea-people. What is left of them flees either westward over the waters or southward. I ask you, my Lord Royance, as one who has ordered battles, is there truth to that old saying, 'He who fights my enemy is—for a season at least—my friend'? These sea-people are fighters, well we know that. And those whom they fight must be our enemies as well as theirs."

Surprisingly, it was Gattor who spoke up. He seemed determined to remind everyone of his presence. His voice fell unpleasantly on the ear, so nasal and high-pitched it was almost a whine. "Yes, we know," he said. As if by absentminded habit, he fumbled at his belt where hung the sheath, emptied as were all save those of sworn guards in royal presence. "Ask of the merchants, Your Majesty. If it is in your mind to make some sort of alliance with those wave-wolves, I do not think many of the Traders will rally to the cause."

Of course Gattor would think of this. The wealth of his Family had come through at least three generations by means of vague and covert dealings with the Trader kindred. No wonder the lace and embroidery trimming his surcoat were of gold thread.

Ysa decided to risk all, to allow herself the freedom of actually putting into words what she feared. "It may come to such a pass that kin must stand with stranger and make alliance lest both perish."

"Our northern borders are strong. The Bog, Majesty, seems an inviting weak spot, but it will be a trap for any invasion from the south," Gattor said without heat. "Can anyone think that those savages who skulk there will take easily to invaders? All know what happens to any of other blood who dare to enter there." He remained deceptively sleepy in appearance, his hands clasped over his belly.

"Yes," Ysa conceded, "the Bale-Bog may hold. But the invaders' weapons are superior to shell spears and there are ways to be threaded through those muck-and-water paths. Do we dare rely on this stretch of drowned land as if it were a tower-high wall? I promised you bluntness. Now let me be even more forthright. Tell me, my lords, do the Houses continue to keep to their quarreling so that this land is riddled with suspicion among the holdings? Or do we work for a peace to unite us all?"

Harous leaned forward again. "Your Majesty, rumor of war is not proof enough. Have you more to offer us than travelers' tales?" He watched her intently, his greenish eyes alight.

Ysa was instantly on her guard. What did he know; what had he learned? His delving into ancient records was notorious. It was even said that his archives at Cragden Keep contained more knowledge than could be found in the storerooms of the scribes in the castle or the library of the Great Fane, where she had diligently been seeking.

She hastened to impress upon him that she knew her information to be reliable, but without revealing her sources. "My lord, rumor ever suggests a core of fact."

Aloft in the high tower rested her "eyes and ears," and some persons, seeing Visp, would surely make a demon sign and speak of dark witchery. She held her gaze steady until Harous dropped his, though she knew he was far from satisfied.

Royance had remained silent through this exchange, keeping his own line of thought. Now he spoke up. "Your Majesty, can one course a hound among warkats, each taking no note of the other as lawful prey? Yet what you have said carries in it the seed of truth. We all have our observers abroad." Now he looked at each of his companions in turn. "Let us call in what news we can. If it be so dour—well, my kin has raised sword for years against Darthan and Glick, but I will send a herald to both of them with peace cords about his weapon if it be needed that we must fight together."

Ysa kept her face still with an effort. She had him! At least for the moment. She must be careful not to let him slip away. He spoke the truth, and if he could pull together two other kin-lines, long bitter enemies, there was hope for the future.

"I thank you, Lord Royance," she said.

She turned to look at Gattor. He pyramided his pudgy hands, palm to palm, and gazed beyond them, perhaps at something not even present. His continued silence shadowed a threat. At last, he spoke.

"What of Prince Florian? It is past time for his betrothal. I, for one, have heard no talk of an embassy to Yuland or Writham to seek a bride of proper birth. We know that if he is united with any kindred of Rendel, it will fling a glove of challenge into the midst of us all."

Damn him, by the Black Jaws of Labor, he was right! If Ysa didn't know better, he might have been privy to the contents of a certain coffer on a far table in this very audience chamber. Inside rested letters that in themselves bore subtle insult. As far as Yuland across the southern sea and the wealthy island Kingdom of Writham to the west were concerned, enough was known about Crown Prince Florian that no royal daughter of theirs would consent to be sent here to wed. Even to betroth him, let alone to marry him to any Great Family among the nobles at this time, would be to pit them all against each other. Or worse, pit them against the Crown. With such an action, all chance of a solid alliance would be gone. So much for her hopes for uniting the Kingdom by marrying Florian to Laherne of Rowan. At least for now. But there was still time to bend matters, if she was patient enough. A ruse, a subterfuge—perhaps that would unite her nobles.

She rubbed the Rings on her fingers now as if this movement would summon some plan out of this very real problem. Then suddenly an idea occurred to her. She pondered it. No need to rush; it was ever her way in these meetings. However, it might be that time was no longer an ally to her in this one area of concern. She decided to reveal her thought.

"The Sea-Rovers," she said calmly, "owe allegiance to no one overlord. They are counted in kin clans. But each has pride in lineage, and they have their lords and those of their immediate blood. There heads south one of their strongest and most venturesome clans. They hold the Sea Raven as their badge—"

"Not so!" Gattor burst in, awake at last. "Blood-drinking devils. Now it comes clear. I know what you are proposing, and I reject it! In one breath you speak against companying with them against some supposed threat, and in the next you suggest a union! I hold blood debts against their line, for they have taken in the past some five of my ships."

Royance spoke up, his voice measured and calm. "Let us say nothing in haste that needs to be swallowed later. Your Majesty has had some contact with them, these Sea-Rovers?" His eyes narrowed as he studied her.

"Not yet. It is only that I know what may come," she replied. She stared hard at each man in turn. "If that which has come down into the north mountainland cannot be trapped by the Bog and we have no common plan with the Sea-Rovers, and we are not able to put aside our quarrels and ride banner by banner together, then I swear by these—" She held aloft her hands, and the bands of the Rings seemed to spark with fire. "Yea, it is certain that Rendel will fall with all our part of the world. Your vaunted Family and the great strongholds of all the Great Houses will be but ruins manned by the dead. If it takes marriage between the Crown Prince of Rendel and a daughter of the Sea-Rovers, then that is how it shall be."

Royance bowed his head. Then he looked up, and once more the burhawk gazed out through his eyes. "Your Majesty," he said with some force, "has given us much to think on. But we cannot make such decisions without considering them from all sides. There is much to be weighed."

"Just so, just so!" Gattor nodded. "Very much to be thought on."

"I recognize the truth and the wisdom of your words," the Queen said, her voice full of sadness and resignation. Secretly,

Ysa was pleased, for she knew she could not in reality have hoped for more than this. Let them ponder the suggestion of a marriage with Sea-Rover trash; that would serve to make La-herne seem the more desirable. It was no trouble to allow Gattor to oppose what she never intended. "But we have time against us. Consult and plan as you will, my lords. I want a united voice when you return . . . say, two days from now." With a gesture, she dismissed them. "You have your tasks, my lords. Pray do not disappoint us all."

They arose and bowed. With Gattor scowling, Royance having assumed his usual impervious expression, and Harous tapping a fingertip against his belt as if pensively marshaling his thoughts, they started toward the door.

Gattor caught Royance's arm and it was plain he wished some private speech once they were out of overhearing. However, Harous held back. He lifted one foot, fiddling with the buckle on his shoe. Then, when the other two had vanished, he turned once more. He must have additional to tell me, the Queen thought, and wants to say it alone and not as a member of the Council. Curious, she acknowledged him, though a private audience, under the circumstances, went against all custom and protocol. "My lord?"

Harous returned to where she still sat. Ysa gestured, and he once more settled on the low chair.

To her mild surprise, he said nothing at first, but drew from inside his velvet doublet a thong that hung about his neck. The amulet, or whatever it was he wore on this thong, he cradled in the palm of his hand before holding it out for her to see.

It had a gray sheen as though well rubbed, and was fashioned into the shape of a winged creature. Despite the polish, an observer could see that the creature was represented as furred rather than feathered. Its tiny eyes glittered with gems.

Ysa dug her fingernails into her palms to keep herself under control. She recognized that flyer—

"Zazar, Your Majesty." His voice rose hardly above a whisper, as if there might be listeners in the room. "This came from Zazar."

Ysa rubbed her hands together to make as much contact between Rings and flesh as possible. Nothing, however, could stifle the chill that spread through her body as she forced her attention from the amulet to the one who held it. "You have delved far, my Lord Harous."

"It is my passion, Majesty. I find the *now* a ragtag place, but the *before* calls to me. Yes, I have followed some very dusty trails. And some of them have taken me to Zazar."

She did not dare ask a question, for to reveal the least degree of ignorance was dangerous. How much did he know? And how would he use this knowledge? Would it be against her, in an effort to gain power? She felt dizzy, on the verge of falling into a trap. She must summon all her wits to keep to herself as much as possible of her own knowledge, and to augment it with what he might have gained.

"This symbolizes a messenger, I think," Ysa said between tight lips.

"A faithful one," he said, nodding in agreement. "One of several. I have not used it yet. But another has been sent north, Majesty?"

There was no use denying what he obviously knew. "Yes. And the reports I mentioned to you and to the other lords are true."

"It seemed to me that this day we hear the results of such a journey, taken by such a messenger." He rubbed his thumb back and forth over the pendant cupped in his hand. "There are other journeys," he added.

She waited, refusing to ask.

He seemed willing enough to continue. Further, he spoke without pause, as if he expected no questions, but assumed they now worked together as equals—which the little messenger might well make them, at least in this endeavor. "Your Majesty, the Bale-Bog has its secrets. Florian should make a marriage to unite powers, yes. And the maid chosen must be one who will raise none of the Houses to question or support a separate cause. Let us suppose—merely suppose—that one could find a maid of high lineage who had no House left to whom she could appeal for support."

The chill that gripped Ysa was pure ice now. Laherne was surely a bride of high blood, but not one entirely without a House. Certainly such would be the most desirable; had she not earlier sent out tendrils of power, reaching for that same solution, and striven with all her secret means to discover the result of such a search? In the turmoil of the past years, several of the lesser families allied with the four Great Houses had indeed been brought down, extinguished. They were the ones whose heads had intrigued beyond their proper depths of guile. To unite with a daughter from any such, were any of pure breed left, would not avail the royal cause, only weaken it. One does not lean on a broken reed when one needs a wall for defense.

She forced herself to think. The Bale-Bog. Why had he mentioned that? There had never been any House with holdings there, not in the memory of even the oldest man. Many generations had seen the existence of that place. And yet . . . the Bale-Bog. No. It couldn't be. Her hands clenched until the Rings bit into her flesh.

He must have read her sudden thought in some change of her expression. "Yes—Ashenkin."

In spite of her fight for control, her hands jerked.

With an effort, she spoke, pausing between each word as if to impress the force of it. "Such is impossible. There is no Ashenkin."

He quirked an eyebrow in agreement. "Not resident in Rendel, to be sure. But was there not one who was possible, one unknown, one with high blood—"

"Dead!" She rose suddenly from her chair, forcing him to rise also. "The House of Ash is no more, and to think otherwise, my

Andre Norton & Sasha Miller

Lord Harous, is treason! This audience is finished."

She could no longer play the game of light-and-shadow. Her sole desire was to have him away, out of her sight. There was that which she must do, and quickly, if the fear he had aroused was to be laid.

He had slipped the pendant back into hiding in his doublet and now he bowed deeply. But he also dared to speak.

"Remember Zazar, Majesty. I am at your service, whether you believe it or not."

She longed to call for a guard and to have this possible enemy put under arrest and locked away. She did not dare, knowing him to be much too powerful, too dangerous. So she stood, her face once more a mask, as he backed out of her presence.

Once Harous was safely gone, she whirled and hurried to the slip panel in the wall. She had discovered it herself, and told no one. A labyrinth of hidden passageways afforded her the means of going unseen from one part of the castle to another, thus reinforcing her reputation as a powerful woman who could appear out of nowhere at any time. She closed the panel behind her and began to climb the steps, holding her full skirts tightly so as not to smudge them with ancient dust.

It was a long climb, narrower and steeper than the stairway she preferred to use, but more direct. Also, she did not care to be observed at this moment. She stopped twice, pressing her hand against her side to ease a twinge of pain. But finally she reached the tower room and lurched across the floor to her chair, where she nearly collapsed, her strength suddenly drained.

How much did Harous really know? His hints stirred up rage and fear. But if he had the power—and a messenger of his own—

No Ashenkin could possibly live, not one of pure blood. It was so well known that that Bog-folk by custom killed any Outlander—and hadn't her own guards found traces of what had happened there some sixteen years ago? She had never had cause to question it. Questions could only confirm that Alditha's child was half Outlander, half of the Bog. With a twist of her lips, Ysa thought about how some Rendelian men—and women—were said to seek liaisons with Bog-folk for the thrill of danger. And how, sometimes, there were untoward results.

Ysa willed it to be so. She would not abide the idea that her husband had lustfully sown that seed, even before she, his chosen Queen, carried his heir. It had to have been someone else. . . .

She refused to remember how much she had loved Boroth at one time, remembering only the hatred that had replaced it. She could not have abided even a flirtation—and that was all it had been, all it could ever have been, all Ysa had allowed time for it to have been—between King Boroth and Alditha of Ash.

To think that even as Boroth had been contemplating the betrayal of his new-wedded wife, so had Alditha placed horns on Boroth's head! The harlot's passion must have overcome her common sense and she gave in to it elsewhere. No wonder her flight into the Bog had been so precipitous. She fled the wrath of both King and Queen! Ysa stifled laughter that verged on the hysterical.

Still, one must be certain. With an effort, she composed herself and settled back in the chair. Her hands shook as she raised them slowly and emitted a shrill twittering, totally unnatural, from pursed lips. There was sudden weight in her hands, and warmth as she looked down at Visp.

🌿

Ashen ducked through the door-curtain after Zazar and looked around with near consuming curiosity. The area here was both wide and long—or had been once—and once might have been spacious enough to have engulfed the whole of the Bog village she knew. However, here as elsewhere, upper walls and part of the roof had collapsed to fill the cavity. She could also see indications that there had been an effort to preserve what was left.

Many unknown hands had been at work, setting some measure of order out of chaos. Blocks of masonry had been *dragged* to one side and piled along the walls into a shoulder-high secondary barrier, leaving the center cleared of most debris. Nor was this bare. Shelf supports had been pounded into cracks between these blocks, and the shelves were burdened with woven reed bags and others of twisted lupper skin. From some of the shelves hung swollen net bags filled with unknown substances. A few cracked pots sat among the bags, and they were certainly not empty.

There was no hearth-hole in the center of this space. Rather, some of the stones that had fallen—in the far past, judging by the fire-marks painting them—had been set to screen a fire. Also, there were piles of mats, well-woven to fulfill either sitting or sleeping requirements.

Somewhat to her surprise, as awesome as the surroundings were, this was a room that welcomed one. Ashen felt quite at home as she allowed her pack to settle to the floor. Zazar was already at the fireplace, busy not only with kindling from a pile close to hand, but tending to chunks of black stuff that she placed carefully around the kindling. Fire answered her efforts and Ashen drew closer, grateful for the heat after their dank journey.

As she settled down and held her hands out as if to gather the heat closer to herself, Ashen realized that she and Zazar were not the sole life in this chamber. The Wysen-wyf had completed her labors and now she was chirping a series of small coaxing notes. The mat pile nearby stirred as if something had burrowed deeply there. Then out into the open wriggled a creature that faintly resembled one of the shy water-rats of the Bog.

This one, however, was larger than any the girl had glimpsed during her own prowling of the known Bogways. Also, once it was fully in the open, she could see that it was indeed like no rat. It was larger, rounder of head, pricked of ears, and its pelt looked much softer than the bristly fur of the pool-dwellers. It padded to the Wysen-wyf, who held out a hand. It stood up and arched its head to rub against her palm before it settled down on its haunches. It reached its slender forelimbs to grasp Zazar's hand and nuzzled it. Then it began licking Zazar's fingers with an absurdly pink tongue.

Zazar's chirping became a croon, and the creature answered with a series of strange, small cries as it raised its head high enough to look up into the Wysen-wyf's face.

Zazar beckoned, and Ashen obediently drew closer.

"This is Weyse. Weyse," Zazar said in turn to the small creature, "Ashen." She might have been introducing some kin from another Bog village. She touched Ashen's shoulder, her other hand still being held by the little creature. "Reach out to Weyse, girl, that she may learn you."

Just what that meant, Ashen could not guess, but she extended her hand to the furred one, who let go of Zazar to catch it in its forepaws. It leaned forward and sniffed at her flesh for a long moment, and then she could feel the rasp of its tongue on her skin. When it loosed its hold on her, she dared to smooth its head between the pointed ears as Zazar had done earlier.

"Weyse knows you now, Ashen Deathdaughter, and you will find that very useful. But there is more to be done. Listen well."

Zazar rose and passed the fireplace, heading toward a portion of the wall where instead of a shelf, holding cords had been tightly laced to support what Ashen saw to be a number of clay tablets. The Wysen-wyf did not remove any of them; she merely drew one finger along the side of that nested cache as gently as she had caressed Weyse.

"You are not of the Bog-blood, girl," she said. "Nor is this place of the Bale-Bog known in this time to the ordinary folk. There have always been those among us who in blood and thought harked back to another time before the dissolution of the Clasp came." She hesitated for so long that Ashen dared a question.

"The Clasp?"

"Another world, another time," Zazar replied. There was a weary note in her voice. "There was greatness here in the long ago. This place in which we shelter was a place of Seekers of

Knowledge. Then the Law that rules all living things spoke. There is a time of building, a time of abiding, and then comes the fall. Only remnants of what was before remain in bits and pieces. So we seek ever for that which may lead upward once again. The Bog, which was part of a great and mighty empire in the ancient times, was sunken into the dark. Now another time of darkness nears us. You are of other blood, but you were born in the Bog; you know it, and that knowledge will be of importance in days to come. Remain here until you are called."

"Called? By whom?" Ashen bit her tongue, but she could not stifle the questions.

Zazar shook her head. "Ask that of the land, girl. It is not known to me and I cannot tell you. I must return to my own place now, for the Bog-kin are my people, though they have become even less than the underwater ones in what they desire and do. There will be trouble, but that cannot be guarded against, only foreseen. That much I know. Ashen Deathdaughter, do you watch while you wait, and watch well!"

She stooped and caught up Weyse in her arms as one would a nursing child. When she put the furred one down again, she nodded, first to Ashen and then toward the wall where hung the collection of tablets.

"Use your time well, girl. I do not know how long you will have free. I call for you the shielding wings of fortune."

She turned swiftly and Ashen hurried to follow her. It was apparent that the Wysen-wyf was now determined to leave, and to go quickly. As Ashen followed, she tried to stammer out question but they died on her lips as she realized there would be no more answers. There was a finality in what the Wysen-wyf had said. Did she mean that their tie, loose as it had always been, was now severed? How to find the words? Finally, as she unfettered the rope mooring the boat that had brought them, Ashen dared to clutch Zazar's sleeve, and words tumbled out.

"Protector—" from some unknown source, that title came to her "—do you then wish to deny me?"

Zazar looked at her steadily, unblinking. "In this life, we do either what we desire or what is needful. This that I do is of the second sort. You have been all I could have asked for to nurture in my service. I can tell you that we shall meet again, only it will not be as one who teaches and one who learns. And so I wish you good fortune."

"B-b-best of fortune to you also, Wise One," Ashen said. She felt as if the strongest part of herself had been severely shaken, threatened, and yet she could not protest as she saw Zazar board the craft and start to pole herself away. Nor did the Wysen-wyf turn back to look at Ashen, who watched until the boat reached the inlet to the pond and disappeared from view.

Eleven

As the little Sea-Rover fleet sailed on, the watchers could find no great change in the cliff barrier of the Bog except that it stood lower now. Here and there, the cliffs were riven, as if inviting a voyager to a sheltered harbor. And there showed, when the wave-reader used his seeing-glass, more and more cavelike openings through which issued turgid and odorous water to sully the sea. Provisions for the fleet were dangerously low. They had begun to despair, and even to consider invading that uninviting land in search of food. Then, on the third day after the attack of the amphibian, the lookout spotted a disturbance near to shore. As the steersman brought the *GorGull* as close in as he dared, they could identify the frothing water as a school of fish apparently tearing to pieces some bit of prey.

What it was, they could not determine, and to feast on the feasters was certainly a stomach-churning thought, if one allowed it to cross the mind. However, there was little use in being fastidious when starvation loomed to weaken them all. Thus it was decided in council held on the *GorGull*, in communication with the other ships by means of signal flags, that a group from the lead vessel would make an attempt to get closer to that shoreline in spite of what might be spilling from it.

Still using the flags, the helmsman of *Wave Ruler* pointed out that there was also a number of birds to be noted now, and that they could see a pocking of the cliffs in which such might nest. Birds' nests, too, might contain a possible source of food. Or they could follow the inlet ahead, to see where it led.

They drew lots for the four-man crew of the small boat to make the scouting voyage. *Stormbracer*, the largest and slowest of the vessels in the fleet, undertook to sail on southward, leaving the more maneuverable vessels to follow.

Obern was not surprised when he drew the knotted rope from the choosing-basin that First Mate Hasse passed around to all. In spite of the uneasy awe that the monster he slew had aroused, he had been intrigued by trying to imagine what kind of world might lie behind those cliffs and wondering if indeed the creature had come from there. He welcomed the possibility of a chance to find out.

The four selected in the drawing settled to the oars of the small landing boat. Two were seamen used to such maneuvering. Obern and the armsman, Dordan, a sergeant of archers, followed the directions of their seagoing companions and also swung to oars.

Around them, the water grew thick with fish that darted away at their approach. There was a coil of net lying ready at their feet, and one of the seamen was a master at casting it. They headed toward the main disturbance with what speed they could muster.

However, before they reached their destination, a chance current carried a tangled, dull-green mass, nearly a third the size of their boat, across their course. Thorny, spiked branches protruded from it. The men agreed that it must have been torn away from a rooting on the side of the cliff. Dordan fended it off with a push of his oar. Then all aboard had to duck quickly, for out of nowhere, an enormous bird appeared and dived straight at them. For a moment, Obern thought it was one such as had followed them the night of their escape, but this one was mere flesh and blood and brought with it only that measure of fear appropriate to those faced with such a predator.

"Should have known these was big 'uns," one of the sailors muttered. "Seeing them from so far away and all."

The wingspread of this one was wider than Obern could measure with both arms outstretched. Its wickedly hooked bill snapped open with a shriek as it wheeled above them. Thick, dirty-gray feathers covered all but its obscenely naked red head, which reminded Obern of a newly flayed skull.

The shriek was echoed by a second flyer nearby. A third flyer launched itself from the cliffs. Fighting the rocking of the boat, Dordan readied his short-bow. The first flyer bared its talons, and the water reflected the beat of the great wings as it attacked one of the seamen. The man swung up his oar, only to lose it overboard, yanked out of his hands as the bird struck. Dordan let fly, and the thrum of the bowstring was nearly lost in the bird's scream of pain.

Neither sea-sword nor knife could serve well here, Obern knew. Now there were two birds circling overhead, and another was winging swiftly to join battle. Obern held to his oar, though he nearly lost his balance as the first bird crashed into the boat, Dordan's arrow protruding from its breast. The craft rocked perilously and threatened to capsize.

The fate of its fellow served to make the second flyer swerve off. But the other had no such qualms and swooped on them from a great height. It targeted Dordan as if realizing he was the principal threat.

The archer had a second arrow nocked, but the dying flyer struck him a hard blow with its wing, nearly sending him overboard. The airborne attacker screamed, and Obern swung his oar with all his strength, barely taking time enough to aim the blow.

His desperate swing caught the outstretched, naked neck of

the bird. He nearly dropped the oar as the impact jarred him through and through, but he fancied he had heard the crunch of breaking bones. The force of the blow, together with the flyer's own speed, sent the attacker out and away from them. However, they were shipping water and the seamen strove to steady the boat with the remaining oars. Now that they had time to look, they discovered that they were indeed approaching the cliffs, though at an angle which did not aim their craft toward the dark opening looming in the rock barrier.

The dying bird still battered them with its wings, and the two other birds might return. Obern dropped the oar, drew his sword and swung it with a precision unhindered by the unsteady footing.

He struck and struck again, until the bird ceased flopping. He turned in time to see Dordan, spraddle-legged and fighting for balance as he aimed aloft at the remaining attacker. The bird Obern had clubbed with the oar floated near them, its outstretched wings bearing it up; it was slowly drifting shoreward on the waves. The angle of the ugly head told him he had, indeed, broken its neck.

Dordan swore as his arrow brought down only a broken feather. The bird wheeled off toward the cliffs in reluctant defeat. Meanwhile, one of the seamen pulled the dead bird out from under their feet. Obern stooped to help him. The creature was unexpectedly heavy. The other seaman and Dordan made ready to cast the net.

Skillfully, they entrapped the body of the second flyer and dragged it aboard as well. They set a course then as best they could, for the boat was now awkward to steer, toward the churning waters that had been their goal.

It was an awkward business, for they had drifted too close to the breaking waves at the foot of the cliffs, during their skirmish with the giant flyers. The boat tossed in the heavy chop, almost unmanageable. Nevertheless, the seamen and Obern and Dordan used their strength and skill to bring them to the site of the feasting. There were fish in plenty, undisturbed by the battle nearby. What they devoured, strangely enough, did not sink far under that churning mass, but seemed to ride near the surface. Now and then, a chunk of it broke free and floated upward, only to immediately disappear down a fish's gullet.

What they feasted upon so greedily, the men could not fully see. It appeared to be no more than a spongelike mass in which the fish had torn great holes. Those in the boat avoided it carefully as they cast the net.

Their catch was heavy enough when they drew it in to cause Obern to wonder if they would be able to dump its contents or would have to struggle, towing it, to the ship. With muscle-wrenching labor, they managed to collect a mass of twisting, silver fish, enough to cover the bodies of the birds. They dared not make a second cast, for by now, their craft was near too heavy to remain afloat. The waves lapped at the gunwales, and one of the seamen set to bailing lest they founder and sink.

How much of what they carried might be eaten, Obern could not guess, nor how much of what was edible might be palatable. Still, food was food. But that the birds could be formidable enemies was plain. And perhaps even more-dangerous creatures waited behind the cliffs. He eyed those stone barriers speculatively as they rowed back to the *GorGull*. It was just as well that they had not had to try a landing. An unknown land, the Bog—and a forbidding one.

*

It was silent in the high tower room, and time had passed with stifling slowness. Ysa could not afford to linger here much longer, waiting. And the roiling of small fears. Her mind flinched at that word. Fear could not be allowed a place at the gaming table when a Kingdom was at stake. She settled on another word. Annoyances, then. They had summoned a dull pain to settle behind her eyes.

Her messenger was, according to ancient reports, impervious

to most dangers, unless . . . she shifted in the high seat. What did anyone know of the Bog except that it was a watery trap where death openly ruled? Yet she *must* know the results of her seeking, and soon.

Boroth. Despite all her efforts, there was no mistaking that he was slipping every day, approaching closer to a time when he would be utterly useless. This very morning, two of his physicians had called upon her, uttering fell warnings even before she had had time to break her fast. They had stared at her hands during the interview. She knew what they wanted but dared not voice. Was it true, she could almost hear them saying, that superstition claiming that the Rings indeed held the life of the monarch, as well as of the country? And would she not return them to the King?

Even if she wanted to, this was impossible. Without the power of the Rings to aid her, she might as well open wide the gates to all those sly lords and let them pillage to their hearts' content.

Harous. Not merely to pass the time, she had her eyes and ears focused on him. He hunted, they said. But the direction of that hunting was a challenge in itself, and she was certain that in all his twists and turnings and backtrackings, he made sure he rode toward the broken land that bordered directly on the Bog. The Bog— Her thoughts circled back to her messenger, Visp. She had so little time left. To remain here—when the castle, the whole city, knew of Boroth's condition—was perilous folly. Never before had this one trusted companion failed her.

She arose, stiff from inactivity. If she did not go, those from the court would come seeking her, even here, which long ago she had set aside for her privacy alone. Now she approached the southern window where that curious rainbow glimmered, shielding out the world she knew only too well. She raised her hands in welcome, but there was no answer.

At last she allowed the weight of the Rings to drop her arms to her sides. If she left the tower now, it might be long before she could once more withdraw from the sight of the court and return. Yet linger longer, she dared not. Her descent of the main stairway was much more sedate than her precipitate rush up the hidden one.

As she stepped out of the door that guarded the tower stair, Ysa all but bumped into Master Lorgan, the eldest and most assured of the physicians. However, it seemed a random meeting.

"You are needed most urgently," he said. "The warning I gave you this morning—well, we fear the King's condition has grown very grave. He lies at a crisis. Your presence is . . . forgive me, Majesty, but your presence is mandatory."

He bowed, and Ysa was aware that she must make a choice; perhaps a half measure would suffice for the present.

"Good physician," she said. The words came with a trace of unease, which would only be natural, and thus convincing. "How fortunate to find you. Of course I will go to the King's chamber. How could I not? Furthermore, I have been thinking on what you spoke of this morning. You have seen the King's hands." Now she held out her own as if to compare what was present to those that were in the bed. "I tried once, most earnestly, to put the Rings back on him, but failed. If the Rings cannot be forced upon him because of the swelling, perhaps they can be used in another way to his benefit. It will cause no harm to try."

She led the way once more to the King's chamber, where smoldering herbs on the hearth could not overcome the fugue of coming death. Indeed, the physician had spoken truly. There were others gathered in the shadows; some stepped aside so that she could take the step up on the dais and stand beside the massive bed.

Boroth lay on his back, his mouth open a little, drool matting his unkempt beard. His eyes were not completely closed, but Ysa doubted that he saw what was about him.

"My Lord." Conscious of how she appeared to those in the shadows, she leaned forward and reached for one of those puffed hands, closing both of hers about it so that the Rings touched his flesh. "My Lord, by Oak and Yew, Ash and Rowan, take strength! By your oath for the land, call to you what will give you—"

His eyes opened suddenly all the way. The whites were shot with blood. His lips drew together as he turned his head on the pillow to stare straight at her.

In that meeting of the eyes there shone such hatred and rage that she swayed a little. But steadying herself against the edge of the bed, she continued to hold his hand. Was he going to spit out that rage before all these listeners? She was risking a lot because she had no other choice. His bluish lips moved, but if he shaped words, he did not utter them aloud. That he cursed her from within, she had no doubt.

"Oak and Yew, Ash and Rowan," she said again, loud enough to reach at least those closest to her. "Strengthen him—"

She was not to finish that plea. A choking gasp rumbled from Boroth as if his red anger filled his throat but could not be spewed forth. His bloated body shook and the force of the out-flung hand, which he jerked from her hold, sent her spinning until she clutched at one of the bedposts to keep from being thrown sprawling onto the floor.

Though she had often been alone in the Bog, Ashen had known that she did have a hearth-place with Zazar, and that knowledge had been an assurance of security. Now, with a pang that surprised her, she was very sure that Zazar's hearth was no longer hers. She would not see the Wysen-wyf for some time, and this strange straggle of ruins would be her only shelter. She remained where she was on the flattened stones of their landing, watching that cut into which Zazar had just poled the small craft.

Certainly the Wysen-wyf had not given her any real orders of what to do. Ashen shivered. So much had happened in so short a time. The events of the immediate past had been very different to the daily duties she had always known, and this shattered mound of what had once been did not encourage present-day inhabitants.

She felt a stout tug at her leggings, and a small trill echoed in the still air. The creature Zazar had made known to her was demanding attention. Slowly, hoping it would not bite now that Zazar was gone, Ashen reached down and lightly stroked the small head that was turned up so its eyes could meet hers.

Weyse trilled again and gave another sharp tug. It was plain that her new companion wanted her away from the shore, back into the stone-walled maze. On impulse, and because she felt alone for the first time in her life, Ashen stooped and took Weyse into her arms. To her relief and comfort, the little one willingly allowed her this liberty. In fact, it cuddled against her and began to knead her arm with its clever little forepaws.

Carrying the bundle of fur carefully cradled, Ashen returned to the refuge Zazar had shown her and began to truly examine the place.

The first task presented itself immediately. The fire still burned, but low. She remembered the strange black rock Zazar had used for feeding the starting flame. Putting Weyse down, she searched until she found a tightly woven basket, nearly waist-high, heaped with the chunks. She gingerly freed two of the blocks and laid them on the fire, where they caught almost at once. The warmth did help to banish that ever-biding chill and sense of dampness.

Then she began to make a slow circle of the room, leaving Weyse to squat by the fire, holding out those forepaws that seemed curiously like hands in a gesture even more curiously human. At the far end of the chamber, she discovered an improvement that she had never seen in a Bog dwelling. There was a basin set in the floor and above it, protruding from the wall, a hollow tube of the same rock as the walls, from which trickled a steady stream of water.

As a precaution, she tested it with one of Zazar's unfailing herb detectors and found it to be as clear of the dank outside water's effluent as that they had used for drinking and washing. In fact, it tasted better than any she had ever drunk. Then, searching further, she discovered shelves she had overlooked before. They had been erected from large pieces of rubble, but seemed secure enough. On them were closely woven storage baskets, firmly lidded. A random exploration of these turned up dried herbs, most of which she knew by sight. Behind the tall pile of mats for sitting and sleeping, she found an assortment of clay plates that were not scratched, but had oddly shaped drawings and symbols embedded in their surfaces.

The girl helped herself to several of these and sought the fireplace. During the course of her investigation, she had realized, in some surprise, that there were no windows. How was it then that this chamber nevertheless had light enough to rival a gray day outside? She glanced up and saw what looked like smooth, polished pieces of bone firmly anchored in the wall crevices wherever possible. Though they emitted a strange light of their own, they appeared to glow brighter when encouraged by light from the flames. She should have been frightened. Certainly such as these were foreign to the Bog she knew, as was all the rest of this mass of worked stone.

But she accepted the light gratefully now. From her pack she brought out the dried briar fruit and boiled lupper's eggs, along with a packet of trail food—nuts and dried berries mixed with small pieces of smoked lupper meat.

Weyse squeaked. Ashen glanced up to see it staring, large-eyed, at the packet. The little creature licked its lips. Smiling, the girl poured out a handful of the mixture and laid it on one of the plates beside her.

Weyse trilled and moved to squat before the offering. Using both forepaws, the little one scooped up a portion and started eating with every sign of one presented with some dainty. Because the lupper's eggs would not keep well, Ashen ate these for her supper, at the same time examining the plates. No, she was mistaken. They were not clay, though they looked like it. Their inscribed surfaces had a different feel, one she could not identify. However, it was those symbols that held her attention now.

Zazar had trained her to understand many of the swirls, dots, and other markings to be found in the Wysen-wyf's private library. As it was with Zazar's records, many of the signs on the plates were familiar. Here and there, however, Ashen came across a line so different that though she traced it with her finger, no spark of recognition aided her memory.

These were not recipes for salves, recorded methods for treatments of various ills and injuries, the way Zazar's plates were. Instead, they seemed to be, and Ashen was sure she was correct, the setting down of thoughts, as if the one, or ones, who had compiled them were trying to preserve knowledge of a different sort. She grew more and more fascinated while trying to work out the puzzle, unaware that Weyse had padded away after the meal, nor was she aware of anything else about her until the fire burned so low that she shivered. She raised her head to stare around, bemused as one coming out of a deep sleep.

But was the dying of the fire a warning? Suddenly alert, she got to her feet. Those crevice-bones were all aglow, and now fingers of light streamed straight up from them to fight their way through the cracks in the remains of the roof above. Without realizing why she did, Ashen drew her knife. She had heard no bellow from without, nor felt any solid thud carrying through the pavement.

Still, there was that which was totally alien to this place, something that was in a way a threat—and it was drawing near!

She had barely accepted this as being true when a shriek sounded, so thin and so high that she could hardly hear it. It came from overhead, from outside. Quickly she reached the entrance to the chamber. What she had heard certainly could not have been any protest or warning of falling wall or roof. That had been the cry of a living thing, and one in danger and pain!

She picked up a chunk of the rubble and with that in one hand and her knife in the other, went out into the night, drawn almost against her will to answer the anguish in that cry.

She reached the great stone figure that lay facedown. The evening was already well into night's darkness, but because the stones about her produced a similar though fainter radiance to the rods within, she could see well enough to cross the rough footing.

Weyse had bounded out before her and now scurried back to pluck once more at her leggings and urge her to follow, trilling a note of anxiety. Guided by her companion, Ashen rounded the head of the fallen figure to see something lying on the ground. Its wings beat, but apparently it was unable to rise. Weyse pulled her closer.

Ashen hesitated to deal directly with any strange life-form. There were too many deadly ones within the Bog, and many looked no less dangerous than this. But this creature out of the night was certainly too small to be a strong threat, and she could feel its pain and fear in an oddly heightened sense.

Throwing her rock away and sheathing her knife, she went down on her knees. With Weyse crouching on the other side of the injured thing, still trilling, Ashen reached out. The creature slapped her hand away with its flailing wing, but she persisted. Weyse also hunched nearer and copied Ashen's gesture with one front paw. This had the effect of quieting the creature. It stopped its useless struggle of flight and quieted as Weyse leaned even closer. Weyse's trilling was no longer summoning, but held soft reassurance and concern.

In this dull light, Ashen thought it was a bird. However, as it stilled, she was able to touch it, and felt fur. Furred, yet winged! This was another surprise of the Bog. With care, not knowing how it had been injured, she took it up. She must accept Weyse's decision that it was harmless and in need.

Small clawed paws raked at her wrists and once more she heard, and very plainly now, the wail that had brought her here. Sheltering the flyer against her, the girl started back to her refuge, Weyse scrambling ahead. But when they reached the portal of the gray ruins, Zazar's accepted companion—friend, servant?—suddenly stepped out before Ashen, blocking her way, though Weyse had not shown any such resistance before.

Weyse trilled again urgently, pulled at Ashen's clothing, tugging her as if to bring her down to Weyse's own level. Obediently, the girl knelt with some difficulty, for the injured flyer she was carrying had come to life once again in feeble struggles. When that burden was within Weyse's reach, the creature of the ruins trilled a series of high notes. The flyer ceased struggling as Weyse straightened up as tall as it could on hind feet. Then the rounded, big-eared head came forward and it seemed to Ashen that Weyse was deliberately blowing puffs of breath against the small winged body. For a long moment, Weyse continued these strange actions and then looked up at Ashen, its large, round eyes luminous as if they emitted light as well as used it. The creature once more led the way to the portal, making it clear to the girl to follow. The flyer she carried was now quiet, though she could feel plainly the rapid beat of its heart against her hands.

When they came into the full light of the inner room, seeming all the brighter after leaving behind the curious, foggy emanation of the ruins without, Ashen for the first time saw clearly what she held.

It was small enough that when its leathery wings were drawn against its downy body, as they now were, it could be easily held in her two hands. As with Weyse, the forepaws had the look of being meant to take the place of hands. The head was rounded, and its ears were large in proportion to the skull that supported them. The eyes now regarding her were also large and showed reddish glints. The snout between them was long; the mouth was a little open, for the creature was panting.

There was that about it which made one want to stroke the soft fur, to try to comfort the fear that the girl could still sense. She settled down by the fire and with care surveyed its body and wings, unable to find any visible injury. As she did so, she could feel it relax.

That it was capable of any harm to her, she dismissed at once. When she withdrew her hold, it settled down on her knee as if that was where it was at home. However, as she stroked it, it continued to watch her with those large eyes, almost imploringly. She became certain that as with Weyse, this new one was urging some action upon her. To free it? Perhaps. Plainly, even though she could see no injuries, it had been brought down against its will. And to take it out once more, if wounded, could mean its death.

She pulled over a small mat and transferred the now-quiescent flyer to it. Was it hungry? Once more Ashen went foraging in her trail bag, then offered the little creature a handful of the sustaining mix. The small head lowered. It sniffed the offering and with the same pleasure Weyse had shown, snatched up bits in its forepaws and began feeding itself.

Ashen watched it. Was this some other surprise of Zazar's? Weyse had accepted the small creature at once. Well, she could only wait and see. Perhaps in the morning she could loose it if it were not badly hurt and let it go to its own abiding place.

She heaped three of the mats together and selected from another pile a more yielding piece of weaving as a cover before she curled up for sleep. The flyer finished its food and set about using its forepaws, moistened by a long tongue, to wash its face. Then, with a hop, wings raised a little, it joined her, settling down by her shoulder with a faint purring sound that made her own eyes heavy with sleep. Weyse, also purring, snuggled down at her other side.

Twelve

Q ueen **Ysa clung to** the bedpost and then pushed her way
free of that support, refusing any assistance. The physician,
at her beckon, crowded past her to Boroth. She must not let any
weakness show before those gathered there. Turning her head,
she spoke to the nearest, one of the under physicians.

"Go and find His Highness. Let Prince Florian be summoned!"

But her attention remained riveted on the bed. Surely the
King's time had come—and too soon! Much too soon. For
months, she had anticipated what was about to happen here,
had rehearsed it in her mind, but the preparations she had made
seemed too few and feeble now.

The weight of the Rings pressed against her fingers as if they
were a part of some confining chain. She forced herself to look
around. The attention of most of the people in the room was
fixed on the bed and its occupant. She must know who was here
this night.

Grimly, she identified the members of the somber gathering,
one by one. There stood five of the lickspittles who strove to
raise themselves to prominence when there was any gain within

their reach. They would follow anyone with authority. She dismissed them with a glance. Not so another. Royance. The news must have reached him before he left to return to his own holding. Very properly, he remained within reach.

He had the strength and resolution that might be invaluable to her when she needed him to back her—if she could trust him. The alliance with Oak pushed itself to the front of her mind. She identified members of the Council, seldom seen unless the governing body was in session. There, crowding closer to the bed, was Valk, and that was one she could never hope to be any but a determined enemy. Two of his creatures, too, though they did not show themselves to the fore in any distinguished gathering.

But Jakar, Liffin— Her mouth tightened. Yes, word had come only a few turns of the time-glass earlier that they had ridden in with their war trains. They, too, were Council members, but she had not summoned them, nor had Florian the wit to do so. Perhaps one of his playmates with more cunning than he had suggested it.

Too much danger, too soon.

Boroth's breathing came in heavy snorts. Lorgan had tried to get him to swallow a potion one of his assistants had hastily prepared. The liquid only ran out again to wet the King's beard. Boroth flailed out one arm and the cup was dashed to the floor, spraying out its contents.

Once more the blood-reddened eyes opened, searched, settled on her and held. Her hands raised, fisted, before her mouth so that her breath would pass over them and the Rings, toward him. It was too soon—oh, indeed let the old legends hold for a space and keep him from death this night.

"Oak," she said aloud. "Yew, Ash and Rowan, give the strength of your roots to one sworn to your service!"

Boroth's mutely raging stare was on her still, enough to skewer her to the paneling on the wall if she had been made of lesser stuff. She looked at his thick fingers pawing at the covers.

Andre Norton & Sasha Miller

Ysa knew well what he wanted and she did not dare—not now, not when the man who had taken the Ring oath was already as good as dead and buried, trapped in this flabby body, even if the Rings could be once more forced onto his fingers.

He coughed, choked, and began breathing faster. Lorgan had pulled aside the stained nightshirt, baring the thick-haired chest in some desperate measure known to his trade.

A presence as jarring as a belch in the cathedral. "So, the old man's at his last gasp?" Florian lurched up beside her, reeking with fumes of wine and the stale scent of an unwashed body. He grinned down at Lorgan's frenzied labors.

Ysa tasted the bitterness that always seemed to rise when she found it necessary to deal with her son. He had no ability in spite of all her past efforts to prepare him, to at least play a suitable mummer's role befitting their House's only heir. And his actions now before this audience were typical of what could be expected when he ascended to the throne.

He had shed his baby fat, and his straight-limbed body and pleasingly featured face had not yet begun to show signs of his excesses. She could not say as much for his mind. At least Boroth in his early days had had some cleverness. When he was this dolt's age, he had won to himself the allegiance of the major lords, wedded her, gained her respect, and even her love—for a while. Until, that is, he had made plain how little she meant to him save as a breeder. Then love had turned sour, and she had seen to it that all endeavor to sire had proved a failure, producing only this one disappointing lout.

Yes, Boroth had possessed cunning, intelligence, and a kind of rough charm that had drawn men to him. But it was long since he roused to hold his place in the world. Not since that slut— No, do not think of that now, she told herself sternly. The past was past, only the present counted, and it was a perilous present. She knew one thing—if Boroth died tonight, the Rings would go to this youth who stood beside her, a vicious curl of lip raised as he surveyed his father, the King.

If only the legends held true! The Rings would not abide by the unworthy, nor with a ruler who did not strive to hold the land safe. They had accepted her, but would they accept Florian? And if they did not—she drew a deep breath—there would be an end to everything she inwardly knew must be kept.

She dare not risk it. Boroth must live, at least a while longer.

Florian's lips were very full, and like his father's, tended to be loose and more than a little wet. He drew his hand across his mouth, tried to stand a little straighter. Perhaps he was waking from the besotted depths from which they had hauled him.

"He dies? The King my father dies?" He did not ask that of the laboring physician but as if he expected an answer from the gathering at large.

Royance came to stand beside them, Ysa and her son. "Do not despair, Highness. While there are breath and heartbeat, there is still life."

The sound Florian made in answer was a snicker. He turned a little toward her. "Breath and life, and you, my dear mother, strive to keep it so, do you not? Give those to me!"

His hand suddenly shot out toward hers as she held them to show the Rings plainly. But those grasping fingers did not touch hers. Rather, it was if they had slammed against a solid surface, so that he stumbled and would have gone down had Royance not steadied him.

Incongruously, Ysa was reminded of the moment when Boroth had sought to put her hand into the candle-flame, and had been denied.

Florian's face had gone pale, but his eyes showed the beginning of that same rage Boroth had turned on her, making clear to all that for this moment, he was entirely his father's son.

"No woman has the right—" His voice scaled upward.

She must take command and at once. "My Lord Royance, the Prince is disturbed by his Majesty's condition."

Royance nodded. As head of the Council, he would know

that to prolong this unseemly episode before such a company would imperil the uneasy peace.

Smoothly, he drew Florian away from his mother. "Your Highness, it is plain that your anxiety concerning the King has upset you greatly." He turned to that same medical assistant who had served Lorgan earlier. "Please fetch a calming potion for the Prince. He is not well and he needs all his strength."

Ysa expected Florian's easily aroused temper to burst forth, but to her surprise and slight unease, he actually did drink the potion brought by the doctor's assistant.

Still, Ysa did not relax. Florian had tried to possess the Rings and had been rebuffed, not by her, but by that power they held. Even after years of study and experience, she could not understand the full meaning of this. Boroth was dying, all but dead, and his heir must, by custom, try at once to hold the Rings and so hold the land. Would he be able to do it once the King had truly breathed his last? Did the Rings cleave to her now because she was the stronger, the one determined that the House would not fall and bring down with it all their allies? Was she in truth the one they had chosen to rule, despite the fact that Rendel had never, in all its history, had a regnant Queen who had not been born to the role? She must delve into her books more deeply to find the answer to this riddle.

While all this had been going on, the master physician had continued his ministrations, necessitating the use of heated cups pressed against the pudgy flesh of the King's chest.

Now Boroth had been settled once more on the pillows that braced up his thick shoulders, and he seemed to be breathing more easily. Lorgan stood aside, and when Ysa looked to him, he nodded.

He bowed his head toward the Queen, and then toward Florian. "Your Majesty. Your Highness." He addressed those in the room as well. "My lords, it would appear that a crisis has passed. We have successfully drawn off the evil humors, at least for the moment, and the King's vital signs are on the rise. His Majesty needs rest and peace—"

It was a strong hint and Ysa quickly seized upon it. "My lords, your concern means much," she said, turning to those who waited in the chamber. "Be sure that careful watch will be kept and you will be summoned promptly if there is need."

None of them could mistake the Rings that winked from her fingers, and for that moment, she was in command. There were murmurs but no open denial against that softly voiced but firm order as they began filing from the room. Now she was all impatience to get to her tower room to study and to await the messenger and what news it might bring. The need for being there was beating at her.

Royance had taken Florian by the arm. "Come, Your Highness, you have been overwrought. It is necessary to rest against the time when much will be asked of you for the sake of our country and our people."

Florian was blank of face, and he looked neither to his father nor to his mother as he allowed himself to be guided from the room. Ysa wondered at his easy compliance—another small worry to gnaw at her—but put it down to the effect of the potion. Perhaps Lorgan would become an ally as well as a witness. Once more she advanced closer to the head of the bed and uttered the ritual Ring words. Then she spoke to the physician.

"Master Lorgan, there is pressing business vital to the realm. But summon me at once if there is need."

He bowed his head and she walked away stiffly, her whole body aching with tension, to do what was necessary that she do.

❧

There was no talk among the Sea-Rovers of a second land venture; once had been enough, unless actual starvation threatened. Since neither the bird-flesh nor the fish would keep for long, Snolli shared out the food among the people on all the ships, and all ate a good meal for once. Then they tightened their belts again, hoping that those who had gone ahead might have found some food as well.

The small five-ship fleet was strung out now in a line, keeping in touch with each other by mast flags by day and lanterns held before a reflecting shield at night. They sailed in *Stormbracer*'s wake, gradually catching up. By the time they rounded the long, gradual curve of the southernmost part of the land and were truly sailing east, they had the vessel in full sight.

On the third day after Obern's return to *GorGull*, the deep note of the rally horn brought the core of fighting men to a narrow place of assembly near the bow. Obern took his usual place behind his father. Rumors had already spread through the ship that a message of some importance had been received from the vessel ahead, which could barely be made out in the fog of this early morning.

"*Stormbracer*," his father announced abruptly, "has sighted the Ashenkeep outer reef passage. They report seeing one ship in the inner harbor. We shall close in as fast as winds will allow and see what awaits us there. When we left Vold, there was no report from any Trader that the keep had been taken by any of those ever-quarrelsome lords of this land. However, we shall be prepared. Once those headlands are in sight, the deck must be cleared for action, crowded as our people shall be below."

At least the wind was favoring them this morning, and even the fog had begun to lift. They no longer crept with frustrating slowness along that threatening shoreline. As they left the Bog behind, the waves were no longer stained with the murk of those unclean waters. Obern watched the cliffs disappear behind them, an odd mixture of feelings inside him. His experience, short as it had been of what might lurk there, was a warning that any intruder would recognize. At the same time, there was another small part of him that continued to wonder just what did lie behind those cliff walls, and what other manner of monster could issue from one of those many fissures and caves.

The noncombatants obediently went belowdecks, and the warriors made their preparations as best they could on the crowded deck, waiting to stand to arms if need be when they reached their goal. Waiting—and facing—the unknown always stirred a man's blood. Obern found himself touching the hilt of the Rinbell sword, and drawing his knife upward in its sheath, then slamming it back again in sheer nervous energy. To thread their way through the reef passage, they were having to head farther out to sea, and his father and Captain Narion consulted several times.

Snolli held one of the treasures of his House, a rod that featured a small lens sealing one end. A man could look through the other end and that which was afar was instantly near. Who had designed such a wonder, no one knew, only that it had reached Vold as some long-ago booty or trade.

The High Chief gave an exclamation and passed the seeing-rod to the captain, who gazed for a moment and then shouted orders. The sailors jumped to, skillfully bringing canvas to bear, and the *GorGull* followed *Stormbracer*, slipping through the opening in the reef as if she were a maiden running to the arms of her lover.

Behind them, Obern, even without the use of any such seeing-aid, could now make out one ship and then two follow safely, with a third drawing closer, and the last waiting its turn. They had reached their goal—at least they were within distance that they could send out scout craft and learn if there would be any danger.

But it was past sunset before their small fleet had drawn together. Snolli prepared to visit *Stormbracer*, swinging easily down into the waiting small boat. Obern followed his father. That the High Chief would take such action at night brought home their own needs. This day, before coming into the harbor, all but the women and children had hungered. Trailing-lines in the water had brought in no fish, and the last of the carefully hoarded supplies from Vold were gone.

The oarsmen sent their small boat across the water to the larger vessel, where the shield lantern offered a wavering beacon. Obern looked at the land. He could see an ominous breaking of waves over reef teeth. This was just the outer harbor. Somewhere past that maze of danger there was a closer passage that had been used aplenty, wherein lay the ship that *Stormbracer*'s lookout had sighted.

Once more there was an assembly lighted by a single lantern, and among the captains who had come to this meeting, there was a man Obern had never seen before. Yet his kind he knew well. This was one of the far-faring Traders who had loose alliance with the Sea-Rovers. Obern relaxed, just a little. Traders were no enemies. At least, that had always been the case so far.

His father greeted the stranger, sword hand outstretched and open. The other man's hand met it palm to palm.

"Good roads, open seas to you, Trader Stanslaw," Snolli said in greeting.

The lean, dark-skinned man answered as heartily. "And may the same be given you, Lord Snolli. Your captain has told me foul news. The north marches again—"

"And again, and again!" the High Chief returned harshly. "No more shall you find a ready market in Vold, or in Shater, Dosa, or Juptue. Ruins. That's all that's left. Just smoldering ruins."

The Trader nodded. "Yes, our world is sadly threatened. They say in the Far Islands that the land and sea will rise in time against all our kind if we do not cease our quarrels. Yet no man with half his wits could try to treat with such as those of the ice-bound lands. However, you have not come to a place much better. Be warned of that." He waved one hand shoreward. "Ashenkeep stands open for you; in that much, you are favored. But the land itself seethes like a pot coming to high boil. King Boroth, it is whispered, approaches close to his end. His Queen holds the power for now. But these high-nosed lords do not bow knee to a woman or willingly hold council with her. And the Prince is of little worth. When Boroth is carried to his tomb—ah, then, my friend, you will see a land bathed in blood as one lord vies with his neighbor, or his neighbor's neighbor, to add to his holdings."

Snolli laughed. "With what bright cheer, Stanslaw, you welcome us. We come from war, to face it once again. Yet a man must have a port he can trust, and this we must hold."

The Trader grinned. "How else could any sea-lord answer? In this much, I can be of aid to you. My own *Galica* lies at anchor in the Ashenkeep moat. There is no one there to meet you with swords."

Snolli had questions, and all listened carefully to the answers the Trader supplied.

"Yes, the keep itself has not been destroyed. It is well-rooted, and they could not bring any war machines through to batter down the walls. It is said that it fell through treachery. There was a strong hatred against the Ashenkin, and many tales are told of why. One can pick and choose, not that it matters now. No, you can walk within and find your own defenses.

"There is this also—the plain beyond has not been taken under shield of any neighbor. It is as if they want nothing more now that the House has been brought down. It is good land and there are beasts roving wild there, for the Ashenkin were noted herdmasters. So be at ease—for now—friend Snolli."

In the morning, the entire fleet, guided by Stanslaw, threaded its way easily into the inner harbor, close to where the waters had been channeled into a moat, and came to anchor at last. As quickly as possible, they went ashore, and Obern, seeing those tall, unshaken walls and the fair harbor below, was set to believe that Fortune had once more turned her face in their direction.

Not only did Stanslaw provided them guidance, he also saw to it that food was ready for the near-starving people of the sea before he went on his way. Fortified, everyone worked with a

Andre Norton & Sasha Miller

will as the days passed, emptying the ships of what they had
been able to save and setting up quarters in the deserted keep
and the town surrounding it.

Within days, hunters and small scouting parties ventured out
into the land beyond. They patrolled west to the river that
formed the very edge of the Bog-land, east to the broken lands
of the mountains, and north toward the country to which they
would be unwelcome invaders.

It was Obern, with the leader Iaobim and two others, who
headed north and west a week later to scout along the scrublands
edging the Bog.

Ashen awoke, startled out of sleep by a soft patting against her
face. She opened her eyes to see not only Weyse crouched close
by, but also the flyer, who was urging her out of slumber by
reaching out a forepaw and tugging at the edge of her jerkin.

"Hungry, little ones? Let me get myself into good order and
we shall break our fast." Ashen laid aside her reed covering and
went to the water source she had found the night before. She
took a handful of wild moss from her pack. It served as a sponge,
and also provided a slight lather that left her face and hands
clean. With a horn comb, she untangled her hair enough to braid
it quickly and fasten it with thorn pins to the top of her head.

As she inserted the last of these, she heard an insistent trilling
from behind, along with the soft purring notes of the flyer, and
hastened back to bring out her supplies to feed the two hungry
little creatures. Whatever Weyse had been accustomed to eating
before her arrival, it was plain to see that the furred one greatly
preferred what Ashen had brought. Taking the last of the boiled
lupper's eggs from her bag, she noted wryly that if she would be
here for any length of time, she must do some energetic hunting.
Neither of her charges would understand the meaning of an
empty bowl.

Whether any of the edible roots and plants she was familiar

with could be found here, she did not know, but the night before, she had heard the peeping of luppers, and she was well acquainted with the snares one set for them. In the meantime, she must fully explore this chamber and make sure of just what she now had to hand.

Weyse and the creature she had begun to think of as "Little Flit" remained by the fire she had coaxed to a higher flame. The black stones Zazar had set there burned much longer and stronger than the squares of peat and dried reeds that never fully warmed any Bog dwelling, but filled it with smoke instead. There seemed to be a goodly supply of that fuel in a small bin at the back of the chamber.

Today she did not pause by the marked plates, but rather, picked and probed into all the containers resting on various shelves. Some of the contents she knew by their scent—the familiar materials used for healing. Others she was wary enough not to dig fingers into.

Having made the survey of her new quarters as best she could, Ashen determined to see at least part of the broken buildings around it. As she moved toward the entrance, Weyse flashed ahead, and Little Flit leaped with a flutter of wings to settle on her shoulder, where it nuzzled her cheek and made its purring sound.

Ashen discovered, as she reached the outside, that the morning was well advanced. The clouds, which had blanketed the path yesterday, were gone and the sun had an unusual warmth for this time of year. The Bog-land had crept out of the icy cold but a short time past.

She clambered with care over tumbled walls and peered into a number of hollows, which she believed had once been dwellings. Weyse seemed to take great delight in scampering ahead and trilling at her, then running back as if to show off. This stream of harmless mischief amused her. The three of them were in no way challenged, and even the stinging flies that customarily appeared with the sun did not attack them.

There was certainly little to be discovered. One pile of rubble was like another. Ashen tried to imagine what manner of people had once settled here. She could not picture the Bog-folk accomplishing such finished labor. But Zazar's tales of other times and peoples long since vanished seemed fitting to this ruin.

With some effort, she made the circle of what she was sure had been an outer wall. Taking time to climb and perch at intervals when there seemed suitable footing, she scanned the shoreline. There were clumps of the reeds common to the waterways everywhere, and once or twice she sighted the rise of a bush.

She reached at last the landing to which Zazar had brought her, and it was there that Weyse again darted to hide behind the rocks, chattering in a high voice, while Little Flit stirred on her shoulder. The girl held up her hand and the winged creature moved onto her palm, the tiny nails of its paws pricking her flesh. Turning its head, its eyes met hers and held.

"Go—go—Visp go—"

It certainly had not changed its trilling purr for words, yet that message was in Ashen's mind. The little creature shifted to give its wings a chance to stretch. Once more it stared at her, though this time there was no message, unless it was one of farewell, and a moment later, it took to the air, soaring up and up.

She watched it level out for distant flight. Then Weyse pulled at her leggings and chirped in a way that clearly indicated it was delivering a warning. Its claws were tightly anchored in Ashen's tanned lupper-skin clothing, and the little creature jerked as strongly as it could to bring her to the right, close to a tall heap of tumbled stones.

"Very well, my friend, we will take cover." Ashen could not believe that Weyse could understand her. Nevertheless, she gestured, and to her astonishment, her companion answered with a humanlike nod.

There must be very good reason for Weyse to behave in such a fashion. Ashen found as good a spot as she could where she might see and still be hidden. She hunkered down and carefully drew her knife. When she looked up, she discovered that Little Flit had disappeared. The creature might as well have become invisible, for not even a speck in the sky marked its passage.

Her hiding place was just opposite from where Zazar and her craft had come and gone, and the girl was sure that whatever Weyse considered a threat, it was coming from that general direction.

Ashen had not long to wait. The grunting speech of Bog-folk carried across the water, and a moment later the first of them came into full sight. They had not traveled by boat as had Zazar, but rather they must have followed an overland trail. They could not go more than two abreast in the narrow strip between water and brush.

The band was unusually large for a hunting party, but it was fully armed. They crowded forward, excitement and surprise showing on their broad faces as across the stretch of open water, they glimpsed the ruins of what Ashen was already thinking of as her city. She saw also that at the rear of their party, two were dragging along someone entwined in a net of the type used for Outland prisoners.

These were not strangers from some distant kin-hearth. She recognized Joal. Behind him, Tusser pressed forward, but carefully kept to his place behind the one in command.

Joal uttered the summons call peculiar to their village. "Aaauugh!" He did it a second time as she tried to see the captive more clearly.

Who could it be? Surely not Zazar. Ashen could not believe that Joal would ever dare to handle the Wysen-wyf in this fashion. Weyse clutched at her knee again, but she was not in the least inclined to show herself. She put her hand on Weyse's head.

"Witchling, demon-born—" Joal no longer gave the recognition signal of those with whom she had always lived, but shouted aloud the slime words that she knew with a cold certainty were meant for her alone.

Weyse pressed tightly against her as if to stop any move she would make, but Ashen knew far better than to let any of that company see her. So far, she felt reasonably safe. There was no sign of a boat, and she was well aware that none of them would dare venture a path over an unknown stretch of water. Rubble, once walls, formed a barrier around the pool and it would take the Bog-folk a long time to pick their way across it.

"Demon, your shield be gone!" Joal's voice created thunder in the air. "Zazar no longer treats unbeknownst with Outlanders. We knows her secrets, all her secrets. See you who tells them— with a little sharp coaxing!"

He gestured, and the two holding the netted captive halted. Grabbing one edge of the net, Joal stripped it away to reveal Kazi.

The woman's face was a mask of fear; she was in such a condition of fright that those guarding her had to hold her on her feet. Joal grabbed a handful of her mud-stiffened hair and jerked her forward as she wailed in pain and terror.

The chief's spear thudded against her ribs, and once more she howled.

"Speak," he commanded. "Where is lover of dark demons who was of your hearth? Does Zazar now still walk mighty in our land?"

"Noooo!" she wailed. "Zazar is gone."

Again he struck her. "And where has she-snake gone?"

"To the under-ones—" Her words ended in a screech.

"And her secrets? All her secrets, child of worm?" Joal continued ruthlessly.

"All gone, all forgotten, Great One—except for what lies in head of Deathdaughter."

She sagged. Her guard stood aside and she fell to the ground, face down at the headman's feet in the old formal petition for clemency.

He rolled her over with a kick and looked again toward the isle of ruins.

"We make our land clean, Deathdaughter. You be filth of Outlands and so shall ending come—in the jaws of under-ones."

Tusser put a hand on his father's shoulder. "Need boats," he said, his voice carrying clearly. Joal shook his head.

Ashen knew that despite the difficulty of the path, Joal was ready to start toward her then and there. And she could not get back to where she might lose them in the maze without being seen. Joal began to climb over the uncertain footing of the rubble, and behind him, the warriors took up a war-chant. Then from a distance there came another sound, one Ashen remembered hearing only once before in her lifetime. Someone, somewhere, was beating a battle drum, an alarm that spoke of invasion.

Those on the shore wheeled in the direction from which they had come. Joal's thick lips lifted and his teeth showed like those of a garlizard. Old custom remained strong. That signal, which would be picked up and passed from village to village, told all that one of their worst fears—a full invasion—might soon be upon them.

They were off without another glance at the isle, disappearing with what speed allowed them by the brush, leaving Kazi, still trapped in the net, to lie where she had fallen.

That they had actually tracked her during past explorations, Ashen could not be sure. That Kazi had guided them here, she could believe, if this was a place known to her as well as to the Wysen-wyf. Kazi had been far longer a companion to Zazar than she, and indeed, perhaps the two had shared secrets the girl had never learned.

Despite the departure of the hunting band, Ashen could not be certain that Joal had not left a watcher to spy. For the moment, she was safe, but she knew that when they returned, they would bring up one of the boats to reach her. She watched Kazi, wondering whether or not she dare go to the old woman's aid. Wondering whether or not she even wanted to.

The woman stirred; now that those who had handled her were gone, she fought to throw off the net that bound her. Ashen's lips tightened.

Kazi was not trail-wise; her crippled foot had always kept her close to the village. She had no supplies or weapons to support her now. There was no kin-debt between the Bog-woman and Ashen. And if Zazar was dead because of some tattling of Kazi's, better that Kazi suffer one of the many deaths lurking here.

Still, Ashen hesitated. She could not be sure of any betrayal from Kazi. Also, in her morning survey, she had found no other boat. No more than Joal did she want to risk a swim or a wade through the water—and that for Kazi. However, something within her balked at leaving the crone there, abandoned to her fate. Yet she did not rise from her hiding place to show herself to the woman, now freed of her bonds and crouching on her knees.

Thirteen

O bern lay with the others of the scouting party, belly-down on a ridge that edged the river. The shadowy murk of the Bog stretched before them, warning them away by its very appearance. All had heard the tales of the monsters to be found there, and indeed, they had seen such for themselves in the thing from the sea and the attack from the cliff birds. By its very nature, the Bog was locked in against invasion; who knew what had come to live in its mysterious depths and its formidable cliffs?

To the south, a muffled roar spoke of the swallow-hole they had discovered. There the river vanished, to be spewed out eventually into the great waterfall that marked the end of Bog-land and the beginning of New Vold.

Another matter closer to hand presented a more urgent interest. Below the ridge that concealed them, three men sat at ease about a small fire. Plainly, by their body mail and weapons, they were part of a war-band. Behind them grazed four horses, saddled and ready for riding.

"War-party, not hunters?" Obern said to Iaobim in a low voice. If these were on the same errand as he and his companions, they would not be thus in the open, where they could easily be picked off by an archer before they could mount.

Iaobim nodded. "They wear the same badges," he pointed out. "A landeer on a copper background. Serve the same lord. But if they have lately come, they may not know this is no longer Ash-land."

"They watch the Bog now and then," the man beyond Iaobim murmured. "But those who live there do not come to this side of the river. There is ever a barrier against Bog-folk, it is said."

Plainly, the three were waiting for someone—the rider of the fourth horse. One of the men by the fire got to his feet and turned to stare intently at the forbidding brush-grown land beyond. Then, not only the three below but those concealed on the ridge above heard the thudding beat of a chorus of drums, all sounding the same rhythm, cut at intervals by a screaming blast of high-pitched sound as if from a war-horn.

The three soldiers stood together, and by their gestures, seemed to Obern to be in dispute. At length they went to their mounts, and leading the extra horse, moved closer to the turgid stream that separated Bog from free land.

The din of drums continued. They might be heralding the approach of a whole army. Those who waited rode slowly back and forth along a small stretch of the river, their heads turned, always alert to what might approach from the unknown north.

Then the brush on the far side of the stream stirred into motion. Someone, or something, was forcing a path through. The horsemen pulled to a halt, facing that agitation. A section of brush fell forward into the stream, displaying a figure wielding a sword-length tool to clear the way.

A moment later, that figure emerged on the far side of the stream. However, from what Obern's party could see from the ridge, this one did not resemble those who waited. A tall person walking erect, yes, but veiled from clear sight by the thick mist in constant curl about it.

With no hesitation, the newcomer took a stride or two along the bank and then deliberately, if slowly, went into the water.

Either the river was a shallow one, or this was a ford. Though the water washed at knee-level, the misted figure could wade through it easily. Obern fancied he could see where the murky slough of the Bog ended, about midstream, and clean water flowed.

A spear flew from the brush behind. The hair rose on the back of Obern's neck as he watched it fail to penetrate the mist but instead, drop into the water as if it had struck against a wall. One of the men waiting produced a bow of a sort Obern had once seen on one of the Sea-Rovers' southward raids. Its limbs were small and fastened crosswise on a thick stock, and he knew it to be clumsy, but immensely powerful. The arrow it now released sped almost too fast to be followed, straight into the brush through which the wader, who was now hoisting himself up on the near bank, had come.

The mist suddenly winked out to reveal a tall man. His mail shirt reached past his thighs, and it gleamed brightly where it was not covered with a badly torn tabard of the same rust color as the other men's badges. In place of a helm, he wore a band of metal around his head and in that, just over and between his eyes, was an oval of light. The soldier leading the extra horse rode forward. Still ankle-deep in the water, the man put foot to stirrup, and this light wavered and died away entirely as he swung into the saddle.

Wheeling around, the whole party rode at a brisk pace toward the east. Soon they rounded another ridge, disappearing from sight. The sullen drums continued their boom and now other figures broke through the brush that cloaked the Bog.

These newcomers were surely of another race—squat, dark-skinned men. They seemed clad in mud, and displayed no body armor. They were equipped with spears and small oval shields; several had head coverings serving as helms. Their rage was apparent as they waded ankle-deep into the water, and some of the leaders hurled their weapons across the stream. Their shouts of frustration rose above the boom of the drums. But they made no attempt to go any farther or to use the ford to strike out after the horsemen. The stream might have been a wall forbidding their intrusion into the land.

🌿

Once more at her lookout post aloft, Ysa took her chair. But there was no relaxation from the tension that held her. She must concentrate more deeply than she had ever ventured before to reach her missing messenger—if it still lived. It was a weapon, as strong a weapon as the Rings could be upon occasion, and one she must not lose.

She closed her eyes that she might better see the flyer in her mind. Just so would it look as it came to her once more.

Come! Her reaching thought sought again and again. The Bog—would the flyer have taken a route over that forsaken country in order to return? She knew there was a Power out there perhaps greater than that she had so painfully acquired. She had been careful not to touch it, or to attract it. Could that Power have drawn her messenger? Even now, was it wringing from Visp its purpose, its allegiance to her?

Doubts must be banished. Resolutely she drew the picture in her mind and then called again. So intent was she that her hands came out, though she made that gesture only half consciously, to provide a landing place.

Come! Visp, Come!

Suddenly a small, high-pitched shrilling brought her eyes open. A shadow on the window surface. Then that which she sought came through, showing no harm, and settled on her hands.

Clasping it, she raised the small body so they were eye to eye.

Speak! The unvoiced order was as strong as her call had been. Thought answered as the shrilling cry ceased. They were on their way, those of the far north lands, but their journey was not yet begun. There was yet a little time. Those who had been shaken out of their long-held lands seemed now to be waiting. From Visp's mind, she saw that the ruins of the Sea-Rovers' last stronghold were occupied by the invaders. Did the northern hordes plan to concentrate their hold there? No. If their settlement followed— There was the Bog as barrier, but could that be held in spite of all its traps and the almost insane hatred of its people for Outlanders?

Enough! She must not be led aside from her purposes by such questions. Take one task, one road, at a time and make it as much her own as she could.

But she sensed it was not only news of the northerners that she had been brought. Her flyer had more to tell. Hazy pictures formed in her mind, and for a moment, she felt a pang of queasiness as she seemed to be looking down from some height at a ground shrouded in mist. Out of that arose towers—no, walls. Her sight was so restricted that she could not be sure. But the flyer whose memory she probed was swinging from a straight course toward those walls, exactly as if it had been called! The Bog power—

Suddenly it was as if she had been blinded, and even in this manner of memory only, she felt a blow hurling her down from her course toward the ground. Fear—hers and the flyer's mingled—set her heart beating wildly.

Her mind identified the stones all around as broken walls. But the Bog had no holds, no cities. No man living knew exactly what lay in this place. It must be old, very old, and protected still by some force, one that had identified Visp as a spy and brought it down.

She knew the frenzied struggles of her messenger, shared its terror. Then the body that no longer would answer to the flyer's will was lifted, with care. Visp was being carried toward a larger pile of stones, one that still held the outlines of a building. There was light there, piercing the dark. Fear sharpened. In—no—it was forbidden! Fighting against entry. Then the flyer was lowered and faced another creature, furred, small, but with eyes that promised aid. Visp was held toward this newcomer and felt the touch of its tongue on its head.

Fear was gone; there was nothing now to be a barrier, so Ysa saw the flyer transported into the interior of the building. Visp looked around, and what it had seen became Ysa's vision in turn. The one who had borne Visp hither—a girl, her slender figure clad in the crude clothing known to the Bog. Only, this was no real Bog-wench. Her face was partly hidden. It was—

Ysa gave a small cry, and her bond with the flyer was severed. She refused to acknowledge what she had seen in those short moments. It was just a Bog-woman, nothing more, perhaps some foul half-breed from a Rendel man or woman, strayed beyond the barrier river in search of novelty. She wouldn't have put it beyond even Boroth, had it occurred to him. It was her imagination, stirred by the nonsense Harous had babbled about Ashenkin still being alive. Her eyes—Visp's eyes—were playing tricks on her.

Therefore, Ysa told herself firmly, she had seen a vision, an illusion, an apparition of what Visp in its gratitude only thought it had witnessed. None of it was real. She had *not* seen the Lady Alditha.

Thus the Queen put the matter out of her mind.

❧

Ashen watched Kazi pull herself up and stand, tearing the net from about her. The woman seemed unharmed, apart from fright and a few bruises. Now she turned around slowly as if looking for some path of escape—or was she searching for Ashen herself? From what Ashen had heard Joal say, Kazi was ready now to openly show the spite and jealousy that had so long eaten at her. Had that also turned her against Zazar?

Ashen held her breath, hoping the woman wasn't going to try to find her. At last, Kazi turned and lurched back the way she had been dragged, her twisted foot finding poor support in the overgrown land.

To the King a Daughter

Where would she go? For that matter, where *could* she go? If she returned to the village, supposing that she could get back without falling prey to some Bog creature, would it be only to face again the wrath of Joal and the others?

Ashen turned away in the direction of the heart of the ruins and her own refuge. She knew she must not allow herself to be too softhearted. After all, Kazi had shown herself to be nothing better than a traitor. What was Kazi to her now but an open enemy? Still, they had shared a hearth for many years and the girl was uneasy with her own feelings. Only, what could she do? Even if she could cross the open stretch of water to follow Kazi's trail, dare she bring the woman here, to a place that was certainly one of Zazar's guarded secrets?

She walked slowly, frowning at that twinge within her that said she could not let Kazi wander through unknown perils. Kazi had betrayed Zazar's secrets or— Ashen stopped in mid-stride, stunned. Maybe not. Perhaps the Wysen-wyf had been so mistreated herself that Joal had learned from *her* the way to this place. No. She rejected that thought.

Ashen's pace became even slower. She had reached the giant figure that lay broken. Weyse, who had been scurrying before her, had jumped to take a seat on the cracked stone.

Though it was difficult to read any expression on that round, furred face, Ashen received an impression of concern and uneasiness. How much did Weyse know? The girl was sure that her companion was intelligent—perhaps in a different way from what was familiar to her—but still, keen of mind. Ashen paused by the statue, close enough that Weyse reached out and touched her on the arm, drawing her full attention. Suddenly Ashen felt the need to put into speech her uneasiness.

"Weyse, Kazi will die if she loses herself in the Bog." She thought of that terrible, great amphibian, Gulper, that had pursued her. Kazi would be easy meat for such. But there was water around this island, and no boat to be had.

"Weyse," she said without thinking, "is there any way to get to the other side of that pool without crossing the water?" She wanted to take back the question. After her own exploration, that was a stupid thing to ask.

To her surprise, it appeared to make sense to her companion. Again Weyse made that gesture of the head that Ashen could only believe was a nod. Zazar had trilled to it—no, spoken in an unknown tongue. However, it would seem that Weyse could also understand words it could not utter itself.

"She," Ashen said to herself. "I can't keep thinking of you as 'it.' You seem like a 'she' and so that is what you are."

Weyse gave a jump down from her perch and once more played the guide trick of catching hold of Ashen. But where she led the girl was straight back to the inner room. Was she trying to make it plain that there was no way to go except to this shelter?

Only, once inside, Weyse did not settle down but trotted forward and began to claw at a pile of reed mats stacked to one side. Plainly, the furred one did have some purpose, and Ashen hurried to join her in moving the mats. The floor underneath was paved with blocks set in strange but regular patterns, just as it was all over the chamber. But Weyse was on all fours now, clawing at the stone. A moment later, she had pulled up a ring embedded between two of the blocks. Then she looked at Ashen and gave a vigorous nod.

Though Weyse went back to tugging at the ring, it was plainly beyond her strength to move the surrounding blocks, if that was her purpose. Ashen knelt and reached for the ring, which Weyse yielded to her. She pulled with all the strength she could summon. For a straining moment, nothing happened. Then, with a grating sound, two blocks shifted upward a finger's width. Encouraged, Ashen tried again.

This time she succeeded in pulling the twin blocks aside and uncovering a space below. It should have been pitch-dark, but as she stared down into the cavity, she could see plainly. At least

one, and possibly more, of the same rods that afforded light for
the room had obviously been set there.

Even more plainly, a stone stairway had been set here as well,
immediately inviting one to descend. Ashen settled back on her
heels to consider the situation.

Zazar had put no limit to her stay here. Ashen was certain
the Wysen-wyf herself had intended to return. Perhaps she had
been prevented by whatever deviltry Joal had worked. It might
be that Ashen, if she could reach the land beyond by clambering
down into this way, could serve her Protector better than she
could than by remaining here. And also, she could aid Kazi, as
her conscience demanded.

Making her decision, she rose and hurried back to stow the
supplies she had taken out of her trail pack. Almost as an after-
thought, she emptied her shell water container of what she had
brought from the Bog and refilled it with the good water flowing
from the pipe. Then she closed the pack and hoisted it to her
shoulders. It was bulky enough so that when she returned, she
had difficulty in scraping through the entrance to this secret
within a secret.

Weyse bounded down the stone stairs and pattered ahead.
Plainly she believed she was to continue to play guide. The steps,
so even and straight at the top of the pit, soon turned crooked
and narrow. As Ashen descended, following, even the light began
to fail her. Now she went through thick shadows, for the light-
rods here were far apart. At last, she reached solid flooring. By
the extremely dim light, she could see she stood in a small space
that was walled with stonework, except for an opening directly
before her. This opening was about half the height of an ordinary
door. With a squeaking trill, Weyse popped through into the
darkness beyond. Settling her pack with a shrug, Ashen followed.

🌿

Absently, Ysa caressed the flyer, feeling its weariness as part of
her own. No more questions now; she had enough to think upon.

Nor did she want to risk seeing again the imagined face of her long-dead rival. She rose and walked slowly around the chair to settle her messenger into a nest of clean silken cloth. Then she took a cup and spilled into it grain and fruit bits from nearby boxes she had commanded be brought to the room. Visp trilled what might have been a thanks and set to eating with a hearty will.

Ysa stacked her books neatly, checked once more on the safety of her messenger, and in a black mood, left the chamber. Then she remembered something else, forgotten in the shock of thinking she had seen Lady Alditha alive.

Harous's hunting trip—what exactly was he hunting? What secret was he privy to that had been kept from those earlier days? Did he, or any of the other lords, know or suspect about this imaginary ill-born? Damn Harous and his meddling. Even a rumor would be enough to create trouble. She must summon those who supplied her with information in this land—her land—that she must fight to protect, and have them follow new trails to make certain— She hesitated. What if they learned too much? She believed them locklipped on her affairs, but there was always a chance.

No, for now, she must make fast this land against the coming chaos when she could no longer hold life within Boroth. Florian could not rule; she was sure that the Rings had denied him. The Rings knew only the safety of the land, not the feelings in men's hearts. The lords would certainly not be willing to accept a woman as sovereign, though they saw her as Regent now. She had always been careful to be soft-spoken when with them in Council; nevertheless, she knew she was resented for even the little power she dared wield openly.

Well, they were in error. This land was *hers*. She felt this as fiercely as another would regard a beloved child. Somehow, it had become a part of her long ago and she could not bear to see it torn asunder by warring lords, reduced to a ragged memory of the Kingdom it had been. And to prove that she so believed, she wore the Rings, did she not?

"Oak, Yew, Ash, and Rowan," she said in a whisper as she descended the stair. "Let wisdom come to me in this hour, for I need that which I can lean upon!"

Harous—not only must he be considered, but also another urgent question. The Sea-Rovers were very near their goal. Likely they were making for the deserted Ashenkeep on the coast. Still strong of tower and wall, and with all the sea to serve them, that place was one from which they could well be an ever-enlarging thorn in the breast of the uneasy country. So much, so much to be done and so few of those she could depend upon. Once more she damned Harous for the meddler he was.

Then she forced from her mind the many ominous questions as she passed from the inconspicuous tower door into the corridor, to seek Boroth once again and be sure of how he fared.

Fourteen

Obern debated long with himself whether or not to report these strange occurrences to Snolli. A man, clad first in mist and then in mail? Very odd. And what had been his errand in the Bog that it infuriated so many of its inhabitants, and where had he and his guard ridden off to?

The temptation was strong to follow now. The mail-clad man had had three companions; so did he. They wore armor and his men did not, but surely a Sea-Rover, even lightly clad, was the equal of any of the dwellers in this new land, be they ever so well-armored. If one of them could enter the Bog and emerge unscathed—howbeit with a few spears thrown after him—then four Sea-Rovers could do the same, and more.

"Let's follow," Iaobim said. "We came scouting, did we not?"

The other two men nodded, grinning. "That we did, sir," Haldin said.

"Let us go where the man of mystery showed the way. The Bog-people will go away presently, and then we can follow our unwitting guide's footsteps. Who knows what we'll find once we're across the river?" Roush put his hand on his dagger.

"Sounds like good adventure," Iaobim said.

"Should get to know our land," Haldin said.

"And the people in it," added Roush. "D'you suppose Bog-maidens are as ugly as their men?"

"One sure way to find out," Obern said. "But first we must inform my father."

The others would have protested, but he silenced them with a gesture. Yes, this was a matter for Snolli, and perhaps for all the chieftains under him. But he also decided to petition his father to be allowed to return, to lead an exploration party.

Reluctantly, his companions let go their ambition to head rashly into the Bog. They waited until both the horsemen and the ones who followed them were well out of sight. Then the four men began making their way down the ridge and toward the ford in the river separating Ashenhold—the land they were calling New Vold, now the province of the Sea-Rovers—and the mysteries of the Bog.

Upon his return, Obern discovered that his lady, Neave, had fallen ill, no doubt as a result of the hardships of the voyage. The boy, however, seemed to be thriving. He could not stay, but left Neave in her maid's keeping; he was needed elsewhere, and judging from the tenor of the summons, on more important business than men clad in mist.

After the formal custom when discussing a matter affecting the whole of the kin clan, High Chief Snolli had summoned all the heads of households to a conference. In battle, his orders might be supreme, but in decisions as sweeping or perilous as this one might be, he needed to consider the corporate will of his people.

The keep that they had claimed as their own was both spacious and beautiful, with its symmetry of towers and strong gatehouses. Swans still swam in the moat. However, the building lacked furnishings; they must have been looted long ago. So those in attendance were seated on the floor in a half circle, facing their lord. Only Snolli occupied a chair, one he had brought with him on their flight. He held the speaking-rod for all to see.

"There is this," he said, using the formal tone and manner of one choosing his words carefully. "We are not the only ones of our people who lived past the fighting. Though we thought all was lost, the *Orceagle* is newly arrived at New Vold. It followed our wake and is even now tied up at the gate, being small enough to navigate the moat. On their way, they met a Trader whose ship was newly out of Rothport. He had news of what passes now with these Rendel lords. It is no secret that King Boroth is ailing and not far from death. His Queen holds the land together, but for how long is a matter for wagers. The Prince is a nothing, and it is said that he and his mother are no great friends. There are several strong lordships, and over the past few years, they have been increasing their power and the number of their house armsmen."

He got up and began to pace back and forth as he spoke. "It's clear to see that these lords will be at each others' throats the minute the King draws his last breath. It is also said that the Queen has strange powers and that these alone now keep his spirit in his body.

"So far, none of the neighboring Rendel lords have appeared to notice that we have taken what was abandoned and now abide here. Nevertheless, it is in our best interests to have our new land lawfully. Our scouts have ridden to the old boundaries of this hold, and only once has there been a coming of those of the Kingdom—not aimed at us, it would seem, but at the Bog." He nodded at Obern, who nodded in return, rose, and took the speaking-rod. Then he told the assembly of what he and his men had seen.

When he had finished, he handed back the speaking-rod to his father and sat down again amidst murmurs of speculation, quickly stilled as Snolli looked at each of the men in turn. "It is plain that we cannot hope to escape their notice forever. For our own sake, we must go to them, make an alliance. We cannot afford to wait for them to realize that we are here and intend to stay. Then there is this—we may be put to the Queen's purpose rather than our own. She may attempt to gather these lords to her service, if only temporarily, by pointing them at us—an invader Foulness, or so they will claim. The Sea-Rovers are not universally liked."

There was a murmur of laughter at that. Snolli smiled also, and then took up his thought again.

"No one has, to our knowledge at least, tried to make peace with those of the Bog or to gather allies there. It might be well for us to make a pact with the Bog-men. This lord who invaded the land was within their territory, and seemed to be driven out unharmed. What he did there, or what his errand was, who knows? But that he had a strange protection against the dangers of that country was plainly seen by Obern, as he told you.

"Our greatest need is closer to hand. For the sake of the future, we must put our new land to our use, and not risk being driven out again. Cattle are wild here, perhaps left to roam when this keep fell. Go outside the walls and you will see the remains of fields waiting for the sowing, and that should be done soon. We are farther south than we have ever lived before, so the growing time may be lengthened. Even if it is, we must think of plowing as well as the capture of the straying beasts."

He paused, and it was Kasai, the Spirit Drummer, who spoke then. "Why is it that this land lay fallow for so long?" he inquired as if of them all. "We have a good harbor—the Traders have made use of it during the past years. There are no survivors of those who dwelt here, and yet the boundaries appear to wall out neighbors. This is something that it might be well to investigate."

Snolli nodded. "You have the Sight, Kasai. What has that made plain to you?"

The small man seemed to hunch together. He didn't need the speaking-rod to make his words come easily. His hands slipped over the skin surface of the drum that was ever with him, but they did not touch to bring forth sound.

"This is a place of shadows," he said. "Dark shadows. Just as we sensed the evil of the Lizard-riders, so some like taint holds here. . . ."

Snolli leaned forward, frowning, his hand going to his sword hilt. "The evil ones have been here?" Those seated on the floor before him shifted in their places, several looking over their shoulders as if expecting to see threatening shadows.

Kasai shook his head. "Not the Lizard-riders, no. We know the stink of them too well, and all would have sensed it when we came ashore. But this much is certain. There was a wrong done here, such a wrong as has made those of this land desert it."

Though he was but his father's backshield and had already fulfilled his duty at the assembly, Obern could not stop his own question from being voiced. "Can you draw out this wrong from the past and make it clear to us, so that we know what we face? And perhaps banish it? Does the Sight allow that?"

His father did not frown at him in rebuke. Therefore, Obern thought, Snolli must harbor a like thought.

"No one can measure the depth or the width of the Sight," the drummer replied. "As yet, what I sense is a shadow. I can not even say whether it will engulf us or holds only for those of this land and blood. There is this, though." He straightened a trifle. "there is Power in the Bog. That, too, I can feel. It is not turned to harry us, not yet. However, we must remember this lord who went into the Bog with strange body protection and then returned, and most of all, we must ask how the weapons of those who hunted him out failed to bring him down."

Snolli nodded. "This is a fishnet that is tangled near past all our smoothing." He began to tick off points on his fingers. "Our concerns here in our new home—acceptance, food, and shelter. The borders to be watched against the coming of some lord who has just noticed what we have acquired. The Bog. If so much Power does lie within, perhaps this unknown that Obern saw went to treat with it and add it to some alliance.

We cannot know. For the present, we can only scout and make sure that nothing comes upon us from either the east or the north."

A gray-haired man, Baland, under whose management their source of supplies had been centered for years, got up from his place, took the speaking-rod, and began to speak. "Chieftain, we have six oxen taken by one of our hunting parties. They are ready for the yoke, though they are old. We can begin to break ground and should do it now. Let the herdsman and drivers go armed, and we also shall have our scouts on duty. We hungered much on our voyage, and our women and children suffered greatly. I say let us delay no longer in this matter lest we know the sharp pinch of belly when the cold season comes. This is rich land; it was well-worked in the past and we can make it open for seed again."

Snolli took the rod that Baland handed him and looked from face to face. "Is such the will of all here and now?" he asked.

One hand after another went up, palm outward, in assent.

"So be it!" With those words, Snolli recognized what would now be their accepted choice, the details of which would be worked out in turn with the separate deputies gathered here.

Most of that company now withdrew. Obern lingered, as was his right as Snolli's son, and listened to the reports of those who remained to offer their suggestions as to what was needed and when. He listened, but his thoughts drifted elsewhere, and he was remembering in detail that crossing of the Outlander at the Bog-river ford, his armor appearing to be of mist alone.

How had that peculiar armor been summoned? It was no defense Obern had known before, and yet the High Lords of his land were constant in their search for new weapons and more-effective defenses. Had Snolli's suggestion been correct? Had that lord entered the Bog to make contact with someone—or something—within those forbidden ways?

Any notion that they themselves would dare to invade the depths of the water-soaked land would be utter folly until they knew something more of what had to be faced there. That would mean scouts. And that, Obern determined, meant him.

He summoned to his mind's eye what he had so far seen of the eastward stretch of their new land. Still, his thoughts kept straying to the west, and he surrendered to his curiosity. The cliffs that walled the Bog from the sea, yet allowed its waters to stain the outer waves, offered no way that even a light skiff could be taken through one of the cave entrances.

There was no sea route in. Therefore, if one did not enter from below, how would he know what lay above? Their old homeland had once, as they believed, also been well guarded by heights. He himself had been on scout in the vicinity of the two passes that only days later were seized after a desperate battle with the Lizard-riders. It was mere chance that had kept him out of that fight, but he had listened to the tales the survivors brought back. The Lizard-riders' monstrous mounts had shown raw ferocity in an ugly tide that could not be stemmed. They had climbed the keep walls relentlessly, and nothing seemed capable of holding them back.

Across the border river, the Bog cliffs began. So here also there might be a chance to work one's way up from these lower heights, which the keep held still impervious, to a ridge from which something of their neighbors could be seen.

He was so deep in his inner speculation that he was unaware that the last of those conferring with his father had gone until Snolli turned in his direction.

". . . is it not so?" His father's voice was raised with a sharp abruptness, which brought Obern alert, aware that Snolli was watching him with a suggestion of a frown on his face.

"Sir?" Obern knew he was revealing his lack of interest in the scene just past.

"Have your duties rested so hard upon you that you have to doze off in my presence?"

"I was thinking, sir," he said.

To the King a Daughter

"And what are your so weighty thoughts?" There was certainly irritation in Snolli's question.

"The cliffs, sir," Obern said. It could be that any suggestion of what had caught his attention might indeed be a reckless and worthless one. Yet he must explain, as was the duty of any summoned to conference. "Fritji said something that put my mind to thinking about where to send someone to scout out the lay of the Bog-land."

Swiftly he outlined the idea of a search along the cliffs. "With the long-see glass, perhaps. Much can certainly be sighted with that." Now that he was voicing it, Snolli's permission for the prospect seemed more attainable. His enthusiasm dimmed when his father made no immediate answer.

Obern was tempted to add to his suggestion but was well aware that Snolli, as a true warlord of great experience, might consider the ills of such an expedition greater than any gains.

At last, Snolli spoke. "We shall think on this."

Obern felt the trickle of excitement. If Snolli would seriously consider such an action, then surely— He set an instant guard on his tongue. Though he had thought to petition his father to be allowed to volunteer as part of this dangerous scouting expedition, this might doom him to having no part in it at all. It could well be that the warlord might think it better the duty of one of his second chiefs.

His father got to his feet and went to the window, which looked to the west. From his belt he took the long-see glass and pointed it toward where the Bog cliffs gave way to the lower cliffs on which the hold was rooted. Obern hesitated for a moment and then came up behind Snolli. Perhaps his father would allow him to use that spying tool himself; perhaps with it, he could indeed see some way of traveling along the loftier barrier.

"It will be thought upon," his father said without turning. "Go and summon Kasai now."

Frustrated, Obern went in search of the Spirit Drummer, but

Andre Norton & Sasha Miller

he was aware that Snolli was once more inspecting the far distances with his precious instrument.

❦

Ashen, standing in the mouth of the passage with the opening behind her, faced what seemed to be complete darkness. There was no glow ahead, no matter how faint, to suggest that some of the strange illumination-rods had been set there. As she had ducked through the doorway, she had seen Weyse disappear down the corridor with a suggestion of confidence. The creature appeared to know well what lay ahead. Ashen shifted her pack a little and resolutely stepped into the dark hollow of the hallway.

Here the air felt dead, and there were odors that the girl identified as having to do with some of those stagnant waters that all tried to avoid. She reached out to touch the wall on her right and quickly drew back again. It had been like pushing her finger into a blot of slime.

From ahead there came a trilling call. Ashen quickened her pace at that summons. She took care also, for she was apprehensive that the slime curtain on the wall might have spread to the flooring underfoot.

However much she loathed the feel of what she must touch, she once more reached for the wall and continued to run her hand along it, hoping that touch might take the place of sight and she could discern any change in the passage.

Her knuckles cracked painfully against solid wall where none should be. Of course, she told herself, here the passage made a turn. Again Weyse's trill beckoned her ahead, from the left. Ashen turned in that direction.

At last she glimpsed light of a sort. She hurried toward that wan break in the blackness and found herself out of the passage and in a chamber that seemed larger than the one she had just left above.

Weyse was there, waiting, but now came running to stand

up and pat Ashen's thigh. The little creature looked up at the girl with those compelling round eyes, and Ashen felt that the small one was not at ease here but needed the presence of another for reassurance.

The light came from a series of the now-familiar rods, though some were dark and useless, perhaps burnt out. Each was set at the end of a heavy, rectangular stone case. The smallest of them looked longer than Ashen was tall. There were two rows of these, with an aisle between them. Weyse pulled her toward it.

The cases were ornamented. The sides and lids of each showed a multitude of symbols. The suspicion that she had intruded upon a place of the resting dead made Ashen shiver, though she had never before heard of such preservation as this.

Willingly enough, she followed Weyse down that aisle, curiosity pricking her. If these coffers did enclose the remains of those who had built the ancient city, could they reveal what manner of people they had been? In none of the engraved slates Zazar had stacked were there any representative pictures—only the stylized script. Bog-folk fed their dead to the underlurkers, paying them little honor at life's end.

Ashen counted fifty of the cases, standing twenty-five to a side. Each she studied, and each differed from its neighbor in some manner of adornment. Then she and Weyse reached the other side of the chamber. Another wall faced them, and a second dark opening. Weyse did not run ahead now; rather the small creature kept within paw's distance of Ashen. Now and then she reached out to touch her, as if seeking assurance that the girl was still close.

The passage beyond was as dark as the one Ashen had just come through. Once they left the dim light of the chamber, she had to take all on trust. She could not be sure of the direction they had come, but she had a suspicion that she might now be beneath the lake itself.

Again, a faint light shone ahead and, leading upward, was a stone stairway similar to the one she had earlier descended. Now

Weyse did leave her, scrambling ahead with a vigor suggesting they might soon be out of this underground maze.

Come out they did, though not through any lifted blocks of stone this time, but by having to squeeze cautiously through rubble. Twice Ashen needed to dig a way clear toward what she was sure was a patch of daylight.

She was right. By the look of the vegetation beyond, they had come at last to the outer Bog-land—another island, or a stretch of firm ground, on which there was the drift of time-shattered ruins such as occupied the island behind, but a much smaller collection.

Ashen halted. There might be a very good reason to return here in the future, and she must put her hearth-marker to work. Drawing it from her belt pouch, she laid it on top of a small portion of the ruined wall in a direct line from the point where they had emerged. She touched the marker to set up future guides. Taking a deep breath, she closed her eyes and put her hand firmly on the square. She pictured with the best of her ability a mind point, which she hoped might activate the power of this guide.

There stood that stone, thus, a rounded one still surmounted by what looked like a pair of carved feet, though they supported no legs or body. So and so and so!

Ashen kept her eyes closed so as to channel her force without a chance of being disturbed. Whispering, she recited the formula, one of the earliest she had been set to learn. With a lightening of the heart, she felt the bit of wood under her hand begin to warm.

When the girl uttered the last of the strange words of a long-forgotten tongue, she remained silent for a moment. Her success in this incantation gave her an exuberant feeling of accomplishment. Zazar had taught her only a limited number of such feats, and she had never learned the reasons for certain actions. Now she was glad indeed that this one was a part of those she knew.

Feeling a bit more secure, and with the guide restored to her pouch, Ashen looked around for Weyse. But the little one had vanished, perhaps gone ahead again. She tried to reproduce the trill the other knew, and at the same time, to picture in her mind the creature she called. No answer.

She took a step forward and nearly cried out. A body! No, more accurately, what was left of a body. Cautiously, she circled the bones, all that remained of what had once been a man. Then curiosity overcame caution. Some of his clothing was yet there, rich goods of a kind she had never seen before, in a deep plum red, but shoes, belt—anything made of leather—had vanished along with his flesh. Steadfastly, she refused to think of what sort of scavengers had been lured here to dispose of the remains. One of his legs, she noted, had been broken, and she was suddenly sure that this had not happened after his death. He still wore an armband, however. She reached out to touch it and it came into her hand so easily that the dead man might as well have given it to her.

It was carved from what appeared to be a single piece of milky, translucent crystal, shot through with subtle rainbow hues that glinted as she turned it in her hand.

"I will wear this in your memory, whoever you were," she said aloud. Then, feeling a little foolish for speaking to the dead, she put the ornament on and began looking for Weyse again.

To no avail. When she realized that she was indeed alone, Ashen felt uneasiness creeping back. Though she had made a number of journeys into the unknown when following Zazar, this was different. She found herself sensing a loss such as she had never felt before. She held Zazar in awe, but she did not believe she had any heart ties with the Wysen-wyf. Kazi, of course, had always been hostile, as had the rest of the Bog-folk. Weyse, whom she first thought to be an animal, had, without her realizing it, come to be a companion she was learning to cherish.

Twice she attempted to give the call Zazar had used to summon the small guardian of the lake ruins. There was no answer, so Ashen accepted what she believed to be true. During the time

Andre Norton & Sasha Miller

when she was setting the hearth-marker, Weyse must have retreated to the passageway and was heading back to the island
refuge.

Now her errand was plain, as plain as the fact that Weyse
had set her on her way. She must go and try to help Kazi and,
through her, find out what had happened to Zazar.

The usual pallid sun shone biliously overhead. When it lit
the Bog, its rays seemed to have to beat more heavily to force
their way groundward. She looked back beyond the debris of
stone and sighted the island. Moving toward the left should bring
her, in time, to traces of Kazi's path, which she could follow.

At least the drums had stopped. But that could as easily be
a threat as a blessing. An alarm so short might mean the promised attack had been warded off and that eventually Joal and his
followers would return. She must be on the move. Though Kazi's
pace was limited by her crooked foot, she might get too far ahead
and then Ashen could miss the trail.

Once out of the sprawl of stones, she found the footing was
firm and she could make better time. At intervals she took a
bearing on the island until she could see the landing where Zazar
had tied up the boat. There the brush had been freshly chopped
away, and over there, Joal had come into view.

Using all the craft she knew, Ashen picked up the traces of
Kazi's trail. Clearly, the woman's passage had been difficult. She
had fallen at least twice. Also, those who had brought her here
had not followed any real trail of Bog setting, and this land was
one of rough footing. In addition to the massed ruins of the
islands and those heaped about the door from which Ashen had
emerged, other fragments of stone studded the ground. She must
use caution.

Ashen lost sight of the lake. However, in this place the way
was well marked with torn brush, some of which was bannered
with small fragments of Kazi's tunic. The ground was rising now.
Ahead, the growth was higher than any Ashen had seen elsewhere. Some of the brush was taller than she was, and branches

spread above, many of them woven together. The sunshine was faded into a near dusky twilight.

A scream, no cry from a great predator, but distinctly from a human throat, rent the air. Ashen stopped short, her heart thudding with fear that the woman she sought was now cornered by some Bog-monster.

Ashen had no spear, only the knife at her belt. To go bursting ahead in the direction of that cry might well plunge her into such peril that she could not aid either herself or Kazi. A second scream followed on the first, and she found she could not withstand the plea in that outcry. She worked her way through the choked growth until that ceased abruptly and she found herself on the verge of an open space.

It was not unlike the pavement of the glade where the stone monster had waited. But there was no image here. Instead, two figures struggled together. Kazi had been beaten to the ground, and she rolled and caught at the ankle of the one standing over her.

Kazi's captor was like no Bog-man Ashen knew. A thick mist enveloped him from head to foot. Shocked, she recognized a similarity in this to her own power-stone. Obviously, he wore an amulet with powers somewhat akin to her own. Instinctively, Ashen clutched the stone hung from the cord around her neck and as she touched it, she began to see more clearly until the mist no longer entirely shrouded him.

Outlander! He was tall, and he must have an additional protection over his head, so shadowing his features that Ashen could not see them clearly. His shoulders and body were clothed to mid-thigh with something bright that reflected the weak sunlight. Over that he wore the remains of a sleeveless garment, so torn by branches and thorns that any symbol it might once have borne had long vanished.

Ashen barely had time to see this much when he leaned over Kazi again and landed a blow on the woman's bloody face with a fist gloved in the same glistening material as the bright garment.

Kazi did not even scream. She flopped back and lay still. The attacker prodded her with his booted foot and when she did not stir, he stooped closer and with one hand, tore her upper garment to bare her to the waist. Again his gloved fist descended, and Kazi's head jerked as he applied strength to tear free a cord from about her neck, and the bright object that hung from it.

Ashen could guess what it might be—that round metal ornament she had never been allowed to see clearly. In fact, she was sure that Kazi had always taken care that she did *not* see it.

The man stood for a long moment studying what he held. Then he turned abruptly to stride away southward. Kazi lay limp and unmoving where his last blow had stilled her.

When she was sure the Outlander was truly gone, Ashen sped across the glade to Kazi, who lay sprawled, a rock still in her hand. The crone had tried to defend herself, that much was obvious. But a single glance at that bruised face was enough to freeze Ashen in place. Even muddied and blood-stained, it was clear that Kazi's forehead had been crushed. She stared upward with unblinking eyes. Ashen felt for that place on Kazi's thick neck for the telltale throb of her lifeblood, as Zazar had taught her long ago. There was nothing. It took a few moments to register on Ashen that Kazi had been wantonly killed by the Outlander, one who had somehow known about that object she treasured and was determined to make it his own.

Slowly she straightened the thick body so that Kazi, save for her battered face, looked as if she were at rest. But Ashen had no intention of following custom, somehow dragging the body to the nearest water and pushing it in to become food for the underwater ones. Instead, she gathered some of the numerous stones in the clearing and covered Kazi's body with them.

Kazi had been her first and best hope of discovering what had happened to Zazar. Now she must accept that perhaps she would never see the Wysen-wyf again. Then she knew what she would choose to do. The Outlander—whence had he come to plunder Kazi, and how had he known what she carried?

The Outlander might be the clue to much of the puzzle. The hunters were out and he would be viciously tracked were he to be detected, but that he had come so far into the Bog without being cut down meant that he had some measure of potent protection. Once more she fingered her own amulet. How had any Outlander been able to use what she had always thought was Zazar's own well-kept secret? Though she might be striding straight into great danger, she could not deny that she must learn all she could. And now she searched for the Outlander's trail, determined to follow.

Fifteen

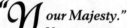

"*Your Majesty.*"

Ysa recognized that voice, even though it was muffled behind one of the long strips of tapestry that gave a touch of color and comfort to her in the most private chamber in her apartment. That this messenger chose to come by secret ways and while daylight lingered was a warning. She gave a quick glance about the room. Quickly she rose and shot the bolt on the one obvious door and then went to her chair.

Though she had already dismissed her ladies-in-waiting and her bedchamber women, she wanted no intruders at this time. To depend on the sort of servant who was now at hand always made her uneasy. Tongues that repeated messages might do so to more than one person if there was urging strong enough. Still, the one known as the Queen of Spies had always been discreet.

Now she turned and spoke a name. "Marfey."

She knew where to look—toward the secret door. Through a slit in the hangings on which the pattern concealed all but from the most seeking eye, there limped a thin, stooped figure, bundled in patched garments, all too large for the bony body they hid.

The newcomer reached up one grimy hand to push back

matted hair of a shade close to dust, displaying a pinched face disfigured with a darkening bruise.

It was hard to tell the age of the woman, just as it would be difficult to say that she was more than one of the street beggars, even in greater distress than most of them. But once inside the curtains, Marfey grinned at Ysa unexpectedly, as if delighted by the effect her appearance had on the Queen. Ysa had seen this servant of hers in very different disguises and was always a bit startled at the many transformations Marfey, Queen of Spies, could summon to her use.

Ysa waved her agent toward one of the tapestry-pillowed stools. Marfey straightened up and walked toward it. She moved with a slight limp, but firmly, her cringing-beggar role discarded. There she seated herself as if she had every right to claim such an honor and shook the pebble out of her shoe. Ysa realized its presence was no accident, but insurance that Marfey not forget her role.

The Queen leaned forward a little, disregarding the stale smell that came from the woman. "What have you learned?"

"Lord Harous has returned from his hunting."

"And what was the result of his labors in the hunting field?"

"He was unlucky, but perhaps he had foreseen his lack of game. The three men he took as his guard did not bring the pack-pony they had had with them when they rode out. Yet he did not seem downcast when he came back, but rather as one who had achieved some return for his efforts."

Harous to the Bog border, returning apparently pleased? Ysa did not find that thought comforting. Whom had he met? What had he learned? Now she spoke swiftly.

"Marfey, there is—" She taped a finger against the arm of her chair, her mind searching for the name she needed now. "Yes, that's the one. The Lady Marcala of Valvager has the right to claim a place in our household. It is reported that she is somewhat wanton in her behavior but that her beauty makes up for all but the most glaring of excesses. His Highness might be interested, but Marcala is distant kin-cousin to Harous. He has not seen her in some years, but should be well disposed to tighten kin bonds. Marcala, as free-living as she is reported to be, might consider Harous a better catch in contrast to spending lazy hours in Florian's bed and then being discarded as soon as another fresh and youthful face appears."

Marfey listened, her expression not giving away her thoughts. When the Queen had finished, she nodded briskly. "I understand," she said.

For the first time, Ysa smiled. "Child, you must certainly be glad to put off these smelly rags and go before the world as it is your right to appear."

Marfey shrugged. "Your Majesty knows that what small talents I have are always at her service. Only, tell me as much as you can about this Marcala. You say she is from Valvager. I take it she has not before been to court—"

Again Ysa smiled. "She has been twice proposed to be one of our household, but the stories about her suggested she was not to be trusted. Living at the far eastern border, she is not known to most of the noble kin, since there are few holdings there and most of those are held by lesser folk who would not know our household." She held up her hands and began to tick off points as she spoke, as if to emphasize the importance of each. "She has black hair. By the left corner of her mouth there is a small, dark mole that is said to enhance her charms rather than detract from them. She dances well, and ever has an eye for a well-built man. Her favorite colors are violet, deep rose, gold, and the peach-pink shade of vaux lilies, for which she has a great liking and wears in her hair whenever there is a chance to do so. Also, she wears perfume made from these flowers."

Marfey nodded at each point. "All well and good, but it would be better to have a likeness," she said bluntly.

Now Ysa's smile widened. "That is how I was able to describe her to you so closely. Go to the table yonder and open its drawer.

You will find a miniature of the lady, limned only this two-month gone."

Marfey obeyed quickly and pulled out a small, framed portrait. She studied it closely. "Well enough," she said at last. "Your artist was cunning and skillful."

"And you are close enough to pass for her, to those who have only the image to rely upon. You will leave the city within the hour," the Queen continued. "You know of the summer lodge at Bray. The court has not used it during late seasons as His Majesty has had other pursuits on his mind. Go there. You will find a woman, Tethia, in residence. She is of my own kin. Say to her, 'The day comes, let all hearts be glad.' You recognize it as a line from a song popular a season past. In response, she will give you the line that follows. She will also supply all that you need. The lodge is near the highway Marcala would follow coming from Valvager. You will be provided with a maid, a wardrobe, and a proper escort. It will be made known to the court that you are soon to arrive. Once back within these walls, the game will be largely yours. Harous is no womanizer, but he is unwed, and he well knows his duty to the lordship and that he must follow it soon. I leave it to you, child. What is to be learned is what connection he has with the Bog. This is of the highest importance."

"Yes, Your Majesty." The young woman rose and made a deep court curtsy hardly in keeping with her present appearance. Without saying good-bye, she slipped through the slit in the hangings and was gone.

Ysa likewise arose and went to draw the door bolt. Time, time, she thought. Often her friend, it could well be her enemy. Boroth lingered, to be sure, but only because he drew upon the Ring power she directed to him. And she knew her own growing exhaustion every time that Power was drawn upon. She had eyes and ears on Florian and knew well that he was not as apt for feminine company these days as he had been. Rather, while there were still convivial gatherings in his chambers, his guests were of a different type—gamblers in more ways than one—and the drink flowed ever more freely. Most of Florian's cronies were younger sons of various lords, and several of the Houses they represented were no friends of hers. She kept what attention was possible on their comings and goings and had hinted to Royance that there might be trouble brewing.

Like her, Royance wanted no power struggle when the King died, and he well knew Florian's nature. Since he had seen the Rings refuse the Prince's touch, Ysa knew that he would most gladly support any project that would continue peace, and upon that fact she was determined to depend.

The sun was strong, its light reaching out over the rough walls of the cliffs that would be the Sea-Rover scouts' road on this day. At present, nobody stirred among the jagged jawline of stone. Besides Obern, there were three of them—Dordan, Kather, and Kasai—to the fore of those who had come from the hold. All were clad in mail. Obern did not glance at his companions. His attention was ahead of them, to that perilous trail to the land-bridge he had argued was worth the trying.

At least on their departure, Snolli had not uttered any advice, and that strengthened his son. That his father was silent made it clear that he trusted Obern to be cautious and to show the same inner steel that would be his were they advancing on some enemy holding.

Snolli had, however, given the old farewell: "Go with wind in the sails and waves favoring."

Obern had half turned and lifted his bared sword in response. Then he had started toward what he had marked by careful observation since this action had been agreed upon as the easiest of possible paths.

It did not take them long to reach the beginning of unknown territory. They needed to descend and then climb again. Soon they reached the swallow-hole where the border river vanished. Beyond that, the waters would emerge again before being vomited out seaward in the waterfall they had seen marking the very edge of the Bog. Light wisps of mist veiled part of the Bog-land but did not rise to cloak the clifftop. Without hesitation, the scouting party crossed the land-bridge. Now they were technically in the Bog, going parallel to the river but not yet beginning to mark the reach of the land beyond.

"No drum," Dordan said in a reminder. Kasai, whose drum was slung by a cord over his shoulder, had halted. Facing the near-obscured Bog, he drew several deep breaths, sniffing the air, as if by so doing, he could gain necessary knowledge.

It was Obern who read the uneasiness in the Spirit Drummer. "Perhaps the mist gives us cover for now. That means we use it before it is swept away."

"Down there—" It was part of a question, and the archer Kather had turned back toward the river, beyond the stone land-bridge.

Obern shook his head. "Better to see what we can—" He halted in mid-speech, for a thread of mist flitted away and he could see the riverbank, and so learned that his party was not alone.

By their dress, he recognized the six men as being from Rendel. As with the group he had seen before, they had more mounts than men; these they had picketed not far from them. And now most were gathered about something spread on the ground—an open chart, Obern suspected. He recognized the one to whom the others deferred; he was using a belt knife to point out portions of the chart. The last time Obern had seen this man, shreds of mist were clearing from his person. Now he was speaking without interruption by his companions. Though Obern strained to hear, they were too far away and the river noise provided a cover for any sound coming from their temporary camp.

Obern made a hand signal and his party faded seaward. Within a stride or two, they could no longer see the men from the Kingdom, nor, Obern was sure, could they now be sighted from below.

"Hunters—of trouble," he said in a low voice, nearly drowned out by the river. All the information they had gathered from traders and their own scouting had always been firm that the Bog was forbidden to Outlanders. Yet it was plain that those below were consulting some guide, and where would that take them? Where else but to the Bog? He stopped short. He could be mistaken regarding their errand. All the Rendel men were on the unforbidden side of the river. There had been no hint that the Sea-Rovers' own taking of the deserted keep had aroused any interest among their neighbors—if there were such within easy distance. But were the ones they had seen now come to scout in turn?

Kasai had joined him. "Scouts—the keep?" Obern asked. The drummer shook his head.

"Not so, I think, though we must never overlook any possibility."

"That one with the chart—I think he has ridden this way before with the Bog his goal."

"I think that be his goal again. There must be some weightful need to make sure of something within those waters and Bog nets."

Obern nodded. "So be it."

If the man from the Kingdom was going again into the forbidden land, it would be wise to keep an eye on him as long as they could. With caution, they worked a little northward, stopping now and then to watch the party below and to the south. The fog wove curtains that served to conceal the strangers, but not so completely that those above did not observe when the chart was rolled together and they stood facing the river and what lay beyond.

It was time for using any cover that was available. Belly-down, the Sea-Rovers wriggled painfully through the bits and rasps of rocky edges to a spot on the lip of the inner cliff. There they had a good view of the men from Rendel.

The leader of that party had opened a pack and was now groping in a bag. What he drew forth, Obern could barely make out. Then he saw a disk dangling from a cord that the man put over his head so that the pendant lay on his breast. A spear stood nearby, its point lodged in the ground. The man pulled out the spear and with this in hand, walked toward the river, avoiding the land-bridge. The water rose about his legs as he went, and the current was rough enough to push him in the direction of the distant waterfall. He used the spear as a support and fought his way to the far bank, almost directly below where Obern and his men lay hidden.

When the man won to that and was out of reach of the water, he touched the pendant on his breast. It was as if that act summoned all the tatters of the still-floating mist. His body was swiftly enwrapped, but not past the point where he could not be seen as a core to that cloaking. It was apparently thicker than the Bog-mist and once he was so cloaked, he moved confidently forward.

Those on the clifftop glanced at each other silently. Just as Obern had reported earlier, the man from the Kingdom had gone into the Bog. Were there any sentinels there to sight him? No drums had yet sounded.

No drums, no. But from the sky overhead there came a screech such as pained the ears of any listener. That horrid sound Obern well knew. He looked upward; above them whirled and circled three of the birds they had once before met in battle. He had time to think, a little confusedly, that such as these must hunt in bands of three.

Kather already had arrow to string. And Dordan had a similar, smaller bow to be used at close quarters. Obern drew his sword without any conscious thought. Prudently, they scrambled for what cover the outcrops nearby provided. They didn't bother to hide from their quarry now. Let the men from the Kingdom defend themselves without their help.

The birds wheeled in a circle above them and it was plain that the interloping Sea-Rovers, not the men from Rendel, were the targets. Suddenly one bird broke from the circle and dropped, its great wings, each the size of a standing man, tucked against its sides. Its hideously gaping beak opened to screech its war-cry.

The cry continued in a rising scream. An arrow suddenly struck one of the giant clawed legs but fell away without penetrating. The feathers and skin must provide good armor.

Obern suddenly realized it was not plunging for the archer who had marked it, but toward him. He took a step back and half crouched, his sword ready. He swung the weapon when he thought the bird within range.

The big head was thrust forward, curved bill threatening. Obern's attack connected with one of the legs extended to claw at him. Just as the bird's feathers had protected it, so now did his mail keep his flesh from the tearing hold the creature strove to set upon him.

If only he could have struck steel against the scrawny neck! As it was, he failed to deliver a meaningful blow. The force with which the bird met the plunging attack was more than Obern had expected, and he staggered. With a whirl of feathers and a second screech, the creature swerved to settle on an outcrop of the cliff just above their refuge.

Obern could not recover his balance. It was as if his feet refused to obey his frantic inner orders. The edge of the cliff dropping before him, he tried to throw his weight backward. The rubble underfoot betrayed him. Out he flailed from the perilous footage, out and down. There was only a moment of realization and then— Blackness, a far-off suggestion of fiery pain—

—nothing at all.

Sixteen

A shen could see where the Outlander, Kazi's murderer, had fought his way through the brush, leaving footprints in the soft land here and there where water oozed to puddle. He had changed course abruptly and was headed now southward toward the edge of the Bog. But the drums still rolled and the girl well knew that there were guardposts in plenty, any one of which could harbor those to pull him down.

She herself habitually used the valuable trail knowledge Zazar had imparted to her to avoid such posts. For those were carefully guarded secrets, each set by one village alone. Now she must depend on the fact that she had read this trail before her correctly and go in just the opposite direction.

The Bog-folk kept open hunting trails toward the eastern cliffs. She had, in her own secret expeditions, ventured only a little toward them. The border river took an underground way, close to the rock walls, before it at last plunged into the sea, a much larger body of water she had only heard about, never seen. Was there, or was there not, a way she could reach the sea and then return, with the river as a guide?

She could only try, taking every care and remaining ever

alert. The drums still sounded, which meant the Bog-folks were alert. However, she believed that the intruder would take the quickest way out and not risk getting lost in an unmarked mire.

Tightening the straps of her backpack and making sure its weight would not trouble her, Ashen then cut from a nearby willow a branch as thick as she could find. With that in hand, she turned eastward. She could see her destination, the shadow across the horizon that marked the cliffs.

The signal drums had started up again, but they kept to a steady beat, one that did not summon the Bog-folk to fight. This tempo was far less vigorous than battle call. They were tracking. There had been no sound of war-pipes, so she could guess that the invader had not been brought down. However, since he had headed south before turning east, she imagined that she would be less apt to run into any tracking party. And also, she had the amulet, Zazar's gift. And she was sure that the unknown killer of Kazi had depended upon some similar ancient secret to mask him from Bog perils. As Ashen went, using her willow branch to test any suspicious-looking footway, she continued to wonder about Zazar.

There had been several times during the years when certain strangers, well muffled against any recognition, had come to Zazar's hearth and spent time in whispered conversation with the Wysen-wyf. Until now, Ashen had dismissed the suspicion that such were Outlanders. However, now it appeared that Zazar's powers were so great that she could promise them safe passage.

Ashen pondered over what network the Wysen-wyf had maintained through such secret visitations. Outlanders? If Joal had come to suspect Zazar treated with such, there was no wonder he had turned on her, forcing from Kazi what information he could.

The drums stopped. The sudden silence broke Ashen's speculations. Either the invader had been captured, which she did not believe, or he had by some unusual means escaped, a chance she found hard to accept.

The probing she made of the damp moss underfoot struck now, only a short way down, a firm surface that might be rock. Perhaps it was a pavement, similar to that with which she was already familiar. Since it seemed to stretch ahead in the direction she would go, Ashen kept to it. Twilight was beginning to close in, and she hoped to find some shelter before the full night-dark was at hand.

Two pillars, a space between them, loomed out of the tangled brush ahead, and it was toward this that the hidden path led. There was evidence suggesting that a stone had once lain atop the pillars at the crowns. More remains of the long-ago ones, Ashen thought. Beyond the pillars there was a fringe of reeds and another of those turgid, slime-spotted pools in which anything might lurk. In this pool, barely breaking the surface of the water, there was a series of stones ringed with green slime. She knew about these, and had used them elsewhere before.

Footage of a sort, yes. But she feared the slick surfaces could betray anyone treading such stones. The pool was not far across, but it was long. A narrow tongue that Ashen could make out in the fading light as soggy footing waited at the other end of those stones.

She must make up her mind and move soon, for there was no hiding place to be sighted. To go around the pool might be a lengthy journey. The last full light of day could linger long enough for her to try the stones, and she reversed her staff to use the other end, its twigs branched close together. Then she thudded this bushy end on the first of the stones, testing its support. It seemed firmly rooted.

She stood thinking, surveying what lay ahead. Reluctantly, she produced her amulet. The girl rubbed her forefinger across the amulet and repeated the singsong words to activate it. Mist arose on either side but did not blind her to the line of stepping-stones. She gained the first stone and steadied herself quickly as a patch of slime threatened her footing.

Slow means sure, she warned herself, taking every precaution to test the stability of each stone as she advanced. There were winged sparks flying about now—the night-hunters of the air. But such were not to be feared; it was well known that the only peril these threatened was to mistake them for watch-lights marking a trail.

Ashen was breathing hard. Drops of moisture gathered under her arms and along the edge of her hair as she finally reached the far side of the pool.

She stumbled onward, putting a stride or two of distance between herself and the water before she turned to glance back, remembering only too well her encounter with Gulper, who had arisen from just such a pool.

The lights on wings swooped low over the water, giving a measure more of sight. Then the water suddenly rippled. There snapped above the surface what looked like an end of rope. Upon sighting that, Ashen fled, no longer sure that she was on any hidden way. However, here the brush did not grow so thickly, and there were no tangles of willows. The mist surrounding her provided a fraction of light, so she could determine that here there were more tall-standing stones. The cliffs were visible against the rapidly darkening sky.

She wound her way around piles of broken stone, not as thickly massed as those in the city on the isle, but still urging caution. As she went, she listened. The other dwellers in the Bog were beginning their time of twilight hunting. There were coughing roars, shrill peepings. Once she crouched tight against another pillar of stone while there came a loud splashing from close by, coupled with a bellow. But that sound led away from her and after a tense wait, she continued.

She caught, beyond the stones, the gleam of what could only be a watch-fire, and that drove her southward to avoid discovery.

At length, her body aching from the strain, she heard the flow of water. If she had reckoned true, that must be the river bounding the Bog here. With a scramble, she fought her way through more brush, to come out at its bank.

However, she could not use it as a guide, for she had reached the swallow-hole. Water tumbled through a veiling of mist into a gap in the earth and was gone. But she had also reached the edge of the cliff. It loomed as a dark wall beyond the hole.

The inner wall of the cliff showed other cracks and fissures in addition to that through which the water poured. Ashen went carefully, step by step, hoping to flank the stream, her goal still the cliff. Evening was gathering in, and from behind there came the louder sounds of the Bog's night-waking. She must have some shelter should any of the under-hunters come forth, seeking prey.

To the right of the stream-swallowing opening was a darker shadow, hinting at a cave. Shifting her pack, she looked for any hand- and footholds that might take her aloft.

The harsh edges of the rock scraped her hands painfully, but she was able to draw herself up and found that indeed there was a narrow fissure before her. A heavy roar from below gave strength to her faltering limbs. She vaulted up and fell sprawling into that opening. Nor did she try to look back, but rather, pushed inward as fast as she could.

Here the rock was not rough; some force in the past might have smoothed a passage. But the darkness was thick. She became aware of unfamiliar smells, curiously fresh, that must be borne from the sea beyond. Using her staff, she struck ahead, hoping to find the end of this pocket. Her explorations told her that she was indeed in a hollow of size enough to hold her without cramping.

A fire was out of the question, but she still had some dried trail food that she chewed vigorously as she tried to plan ahead. It was probably true, Ashen thought, that she had lost the trail and was no longer headed in the direction of the man she had followed. She did not hear the voice of any drum from the outer air, but that did not mean that the Bog-folk were not alert and on guard. Best remain in this pocket of safety until the coming of morning, when her eyes could serve her better.

She loosed her woven ground-cover roll from her pack and spread it out by touch. This would not be a soft bed, but what strayer in the Bog dared hope for that? Taking a small sip from her water carrier, she swished it about in her mouth before she swallowed it, then stretched herself on her sleep-mat and closed her eyes firmly.

The dark enfolded her like a second mound of blankets, and she realized that her journey had tired her to the point that she was assailed by various aches and pains. Hunching up, she fumbled in her pack and carefully loosed one of the small bags lashed so carefully inside.

Though the dank breath of the Bog and the play of sea scent surrounded her, Ashen could also smell the pungency of the herb within. With infinite care, she got the bag open, working blindly and afraid that she might waste its contents by spillage. With forefinger and thumb, she pinched the roughness of dried leaves and transferred them to her mouth. Then she closed the bag and returned it to her stores.

Ashen would have liked to spit out the small mouthful, as its acid taste burned her tongue and the insides of her cheeks. Instead, she forced herself to chew it into a paste and swallow. Now her mouth felt numb. She settled back on the mat and waited hopefully for sleep.

The soothing curtain of unawareness she sought did not come. She twisted and turned on the mat, trying to make herself more comfortable. Sounds from the Bog echoed, indicating plainly that the under-ones were out in full hunt. Ashen shivered suddenly as she thought of some one of the smaller monsters tracing her by scent and climbing to claw her out of this refuge.

But gradually she became aware of something else. It was no warning from without such as she now listened for, but rather, an uneasiness, as if there were some warning whisper in the blackness about her. The sense of it was beyond her power to understand.

At length, that strange message, if message it was, drowned out her surroundings. She lay quiet and slowly repeated scraps she had gleaned from the rituals Zazar had recited when they were together. Though she could not really believe that any aid from such bits of ancient and nearly unintelligible petitions could be summoned, she did discover that the sense of dread was retreating. She relaxed a little, knowing that there had come a kind of reassurance, not from her own thoughts, but out of nowhere.

Zazar? she wondered drowsily.

She opened her eyes once more to find herself surrounded by light coming through the opening in the wall's fissure. The light was dim, but enough to let her see around her. And now she discovered a second opening in her refuge—little more than a slit in the wall facing the break through which she had crawled. It had been easy to miss in the dark.

She sat up and studied it closely. Again she knew that strange sensation, as if a distant cry was summoning—

But Ashen did not have long to try to understand. Another cry, this one not imaginary, arose from just outside the cliff's opening. She had a jumbled impression of a huge head darting in and out of the aperture before she could see it plainly. Again the cry sounded, shrill but as threatening as any bellow she had ever heard. The river poured seaward not too far away. Was this some lurker in the waters emerging to edge across the cliff wall, having scented her?

Ashen drew her knife. It was clean-bladed and as sharp as careful honing could make it, but for her to use it effectively, she must be very close to her attacker. Her only other weapon was the staff she had used to test her Bog-going.

Another screech echoed, and again something thrust in toward her. This time she could see what it was, and she drew a sharp breath. This creature was one of the giant Bog-birds. Years ago she had seen the large body that had taxed two hunters to drag back to the village, while their companions supported

Andre Norton & Sasha Miller

Batyon, who had met the bird and had his face nearly torn off. And another of these giants was now, apparently, intent on making her into its breakfast.

At least she knew exactly where she was now. Lucky for the Bog-folk that these birds were to be found only amid the southwestern cliffs and it was seldom that any villager ventured in that direction.

Again came the frustrated screeching. Ashen fingered the staff. If it had taken four hunting spears to bring down the creature Joal's people had killed, of what use would this be, having no hard shell or honed tooth-point to pierce the heavily leathered skin? Inevitably, she would be the bird's meal, unless— She turned once more to the other break in the crevice wall, visible only because it made a more profound blackness against the dark rock. There was no light in it.

Rolling the sleep-mat, she lashed it to her pack. It would not do, she decided, to try to shoulder it. The other opening looked to be narrow and perhaps she would have to drag the pack to work her way through.

With a last screech ringing in her ears, she started into the unknown. It turned out to be a kind of tunnel, not wide, but much longer than it had appeared from her sleeping place. Within a very short time, she was aware that the sharp scent of the sea was growing stronger. Since there was no light, she must move cautiously. Once, she tried to see if her direction amulet would aid her, but it remained stubbornly dull. She used instead the staff to tap out a way ahead, hoping that she could avoid any perilous surprises.

Ashen went slowly and with all the care she could summon. Then she became aware that her passage was tilting upward. She could no longer glimpse any light ahead; if the tunnel opened out on the sea face of the cliff, her goal still lay far ahead. Her staff struck an obstruction and she prodded both high and low. To her dismay, there seemed an unbroken wall facing her now. But as she continued to probe, she encountered no barrier to the

right. So, the way turned here. But now she faced another difficulty. The tunnel ended abruptly. Her staff slammed against
what could only be a rise, and a moment later, she used one
hand as well as the willow branch to explore. To her astonishment, she found a set of stairs leading upward.

As she sat back on her heels to consider the wisdom of struggling up those stairs, she caught a glimpse well above her of a
faint lightening of the heavy gloom. With this for a guide, she
pulled up from one stair step to the next.

The grayness lightened and became weak daylight as she
reached the top and saw before her another rock-walled pocket
similar to the one in which she had taken refuge the night before.
However, at the far end of this there was a much larger break
for an exit, higher up on the wall, and into that there streamed
daylight, as well as a steady pounding noise and a refreshing sea
scent.

Ashen climbed out from the passage. As she got to her feet,
she saw that against the wall to her right there lay a collection
of bones, and she recognized another skeleton.

Not yet ready to examine this fresh mystery, she settled
down to rest, as far from the remains as the cave would allow.
The journey had exhausted her, and her stomach was demanding
food. While she pondered that bundle of bones, she hunted for
a portion of trail fare—there was little of it left—and allowed
herself two sips of water.

These remains were similar to the other skeleton she had
discovered. She could understand the impulse to leave the first
one near the burial chamber in the stone ruins, in the company
of others and in a place built for it—but this one was not the
same. The first might well have met with an accident, but what
had befallen this one, and why the bones had been so left, she
could not guess. This one's skull was separated from the rest of
the bones and had been set upon a pile of old ashes, to stare
eyelessly at the rock overhead. Finally, she rose and moved to
kneel down beside the remains.

The daylight reached in with probing fingers now; the air was brighter. A spear lay nearby, its shaft broken into several pieces. He had been buried with his weapon, set to watch—but to watch what? Had he been a sacrifice? What had caused him to be left here, his skull set apart from the rest of him?

Ashen could no longer look at the dead. Bare bones had little resemblance to the here and now. But the fate of this man spurred her onward. She got to her feet and went to that opening into day, turning from death to life as she looked through the doorway toward the sunlight and pounding sea below.

There had been once, she discovered, a kind of perilous path hacked into the rock a foot or so below the entrance. But it did not extend far. Some long-ago slide of rock had destroyed the way, shearing it off. She crept halfway through the opening and looked out upon what she had only heard about—the sea.

Even the stories had not prepared her for this vast, incredibly blue, marvelously clean stretch of water. It washed below, striking the root of the cliff with continued hammer blows. And, jammed amid a tumble of rock, perhaps those same stones that had been loosened by the past slippage, there lay a strange tangle of salt-bleached wood, as if some craft had been pounded to its ruin here.

There was no way down. She was on the very verge of the opening now. But, she thought, what about up? Yes, that way promised a path, not so evident as the beginning of the way down showed, but one she believed could be followed.

There remained the birds. She huddled down and set her thoughts to them. She looked out at the water, attracted by a movement. Something bobbed on the sea, and she realized it was a sailing vessel, like the wreckage below, only still whole. By dint of shading her eyes and straining to see, she could make out people on it.

Then, in a flash of insight, she realized the meaning of the tableau she had stumbled upon, and began to shiver anew. The wreckage below—obviously a large boat like the one now bobbing on the sea—had been lured by a light set to entrap it. And the man who tended this light had been killed and set as a warning least others practice the same deceit—

It really was a completely different world, outside the Bog.

Then came another outcry—but this one was from a human throat, not a scream but a shout. A man's voice, echoed by others, and the screeches of attacking birds. . . .

Seventeen

sa sat a little apart from her ladies. On her knee was a
stitching frame upon which was fastened a section of a
roll of cloth marked with embroidery patterns. She frequently
found that planning came easier somehow when she was staring
at needle and thread. Not that she ever accomplished much with
her stitchery. Now she waited, her needle idle.

All had gone well, at least so far. She had her private news
of Marfey— No, she must remember. Marcala. The lady's cor-
tege, supposedly from the east, should arrive within this turn of
the hourglass.

Harous had not yet returned from whatever business—it certainly was not hunting—that had drawn him to the border of
the Bog-land. Perhaps Marcala could satisfy her curiosity on that
question. Ysa had long speculated as to his choice of prowling,
to no avail.

There was a respectful scratching at the door, and the Lady
Grisella, nearest that portal, went to answer. A moment later,
she turned and curtsied to the Queen. "Your Majesty, the Lady
Marcala desires entrance."

Ysa nodded, and as the ladies murmured to themselves, Grisella moved aside to admit a woman whose appearance put all within the room into dull shade. Even Ysa in her crimson velvet felt somewhat eclipsed. The woman's violet gown was of rich stuff, and vaux lilies were worked on it in a peach shade shot with silver threads. As counterpoint, the fragrance of the same blooms wafted delicately with her every movement.

She indeed proved true all the whispers about her legendary beauty. Such were not rumors at all. There was also floating about her, like a shadowy cloak, a seductive quality that was not quite by conscious will but exuded from her inner person, an enticement that worked upon men and women as well.

She dropped a deep curtsy before the Queen. Ysa did not rise, but waved Marcala closer.

"Welcome," she said in greeting, her voice cool and detached. Word of Marcala's arrival was already about, and she must make sure that no one at court could claim that the Queen favored a lady who caused such whispers as people spread only behind shielding hands. Ysa made another small gesture, and the least of her waiting ladies brought a stool for the newcomer—pointedly not the low chair to which her station entitled her. The visitor was not smiling, and the Queen knew very well that Marcala was aware of the gathering resentment among her ladies.

Ysa had no time to add anything to her greeting, for another scratching sounded at the door. She nodded to Grisella, who had taken up again her station nearest the door, to answer.

If the arrival of Marcala was a surprise to her women, the man who now entered had the effect of a thunderbolt. Royance strode in, bowed, and then stood awaiting acknowledgment of his presence. His very bearing radiated confidence, but as far as the Queen was concerned, he brought uneasiness with him.

Ysa struggled to remain impassive, though inwardly she was close to screaming at the terrible coincidence. There were too many questions that Royance might ask. Her only course was to refuse to allow him to voice any of them in this company, and that was what she now chose to do.

"My Lord Royance, give you sun for the day," she said, granting him the most formal—and least meaningful—greeting.

"May the sun be warm, the day bright for Your Majesty," he replied in kind. But he divided his gaze between her and Marcala.

There was nothing for it but to be gracious. Ysa indicated the newcomer. "My lord, this is a welcome addition to our court, the Lady Marcala of Valvager." The lady was already on her feet and dipped a curtsy of just the proper depth.

"Bright welcome to you, Lady," he replied. But he was eyeing Marcala as suspiciously as if she held some stealthy weapon in the wide folds of her skirt.

"May the sun be warm on you, my lord." Marcala's voice was soft, and Ysa thought she heard a murmur of beguilement in it. She would have none of that. Marcala was playing the role intended for her, yes, but she was to have only one prey here—Harous.

Ysa could guess also that it was not the newcomer who had brought Royance to her chamber. He would not have sought his Queen out unless it was of the utmost necessity. To end the flirtatious by-play, she decided to take the initiative.

"My lord, it is well you have come." She turned to her ladies. "I will speak with my Lord Royance in private. You may all withdraw." They left quickly, Marcala at their heels.

The Queen waved Royance to the stool her new lady had just vacated and dropped her needlework into the sewing-box table at hand. Royance raised one eyebrow and pulled up his accustomed low chair instead.

"You have news for me?" She took the posture that she did so often lately, with hand laced over hand as if the double touch of the Rings was somehow needed.

Instead of answering directly, he addressed what had surprised him. "Your Majesty has added to her household."

"What aid any can give in this uncertain time is to be cherished," she replied, thinking quickly. "If rumor is true, the Lady

Marcala is no innocent bud; there are stories in plenty to assure us of that. However, I am told she has tried to mend her ways and has striven for many months to be as she is today, accepted here. I have very little support in the eastern land and I am willing to allow her to prove herself. To have a source of information from that direction is good—at least for the present."

Royance had taken his favorite posture of hands with fingers steepled, as if to mock some position of petition.

"Your Majesty is ever alert to what can be done," he said, but there was a tone in those words that warned her.

"Yet I feel, my lord, that your approval is lacking. This lady is what she is."

"And," he said, "His Highness the Prince is also what he is." He was becoming harshly honest. The words hung heavily in the air, full of meaning.

Yes, perhaps he had a point. She thought again. Since most of those who had influence at court already knew that Florian was no prize in any matrimonial race, it could be gossiped that she had arranged what she could to see him married, even though any alliance she made with the Lady Marcala on his behalf would certainly have been lack-witted.

What Royance did not know—what even Marcala did not know—was that she had already determined that dalliance with Florian could lead to an aroused interest on the part of Harous. That portion of the planning she intended to keep to herself. Royance's arrival was premature, though not entirely unexpected. Now much depended on just how much he would believe of what she would share with him.

"I am not matchmaking. Such a plan," she said evenly, "would serve nothing. Do you believe that the Council would accept such a suggestion? I think not."

He surveyed her and then slowly nodded. "Your Majesty is correct, of course. I think, however, that you do plan some twisting of fate on your own."

"If so," Ysa returned, "when the time is right, be sure that you will be made aware of what is happening." She smiled inwardly, secretly delighted. This was something she had not even considered before! Marcala's presence would make the choice of Laherne as Florian's bride even more desirable, if she were clever about using the opportunity. And she would be. "Now surely, the story of this lady's arrival is not all that brought you here?"

For the first time, his thin lips sketched a shadow of a smile. "You are correct. There is something else. There is a stirring along the Bog borders. Recently—"

"Recently there have been hunting parties in that direction, I know." She waited to see if he would mention Harous.

"That, and the fact that the Sea-Rovers have settled into the Ashenkeep. They patrol the lands of what remains of Ashenhold, but so far, they have not in any way approached us. I have had report that their leader is a High Chief known as Snolli, and if so, we may eventually have to deal with a very wily and well-experienced warrior."

"Have the Sea-Rovers shown any desire to enter farther into Rendel? Such has not been reported to me." For an uneasy moment, she pictured Harous meeting with this Snolli, and not to any good for her own cause. She had at least two lurkers combing the district by the sea, but they had not reported any sight of Harous in the eastward direction. The man was far from a fool and could, she was sure, detect any eyes she tried to put on him while away from the city. So much would depend on Marcala. . . .

Royance faced her squarely over his steepled hands. "There has been no direct contact with the Sea-Rovers. Perhaps we should move in that direction ourselves—"

He never finished his thought. There was no polite scratching this time. The door to the Queen's chamber crashed open and Florian stood there.

He swayed a fraction, and by that and his flushed face, Ysa guessed that he, as had become usual, was following his father's search for strength from a bottle.

"You have some message?" she asked in the coldest voice she could summon. "It must be important indeed that you forget all courtesies, Florian, and interrupt my conversation with the Lord Royance."

The sneer on Florian's face was very clear to see. He sketched a bow that nearly cost him his balance. "Lady Mother, we are in perilous times."

"Yes," she returned, and waited. He must be made to say what had brought him here.

"The King holds to life by a weakening thread."

It was not like Florian to be so roundabout. Perhaps it was a sign that he was unsure of himself.

"The King lives." Her voice was colder still. She raised her hands so that the light in the room winked on the Rings. "By the aid of fate, he shall be with us for a time, and we cannot guess when he will go."

"It is against all custom, Madam Mother, that he leaves the rule in your hands. He has a son, come to man's age, or at least near enough. I would be what is proper—Regent—until he departs."

He staggered a couple of unsteady steps forward, but Royance had risen and now put himself between the Queen and the Prince.

"Your Highness, as you know, this is neither the time nor the place for such an act." He might have been speaking to some underling who had presumed far too much. "The passing of the Rings must be done before the full Council. Do you call for such a meeting, then?"

Ysa did not await her son's answer to that. Instead, she caught and held his eyes. "You have made this demand before, and also while you were in your cups. The Rings rejected you then. Do you think they will come freely to you now, and are you willing to take that risk before the great nobles of this Kingdom? That previous attempt could be excused, covered up. But

Andre Norton & Sasha Miller

to make another, and to be so disowned again, will be known throughout the realm only too quickly."

He licked his loose bottom lip. Beneath his rich short cloak, his shoulders hunched.

"Listen well," he said. A small spatter of foam appeared in one corner of his mouth. "There is no doubt that I am who I am. There is none other who can take my rights from me." He swung around to face Royance more squarely. "You are the premiere lord here. The rules of law are known to you. Will you permit the Queen to break those that are the most important? Think on this, my lord. How many of those Houses will raise a Crown chant for a woman? I am your only choice. Remember that!"

He slewed around again, keeping his balance only by chance, and staggered out of the door. Royance spoke first into the shocked silence.

"Your Majesty, unfortunately, there is much in what he says. Also, he is stirring up a pot of trouble, news of which is already spreading beyond the palace."

She looked at him straightly. "The Rings have refused him once, even at the hour when the King seemed to be dying. Would you have me summon those of possible descent and have a choosing before the Council?"

He shook his head. "There must be truth between us on this matter. Perhaps it will come to that," he said heavily. "There is no other heir—"

"Alas for our country, you are correct, my lord."

She refused to allow herself even to conjecture on an alternative. No, there was no other possible heir in the direct line.

❧

Kasai had volunteered to bring Snolli the dreadful news, and the others concurred gratefully. Only the Spirit Drummer could do this and not risk the worst of Snolli's wrath. Now he knelt uncharacteristically before the High Chief, his head bowed.

"If you have bad news for me, Spirit Drummer, then spit it out," Snolli said.

"It is more dire than you can imagine, Chieftain," Kasai replied. "Obern is dead."

Snolli didn't stir in his chair, though an observant onlooker might have noticed that his fingers tightened on the arms. "Did he die well?"

"Very well, Chieftain. We were attacked by three of those terrible birds we saw once before as we sailed along the Bog-cliffs. Bravely, he drew the wrath of one of them and gave the rest of us time to make our escape."

"I see. Then he will be mourned properly."

"There is further news."

"Another death?"

"No, Chieftain. On our way back to the keep, we met some of the men from the Kingdom, very important men to hear them tell of it. They wait outside. I told them you might be occupied with mourning."

"No, this is not yet time for it. Tell these very important men to come in."

But as the company of a dozen Rendel men entered the chamber that Snolli had set aside as the one where he conducted the business of New Vold, he drew a trembling hand across his eyes. Then he arose, as was proper, and offered the weaponless hand of friendship to the one who, in spite of his youth, seemed to be the leader. All frills and lace and perfume and velvet clothing, the young man touched Snolli's hand with just the tips of his fingers.

"I am Prince Florian of Rendel," the young man said, using the Trader speech that was universally understood. His accent was heavy and more than a little affected; obviously, this was an unfamiliar language to him. "And I am addressing—"

"Snolli, War Lord, Chieftain of New Vold."

Florian smiled. "New Vold, is it? We have long known this fragment of land as Ashenhold. But no matter." He turned and gestured.

One of the men with the Prince stepped forward. "I am Count Dakin, one of Prince Florian's friends. The Prince is not fluent in Trader speech, though he understands it well enough. Therefore, I will speak for him in important matters. We come in peace. As you can see, all swords are fastened with peace ties."

"I knew this before you came through the door. None of my men would have allowed you in without this token of your intent." Snolli allowed himself to smile. "They think to protect me."

"Oh, I have no doubt that you are still a ferocious warrior, for all of your years," Florian said with the carelessness of youth.

Snolli frowned, not bothering to try to hide it. "You must know that you come at a poor time. Under the best of circumstances—which these are not—I have little patience for mincing court manners. Therefore, I must ask you to state your business plainly."

Florian seemed a little taken aback. He looked around, obviously annoyed at the stark room and the lack of comfort, but he swallowed any rash comment he might have made.

Dakin took it up smoothly. "Then, plainly, my Prince's business is this. He seeks a treaty with you. We have common enemies, and as the saying goes, the enemy of my enemy might not be my friend, but in parlous times, that will do just as well."

Snolli's eyebrows rose. "It is worth thinking on, friend Florian. Prince Florian," he corrected himself, noting how the young man's face darkened. The young royal was quick to take offense. That was valuable information to have. "Please forgive a father who is a little addlepated at the moment. My son is newly dead—"

"My sympathies on your great loss," the Prince said.

"How great you cannot know unless you have sons of your own."

"Not that I know of. I am still unwed."

The Prince actually sniggered at his own jape, and several of his men smiled as well. Snolli made sure his own expression did not change.

"Thank you for your understanding," he said. "Please know that a treaty between ourselves and the Kingdom of Rendel is something we desire very much. Excuse us for the moment, though, for before we can work out the terms, we must undergo a period of mourning. If it helps, think of my dead son as a Prince of our kindred—a standing similar to your own position."

Florian couldn't be insulted by this, though Snolli knew he would like to be. Dakin touched Florian's sleeve.

"We can leave the draft of the treaty with these good people and meet with them at another time, when they will not be distracted by sorrow. By then, they will have had time to look over the terms—which they will agree to, of course—and also to prepare a feast for us all. What say you, sir?"

"Oh, very well," Florian said, a trifle peevishly. "Still, it's a long ride back."

"Give your paper to Kasai, here. He is one of my trusted advisers. Baland, who serves as what your people might term our seneschal, will gladly provide you with food and drink, such as we have. We fled our homeland with little more than what was on our backs, and our stores were much depleted on our journey. As you can see, we have not even enough chairs to allow all of you to sit in comfort, nor a table around which to discuss your interesting offer. Still, what is in our power to share, that we gladly offer you."

"You are very gracious," said the man who had spoken for Florian. "And chairs matter not at all to great princes. Thank you—what title should I use for you?"

" 'Chieftain' will do. It is what my people call me."

"Then thank you, Chieftain. We will leave you to your mourning, and will look for a messenger in due time to tell us that our negotiations can be mutually agreed upon."

With a courteous bow, Dakin pulled a roll of paper, tied with red ribbon and heavy with wax and seals, out of a carry-bag and handed it to the Spirit Drummer. Then the men left the audience room, all but shepherding Prince Florian ahead of them.

As the Prince departed, Snolli could hear the youth's somewhat nasal voice raised in complaint. The Trader speech was indeed close to the common tongue used in Rendel. He could pick out a few words, and knew that Florian was unhappy because there was to be no feasting, no drinking, and no opportunity to sample the charms of the Sea-Rover maidens.

Beside him, Kasai spoke up. "I don't need a Spirit Drum to tell me about that one. He is trouble on horseback, Chieftain."

"Nor do I need you or your drum to tell me this, for I knew it from the moment I set eyes on him. Prancing catamite. He is as bad as the stories have him. Worse." Snolli sighed heavily.

"I wonder, too, at why they come seeking treaties from us, when by all right and custom, it should be the other way around. After all, we could be considered intruders here," Kasai said. "You'd think they'd want us gone, rather than offer us the hand of friendship."

"Be that as it may. Sometimes we needs must treat with those we would otherwise despise, and this seems to be one of those times. Furthermore, we have not yet even read the proposed treaty and have no idea of what it contains. It might very well not be to our liking. However, that is a matter for another day. Now. Are the scouts who were with Obern close at hand?"

"Outside, and if it hadn't been for Prince Florian barging in, they would have presented themselves to you long before now."

"Give them food and drink as well, and tell them that I ride with them within the hour. We must bring Obern's body back for a proper burial."

"Yes, Chieftain, though I suggest you wait until morning. Night draws on."

"No, I must go. You will stay here, though. I want you to look over this treaty so that we can discuss it when I return.

Oh—please send a messenger to Neave and tell her the sad news."

Kasai nodded, and left the audience chamber, treaty paper in hand.

It was a very long night for Snolli, and a long ride to the place where the Sea-Rovers could cross over the river into Bog territory. Among the Sea-Rover kindred, it was customary for warriors to have little to do with their children. Snolli hadn't realized until Obern's reported death how fond he was of the youth. Obern had always been there, solid, dependable, reliable—the best backshield any father, let alone a chieftain of Snolli's rank, could hope for. New Vold would be poorer for Obern's absence. He resolved to pay a little more attention to Obern's son, once the child was old enough to be interesting.

But though they searched the place where the attack had come from the giant birds and found the spot where Obern had last been seen, just before he fell, they could not locate a body. Kather volunteered to climb down the cliff-face and search, while the others stood watch to guard him from any renewed attack from the foul Bog-birds that might come. Despite his best efforts, he found nothing.

"There were crushed leaves and broken branches to mark where he fell, but no body. We fear that it has been taken," Kather said, panting, when he had once more regained the top of the cliff. "Some say there are evil things in the Bog that scavenge what they can find—"

"Speak no further," Snolli said, his voice strained. "I will not admit that my son's remains have been eaten by monsters. Let us say instead that he is lost to us now, but that someday we will find him and give him a proper burial."

The search party bowed in agreement, though more than one face in the company bore an expression of skepticism. And in his heart, Snolli knew that what he proposed was naught but mere pretense.

Eighteen

ith **Royance and Florian** departed and her ladies not summoned back into her chamber, Ysa sat thinking hard, tapping one fingernail against her teeth. Though she had rid herself of her son for the moment, none of her worries had lessened. Indeed, if anything, they had magnified.

Yes, she thought, she must turn again to her messenger. She must know if what she only felt was true. The strategy of waiting and watching was not going to serve her in this coil. She sensed that time would not favor her, and she knew she must do whatever was available to her that she might keep abreast of the rush of events. At that moment, she felt that she dared anything—even a betrayal of most of her long-held secrets, if necessary.

She made a hurried trip up the secret stairs to the dizzying height of the tower and sent Visp on its way. Then she returned to her chamber, summoned her ladies, picked up her embroidery once more and settled down to wait.

While she waited, to all intents serene and untroubled over anything more serious than the selection of a color of thread for her needle, she pondered far more weighty matters. That brief episode between the Lady Marcala and Royance—Ysa could tell that this was not fated to be an isolated incident. Also, she knew that Marcala was not entirely averse to the attentions she was sure to attract at court. That must be remedied.

Ysa had long before determined to work a spell to ensure that Harous was attracted to Marcala. It would be only prudent to secretly include a little magical extra to cause Marcala to be equally attracted to Harous, to the exclusion of anyone else. Forestalling problems, Ysa knew, was much better than solving them once they had arisen.

Pleading fatigue, the Queen dismissed her ladies and ordered a hearty dinner brought to her chamber. When the maid had set the tray on the table and started to leave, Ysa stopped her. "Where is the Lady Marcala?" she asked.

"Downstairs, in the dining hall, Your Majesty," the girl replied, a little disconcerted. Ysa had never spoken to her before.

"Go to her and tell her that I wish to speak with her before she retires. Say, at the eleventh hour."

"Yes, Your Majesty," the girl said, dropping a deep curtsy. Then she went to do as she was bid.

When Ysa had finished all the food on her tray, she made her way once more up the steep, secret stairs. By now, Visp must have returned. And indeed, the flyer came through the window almost before Ysa's breath had returned to her from the strenuous climb.

She put out her hand and Visp landed on it. She gazed into the creature's eyes and began to see what it had learned on its flight.

Indeed, events had marched even more swiftly than she could have imagined. Her heart began to pound.

So. Those Sea-Rovers who had taken the Ashenkeep for their own were on the move also? Ysa watched them venture on the broken trail of the clifftop. And also she saw others, men from the Kingdom, and recognized Harous. Then—danger! From overhead! Involuntarily, she flinched. With Visp, she flew high and invisible, away from claw and talon.

Though she had never before sighted the giant birds that infested the Bog-cliffs, she had heard of them and knew just what a danger they could be. More than one trading ship, sailing in those unfriendly waters, had reported attacks.

She knew when Visp went invisible, for the colors faded. She understood; once before, the flyer had been in peril from creatures that far outmatched it in strength and ruthlessness. Ysa watched through Visp's eyes as one of the huge birds concentrated its attack on a man who could only be the leader of the keep force. And she watched him fall.

He must be dead. This could be an aid. At the least, it would be a warning to those adventurers to stay far away from Bogland. An alliance there— No, it must not happen.

She started to turn away, to end the connection, but there was more. What else, Ysa wondered, a little dazed, could there be after the propitious moment of the fall of the seaman? For a moment, she was dizzied by a rapid spin of one vista after another. She saw movement at the dark edge of the cliff break.

The creature who was her eyes wheeled down and down until the Queen might be standing on a level with a woman. No, she was little more than a girl. With a chill in her soul, Ysa recognized her as the one who had nurtured the flyer when it had been knocked from the sky by a mysterious surge of power.

Come away, she instructed Visp urgently. But that was foolish. She was not seeing contemporary events, only the remembered ones. And, she sensed, the flyer felt a certain affection for the girl, regardless of its obligation to herself. Ysa closed her lips firmly and let what the flyer brought her unfold. Even here, unwanted and unwelcome though it might be, was knowledge. The first glimpse of the girl, when she had been tending the downed flyer, had not been enough to do much more than confuse Ysa with the possibility that Alditha still lived. This girl was much too young to be Alditha, though she could surely be of Alditha's blood.

Ysa drew a deep breath. *Whoever she was, this person had power of a sort.*

Power answered to power; there was no denying that. But what touched her through the strained method of this oblique meeting was something she could not name or understand. It flowed from a source other than those ancient books and rituals that were her own fount of learning. Untaught and undeveloped, nevertheless it was there.

Then, some movement, some glimpse of features—Ysa's lips shaped as if she would spit and cause her spittle to somehow reach that girl. The Queen cursed herself for a fool, for having hidden the truth from herself, hoping it was not so.

She watched—she had to—the dim picture unfold. One who should never have lived sought and found the fallen Sea-Rover, tended him with the surety of one who had a healer's training. And as she watched, she ground her teeth with fury. Why hadn't the wench died according to plan? And why hadn't the leader of the intruders from the Ashenkeep died as well?

Queen Ysa stopped her teeth from chattering with an effort of will. Outlanders were prey in the Bog; all knew that. Then how—

No, she told herself firmly. Her nerves were playing tricks on her. With equal resolve, she faced what must be the truth. Alditha was surely dead, long ago. Could this be Alditha's daughter? With growing certainty, Ysa knew that this was who the girl must be. Bastard if so, and no clear claim to anything but a fast death if discovered.

Ashenkin had disowned Alditha for her folly in companying with a man, his identity unknown, without being wed. And because of her, they had been brought down. Ysa grimaced. Yes, the House of Ash had fallen and she, the Queen, had had a strong hand in its fall. She knew that those who wore the Ash badge would not have shielded Alditha had she reached them. But who in the Bog would have offered her refuge? And the child—how had she survived all these years in the Bog?

Now Ysa's grimace became the stronger. What of that other power she had long sensed rooted there? An enemy? Was this bastard a tool, held against a day when she might be used against the Queen by that opponent? The very fact that the wench had survived in a place where death was all but automatic meant that someone of outstanding authority had decreed that she live on.

That, or she was one of the Bog-folk, at least in part. How else could she have been accepted by them and allowed to live— that slut, that abomination? It was the only explanation as to why she could move freely about as she did while Ysa watched her through Visp's eyes. Ysa almost wished she had seen more than the girl's face. It must have sat, incongruously, above a stunted Bog-woman's body, the Ash connection plain only as far as the neck.

So. It had been the wench's misshapen hands that tended the flyer after it had been downed by that strange stroke of power. The girl's doing? No, she thought not. She herself had had to strive for years to learn what she now knew. This girl . . . Ysa summed up the years. Sixteen. Yes, sixteen. A child—a stupid bastard child!

Would the girl be able to accept help and return the injured man from the keep to his own? It was bad enough to risk alliance between the newcomers and Bog-men, but to have such a grotesque one as this outcast make a common bond with them— that could prove to be a failure, dire failure, of all she had fought for during these years past. Ysa fancied she could feel the Rings grow a little looser on her fingers, as if they foresaw a time to leave her flesh and bones for those on another.

No!

A sudden curtain of darkness fell, and she knew that Visp had been released from her control. Ysa could no longer see beyond her present time and place. She gave the flyer some food and settled it into its silk-covered shelter. Then, falling back against the support of her chair, she stared at the wall—a wall on which she could suddenly picture peopled by one dire happening and enemy after another.

Harous had gone hunting along Bog borders. Did he know of or even wonder about this girl's existence? That worry, at least, could be laid to rest. He had been a child, not of an age to be at court, when Alditha's embarrassment was being whispered about behind hands. And how much of that strange power did the abomination possess? Ysa must learn. She willed herself to patience. Now that she knew what direction she must search for the knowledge she needed, she could afford not to be hasty. In fact, haste was her worst enemy.

There was another matter at hand, and what she would do now needed other aids. She pulled herself wearily from her chair. Once more she must descend, and then re-climb, those steep stairs.

The Lady Marcala was waiting for her. "Come with me," Ysa said without formality. "I propose to accomplish some arcane matters, and I must needs draw upon your strength."

"It is yours to command, Majesty," Marcala said. Without further comment, she followed the Queen up the stairs to the tower room.

Ysa opened a book on the table to the place she had marked. "Stand behind me, with your hands resting on my shoulders," she told Marcala. "Your strength will flow into me at need."

The younger woman did as she was told. Ysa began to read aloud, but softly, from the book. Some of the things she might do this night held deadly peril. She had read, she believed she had understood, but she had never put that understanding to the proof.

Mist began to gather above the table, as if a window were opening to another world. Ysa glanced quickly over her shoulder, but the look on Marcala's face told her that her assistant did not see the blurred spot in the air. Emboldened, the Queen read on, louder, and then with a sudden, soundless *bang!* she found herself in what looked to be a cave. In the center of the cave writhed a pillar of fire, and captured within that pillar stood a Bog-woman.

No—not a Bog-woman, but similar. This one was ancient without being old, and her bearing even in captivity spoke of the kind of power Ysa understood.

"You are here. Help me," the crone said. She held out her hand for Ysa to take.

The Queen hesitated. "Who are you?"

"The one you were sent to aid. My name is Zazar."

Zazar! For a moment, Ysa only stared, uncomprehendingly, at the legendary figure.

"Well, what are you waiting for?" Zazar said impatiently.

Reluctantly, Ysa reached out one of her slender, manicured hands toward the crone's rough, wrinkled one. But before she could touch it, another noiseless explosion deposited into the cave the young woman Ysa had seen earlier. She did not look as Ysa imagined; the spell must have put a glamour on her, so that she appeared fully human.

"Zazar!" the girl exclaimed.

"I should have known it would take both of you," Zazar said, as unconcerned as if what was transpiring were commonplace. As far as Ysa knew, perhaps it was. "Well, come on then." Zazar held out her other hand.

The girl took it without hesitation, and after a moment, Ysa took the one that had been proffered to her. As casually as though she were stepping from a boat onto dry land, Zazar moved out of the fire and it died behind her.

"I suppose you should know each other's name, since you are going to meet in the outside world sooner or later. Ysa, this is Ashen. Ashen, this is Ysa."

Then the cave and its inhabitants blinked out and Ysa staggered back into Marcala's arms. "What happened?" she asked shakily.

"Nothing," Marcala said, puzzled. "You were reading, and then you stopped, and then you nearly fell. I caught you."

"No more than that?"

"Should there have been?"

"Of course not. No. Nothing."

"Are you all right?"

Ysa gingerly tested her limbs. They were weak and shaky, more so than she had ever experienced before. She knew that her spell-casting had had far-reaching results beyond what she knew, or was likely to know. Something sour rose in the back of her throat. "I must sit down. I feel ill."

"Can you make it down the secret stairs?"

"I don't think so. Please use the main stairway and send servants to help me. I must get me to bed."

※

Ashen had chosen to climb the way up over the clifftop, for no one could descend it in any safety. On the other side of the ridge it proved much easier to go down than it looked. Then she became aware that the steady beat of the sea was being overborne by the sounds of screeches and shouts—the latter from human throats. She quickly went to such cover as she could find, at the base of a tall outcropping that might have been set there as a signal for those out on the sea.

She quickly discovered that she was not the only one to take to this rough sky road. Coming from the south was a party of four who, by their clothing and armor, appeared to be Outlanders. Panic rose, blocking her throat. Was the man she had followed here one of that company?

Whoever they were, they were being besieged. The birds had already attacked them before she reached her perch. She was just in time to see that one of the men had lost his balance as a result of that attack. As he fell, she noticed that two glittering objects also fell, though in different directions. Ashen had no idea of what they might be, and she knew there was no aid for the man. His body was over the cliff rim and down, not toward the sea, but on the Bog side.

He had disappeared into a clump of tall, reedy ferns and lay at, or close to, the foot of the cliff. All she could see from her position was an outflung arm. Some distance away, one of the bright things that had glittered in falling caught the light. A weapon he had carried? Those with him could offer no aid, for the birds were in full attack. The three left in the party separated and withdrew to hunt what cover they might as they defended themselves. One man stood up to use a weapon of a sort that Ashen had never before seen. He held a bent stick with a string taut between its two ends, and another smaller stick pressed against the string. He pulled string and stick back and let go, and the small stick lodged in the base of the long throat of one of the screeching birds. It fluttered down almost over Ashen's head in a losing attempt to remain aloft, and she watched it disappear into the waves below.

The other birds seemed to realize their danger and broke off the attack. After a time of fruitless searching for the comrade who had fallen, the men gave up and left. Ashen realized that the ferns hid the body entirely from view except from this one spot where she herself lay hidden. She realized also that she had far less-proper weapons to defend her own refuge if the birds should return. There was nothing to be done but to go back through that passage inside the cliff and strive to find a safe way of returning to the Bog.

As she retraced her earlier path, she thought about those men. They were certainly Outlanders, and since the man she trailed was clearly one also, it must be that he was from the same place. It had been a very long time since the outer world had striven to enter the Bog. What was the reason for the appearance of an armed party now?

She could still hear the birds' screeching as she emerged from the fissure. Dropping her pack, she wriggled forward as close to the edge as she dared. There was no way to view the clifftop from the lower position, nor could she sight where the Outlander had fallen. At least the birds did not seem to have spotted her when aloft, and there might be only a long wait before her until she could seek cover in the Bog.

The sounds of the battle were still loud. She realized that the birds had merely shifted the focus of their attack and now those fierce shrieks were challenged by a different means of defense. A drum was sounding, but this was not the raucous rhythm of the warning Bog-drums. Ashen clasped her hands to her ears. The sound struck into her as it must be assaulting the birds, touching some sensitive place. And on her breast, her amulet, though not a guide, showed a spark of awakening color.

No normal beat was this, and while it had been low and only half audible in beginning, it now seemed to fill the entire Bog-world. There was a last burst of screeching from the huge birds and then it seemed that all sound died away. At last Ashen could venture to take her hands from her ears. The drum was still sounding but softly, and not as body-shaking as it had been. The screeching had ended as if the birds had been wiped from the sky into nothingness.

Greatly daring, Ashen crept outside the aperture and a little way up the cliff-face. She still could not see the battle site above, but now, except for the continued beat of that rhythm, there was no other sound. The beat began to grow fainter, and she felt a release of the strange uneasiness it had awakened in her. Something shimmered in the air just ahead of her, but when she tried to see what it was, the shimmer vanished.

She lay down where she was, listening intently. There were no more bird cries; the drone of the drum had faded. At last she felt it safe to make her move. She crept to the top of the cliff. The men, the birds—and the drum—were all vanished.

Good. Ashen dragged her pack to where she crouched. She took out a length of vine rope, closed the pack, and attached the line to it. Carefully she worked it over the edge and let it fall into the open, keeping a good grip on the rope until it paid itself out. Below, she saw the pack turning slowly, close to the rise of rubble skirting the base of the cliff. Guiding the burden closer to the barrier, she loosed it, and it landed easily. Then she began to climb down after it.

Still she listened warily but heard no bird call as she set foot on the Bog-land. The thud of the drum had become only a faint murmur in the distance.

Ashen re-coiled her rope and stowed it away. She shouldered her pack and as she did so, took her bearings in relation to where the man had fallen, near where the river ran loud, rushing into the sea.

There was nothing to do for the Outlander. Surely he was dead. She had sealed the amulet to the land entrance of Zazar's island. To return as speedily as possible was surely all one could do—

As she moved, she thought of the place, sighted from above, where the growth hid the body of the invader.

Undoubtedly he was dead.

Prudently, she decided to retrace her earlier trail. Still, when she chose her way, she headed in a different direction. Twice she had to delve deeper into the Bog-ways to locate a path. Now and again she glanced toward the clifftops, but as far as she could see, there was neither bird nor Outlander to mark her.

Unexpectedly, she found one of the things the man had dropped. It was metal, long and deadly, and she recognized a kind of knife, superior to any she had ever before seen. Though unschooled in the use of such a weapon, she fastened it to her pack, where it would be out of the way, and took it with her.

Then she reached the place where the man had fallen. His arm, thrust from the edge of the torn and tangled reed ferns, still lay as unmoving as when she had first sighted it. It would not take long for the scavengers of the Bog to light upon the body. Teeth and claws would strip away flesh, then crush the bones. Eventually, there would be no trace.

Ashen swallowed. No kin of hers lay here. Should it matter what became of an unknown intruder? Even his own kin had not been able to aid him.

Unbidden, a thought came to her mind: What if she had gone immediately to aid Kazi? Would the woman still be alive?

Slowly she approached the place where the man lay. What if he were not dead, only injured? Ashen's hand went to the hilt of her belt knife. To lie helpless when the eaters came—

She pushed aside the battered reeds and now she could see him plainly. The other bright thing must have been the protective covering he had worn on his head. It was gone, and a sticky patch of blood had matted hair that was almost as bright as those round pieces of polished metal Zazar kept carefully among her personal possessions and that Ashen knew were an important part of life in the Outlands. The locks so exposed were not as red as a flame nor as yellow as marshroot, but held something of each color.

Something awakened her healer's notice. Ashen squatted down on her heels and shifted her pack from her shoulders. She leaned forward and gently touched the man's hand. It was not cold as she had expected, but warm. Could it be that he still lived? He had certainly fallen far enough to have been fatally wounded, but the soft, ferny growth must have cradled him from greater injury.

Now her touch moved swiftly, her fingers finding their way above the collaring edge of his flexible metal shirt to locate the pulse of life. It was steady. Perhaps fortune had favored him after all and his hurts might be tended. Suppose he could be taken care of until his companions returned? But as he lay now he was helpless Bog-bait and she could not defend him.

Nevertheless, Ashen went to work as if this were some Bog-man whose clan had called for her aid. She worked swiftly but steadily with what aids she carried, making sure the proper step had been taken before she went to the next.

One of the bones in his forearm was broken and she could not free it from the metal garment he wore. But she could bind it so that any move he might make would bring no further harm.

Now that she had rolled him on his back, she could see his face clearly. She worked with a pad of moss sodden with one of Zazar's potions to cleanse and examine the head wound. When she touched it, he moaned faintly but did not open his eyes.

Indeed he *was* different from the murderous Outlander she had trailed here. This one was younger than the other, she decided. She found it pleasing to look upon the face she had wiped free of blood. Of what clan was he—or, being an Outlander, of what Family? She finished bandaging his head, tore up a mass of leaves and pillowed him on it. Could she now get some restorative into him? She was growing increasingly uneasy. To linger here with the scent of blood ever present was risky. What—

His eyes opened and he stared up at her. It was as if he could not see her, but searched beyond for some face or familiar surroundings. He spoke, his voice quavering a little, though his words had no meaning for her. This must be speech common to his kind. She started to put her hand on him, but did not complete the gesture. They were strangers to each other. How could she offer him any soothing heal-touch?

He was still staring about him. He looked past and through Ashen as if she were invisible, but his voice had steadied and taken on a demanding note. If he questioned now, he received no answer.

Ashen searched in her pack again and took out a small clay bottle, well wrapped in shielding moss. Taking the stopper from it, she determinedly raised his head and put the bottle to his lips. He swallowed without protest. This time when he looked up, he appeared to see Ashen. There was a slight frown on his face, as if she were very strange to him.

"You are hurt." She spoke slowly, giving room between each word for him to comprehend, if he was able. "Lie still. Rest."

His frown grew deeper. He tried to move his head and then groaned and closed his eyes again, not to reopen them. She sat still. It would seem that she must see him to some place of safety—but where did such exist, and how could she get him there?

Nineteen

In the still, deep hours of the night, Snolli sent for Kasai. He came quickly to the Chieftain's bidding, knowing that something dire must be eating at Snolli for him not to wait until morning.

"I am here," he said as he entered.

Snolli sat close to the fire. He glanced up at the Spirit Drummer's words. His face was drawn and haggard, and he looked like someone who has witnessed that which no man should ever see. "I want you to perform a drum spell to find Obern," he said. "I will not rest until his body has been found and buried decently. His spirit will haunt me forever if he is eaten by fell creatures in the Bale-Bog."

Kasai nodded. "The matter has been weighing on me as well, Chieftain," he said. "I have been disturbed enough that I could not give my full attention to the treaty from the Rendelian Prince. And yet there is something we do not know about Obern's disappearance—"

"We know that he was attacked and fell, and that despite our searching, we could not find him. What more do we need to know? It is time to use the Spirit Drum."

The drummer took his instrument, never far from his hand, and began to whisper his fingers across the surface. He searched, he probed, he sent out tendrils of thought—

—and found Obern.

"He is alive, Chieftain," the small man told Snolli. "He is not unharmed, to be sure, but he lives."

The leader of the Sea-Rovers merely nodded, but Kasai knew he was keeping his face impassive only by great effort. "What else?"

"I will try to See for you, Chieftain, though these are perilous waters to navigate. He is under the protection of some mysterious power, something I have never before encountered."

"Because I am your Chieftain, and for whatever love you bear me, See what you can, Spirit Drummer. I must know."

Obediently, Kasai began moving his fingers across the surface of his drum again. The whisper of sound drew him inexorably into a spell not entirely of his own making, a place where time and the constraints of the world meant little. Tonelessly, he began to sing in droning counterpoint to the drum. "He lies now in a woodsy bed, and a woman comes. Someone protects him—"

"The woman?" Snolli clapped his hand over his mouth, knowing that he must not interrupt the Spirit Drummer when he was in such a state.

But Kasai was deep enough into the dream that he was not disturbed. "Protects, protects, I know not who or where. Soon he will lie in a house not a house, in a city not a city, in a land not a land. Someone seeks him. A man of light, followed by men of darkness."

"But he is safe?"

"Safe enough. For now. But what is to come— The man of light is not his friend."

*

Ashen had to face the possibility that the man she was tending just might be the one who had murdered Kazi. There were certain differences—the flexible metal garment, for example. This man wore no covering over it, though that might not mean anything. Curious, she examined the metal shirt. It was not a tunic, for it crossed in front and was held in place by a wide leather belt. Its flexibility came from the myriad small rings woven in and around and over themselves. It was armor, not the shell-strengthened leg shields she was familiar with, but armor nonetheless. The shirt, Ashen understood at once, would provide good protection even from knives and spears. Or even from the kind of long metal weapon she had rescued from the underbrush.

The man moaned. He was waking up again. This spot, at the base of the cliffs, was no place to linger. Perhaps with her help, he could walk. With luck, they could get back to Ashen's refuge in the building on the isle. There, they would be safe.

She was very glad that she had set her guide for the island. Perhaps her way back would be easier.

"Come, stranger, we must go where I can tend you better," she said to the man.

He looked up at her uncomprehendingly, but she did not believe that he did not understand her words. Rather, his eyes were more those of a child. It must be the head wound; it had knocked all the sense out of him, at least for the time.

"You will be yourself again soon, but you must come with me." So saying, she took the man's hand and helped him to his feet. He obeyed without protest and she was relieved that in his present childlike state, he would follow her.

But when she attempted to locate an easier path back to the isle, she met with disappointment. Everywhere but along the route she had come she encountered impassable tangles of vegetation, dank pools, and the kind of footing that would drag both down to be seen never again. Sighing, she turned back and began retracing her steps. How she would manage when she returned to the pool with the stepping-stones across it, she did not know.

With her aid, the man gained the relatively high ground from which she had spotted the fissure in the rock beside the swallow-hole where the barrier river emptied.

"That way," she told him, pointing.

He nodded; this was a good sign, the first indication that he might recover. He must be strong as well as—she had to admit it to herself—handsome. He was the most handsome man she had ever seen. But then, she told herself, he was also the only Outlander man she had ever seen clearly. She found herself hoping that he was not the one who had murdered Kazi. She didn't know what she would do if she learned that it was he who had done such a foul deed.

They walked on, with the barrier river to their right. Ashen consulted her guide now and then for the signal to turn back toward the Bale-Bog, toward the island. Then a movement caught her eye. Immediately she crouched behind an outcrop of the reedy fern that grew so plentiful in the Bog, and pulled her companion down with her. She put her finger to her lips, signaling him to be silent, and he obeyed.

Someone was wading across what must be a shallow place in the river's bed. Cautiously, Ashen raised her head until she could part the ferns and see without much danger of being detected.

She almost cried out. *This* was the one whom she had seen before. No mistaking the bright metal garment, the colorful cloth covering, the light surrounding him, the mist about his head. Several men, similarly clad, followed him.

A chill went over Ashen, coupled with immense relief. The man she was succoring, then, was not the one who had killed Kazi. She turned and, impulsively, squeezed his hand. He looked at her with wide, uncomprehending eyes, but returned the pressure.

Ashen's relief turned to near panic. Why was this man, this killer, coming back into the Bale-Bog? What could his errand be this time? And what if he picked up her trail? She watched until he and his followers disappeared into the undergrowth. If luck was with her, he would take a direction different from the one in which she wanted to go. And if he did venture in that direction, his path dictated by the land itself even as hers was, the interlopers might make enough noise that she could trail them and yet be safe. After all, staying behind them was the best way to keep the Outlander and his followers from creeping up on her and the injured man, whom she was more than ever determined to nurse back to health.

❦

Queen Ysa had lain abed for a week, too ill to rise. Master Lorgan, the chief physician, had tried several remedies, to no avail. Finally, she sent him away, stating that time alone would cure her.

Now she wearily dragged herself from her bed and, to lighten her spirits as much as possible, dressed in her favorite gown—deep green taffeta, with a creamy-white underdress heavy with lace and embroidery. A glance into her mirror told her that despite her fatigue, her appearance had not suffered greatly from the activities of that dreadful night. But her hunger—though she had eaten enormous amounts of food all through the time of her illness, she was still ravenous! Anxiously, she examined her image once more, this time for signs of impending obesity. She found none; indeed, she might even be a little thinner than before she had wrought—whatever it was that had put her into contact with the Bog-witch Zazar and the bastard child of her hated rival. She could not bring herself to say the girl's name, not even to herself.

She gave orders for her breakfast to be brought to her. When the tray arrived, she ate everything on it, even the last drops of the cream for her porridge, laced with honey and spices, and wiped the bowl with a fragment of bread.

She knew she must go to check on the King. Who knew how much his condition might have deteriorated while she lay ill? She did not look forward to the meeting. If it still had not been morning, she might have fortified herself with wine beforehand.

For the first time, Queen Ysa had a glimmer of understanding of both her husband and her son, but this insight brought only contempt in its wake.

Let them indulge weaknesses, she thought scornfully. She, Ysa, Queen of Rendel, First Priestess of Santize, was stronger than either or both of them. No mere accident, no backlash of magic, would be enough to halt her. Not for long, anyway.

She checked to see that her toilette was complete, and her appearance enough to still any wagging tongues who would have it that she was sickly and incompetent, her Regency, therefore, likely to be set aside in Florian's favor. One more touch. Perfume. Her hand lingered over her favorite spicy scent, and then she changed her mind. She selected one that Boroth had given her long ago, its aroma reminiscent of aldyce flowers. She had never cared for it, but he always liked it. Perhaps if she wore it again, his mood would be lighter than it had been the last time she had seen him. Then she swept out the door of her chambers toward Boroth's suite, at the opposite wing of the castle.

The usual complement of hangers-on, vultures watching to mark the exact moment when the King would die, the physicians and the servants, filled the chamber. They had begun almost to live there, Ysa noted, having their meals brought to them so they would not miss a moment of what was happening to the King of Rendel. Master Lorgan glanced up, and his face lit in a smile.

"You have proved yourself a better healer than I," he said. His voice held a note of what seemed to be genuine pleasure. "But I am sure that our sovereign lord has missed your presence. Please, come and gladden his spirits as your appearance gladdens ours."

With a bow, the physician indicated the bed where Boroth lay, his eyes closed. He had on a fresh nightgown, and a basin of water sat on a table nearby, indicating that the King had been newly bathed and tended. He seemed almost in a coma, and his breaths came thickly.

"The King sleeps?" Ysa asked.

"He rests. I think the number of people in his chamber wearies him."

"Then send them away," she said, pitching her voice loud enough to be heard. She glanced around imperiously. "Know you not that you burden the King with your presence?"

Reluctantly, the company began to depart. When all were on their way toward the door and only Master Lorgan, his chief assistant, and the King's body-servants remained, she approached the dais on which the great bed stood. She bent over Boroth and as she did, a cloud of perfume enveloped them both.

He opened his eyes and gazed at her unseeingly. Then his loose lips curved upward in a faint smile. He took a deep, clear breath and spoke. "Alditha. Alditha, my love. You have returned to me again. I have missed you."

Shocked beyond measure, Ysa recoiled. With an enormous effort, she regained command over herself. Distasteful as it was, Boroth's current confusion might lead him to reveal important and useful information if she were adroit. That his thoughts were muddled was only to be expected, considering his physical condition. But what had caused him to confuse her, his lawful Queen, with that hateful Ash whore? What was different this time from many times before? Then all at once she understood. The perfume. It must have been *her* scent. Of course. Aldyce flowers were blue, the Ash color. And Boroth had given it to her, to Ysa, perhaps to remind him in the night. . . .

She resisted an impulse to snatch the sponge from the basin and scrub the hateful stench from her skin.

She made herself approach the bedside again, and even to speak to him in a low, sweet voice. "Yes, it is I, your beloved," she told Boroth. She leaned over to kiss his forehead, making sure that he breathed the scent of the perfume again.

"It has been a long time since you were with me. Why were you gone so long?" he asked.

"I am returned. Have you—have you any message for me?"

"Only that I love you. And will forever. Oh, if I had but met you first—"

"And?" Ysa prompted. The word almost stuck in her throat. There had been more between them, Boroth and Alditha, than a mere tumble in the bed for Boroth's swinish pleasure. She pushed the thought aside. Later, she would think of it. "Yes?"

"How different all would be. But I tried to protect you. You know that, don't you."

"Of course. I fled your jealous wrath—"

"Never!" He roused himself a little. "You went pursued, yes, but not by me. Have you forgotten?" Then he opened his eyes wider, and a certain focus seemed to come into them. He stared at her, recognizing her at last. "Ysa," he said, with a world of bitterness laced into the word.

"Yes, it is I, Ysa, your Queen," she returned with equal bitterness. "And by law, your rightful wife. Your beloved, and not that harlot you coupled with, almost in my face."

Boroth did not answer, but merely closed his eyes and turned his head on the pillow.

Biting down her impulse to leave him as she found him, Ysa nevertheless summoned the will to perform the ritual of the Rings. Then she all but fled the room, her fatigue and illness forgotten in her rush to return to her chambers and destroy every drop of the hated scent that had brought Boroth out of his stupor.

How they had managed to make it back to the ruins on the island, Ashen could not have told. Partly, she put it down to the mysterious Outlanders' choice of another path, heading north, which allowed her to lead her charge more quickly to the place she had come to think of as a refuge. It was well past midday by the time the two of them stumbled into the chambers. The fire had gone out, and it was dank and cheerless within.

She settled him onto a pile of reed mats. Then she found

more of the black stones, lit a fire, and when she was certain it was taking the worst of the chill from the air, began to loosen his clothing. Surely the woven metal shirt must be uncomfortable to lie upon. She got it off by unbuckling the belt and easing the garment out from under him. Then she folded it and laid it aside together with his long knife. Quickly she splinted the broken arm.

His boots were another matter. There must be some trick to removing them, and she did not know it. Reluctantly, she had to leave them on him, knowing that his feet were likely to be numb in the morning. To her delight, Weyse came out of the shadows. The little creature had obviously been waiting for her here in the refuse and now hovered nearby, sitting on her haunches and rubbing her paws together. Then she came closer and began sniffing at the man's head wound.

"Let me clean it properly," Ashen told her.

She began rummaging through the pack, drawing out packets of herbs. Then she gathered some water in a pot, added a pinch of this and a palmful of that to the water, and set it on to heat. When the mixture had steeped long enough, Ashen dipped a cloth in it and began to wipe away the blood that matted the Outlander's reddish-gold hair. To her relief, she found that the wound itself was not deep—head wounds, she reminded herself, always bled freely—though there was a lump on the man's forehead the size of a vorse egg. Almost before she had finished, Weyse waddled up to squat beside the man and examine the lump with her paws. Her touch was so gentle that he didn't even moan, though he had protested feebly while Ashen was cleaning the cut.

"I do think he will be all right," she told Weyse. She wrapped a strip of clean cloth around the man's head. Then she emptied the pot of the herbal mixture and filled it again with water, preparatory to brewing a strengthening broth. When it was done, she gave it to the man and he drank it, after which he fell into a deep sleep.

Tired from her exertions and the strain of trying to avoid the other Outlanders, Ashen lay down upon another pile of mats. Perhaps she could sleep for an hour. She was too tired to eat, though she did give Weyse some of the trail mixture the little creature loved. Ashen held out her arms, hoping Weyse would come and warm her as she had done before, but Weyse appeared determined to hover near the Outlander.

"Very well," Ashen murmured sleepily. "You tend him now, and I'll take care of him presently." Then she pulled a reed covering over herself and fell asleep.

She awoke abruptly to the sound of a man's voice, raised in what was surely anger.

It was the Outlander, fighting free of the reed mats that he had obviously disturbed in a restless sleep. He tore the bandage loose from his head, stared at it, and flung it away. He pointed his finger at Ashen and shouted something at her. She could understand perhaps one word in three, but grasped that he held her responsible for his injury.

"No, no, it was not I!" she said. She scrambled up from her own mats and started toward him. "You fell—"

But he was already dashing toward the door and into the deep twilight as fast as he could go. By his gait, she knew that true to her prediction, his feet were numb and without feeling. She followed and caught up with him just in time to see him climb up onto the top of a ruined wall. He took a step forward. One of the stones shifted, and to Ashen's horror, he fell. She heard a dull *thunk!* as his head hit another stone.

Certain that this time he had killed himself, she ran to him. "He still breathes," she said, as much to herself as to Weyse, who had bounded after her.

Necessity lent her strength. Somehow she managed to drag him back to the sheltered room again. There she stirred up the fire and examined the wound on his head. The herbal mixture had started the healing well, and by chance, he had not re-opened the cut when he fell. Also, the splint was intact. But there was another, even larger, lump on the side of his head where he had struck it on the rock. His lips were bluish and his breathing slightly labored.

If only Zazar were here, Ashen thought. She would know what to do.

She tended the man as best she could until far into the night. Then, despairing and certain that he was in danger of dying before morning, she decided on a risky action. If Zazar would not come to her, then she would go to Zazar.

For the first time in her life, Ashen deliberately chose to invoke magic. Using ingredients at hand and others she identified by smell from various jars on the shelves, she stirred together a mixture such as she had seen Zazar use on rare occasions and dissolved it in water from the pipe. Then, hoping she had done it right, she drank the potion.

The room around her dissolved and when she could see again, it was by the light of a pillar of fire, in which stood Zazar.

"Zazar!" Ashen exclaimed, astonished. How could this be? Zazar seemed unable to move. She should have been writhing in agony from the flames, yet she appeared only a little exasperated.

"I should have known it would take both of you," Zazar said. Only then did Ashen notice that another woman was with them, a woman dressed in the most beautiful, lustrous clothing she had ever beheld. Ashen could only stare in wonderment. "Well, come on then." Zazar held out one hand to her and the other to the beautiful stranger.

The girl took it without hesitation and after a moment, the woman took the other. Then Zazar stepped out of the fire and it died behind her.

"I suppose you should know each other's name, since you are going to meet in the outside world sooner or later. Ysa, this is Ashen. Ashen, this is Ysa."

Before Ashen could tell Zazar of her need, and of the reason for her trying to contact the Wysen-wyf, she was back in the ruined house on the island.

To her astonishment, the man had awakened and was now trying feebly to sit up. She rushed to him. "No, you mustn't. It's too soon."

He looked at her clear-eyed. Though it had undoubtedly brought him close to the edge of death, the second blow to the head seemed to have had the effect of restoring his senses. Then he spoke, and again Ashen could understand enough of his words to know his meaning. "Did you hit me?" he asked. Gingerly he touched the rapidly healing cut on his forehead and the big lump on the side of his head.

She laughed, surprised that she could. "No. I saved you." With the use of pantomime and by repeating words over and over until he understood them, she got him to understand the circumstances of his fall over the cliff.

"Ah. The birds' attack. Yes, I remember now. I thought I was dead."

"You nearly finished the job on yourself when you fell again, just a little while ago."

"I didn't know where I was. And you were just sitting there, unmoving."

"Yes." Ashen decided not to try to explain these circumstances to him. Later, perhaps. "I am Ashen," she said, pointing to herself. She looked around, hoping to find Weyse, but the little creature had disappeared.

"Obern," the man said, likewise indicating himself. "Do you live here?"

It seemed simpler to agree than to explain the circumstances that had brought her to this place. "Yes."

"I am from the Sea-Rovers. I must go home, for my father must think me dead by now."

She had no idea of where his "home" was. They sat there for

a moment, Ashen feeling a little foolish and wondering what to do next.

That question was answered by a commotion from outside. She looked up and saw a flickering light on the door-curtain. "Wait here," she said to Obern. She followed the words with a gesture, in case he did not understand. He nodded.

Cautiously, she went to the doorway and pulled the curtain back a little. The light still shone, but it seemed far away. Still wary, Ashen stepped just outside and looked from side to side. When she saw nothing, she took another step.

With a rustling noise, something fell over her head and the sheer weight of it bore her to the ground. She recognized a net, but one much heavier than any the Bog-folk could make. Still, she fought to get free of it. Two men came forward and whipped ropes around her, binding her firmly.

Then someone walked into her area of vision. "Caught you at last, Bog-sprite," the man said. His face was hidden by mist but even if it had not been, she would have recognized him as the one whose face she could not see, back at that dreadful place where Kazi had died. "You, Ralse, see if anybody is inside."

"No, there is nobody there!" Ashen cried. But they entered the room anyway, and presently they returned with Obern, bound as she was. Then their captors carried them to the familiar landing place, where a raft awaited. The men tossed both onto the raft, which they began to pole away from the island.

Twenty

The Lady Marcala felt pleased with herself. Not only had her ruse fooled everyone at the court in Rendelsham, but also Harous now seemed to be completely enthralled with her. And there was no doubt about it; Harous was the most attractive, most desirable noble at court. She had been staying in his residence in the city, and was now seriously considering his offer to be his guest at Cragden Keep. There was, she knew, nothing the least bit improper about such an invitation; after all, Marcala was his distant kinswoman. Such arrangements were commonplace among kindred.

Of course, if their relationship should wax and grow warmer, there was nothing to prevent them from evading the servants' eyes and discovering, privately, where such tender feelings might lead. That kind of arrangement, as well, was commonplace.

And also, she thought, she would be fulfilling her obligation to the Queen. That one was walking danger. It always paid to be on her safe side. Therefore, with such good reasons in favor and none in opposition, Marcala decided she would accept Harous's kind offer. The Queen would want to know.

On her way to Ysa's chambers, to Marcala's displeasure, she

encountered Prince Florian. At least he didn't seem quite as drunk as he usually was. This, however, had no beneficial effect on his manners, she noted.

"Well, lovely lady." He stepped in front of her, putting an arm out and barring her passage. "What are you up to this fine day?"

"Nothing, Your Highness," she said. "I was just on my way to see your mother, Her Majesty the Queen."

"And did she send for you then?"

Marcala didn't answer.

"Perhaps you would prefer to spend an hour in my company instead?"

"My preferences are of no consequence, Your Highness," she answered. "Now, please let me pass. Her Majesty will be expecting me."

"Your preferences do not matter, but mine do. What would you say if I told you I *prefer* that you walk with me? Or that you go riding with me?" He licked his loose lips. "Ah, there's a turn of phrase. What a ride I could show you—"

"Please, Highness! You forget yourself!"

"Don't play the innocent virgin with me, Marcala of Valvager. Your somewhat soiled reputation precedes you. I daresay that even you could learn a trick or two from me, though, if only you'd—"

Marcala saw her opportunity and ducked under the Prince's restraining arm. "The Queen . . . my duty . . ." she said, already running toward the safety of the Queen's door.

"Well then, give my Lady Mother a message for me," he called after her. "Tell her that I'll have her barred from my father's bedchamber! Everyone at court knows that she's the one keeping him alive—"

But Marcala swiftly closed the door, shutting out Prince Florian's words. She leaned against the portal, eyes closed, gathering her composure.

"Come in, Marcala," the Queen said. "I take it you have just come from my son's company."

"I have," Marcala said wryly.

"Then busy yourself in here, with me. I am given to understand that you and Count Harous have become the best of friends."

What need, Marcala thought, did the Queen have of her, when obviously Ysa had spies in every corner. "Indeed," the younger woman said aloud. "We have been much in each other's company. When he is not out hunting, that is."

"Oh, I daresay you can persuade him to spend more time at home, if you want to."

"He has asked me to be a guest at Cragden Keep."

"That should prove to be a great incentive to pay close attention to matters close at home."

The Queen, Marcala noted, did not seem the least bit surprised at the information. Therefore, she must have known beforehand. "Then you will not object if I move into the guest quarters there?"

"Of course not. He is your kindred, after all, isn't he? With the passing of years, the connection has grown faint, but kindred is, nonetheless, kindred. And we must all hold dear those friends we have in these perilous times."

"As Your Majesty commands," Marcala said. She dipped a curtsy, eyes lowered. What was it she sensed in the air? She had seen the Queen like this before, and it always meant that something was brewing—something not entirely beneficial to someone. Marcala hoped it was not she who was the target this time. She would not like to cross metaphoric swords with Ysa.

"And also, Cragden Keep is visible from my tower, situated as it is at the mouth of the valley. It is less than an hour's leisurely ride, supposing you would wish to come and visit with me." Ysa smiled, and Marcala had to keep herself from flinching. "If I had a long-vision glass, I could almost see into your window, I fancy."

Or you could send that creature you have in your thrall, Marcala thought. The one you thought hidden in the silk-lined basket. Only I knew. Yes, I knew. Aloud, she said, "I will always be at Your Majesty's command."

Ysa smiled again. "Of course. I have no doubt. Now, come and help me. As you can see, I have been reading and there are books to be returned to the library at the Fane. It is not everyone I would entrust with such a task, for the books are old and fragile. Most of all, they are very valuable."

Marcala nodded. So the Queen had been meddling with magic again. One would think that Ysa had learned her lesson after that dreadful night when Marcala had been afraid the Queen had killed herself. She could still feel the power tingling through her hands where they had rested on the Queen's shoulders. And then, when Ysa had fallen back into Marcala's arms— It was not wise to dabble in such matters. She began to pick up the books from a pile beside the Queen's chair, preparatory to putting them in a basket and returning them to their proper place. One book slipped from her hands and she bent to retrieve it.

By chance, it opened on a hand-colored illustration and, curious and intrigued, Marcala turned a page or two. Then she stopped, astonished. "I recognize this!" she exclaimed.

"What is it, child?" the Queen asked. She held out one slender hand and Marcala gave her the book, pointing out what had caught her attention.

"This. It is very close to something I once saw Harous studying, in one of his books." Marcala glanced at the spine. "In fact, it was another copy of this one. Anyway, this is the picture that caught his attention."

Both women looked at the page. On it, drawn with great skill, was depicted a brooch design. A circle, painted gold, around a golden flame arising from a blue vessel. There was no motto, though there was a place for one, nor any attribution as to whence the design had come.

"That is interesting," the Queen said. She closed the book and handed it back to Marcala with every indication of having no interest in it at all. If she had been with anyone other than the Queen of Spies, the entire incident would surely have gone unremarked. But Marcala's very life depended on her being able to read the thoughts and moods and actions of those around her. Her skin prickled. This was surely part of what was passing in the Queen's mind. She was certain Ysa knew more about this design than she was willing to admit, not now, and especially not to Marcala.

Marcala resolved to unravel this mystery. For the moment, she was safe enough, able to avoid Florian now that she would be living in Harous's keep and under his protection. Away from the Queen's suspicious eye, she would have the opportunity for study, sooner or later. In the meantime, her outward manner was as docile as she knew how to show as she began to pack the borrowed books to return to the Fane.

Ashen raised her head cautiously. She discovered that her captors had dropped her some distance from Obern. She knew, if the men who had taken them did not, that they were all now easy prey for the Bog-folk. The raft was slow and clumsy, while the crude boats the Bog-folk used were surprisingly swift when propelled by a skilled boatsman.

Then, to her astonishment, Ashen saw the man with the mist over his head do something that had every appearance of lengthening the odds on their survival. He picked up a bag, and using a rod tied to it, sucked up something from the interior. When he blew it out over the water behind them, Ashen saw that it was a powder. Raising her head a little higher, she watched the powder dissolve into an oily scum that lay on the surface of the water.

"Fire, Ehern," her captor said.

One of the men with him took a coal from a covered container and touched it to the scum. It immediately burst into flame. Anything following them would be halted, at least until the fire burnt itself out.

The Outlanders poled the raft away from the ruined city and down a side stream so well hidden with rank vegetation that Ashen had missed it entirely when she and Zazar had first come to the island. Here the water was disturbed, and the surface began to dapple with the frequent splashing of ominous things.

"Boggarts," the man called Ehern commented. "More fire, sir?"

"Yes. Give them a stiff dose of it."

Ehern took the pouch and the rod from the man with the misted head and applied the powder to the water. Even with the fire roaring so close that it lapped at the very stern of the raft, the men poling had a hard fight of it to make their way through the mass of underwater monsters. To add to the confusion, over the noise of the fire and the cries of men and dying boggarts, Ashen could hear the sound of drums. She thought they were coming from the direction in which they were heading.

"Good thing this shortcut isn't any longer," Ralse said. He was at the steering pole. "Here's the river. Now we've but to cross it and we're almost home."

"Aye, the powder is nearly spent," Ehern said. He held up the pouch, and from where she lay, Ashen could tell that its contents were indeed sadly depleted.

"Trouble ahead," the leader said. "Look sharp. They're just Bog-runners, but have a care for those we have on board."

Then the raft grated against mud, and before the Outlanders could gain the shore, the Bog-folk were upon them. Ashen's world dissolved into cries and grunts and the clash of the Outlanders' superior weapons against shell-tipped spears, punctuated by the thud of Bog clubs against Outlander armor. Now and then a splash, sometimes accompanied by a scream, marked the fall of someone into the river, where more boggarts, emboldened and scenting blood in the water, came swarming out from the stream they had just navigated their way through. Twice Ashen was almost trampled, and she heard Obern grunt as somebody stumbled over him. Fire crackled again—the last of the powder, Ashen surmised—and men screamed in agony.

Then the battle was over. The remaining Bog-warriors scrambled for their boats and escaped before they could catch fire, still shouting and brandishing those weapons that remained to them. One hurled a spear that lodged in the deck of the raft, between where Ashen and Obern lay trussed like waterfowl. An Outlander wrenched it free and flung it back at the enemy with a curse. Another scream told Ashen that it had found its target.

"We mark you, Outlanders!" The threat sounded from the murk, and Ashen thought she recognized Joal's voice. "And Outlander demon-whelp, too! We mark you well. You be not done with Bog, not at all."

Another company of Outlanders came through the brush. They were armed with more of the bent sticks that hurled other sticks, and they used these weapons to provide covering protection so the people on the raft could disembark. The misty-headed man noticed Ashen staring.

"They are called bows," he said, "and the projectiles are called arrows."

"I could have told you that," Obern said.

The man made a gesture, and two of his followers seized Obern. He grunted as blows fell upon him, but otherwise was silent.

The man removed a shining metal band from his head, and Ashen could see an oval of light on it that faded even as she watched. With the light's disappearance, the mist surrounding the man's head vanished. The thought that this man was even more handsome, more attractive, than Obern crowded into her mind unbidden.

"I am Count Harous of Cragden, a nobleman of Rendel," he said courteously to Ashen, "and the one who has saved you."

A number of rash retorts rose to Ashen's lips—she didn't need saving, she would not be saved by a murderer in any case, and she had not asked for help—but prudently she didn't give voice to any of them. "I am Ashen," she said.

Harous seemed startled for an instant. "Then my surmise was correct," he said, almost to himself. He bowed. "I have reclaimed a prize indeed from the mysteries of the Bog. A new life awaits you, lady. I am humbly grateful that it was I who was chosen to bring it to you."

At this, her temper flared despite her best efforts. "You *chose* to invade my home? You *chose* to snare me and my companion like wild animals?"

"I am not your enemy, Lady Ashen," Harous said. "In time, you may come to realize that. All that I have done, I have done for your betterment. Please believe that."

"If you are not my enemy," Ashen said, trying to keep her voice from trembling, "then why did you kill the servant of my Protector?"

"Who? Was someone killed?"

"I saw it. An old woman, crippled. A man such as you, clad in mist, killed her with his fist."

"I do not make war on women, not even on Bog women."

"Nevertheless, I saw it," Ashen said stubbornly.

"There are others besides me who have the ability to go clad in mist. Ask Zazar. I tell you, lady, I am not your enemy."

The mention of Zazar's name startled Ashen. This must be one of the several Outlanders who had sought Zazar's skills, and what he said could very well be true. She forced herself to use a more reasonable tone. "Then why am I still bound? And my companion with me?"

"That is quickly mended." Harous made a gesture, and two of his men stepped forward to release Ashen and Obern from their bonds.

For a moment, she was afraid that despite his broken arm, Obern would try to fight and that Harous's men would succeed in killing him as two terrible falls had not. She looked at him, eyes narrowed, and shook her head. But he was obviously intelligent enough to be able to assess the odds against him. He stood quietly, massaging his wrists where the ropes had bitten, waiting for what came next.

This turned out to be horses—another animal of which Ashen had heard but never seen, let alone touched. She and Obern were lifted into the saddles on these great, fearsome beasts, and they set off toward a place, Harous told her, known as Cragden Keep.

*

"The catamite's lapdog is here," Kasai told Snolli sourly. "He wants to know about that treaty."

Snolli looked up from the pile of records he had been going through and tried to work out what Kasai was saying. He hazarded a guess. "By that, I take it you mean Prince Florian's translator."

"None other."

"Bid him—no, *ask* him, very politely, to come in." He smiled a trifle wanly. "At least I have a place for him to sit now." He indicated several chairs of varying degrees of crudity that surrounded an equally rustic table.

The men of Rendel must have been waiting just outside the door. Dakin and four men entered almost before Kasai had had time to notify them of how the High Chief of New Vold eagerly awaited them.

"Chieftain!" Dakin said. "How good it is to see you again."

"It is good to see you as well."

Snolli indicated that the small company of men should seat themselves at the table. He gestured for wine to be brought and noted how they struggled to hide their dismay at the indifferent quality, and that Dakin succeeded while those with him failed.

"Thank you," Dakin said. "Your hospitality is gratefully accepted. Shall we begin our discussion without all the pretty, time-consuming formalities?"

"I have never had much time for those," Snolli said. "I greatly prefer to talk man to man."

"So, Chieftain, man to man, have you decided to sign the treaty with the Prince?"

"I beg the Prince's indulgence. The time of mourning for my son is not yet past. Let us but accomplish this and I will ride with a few of my men to your city, and there—"

"It is better done here, Chieftain."

Snolli looked at Dakin thoughtfully. So, he said to himself. This is something that must be kept secret, here at the far end of the Kingdom. This man is under orders about something the Prince does not want his mother to find out about.

"Then leave one of your men here as my honored guest and I will send him as messenger as soon as the time arrives when we shall make pact with your people and your Prince," Snolli said. "If you are concerned about him, take one of my men with you when you go, as surety for his safety."

Dakin stared at Snolli for a long moment, and then nodded. "I will stay," he said. "None of my companions know your language very well."

Snolli nodded in turn, aware that he was accepting a spy into his midst. "And for us, I will send Harvas. He is a wave-reader whose ship is no more. He will be glad to have something to do."

And also, Snolli thought, he will make as good a spy as you, Dakin, or perhaps better. Understanding each other perfectly, the new "guest" at New Vold Keep and the High Chief clasped each other's forearms in the grasp of friendship.

"Only, let me inform my men and take a few belongings from my saddlebags."

Thus Dakin confirmed that this had been at least a contingency plan all along. Inwardly, Snolli smiled. These people thought themselves much cleverer than they were. He wondered if they were taken in by the Sea-Rovers' rough clothing and sometimes questionable manners, supposing by such outward signs that the people themselves were not worthy of any great effort when it came to deceiving them. Well, they would learn better. Snolli resolved to take a good, hard look at that treaty at the first opportunity. There might be traps laid in it.

"I am sorry you had such a long ride for nothing," he said as he and the Rendelians left the keep by way of the northeast gate. There their mounts waited, along with an armed escort.

"I only do my Prince's bidding," Dakin said. Then he issued orders to the waiting men. One of them led out a pack animal— laden with the "saddlebags" Dakin had referred to earlier, Snolli noted.

He gestured to one of his own men to take the animal to the stables. "Put those bags in the new guest apartment in the west tower," he said. The man departed promptly.

Then Dakin gave a few instructions of his own. Snolli could understand enough to know that he was telling the men to ride swiftly to Rendelsham and report to Prince Florian. The lieutenant in charge touched the rim of his helmet in salute, and then the troop mounted and started off, back down the road whence they had come.

"Now I will leave you to get settled while I take care of some business I was about when you arrived," Snolli told Dakin.

"As you command," Dakin replied. He bowed and without protest, followed after his belongings.

Snolli issued a few orders and then went in search of Kasai.

"We must be certain of what has become of Obern," he told the Spirit Drummer. "I must know. I want to see with my own eyes."

"First, let me use the Inner Sight," Kasai said. He began whispering his fingers across the surface of his drum and then slipped easily into the trance. "He lives. He goes into danger. The woman who saved him is still with him."

"Where? At the place Obern was last seen?" Snolli asked carefully, so as not to disturb the spell.

"To the north of that place."

"Can you guide us there?"

"Yes." As if he sensed the Chieftain's urgency, Kasai came out of his trance as quickly as he had entered it. Perhaps he had entered only deep enough to learn what was needed. "If we ride now, we might sight them before they have gone so far that it is not safe for us to follow."

"The horses are already waiting."

Snolli and Kasai and the four fighters with them cut quickly across the land toward the west, so as not to tread on the heels of the Rendelians they had sent back toward the capital city. When they reached the barrier river, Snolli recognized that it was somewhat to the north of the place where they had been earlier.

"If my dream was true, the river bends somewhat more to the west, up ahead," Kasai said. He shielded his eyes with his hand. "There is where Obern and those with him will come out. If they have not done so already, that is."

"Then we shall find their tracks if they have gone ahead of us."

The Sea-Rovers set spur to horse and made as much haste as they could along the riverbank. True to Kasai's Sight, the river did bend westward, growing narrower but deeper at this point. Here it could be navigated by a small boat; Snolli wished he were on one, and not mounted atop this horse. He eased himself in his saddle, hoping he was not developing a blister on his backside. Sea-Rovers rode well enough at need, but their preferred place was on the deck of a ship.

Dordan interrupted Snolli's thoughts. "Look ahead, Chieftain," he said, pointing. "That smudge of smoke in the sky. It is like a beacon to us. And look also—a raft. And men getting off it, on this side of the river. There has been a battle, and recently, or I miss my guess."

"Yes," Snolli said, following the direction Dordan indicated.

"Let us take cover, for there are many more of them than there are of us."

Quietly, the Sea-Rovers dismounted and looped the reins of their horses over low branches near the river so the animals could crop early grass if they wished, and could drink at will. The thirsty beasts promptly began to do both. The Sea-Rovers loosened their weapons, for defense in case they were detected, and began to creep close enough that they could see what was going on. The fire that had caused the smoke had died away by now. Curiously, there seemed to be no charred ruins. It was as if the water itself had been burning.

"That is the misty man," Dordan said.

"He isn't misty now. Could be anybody," Kather said.

"Whoever he is, he has Obern with him," Kasai pointed out. "He has a bandage on his head, and his arm is in a rope sling. And there's the woman I spoke about. Not much to look at."

Snolli pulled out his far-see glass. "Not so bad, close up. Pale, though." He shifted the focus to Obern. "Obern seems undamaged, considering that he fell from a cliff and nearly got eaten by the giant birds."

Dordan held out his hand for the glass, and Snolli reluctantly handed it to him. "Wonder where they're taking him," the archer said.

"North, to all appearances. Wherever else that might be, at least he lives. We can find out later, when we have finished our dealings with Prince Florian." Kasai spat to emphasize his displeasure.

Snolli took the glass back, scowling. "Florian. I would not be surprised to learn that our lace-bedecked Prince has a hand in these doings, somewhere and somehow."

"It is strange," Kasai said. "We postpone signing the treaty because we think Obern is dead, and then Obern shows up, very much alive and under escort northward by the misty man and a woman with hair so light it is almost silver-gilt."

"Our misty man may well be in the Prince's employ." Snolli

folded the glass with a decisive snap and got to his feet. The men and their captives—for such they surely were—had by this time gone far enough distant that the Sea-Rovers risked little in the way of discovery. "We cannot trust the Prince. That much is certain. In my heart of hearts, I feel that he has been deceiving us."

Twenty-one

Q ueen Ysa, despite all her will and resolution, was still not
   fully recovered from the terrible effects of her last attempts at spell-casting. From time to time and unexpectedly, she
faltered in midstep or, suddenly dizzy, nearly fell from her chair.
Her appetite, formerly robust at all times, now came and went.
What, she wondered, had she summoned that it had struck her
so hard? She could only hope that her illness was not a permanent one.

It was enough that the King continued to sink, day by day,
and that she was in no way ready for the possibility that Prince
Florian would take his place. Florian was at that most awkward
age, when he was not yet judged mature enough to rule—he
would never be that, no matter his age!—but was too old to have
all his actions approved by a Council of Regents. And as for his
being guided by his mother— Ysa laughed shortly to herself.
How, she wondered, could she manage to keep him from the
throne . . . unless she had him killed?

She should have shuddered at the very idea, she thought. It
was a measure of her utter disdain for the son she had borne
that she did not—indeed, that she lingered over the thought long

enough to ponder how it might best be done and not implicate the one who instigated the deed.

"The land comes first," she said to herself, clasping her hands so that her fingers rubbed against the Rings. "Ever the land. We Kings and Queens—aye, and Princes, too—we come and go, but the land must be preserved."

A discreet rap at the door to her chamber interrupted her meditations. She looked up, welcoming the respite from her increasingly gloomy thoughts.

Lady Grisella entered. "Lady Marcala has come from Cragden Keep and begs an audience with you," she said deferentially.

"Bid her enter!" Ysa said. This was an even more welcome interruption than what she had expected—some bit of court business in which she would have had to feign an interest. "Bring warmed wine and spice cakes, and then leave us alone for a while."

When Marcala entered, Ysa was struck once more by the way her Queen of Spies had taken on the role of noblewoman so completely that she seemed to have been born to it. Marcala curtsied and then took the low chair Ysa offered her. She accepted a flagon of hot wine Grisella provided and drank gratefully. "The air still has a chill in it before noon," she said, "though the afternoons are warm enough. Thank you for your thoughtfulness."

"You bring cheer and light to the court," Ysa said, mindful that Grisella had not yet closed the door behind her. "Now, tell me how it goes with our loyal friend, Count Harous."

The door closed with an audible click and Marcala looked around to make certain that nobody remained within to listen. "I have had word that another guest is expected at Cragden Keep," she said in a low voice. "Two, actually, and both very important. One is a lady. Count Harous sent a man to tell me to make ready a guest apartment."

"And what is this lady's name?"

"I do not know yet, only that Harous is returning from his latest hunting trip—" she said the words with a certain edge of distaste "—and is bringing her back with him. Also, there is an unknown man with Harous's party, and his name I do not know either. But I thought the word of their imminent arrival would be of interest to you. Then too, I wanted to visit the court and perhaps gain a little more perspective. I find that I am longing for Harous's return more than I should."

"There is nothing wrong with that," Ysa said soothingly. "After all, you are young, and he is handsome, and he is probably the best catch in all of Rendel, if you don't count the Prince."

Marcala looked at Ysa sharply, and then began to smile. "And, of course, Prince Florian is far, far above me," she said, laughing.

Yes, Marcala's arrival had brought Ysa some much-needed amusement. "Far above everyone we've yet proposed for a bride," she said, and this time, the ladies laughed together.

"I have more news," Marcala said as she helped herself to a spice cake. "But it is only gossip so far."

"Tell it to me anyway."

"I have heard that deep in a hidden room of Cragden Keep, Harous has put certain records under lock and key—records that he unearthed months ago. Nobody knows exactly what those records are, only that he goes to this room from time to time and reads through them. It's said they are so dusty that the entire castle needs cleaning when he's finished."

Ysa nodded. She had heard much the same thing but had had too much on her mind to devote any time to investigating the intrigue. "You must find out what Harous thinks is so important that he must lock it away. I know that you are able to do it. Do not be in such haste that you reveal what you are about, but do not delay, either."

"A little of this I have done already."

"Good. Now, in the meantime, share the midday meal with the court. Then you must return to Cragden Keep, for I think it

would not be well if Count Harous found you missing when he
came home with these mysterious strangers."

"Yes, Your Majesty," Marcala said. She arose, dropped another curtsy, and left the chamber.

I will go and see the King again, Ysa thought. With Marcala's
visit and the fresh riddles the woman brought concerning Harous's doings, she felt almost invigorated once more. Then, her
duty done to Boroth, she, too, would take a meal, this time in
the Hall, and furthermore, she would eat heartily whether she
wanted to or not. She needed to have the people see her in her
strength.

🍂

Ashen could not contain her curiosity as they rode through country totally unfamiliar to her. She could not even remember
having read about such a land, or recall Zazar mentioning it,
other than to tell her that there was an entire world outside the
Bale-Bog and to predict that Ashen would someday have to live
in it. Now that this prediction seemed to be coming true, Ashen
knew she must devote herself to learning the ways of this new
life as quickly as possible.

Obern, she observed, was not nearly as overawed as she. And
yet he, too, gazed about with keen interest. That meant that he
was not totally unfamiliar with the Outside, though he did not
know this portion of it. She tucked that observation away, to
think about it at some other time.

It was a fair land, she thought, if utterly strange to her. It
was so dry! They could have gone anywhere, it seemed, and not
be in danger from pools, or giant luppers, or the sucking mire.
There was, however, a road, and they kept to that rather than
ride crosscountry. She had never seen such a road before and
knew only the uncertain paths through the Bog that disappeared
and reappeared at the caprice of the water.

Gradually, she realized that they were passing through places
where food was actually being grown, as opposed to the necessity

Andre Norton & Sasha Miller

for people to go out and gather what they needed for the day. She saw men and women working in fields, and knew that they were cultivating far more than they could eat. Where did the rest go? She answered her own question. To feed others, such as Harous. She could not imagine this handsome and obviously powerful man digging out weeds in an expanse of fair grain.

The land rose and fell, and though she recognized mountains similar to those that ringed the Bog, she had never before seen any that belched fire and smoke. Several of these lay on the horizon, and now and then a faint tinge of something tainted the air. "Sulfur," Harous said when she asked him about it.

Harous seemed agreeably disposed to having her ride near him and to answer many of her questions. Luckily for Ashen, she was accustomed to having only a single explanation, if that, from Zazar, and her memory was excellent. She took it all in thirstily. He identified the weapons she had never seen before— crossbow, sword, dagger. The armor was called chain mail. It was put together in a pattern similar to knitting. She would learn about knitting and other work with needle and thread. Sometimes, in jousts—yes, he would show her a joust later—the chain mail was augmented with plates of metal.

Ashen realized, without being told, the benefits of the sort of shirt that she had removed from Obern. He had called himself a "Sea-Rover." That must mean he was one of a group of people who lived on, or at least close to, that vast body of clean water she had glimpsed from the clifftop. If someone wearing that kind of armor happened to fall into the water, it would be much easier to free himself than with the metal tunics Harous and his men wore, and thus save himself from drowning. Later, she would find a way to assure Obern that his belongings were safe; at least, she had not seen any of Harous's men carrying them out of the ruined building that had been her home. She took up her questions again.

No, they were not yet at their destination; she would have a fine surprise when they reached it. Yes, it was a kind of city, similar to the one in the Bog where she had been living, for it housed many people; it was sometimes called a castle, sometimes a keep, or a stronghold. No, it was not in ruins but whole, and that was where he lived, with others. No, it was not the greatest one in the land, but possibly the strongest. This was because his castle, Cragden Keep, was the great fortification that defended the capital city, Rendelsham. It was called that because the country itself was Rendel. No, it was not his only residence. A hunting lodge lay off to the west, but they were not going there. Also, he had a house in the city itself, where he stayed when there was much business for the Council. The Council once advised the King—the headman—and now advised the Queen, the King's wife. That was because the King was very ill.

And so on. Harous seldom seemed out of patience, but rather, amused by Ashen's curiosity.

"You are indeed going into a new life," he told her. "I will have tutors—teachers—to help you learn quickly what you must know, as a lady of this land. And so you are, because of your birth, though you do not yet realize it."

When Ashen ran out of questions temporarily, she dropped back to ride near Obern, who seemed to be recovering rapidly from his head wounds. "Why are these men of Rendel taking you with us?" she asked. "I can understand my being with them; it is my fate to leave the Bog and go out into the world, as foretold by my Protector. But your presence with me was only an accident."

Obern shrugged. "Accident or not, it seems to have become my fate as well. You must have a strong thread on the Loom, for it drags others with it, will or nil."

And then Obern told her about the Loom of the Weavers, and how this belief in the Loom was common throughout the known world. Ashen listened, fascinated, remembering something of the sort she had learned from Zazar, and then she sought the same story from Harous. Only a few details differed. "And yet I perceive that you think of Obern as not a friend," she said.

"You have keen eyes," Harous replied. "No, he is not a friend, but he is not an enemy, either. I have not made up my mind about Obern. For the moment, he is someone I have decided to shelter, to see what will come of it."

"Like me?"

"Not exactly."

And that was as much detail as she could get out of him on that subject among many, at least for the present. Ashen knew that she liked Obern more, in some ways, than she did Harous, even though Harous was more polished. She had other matters to occupy her mind, however, for they had now drawn close enough to Cragden Keep that it could be sighted on the crown of a hill. Immediately she understood Harous's sketchy description. This was mountainous country, and her unpracticed eye detected a valley behind a wall of the heights. Cragden Keep stood at the mouth of that valley, closing it off as securely as any bundle of reeds ever stopped a jar.

"And the city you spoke of—"

"Rendelsham."

"Yes, Rendelsham. That lies beyond?"

"It sits atop a crag inside the valley. It is strong enough under ordinary circumstances, and the royal residence even looks like a castle. But it is a castle out of a child's storybook and would never hold if war came to this land. You can see it from the battlements. That is the reason for Cragden Keep—to prevent the city from ever having to endure the hardships that fighting would bring to it."

Ashen digested this in silence. Another hour's ride, she estimated, and they would be within Cragden Keep's walls, and perhaps she would even catch a glimpse of this storied castle so she could see it for herself. By Harous's estimate, they would arrive at mid-afternoon.

All her questions went out of her head, however, as they approached the keep. It occupied a sharp outthrust of stone and commanded the entire approach to the valley beyond. It had been whitewashed, though the underlying stones from which it was constructed were beginning to show through, giving it a curiously homey appearance. All traces of any friendliness vanished, however, as the travelers came closer. They climbed a steep ramp, crossed a wooden drawbridge over a ravine so deep it nearly stopped one's heart to look down at it, and entered the gatehouse, a structure whose very size and power made Ashen's heart quiver and her throat threaten to close. It was so long that it formed a tunnel; inside, twilight descended, the gloom lightened by wall torches on either side. Double doors stood wide open, ready to close and bar. The doors were made of multiple layers of wood, and strengthened with metal.

Ashen glanced upward; there in the semi-darkness, two separate constructions like, and yet unlike, doors hung overhead, spaced two dozen paces apart and suspended in grooves that had been gouged specifically for them. Each had sharp spikes along the bottom. She nudged her horse to get out from under one of these enormous, dangerous things before it could fall on her.

"Portcullises," Harous said. He had been watching her, apparently judging her reactions. "If an invader comes through the gate, we can trap him between them and destroy him. They will not come down upon you by accident. And see here." He pointed out openings in either wall. Beyond was yet another wall with similar openings, and she gasped as she realized that a man with a bow could stand protected and fire through both walls at an invader, and that his line of sight would cover almost the entire passageway. "And above."

Now she noticed the holes in the ceiling, through which one might drop things upon someone's head, provided an enemy could even get this far. Again, she nudged her horse forward. At the end of the tunnel, another pair of double doors waited to be closed and barred in their turn. "Surely this great keep has never fallen, Count Harous," she said, trying to keep a nervous quaver out of her voice.

"Once, in the far past, through treachery— Ah, now see who

has come to meet us. The messenger I sent ahead did his duty. It is the fair Lady Marcala."

Ashen looked up and saw a woman, someone younger and even more beautiful than the person she had seen when she had so briefly been—where? In the place where Zazar had been imprisoned in the flame. Marcala approached as Harous helped the girl to dismount. Tired from riding, Ashen moved a little stiffly, but Marcala was all grace and fluidity. She wore a wondrous violet-colored dress that rustled when she moved, and a waft of sweet fragrance preceded her as she came near. Ashen suddenly became aware of her own lupper-skin garments, now shabby and soiled from the journey, and of the fact that she must smell of horse sweat. Not sweet at all.

"Welcome home, my lord," Marcala said, smiling. She turned to Ashen. "And who have we here?"

"The guest whose coming you have had foretold, my dear lady. A little Bog-blossom that I hope you will turn into one of Rendel's finest flowers—never to rival you, of course." Harous took Marcala's hand and brushed his lips across her fingers. "I want you two to be friends."

"As you command, my lord." She turned her smile on Ashen, and suddenly the girl wished with all her heart that Zazar was here with her, to guide her, for she knew instinctively that Marcala would never be her friend. And she had never learned the ways of one Outlander woman with another.

🌿

Reluctantly recognizing that they were—for the moment—severely outmanned by the Rendelians, Snolli turned his horse toward New Vold Keep once more. At least Obern was alive and relatively unharmed. Though how he had survived that kind of fall, from atop a cliff into the Bog, remained a mystery. For the moment, the lad would have to take what came and make the best of it. Later, when he had learned where Obern had been taken, Snolli could mount a proper rescue party and demand his son's return, by force of arms. A certain pride in Obern's abilities rose in Snolli as he realized that he could not have planted a better spy in the midst of the Rendelians if he had plotted for weeks. Between him and Harvas, when Harvas escaped as he was bound to do, they would bring back a good report of how things stood in Rendel. It was always wise to know your enemy.

He jerked his head up, roused from his thoughts. An enemy more immediate was presenting itself.

"Bog-men!" Kather said, putting his hand on Snolli's arm. He pointed. "Looks like this time they aren't staying on their side of the river."

And true enough, a party of Bog-dwellers was paddling determinedly toward the place where Snolli and his men had paused. Six to a boat, Snolli observed. And three boats—

Once more they were outnumbered, but the superior weaponry the Sea-Rovers carried, plus their chain-mail shirts, evened the odds. "Dismount," Snolli said. "We might outride them and escape, but being as we could not retrieve Obern, I am itching for a fight."

The grim nods of those with him told him that his men felt the same. By the time the canoes of the Bog-men grated against the river's edge, the five Sea-Rover warriors had sent Kasai with their horses out of harm's way and put themselves into battle order. Grinning behind their shields, they hefted their weapons in anticipation. Dordan sighted carefully with his bow and dropped the first Bog-man to set foot on land that was not Bog. The rest began yelling and brandishing their spears, only to be answered by bellowing war-cries from the Sea-Rovers. Dordan slung his bow and took up an axe.

Then, even before they could charge, as was their wont, the Bog-men were upon them. Snolli quickly fell into his accustomed fighting rhythm, though he sorely missed Obern's presence as his backshield. Kasai, no fighter, still had a weapon at his disposal. He began drumming, and the insistent, throbbing beat strengthened the Sea-Rovers even as it dismayed their opponents.

A shell-headed spear struck Snolli on the shoulder and jarred him, though it shattered before it could pierce the Chieftain's sturdy armor. He remembered this style of fighting from the reports Obern had brought back; Bog-men jabbed, and threw only at the last. Thus he could tell that the tide of battle had turned in the direction of the Sea-Rovers. "Don't let any of them escape if you can help it!" he yelled.

The Bog-man who had thrown the spear turned and ran, but Kather struck him down before he could reach the canoes, obviously his destination. Others of the Bog-warriors were able to scramble into the boats, push themselves away from the river's edge, and achieve the relative safety of the water.

Kasai ceased his drumming. Snolli straightened up and wiped the battle sweat from his forehead. He glanced at his sword and then cleaned it on a rag he took from the body of his latest opponent. Fewer than half of their attackers had escaped; the remainder lay crumpled upon the makeshift battlefield, proof·of the Sea-Rovers' prowess. One of the Bog-men stood up in a canoe, shaking his fist and screeching defiance.

"Shall I teach him one last lesson?" Dordan asked. He had retrieved his bow and now stood at Snolli's side, an arrow nocked and ready. A trickle of blood ran down the side of his face from where a shell-edged weapon had nicked his forehead.

"He looks like their leader. Yes, take him if you can."

But by this time, the current had carried the boats swiftly away from where the Sea-Rovers stood, and Dordan's arrow only lodged in the side of one of the flimsy crafts. The leader laughed, and the Bog-boats disappeared as the men drove them into one of the innumerable Bog-streams that branched out of the river itself.

Snolli spat. "Another time," he said. Then he turned to look at his men. "Is anybody badly hurt?"

"Just scratches," Kather said carelessly. "We hardly had time to get us a proper heat before they broke and ran."

Snolli grinned mirthlessly, admiring the fighting spirit of the men with him. "They were stout enough. If they had proper equipment, we would have fared far worse. Let's go home," he said, "for we have plenty to keep us occupied there while we wait for Obern to return." He turned to Kasai. "Make note. When we are at New Vold Keep, I want to send two of our ships out to see if there are any more refugees from the north. I have a feeling that before this is over, we are going to need all the men with us that we can muster."

Twenty-two

Queen Ysa's many informants began bringing information to her about rumors of incursions from the Bale-Bog. These incidents became increasingly serious as fighting broke out between Rendelians and Bog-men, not always to the credit of the Rendelians. At first these raids occurred close to the river's banks, and then they began edging ever farther into the countryside. More than once, good farmers, untrained in arms, had been the targets of those whose proper place until now had been the confines of the Bale-Bog.

Worse, the fire-mountains rumbled even more ominously. There was a feeling of anticipation in the air, as if an old evil far away to the north had awakened and was now on the move. The three troublesome windows in the Great Fane of the Glowing began to change more rapidly. The shadow in the milky-white window stirred, as if something was rising from the snow, and what was revealed caused Queen Ysa to order a curtain put over it.

She called a Council meeting at once. Five of the seven were close at hand. Only Erft, pleading his years, had not come to the city to attend the King's dying, and Harous was, as usual, missing because of one of his mysterious outings. Both men, however, had sent deputies—Edgard for Erft, and Chevin for Harous. Ysa occupied the chair at one end of the table; as head of the Council, Royance sat at the other end, opposite her.

Royance called for a map, which was already marked with pins at the places where the raids had occurred. The pattern was immediately apparent; the Bog-men ventured perhaps a league and a half beyond the river's edge. But there was nothing to guarantee that, emboldened, they would not go farther, given time.

"We must begin sending out patrols," Ysa said. "This cannot be allowed to continue. And I expect all of you to respond. This is not a local matter. Ever since anybody can remember, the men of the Bale-Bog have always stayed in their place. However, once they are out, there is nothing to say they can't overrun us should that become their intent. Our good countrymen are all but helpless before them."

"Agreed, Your Majesty," Gattor said lazily. "I can supply ten mounted men from my retainers."

"And I, speaking for my master, Erft, can send twenty. Also, we can supply horses for those who have none. Rowanwald has always been the home of good horse-flesh." Edgard looked around the table with more than a touch of pride.

"The brunt of the attacks have been against Oak-lands, which are protected by Count Harous," Chevin said. "As his lieutenant, I am authorized to pledge as many of his men as are needed for this enterprise. Also, I am authorized to offer those from other holdings a place at Cragden Keep for both bed and table during the course of this action."

The other Council members nodded, and Jakar of Vacaster spoke for all. "This will ease the problems of barracking. In return, I pledge to send food and other provisions to maintain the dozen men I will provide."

"All must be under the command of Count Harous, or, in his absence, myself," Chevin said. "Otherwise, we will be in chaos."

The other members of the Council nodded in approval, and

Ysa felt a certain tension ease. Good, she thought. That makes it easier to direct the patrols. Perhaps this threat had united the ordinarily quarrelsome nobles enough that none would take it as an opportunity to snatch some advantage for himself.

"Let us remember that our goal is to chase away the Bog-men and not necessarily to kill them," said Liffen of Lerkland. He was from one of the affiliated Families of the all-but-extinct House of Ash. Ysa had no reason to like or trust him, but his words were wise.

"I agree," Royance said. "Let us not fan a flame we may not be able to extinguish. But if the Bog-men decide that they are our open enemies, there will be time enough to act."

Ysa let her mind wander while the Council began plotting out the general outlines of what, despite the conciliatory words, was shaping to be a war between Rendel and the Bale-Bog. Harous's retainers would make up the majority of those who went out to chase away—and sometimes to fight—the Bog-men. This meant that Harous himself would frequently be in the field and, as usual, absent from the daily life at the court. He was never one to lead from the rear. With his influence lightened, and with her Queen of Spies at work, Ysa felt safe in putting the problem of Harous's guest into the back of her mind, to think about at another time. This guest posed no threat, at least not for the moment, whereas the raiders did.

Later, if it seemed advisable, Ysa could, as the saying went, "do something" about this miserable half-breed Bog-wench Harous had brought back with him as a souvenir from one of his many mysterious expeditions. Ysa smiled to herself. It was whispered that the Queen of Spies was not above a little light assassination from time to time, if she were paid well enough. And her location was ideal.

Too ideal? Ysa thought for a moment. Perhaps, if it came to that, it should be someone else, and she should leave Marcala out of it. She had plenty of other resources to draw on for this sort of work. Resources that, once used, were expendable. . . .

Yes. Later, a knife in the night, or a poisoned cup, all while Marcala was conspicuously elsewhere. The Queen of Spies was far too valuable for Ysa to squander her in the elimination of a mere half-Ash, half-Bog bastard of a former rival. A dead rival, at that.

So thinking, the Queen dismissed the entire matter and brought the Council's attention to other problems the Bog-men were creating, problems overlooked in their pleasant discussions of war. Where the Bog-men raided, they also burned, and if this were not brought into check soon, Rendel might face a shortage of food.

"Thank you for mentioning this, Your Majesty," Royance said. He bowed his silvery head in acknowledgment. "We must consider the wisdom of taking this disagreement back to the Bale-Bog itself. If they are confined there as before, they will not be destroying our lands."

"And in the Bog, there is nothing worth saving anyway," Gattor said. The others laughed.

Ashen's world became one of wondrous new clothing, frothy white linen, baths in tubs full of water scented with rose oil—and soap!—and a variety of foodstuffs that she had never even heard of, let alone tasted. All thoughts of Obern, of the Bog, and even of Zazar, retreated from the front of her mind as she began to comprehend how much she needed to learn for her new life. When she was not at her lessons, she went for walks along the walls of Cragden Keep, and sometimes for rides out into the countryside. Most of the time, her companion on these rides was Lady Marcala, but occasionally, when he was in residence at Cragden Keep, it would be Harous. She found herself looking forward to these outings with more than ordinary anticipation.

At first, she thought they might even go into the wondrous, gleaming-white city that, as Harous had told her, occupied an outthrust of rock deep in the valley. Not yet, both Marcala and

Harous told her. That time would be determined by how swiftly she learned to behave as befitted her station in life.

Each morning brought a new gift, sent from Harous. One of the first was a dress made of a blue stuff that, like so many of Marcala's dresses, rustled most enchantingly when she moved. At first, Ashen was appalled at seeing how the dress was cut into such a deep vee that it reached the point where the skirt was attached to the bodice. Marcala's garments displayed no such immodesty, having a froth of white to fill in the neckline. But then Marcala showed Ashen the secret of how dresses were worn over yet another garment, cut much more modestly.

These underdresses—in summer made of crisp, lace-bedecked linen, in winter of pure, delicate wool—proclaimed their owner's social station as clearly as did the ornate over-dresses. The longer the garment and the more opulent the fabric, the higher the status of the wearer. Marcala's dress swept the floor, as did Ashen's.

Along with more dresses came shoes to match them, and a gift of pins for the hair that arrived in a jewelry coffer. Ashen immediately placed the iridescent bracelet she had found in the coffer, where it was joined by other trinkets she received. There also she put the power-stone and hearth-guide for safekeeping. Harous sent toilette articles, including the first real mirror Ashen had ever seen, and a pot of rouge, which Marcala showed her how to apply. She received embroidery materials that she was immediately set to learning how to use, and a bottle of perfume that Marcala told her was made from certain blue flowers. Each morning brought a new token, until Ashen was moved to protest.

"Marcala, this is too much!" she exclaimed as she held up a pair of golden earrings set with tiny blue stones that gleamed in the morning light. "I feel embarrassed by it all."

"Oh, that is Harous's way," Marcala said. She tossed her head and Ashen noticed the earrings Marcala was wearing—somewhat larger and more ornate than hers, and the stones were purple. "He is very generous to all his favored guests."

"That you are favored is obvious," Ashen said with conscious tact. "But why am I?"

"There are reasons that will come clear to you in time."

Ashen bit back the question on her lips—how long would it take before all was made clear?—in favor of a show of meekness. This had proven to be the best course to take with the other woman. "As you say, Marcala. I am very grateful for all you have shown me already. I must be a great trial to you, as untutored as I am."

"It is nothing," Marcala said with a shrug. "Now, I have had a place set up in your chamber with a little dish of fruit. Let us practice table manners, and later we will go down into the Hall for the real meal. Be sure to put the napkin in your lap as I have taught you, so that you will keep your dress clean."

There was so much to learn. Washing one's fingers and drying them on the napkin but never with the tablecloth. Bread trenchers in the plates, to catch the juices from the meat. And one must cut the bread with one's knife—another morning gift from Harous, an eating dagger set with blue stones in the hilt—and not with the fingers. In the mornings, you ate your porridge with a spoon, and did not leave the spoon in the bowl. Nor did you lean your elbows on the table, nor did you ever dip the meat in the saltcellar. All bites were conveyed to the mouth with the eating dagger, not with fingers, and even cheese—a real delicacy!—was cut into small bits first, and then eaten.

The early strawberries were just coming into season, and these were in the bowl of fruit Marcala had provided for practice. When Ashen tasted her first one, she almost forgot everything Marcala had taught her about manners, so strong was her desire to stuff her mouth full of the delectable fruit.

"Later in the year," Marcala said with a frosty smile, "there will be apples and pears to eat."

"Are they as delicious as strawberries?"

"In their own way."

Grudgingly, Ashen thought, Marcala pronounced her fit to

join the keep's retainers down in the Hall for the midday meal. "And since you have already gorged yourself on berries, you won't run the risk of disgracing us all by gobbling the meat."

Ashen searched in vain for a trace of friendly teasing in Marcala's tone, though the other smiled.

Harous's chair at the head table was empty, as usual. Marcala took the seat to the right, and Ashen the one to the left. She caught sight of Obern, well down one of the other tables that lined the great Hall, and smiled and waved to him. When she could, she sent a page with a message that she wanted to see him. He rose from his place at once and approached. His injured arm was still in a sling but from the way he moved, she knew it did not pain him.

"Your armor and your sword are, as far as I know, still safe," she told him. "I folded your chain mail and set it aside. Those who . . . who took us away did not even look for it, I think. They were in much haste."

"Thank you, Ashen," he said. "Lady Ashen. I am relieved to hear it. That was a Rinbell sword—counted very fine, very valuable, among my people."

"Perhaps you can go and find it later."

"Perhaps. I thank you again." Then he returned to his place at the lower table.

Marcala watched all this with keen interest, but she said nothing.

After the meal, the ladies went back upstairs, where they cleaned their teeth with green hazel twigs. At least this was nothing new, for Ashen had been performing this ritual ever since she could remember.

As the days passed, she learned about cabbage and onions, lentils and peas, beans and millet. She began to enjoy beef and mutton made into pastries, and potages of meat scraps stewed with vegetables. She learned that in this world one ate a light breakfast of bread or porridge with ale or watered wine at first dawn. She much preferred the diluted wine to the tart ale. Then came lessons, and at midday, the large meal. Supper was at dusk, and sometimes, what was called a rere-supper followed—an occasion for much carousing and gluttony. Ashen retired, along with Marcala, at such times. However, she noted that Obern stayed in the Hall, apparently having made friends among Harous's men.

Some women did stay for the rere-supper, Marcala told her. "There is always an occasion for flirting and courtship. And also there is the music and dancing."

"Music!" Ashen said. "What is that?"

And so, in the afternoons, she learned about music, and also about dancing from one of Harous's personal servants who was noted for having a light foot. Music became almost a passion with her, as if it filled an empty place in her soul she had never known existed. These lessons were the most enjoyable of any.

At night, she retired in her own room in her own apartment to her own bed—a curtained enclosure that she had all to herself, a luxury she never tired of. Before going to sleep, Ashen would fix her mind on Zazar, wondering where the Wysen-wyf was, what she was doing, if she ever wondered how her charge was faring. "Zazar, if only I could talk to you, listen to your wisdom," she murmured.

Sometimes she dreamed of her days in the Bale-Bog, and once in the dream, Zazar appeared, repeating the words she had spoken to Ashen just before they set out for the ruined city, Galinth. "This is the path that only you will walk henceforth." She added, "I have much to occupy me now." Then she faded from sight.

The dream reassured Ashen, even as it left her with unanswered questions. And the days passed in Cragden Keep, one after another. Always, when she awoke at first light, there would be yet another guest-gift from Harous.

One morning this proved to be a gift so special that he brought it to her himself rather than entrusting it to a servant. It was the first time she had seen him except at a distance since coming to Cragden Keep. He wore an elaborately embroidered surcoat with wide, loose sleeves, much different from the fighting gear in which she had first seen him. And much more handsome as well.

"Oh!" Ashen breathed as she opened the package and lifted out a golden necklace. It was an ornament—a gold circle, set with a gleaming blue stone like those in her earrings. On either side, a gold chain, set with smaller stones, was attached so it would hang evenly. Immediately she started to fasten it around her neck, but was baffled by the clasp. Harous took over the task, lifting her hair aside to do it.

"There now," he said. He turned her toward her mirror. "Look. It suits you, even as I thought it would."

And indeed, it looked very fine around her neck. She touched the trinket gently. "Did you have this made?"

"In a way. It is very, very old—when you take it off again, you will see on the back the marks that show it was once a brooch. When I found it, it was broken and almost ruined." He held out some fragments of a dull blue stone. "I replaced the old gem with the sapphire. This is lapis, I think. You may have it if you want it."

Wondering, Ashen took the bits of lapis from him and set them on a table. "But how did you know—"

"I read widely, and study, and remember." He took a carved amulet out of his doublet, where it hung on a string. "And I have powers such as you might be familiar with. Do you recognize this?"

Ashen reached out one hand, but dared not touch. "It looks almost like something my Protector might—"

"Protector? You mean Zazar?" He laughed at her surprise. "Oh, yes, I know Zazar well. In fact, it was she who sent me to find you in the ruined city before the Bog-men could kill you."

"Then you must have been one of the shadowy ones who used to come to Zazar in the night. She always sent me to bed, but sometimes I saw anyway."

"Aye. I have visited Zazar often. We know each other well. You would be wise to obey me in all things, even as you trusted her."

Ashen bowed her head, remembering the mist she had seen surrounding him. Only Zazar could have supplied him with the power-stone—unlike the one Ashen had worn, but with similar properties. "Yes, Lord Harous."

"Good. Now, back to your necklace. This is a symbol of the once-great Family to which you belong. I had the jeweler repair it as much as possible and still keep the worn look that shows it to be a Family heirloom. Observe the design."

Ashen looked again into the mirror. "There seems to be a flame rising from the sapphire—oh, I see! It is a vessel, like a jar. And there is writing around the circle—"

"Yes. It is what is called a canting pun. 'Without flame, there can be no Ash.' What it means is that in members of the Ash Family there burns a bright flame—some members are aflame with loyalty, some with ambition, some with passion." He kissed her neck.

Startled, Ashen watched her cheeks grow red. "T-thank you, Lord Harous," she managed to say. "Thank you for your courtesy."

"Your hair is fair, the way they say your mother's was. Blonde, so light it looks almost silver. She wore it loose, the way you do."

"My mother? Did you know my mother?"

"No, but there are stories. It was said she was very beautiful. You must look a lot like her."

Confused and speechless, Ashen turned away. She did not know what to make of this new aspect Harous was presenting to her, except that it caused a fresh thought to come into her mind. What was his real motive in all he had done? Friend of Zazar or not, surely all this was not out of some goodness of heart. He must expect something of her, and perhaps something she did not want to yield. "I am as I am," she said. "I do not think of myself as beautiful—"

"But you do not object if I do?"

She shook her head. "No, I do not object."

Later, she put the pieces of lapis into the jewelry coffer along with the other treasures she was accumulating.

That day Marcala was very hard to please with her lessons, and Ashen realized at last what was driving her. The woman was jealous. But how could she convince Marcala that she had nothing to fear? Ashen admired Harous, of course, but she knew that her station, such as it was, was far beneath him. After all, was he not a great lord in this land? And was she but a guest in his house?—dependent on him for even the food she put in her mouth, let alone the beautiful clothing she wore. How much higher above her must be the fabulous beings who dwelt in the wondrous castle farther up the valley, the one she could see from Cragden Keep walls, gleaming in the light?

❧

The morning after their arrival at the keep, Harous had sent his private physician to see to Obern. Though he judged himself an unexpected and perhaps unwelcome guest, Obern knew that his captor was intelligent enough to make as good use of him as was possible. Thus it was only good sense for Harous to ensure that Obern would be restored to health.

The physician had removed the splint Ashen had put on his broken arm, replaced it with another, clucked his tongue over the nearly healed cut on Obern's head, rubbed it with a malodorous salve that made Obern wish for the flower-scented potion Ashen had used, and packed up his kit. "Considering the rough treatment you've had, and tended by one not trained in the healing arts, you're recovering remarkably well," the physician said, a trifle disdainfully. "Perhaps it's because of your excellent constitution."

Obern forbore to mention that it might have been also because the one not trained in the healing arts had, nevertheless, a skill that could not be instilled from without. Now, with clothing supplied to him and nothing to do but finish the healing process, time began to hang heavy on his hands.

He took to joining Harous's men at their meals, and to following them out onto the practice-yard where they honed their weaponry skills. In off-moments, he joined them at their games, discovering that one of their favorites, a board game using men and kings, was not far different from one he had always enjoyed.

Before long, he had struck up several acquaintanceships, and his sojourn in Harous's keep became much more pleasant. One of these acquaintances was Ralse, who had been among those in the party when Obern and Ashen had been taken, and there was Ehern as well.

"Hope you bear me no hard feelings," Ralse told Obern. "Following orders."

"I don't bear grudges," Obern said. He grinned. "I get even."

Ehern laughed. "Me, too. I like you, stranger. Where did you say you come from?"

And so Obern found himself telling his new friends about the Lizard-riders, about the warfare in the northern lands, and about the flight for their very lives when they had found the deserted keep and taken it for their own.

"Whew!" Ralse said when he had finished. "No wonder you were so tough on the journey here! Anybody else with a broken arm and a couple of hard knocks to the head would have been a litter case."

"Sea-Rovers are not ones to cry over a few bruises."

"Nor much else, I warrant." Ehern looked at Obern with an appraising eye. "Too bad you're under house arrest. We could use you out on patrol."

"Patrol?"

"Aye. The Boggies have taken to crossing the river, now that we were kind enough to teach 'em how—" Ralse grimaced and spat "—and they are making a right mess of things over on this side. Lord Harous, along with other of the nobles, has to send out patrols to chase 'em back. You may have noted how crowded we are in the barracks these days, sleeping three to a bed."

Obern digested this in silence. "Then," he said at length, "even after I'm healed, I couldn't go on patrol with you? I'd be glad of the chance to get out into the open air again."

"You'll have to take that up with the Count," Ralse said. "As for me, I'd be glad of your company. You seem to be a good sort. But orders is orders."

And so Obern bided his time, waiting. Once, he sent a petition to Count Harous, asking for an audience, but the reply put him off. He wasn't refused out of hand, but the Count had far too many things on his mind currently to give Obern, his honored "guest," an audience long enough for courtesy. Obern must wait.

Wait he did. Occasionally, he caught sight of Ashen, at the noonday meal and sometimes at supper. He was glad when she told him that his mail shirt and the precious Rinbell sword were safe, or as safe as they might be, hidden in the ruins where he and she had been captured. But he was gladder still when she smiled and waved to him. It was Ashen herself that interested him more, to his surprise, for a Sea-Rover valued his weapons above all.

She grew more beautiful by the day. Someone had taught her how to do her hair so that it fell in a bright shimmer halfway down her back. Her complexion glowed; her cheeks and lips bloomed pink. And the clothes that she wore were enough to make any man look more than twice at her. Obern was happy to look more times than that. She had, he must admit, caught his eye. Guiltily, he remembered Neave, and their small son. Those were the ones he should be thinking about. And yet, Ashen filled his thoughts.

Twenty-three

The patrols sent out regularly from Cragden Keep began to have an effect on the Bog-men's raiding. They seemed not nearly so eager to burn honest farmers' holdings, or to cut down any Rendelian who had the misfortune to come in contact with them. And yet, Queen Ysa was reluctant to issue orders that the patrols be lessened, or even discontinued.

Other word coming to her from Cragden Keep was not so reassuring. Every three days or so, Marcala found the opportunity to visit and relay what she was learning about the girl, Ashen, whom Harous was training—for what?

Ysa had to admit that the best time for doing away with this interloper had passed, thanks to the raids of the Bog-men and the growing knowledge of the imminence of danger from the north. Enough people knew about Ashen's existence by now that should anything untoward happen to her, the finger of suspicion would point immediately in the Queen's direction. Now Harous, she was sure, would defend the girl, even against the Queen. If only she had issued orders to eliminate this upstart upon first learning of her existence! Well, another time would come eventually, and with it, the opportunity. She found a certain sustain-

Andre Norton & Sasha Miller

ing hope in the enmity that Marcala had for the girl. Not that she blamed her. Half-breed though she might be, still, Ashen was female, and Marcala knew about the dark ways of men and the unknown and the forbidden. This could be put to use later.

"I know that Harous intends to marry that pale, waterlogged little chit," Marcala said again. She had been voicing that opinion on every journey to Ysa's chambers since shortly after Ashen's arrival. Today she was actually weeping. "Why else would he be treating her as he does?"

"Now, now," the Queen said soothingly. "It is you he loves. I am sure of it."

She realized her potential error immediately, but it was too late to take back the words. Fortunately, Marcala didn't seem to notice. Perhaps the Queen of Spies was too rapt in her own emotions to realize that Ysa had had more than a small measure of influence in making certain of Harous's regard for her, and hers for Harous.

Still, Ysa had to admit that Marcala's fears were far from baseless. Her spell-casting had ensured that Harous love Marcala and that Marcala love him in return, but with the Count, his ambition would always come first. Ashen's heritage might be dubious, but half-breed or not, she was the heiress of the House of Ash. Thus she was valuable because of her claim to the Ashenhold, where the Sea-Rovers now resided. Harous would be perfectly capable of wedding Ashen, despite her unworthiness, and keeping Marcala as his leman. With a twist of her lips, Ysa thought about her own situation and of how Boroth had come to prefer coarse serving-wenches to her own well-bred beauty. Oh, yes, she knew how such things were oh-so-conveniently arranged.

"She's awkward, and she had no manners before I took her in hand," Marcella continued. "Her dreadful clothing. Her hair was a disgrace, and her complexion— Shall I describe her to you?"

"No," the Queen said, repressing a shudder. That was the last thing she wanted to hear. "Believe me when I tell you that I will do everything in my power to see to it that Harous's in-

fatuation with this Bog-creature goes no further than the friendship he claims it to be. And you can believe me also when I tell
you that my influence is not a small one."

"I am grateful, Your Majesty." Marcala dabbed at her eyes
with a finely embroidered handkerchief.

"Now, turn your mind to matters more useful to me. This
man who was captured with . . . with Ashen." The Queen stumbled over the half-breed wench's name. Well, she might as well
get used to saying it, at least for the present. "Tell me about
him."

"Oh, he is nobody of consequence," Marcala said with a
shrug. "He says he is a Sea-Rover. He also claims to be the son
of the leader, but he is probably lying about that."

"Perhaps. Perhaps not. Is his life in danger?"

"No. Harous has been as careful with him as he is about
Ashen. Both receive the tenderest of attention."

"Then the man has nothing to fear as far as his life is concerned. Thus he has little reason to lie. Let us suppose that this
stranger—what did you say his name is?"

"Obern."

"Let us suppose that this Obern is who he says he is, and that
the girl saved his life. We have her, and we have him—at least
Harous does, and I don't think he will test his loyalty to the Crown
by defying us if we decide we have other plans for them. Not if we
are careful about it. I will have to make it a matter for the Council,
I think. Even Harous would not defy them."

"Do you think not?"

Ysa gazed upon her Queen of Spies with great fondness, not
the least element of which was the total reliance on her that
Marcala was now exhibiting. Heretofore, Marcala had been just
a shade too independent, too much her own person. Now she
depended upon Ysa, and that the Queen found very gratifying.
And Marcala had handed her another tool to use at her discre-
tion. Now she would have to decide what use to make of this
Obern.

"I know so," Ysa said with confidence. "In fact— Will you be missed at Cragden Keep for another hour or so?"

"No. Harous is out with one of the patrols, and Ashen will be occupied most of the day with music lessons."

The Queen nearly strangled with hidden laughter over the thought of this uncouth creature strumming a lute, or, by the Wraith of Kambar, dancing! But she kept herself under control. "Good. I will summon Royance and you will tell him what you have told me. Also, you will answer any questions that he has for you. Then we will decide what we shall do."

While the women awaited the arrival of the head of the Council, Marcala took the opportunity to attend to her appearance, wiping away all traces of tears. Ysa noted that her vanity still dictated that she appear as attractive as possible to men, regardless of her feelings for Harous.

As Marcala related her story to Royance, his silvery eyebrows rose higher and higher until it seemed they might almost disappear into his hairline.

"This is very tangled news indeed," he said when Marcala had finished. "And you are sure of all this?"

"When I was not occupied in my role of tutor, I had free time on my hands. There are certain books and records that Lord Harous has hidden away in a room deep in one of the towers, and out of curiosity, I have looked at them. He has places marked that are of special interest. One is the complete genealogy of the House of Ash, showing the line of Kings. Another concerns the signs and symbols of all the great Houses, along with their mottoes and their devices, and a history of all four. Our gracious Queen—" she bowed her head to Ysa "—is in it, as well as our King, dating from the time when they were both mere babes. The Prince is not mentioned, of course, for his birth was past the time of this book."

"Interesting, but not of consequence concerning this girl's identity. Her name is Ashen, but that proves nothing. Did you not say she was reared by Zazar, in the Bale-Bog? There have long been strange rumors about that one. Her interest could be no more than some kind of japery."

"One might think so, if it were not for the girl's appearance," Marcala said. "In these records there are several miniatures bearing likeness to Ash women. The resemblance in this girl's features and coloring is striking. It is plain that she is, indeed, a descendant of the House of Ash."

Royance turned to Ysa. "The probable time of her birth coincides with the departure of a certain other Ash woman, Your Majesty. I'm certain you remember the incident."

"I do," the Queen said, through gritted teeth.

"It was thought at the time that Ash had destroyed Ash. The reports made much of Ash arrows found, and there had been much internal strife in the House. The man who brought back the news was Lord Lackel of the House Troops of Her Gracious Ladyship the Queen, as I recall. Is that not correct?"

"Yes. I sent him because of that very rumor of great conflict between one branch of the House and another. As you know, it is only prudent to stop such before it can erupt into open civil war—though, as it turned out, it was too late."

"I have always wondered. What would you have done had Lackel found the Lady Alditha before her own kindred did?"

Ysa was prepared for this question, having quickly seen the direction Royance's inquiry was heading. "My Lord the King was concerned about Lady Alditha's safety. And so, as his loyal wife, was I."

"Even though the rumor was that Lady Alditha carried Boroth's child?"

Ysa shrugged with what she hoped was a believable carelessness. She was finding it gratifying to say openly what she had deduced some time ago. "Rumors are not facts, my lord. I believe that the circumstances of Lady Alditha's death at the hands of her own kindred pointed rather to something darker—a forbidden entanglement with someone of her own Family. Or perhaps she had formed a connection with a servant or someone else equally baseborn. However, upon pondering the problem, I now think it most likely to have been one of those debaucheries a few of our people sometimes embark on, when, it is rumored, they go to the Bog seeking pleasure. After all, it was to the Bog she was returning and, I think, to her lover. I believe the new Ash heiress is nothing but a half-breed, and it was for this reason that the Lady Alditha was killed."

The Queen's statement filled the chamber with a presence that was almost palpable. Royance grimaced with distaste. "Let it not be so, Your Majesty."

The Queen waved her hand, and then clasped both in such a way that the Rings were visible. "After so many years, does it even matter? There is a wench, and she seems to be of Ash blood. At least half, that is. This is all that is certain."

"Then you deny that she is of Boroth's getting?"

Ysa knew that her next words must be carefully chosen. "I must, my lord. Boroth may have had an eye for other women, but he was not stupid. To have formed a tender alliance with such a highborn lady, especially after having married me, would have been asking for open insurrection. If you count back, this girl must have been born when the King and I were but newly married, a year or less. In fact, I must have been quick with Florian at that time. The King was very solicitous of me, for I carried his heir. Does it make sense that a newly wedded husband, with his wife carrying his child, would have been engaged in such a dalliance? No, my lord, I submit that it does not. I say that the wench's sire was a Bog-man. How else could she have survived where Outlanders are killed on sight?"

She sat back, looking closely at Royance to judge the effect her words had had on him.

He sighed. "I must admit that what Your Majesty says does make sense. But I think also that there is still more to be learned before the matter can be closed."

"It is of no consequence, if you are concerned about the possibility of another heir besides Florian. Even if this girl, Ashen, *had* been sired by my husband—*which I deny*—she could never be anything more than a royal bastard. But, as I said, I do reject such a heritage." Then she brought out what she hoped was her strongest argument, one she had been saving for this moment. "If she were of Boroth's getting, why would Zazar not have brought her forward long before now?"

"That is a question for which I have no answer," Royance said. "Let me do some thinking on this matter in private." He turned to Marcala. "In the meantime, be not afraid, my dear. It is plain to me that you are the best match for Harous. If this girl is not a royal bastard, then her uncertain heritage does not qualify her for marriage to such a high noble as Harous, and I will press my influence on the Council toward this decision. If this girl is a royal bastard, then her blood makes her too important for any of our peerage to marry—with the exception of Florian, and this is also forbidden, for they would be half-brother and half-sister. And I will so say to the Council if this proves to be the case."

The Queen rose, signaling that the audience was concluded. "I knew I could rely on your wisdom and experience, my lord," she said, offering her fingers for Royance to kiss. "I know that both the Lady Marcala and I are very much relieved to know that the matter is now out of our hands and into yours."

He bowed himself out, and Ysa and Marcala looked at each other for a long moment.

"Well," Marcala said at last. "That is something new. I hadn't thought about the possibility of Ashen being Boroth's child."

"Nor should you think on it further," Ysa said firmly. "The matter is closed. Ashen's mother was a whore. It doesn't matter who it was, among many. Now, get you back to Cragden Keep. And do not mention any of this to Harous."

Marcala raised one eyebrow. "Naturally not. He is always the one who likes to be the first to know everything. I will enjoy it when he discovers that this time at least, he is not."

Then she, too, took her leave of the Queen. Ysa paced back and forth in her chamber, too restless to sit and think quietly.

Her worst fears seemed on the verge of coming true. Despite what she had told Royance, she knew that it would be easy to claim that this girl, Ashen, was Boroth's daughter and, further, to put forth the case that she was more fit for the succession than Florian. There were those who might find that such an off-spring—bastard as she was—could be even superior. After all, she had been born before the Prince was, and even though not legitimate, she would then be able to claim royal blood from both sides, as Florian could not. Also, she was the undoubted heiress of the Ashenhold, if she wanted to pursue matters.

Dangerous, dangerous. And despite the danger the girl presented, she was too dangerous to remove. Ysa put her hands to her temples, where a throbbing ache threatened to make her physically ill. Why hadn't she done something about this upstart earlier? Why had the Bog-men begun raiding into Rendel territory now, of all times? It was only this distraction that had prevented her from turning her attention to this awkward situation.

She touched the Rings for comfort. "Oak, Yew, Ash, and Rowan," she murmured. "Help me now."

✤

Royance came away from his interview with the Queen and Lady Marcala a sorely troubled man. He could not shake the feeling that Ysa had not been entirely open and candid with him. He went to his town house and sent messengers out to call various people in for interviews.

When Lackel had been brought into his presence, he questioned him sharply. The one-time leader of the Queen's House Troops, now retired because of an injury, retained much of his old loyalty. Nevertheless, he related the story of that dreadful, stormy night when he had found Ash warriors lying stark with Ash arrows still quivering in them, and of how he had sighted the boat out in the murk, and the body that had slipped into the water and disappeared.

"I thought that was the one we were seeking, my lord," he told Royance. "And so I reported it."

"You did well, Lackel, and no shame to you. Thank you."

Others of those who had been in Lackel's company, when brought into Royance's presence, told much the same story. So much was certain, and no more.

Royance decided to pay a visit to Harous. As soon as one of his men brought word that the lord of Cragden Keep had returned from patrol, he made the short journey and was admitted into Harous's inner chamber at once.

"I would like to meet your guest," Royance said after the courtesies had been satisfied. "Lady Marcala has told me much about her. Also, the Queen is interested."

"She is at her studies just now. But I can arrange a meeting with her later."

"Is it true that you took her out of the Bog?"

"Yes. As you know, I am interested in many things, and when I heard about a young girl who is not of the Bog, yet living there, I knew I had to solve this riddle. And so I became acquainted with Zazar, of whom I think you have heard."

"Yes, the Wysen-wyf. Almost everyone in all of Rendel has heard of her."

"And, I daresay, employed her services. Well, I went to see Zazar, and during the course of other business, I caught a glimpse of this very girl who was the subject of the rumor." Absently, Harous fingered a pendant he brought out of his doublet. "Later, I would have gone back for her, but Zazar had hidden her. I had quite a time of it, finding the hiding place. But I did, and I brought her back here, to where she belongs."

"I see," Royance said. "And what are your plans for her now?"

"First, we must be certain of who she is. That she is of the House of Ash seems certain; the stamp of it is all over her. But who her parents were is less sure. I believe her mother to have been the Lady Alditha, who perished under mysterious circumstances."

"I am aware of those circumstances. And her father?"

"As yet unknown."

"A Bog-man?"

"Definitely not."

Royance sat thinking for a moment. "Would you agree to let the Council question this girl?"

"If you request it, then so shall it be done."

"It could be that she holds more in her memory than we yet know." Royance got to his feet. "The King is close to death. You should temporarily move to your town house, for it would be most unseemly if you were absent when it comes time to proclaim Florian as our King."

Harous made a grimace of distaste.

"Aye, I know. He is . . . well, it seems obvious that the Council will be greatly needed in days to come. Let another take up your duties on patrol. Your presence is more necessary in Rendelsham."

"As you command, Lord Royance," Harous said. He bowed in acknowledgment. "I can suggest two days hence. A banquet, at my town house? With the members of the Council and Lady Ashen in attendance?"

"That will be very satisfactory."

❦

Royance was not the only one to come away from the meeting in Ysa's chamber with a great deal to think upon. Marcala closed herself in the innermost chamber of her quarters, where she would not be disturbed. She held a vital piece of information, hers alone at least for a while, for she knew positively that Ashen was no half-breed Bog-runner. Given that, the possibility that she had been sired by Boroth became much stronger even if only because the Queen denied it so vehemently.

Royance was bound to come and see for himself. Then it would be just a matter of time before he arranged to have that wretched girl brought before the King. These were facts about which Marcala could do nothing.

And she also knew that Harous knew—or had strong suspicions—about Ashen's true parentage. As ambitious as he had always been, no wonder he aspired to this colorless little chit! A close tie to the throne or, failing that, gaining her heritage of the Ash-lands—either way, it would make him the richest noble in the land, rivaling even the King.

Because Marcala believed in knowing her employers, she was well aware that Ysa had always been prone to a certain amount of self-deception. But this—this was on an unprecedented scale! How to turn this to her own advantage? She didn't know yet, but she would find a way.

In the meantime, she must concentrate on blocking Harous's plans. They were sheer folly, and would most certainly end in Harous's death as punishment for his presumption. That she could not endure. But as long as Ashen remained unwed, she would be a target for any other noble with similar ambitions.

"I cannot do anything until Ashen goes to court and is presented to the Queen," Marcala said to herself. But then—ah, then! Ashen must be married, and promptly, to anyone who was not Harous and who did not present such a threat that he would be eliminated by a rival. But who could it be?

Someone with whom such an alliance would be considered an asset, she answered herself, pleased that she was thinking clearly once more. She had heard rumors of a few tentative attempts at a treaty with the Sea-Rovers, who had taken over the old Ashenkeep. Then the answer came to her in such a burst of clarity that she sat back, astonished.

Obern!

The more she thought about it, the more perfect the scheme became in her mind. Of course it must be Obern. He was, if not of royal blood, at least of high birth as the Sea-Rovers counted such things. And his people were already invested in the Ashenhold; it would be only fitting that they join with the one remaining heiress in order to strengthen their own claim. Further, she had seen the glances that had passed between Ashen and Obern, and knew that such a match would not be displeasing to either.

Yes, she must arrange, somehow, for the other players in this grotesque drama to decide to marry Ashen to Obern. And furthermore, she must be clever enough to make them think it was all their idea. The Queen, of course. And Royance. He could be managed easily. She had seen how Royance had looked at her.

Her lips twisted. And if it turned out that the way of the Sea-Rovers was not as refined as that of Rendel, then it was no matter. Ashen would not recognize the difference.

She arose from her chair and began walking back and forth, running her hands along her body. Once all this had been accomplished, she thought, then would be the time to remind Harous that she, Marcala, was still there, waiting and eager.

Harous had always behaved properly toward her. That would change. She resolved to show him that very night some of the delectable personal advantages of choosing her over Ashen. Once she had merely disliked the girl; now she hated her as much as she loved Harous.

Ashen was very excited when she was informed that Harous and some of the members of his establishment were going to be moving to the capital city for a while. She rushed to Marcala with the news, finding her in the solar occupied with embroidering a lady's handbag. "What should I do? What should I take with me? What are you going to take?"

"Nothing," Marcala said stiffly. "I was not invited to accompany you. I have been instructed to stay here and oversee Cragden Keep while Lord Harous is away."

"Oh," Ashen said, a little taken aback by Marcala's coldness.

"But surely—surely this is a position of great responsibility! It shows how much Harous relies upon you."

Marcala set aside her embroidery with a show of indifference. "Yes, I suppose it does. Lord Harous instructed me to help you."

"Yes, yes he did. But if it is an inconvenience—"

"No inconvenience at all. Send a servant for boxes. We must see to it that when you are seen in Rendelsham, you do us all credit."

Overdresses, underdresses, hairpins, ornaments, shoes and stockings. Rouge and perfume. There was so much to take! Ashen had never had to worry about wardrobe matters before, other than to make sure that her leg armor was intact and her lupper-skin garments without rents. Now it seemed that enough boxes could not be found to hold all the belongings she would need for what was bound to be a short stay in Harous's town residence. And yet Marcala insisted that she pack at least six overdresses and a dozen underdresses.

"Be sure to take this one," Marcala said, holding up the blue gown that had been one of Harous's first gifts to Ashen. "It is by far your finest and you will need it."

"Why?"

"There's to be a banquet—a feast—and the most important people in the Kingdom will be there. Just to meet you."

Ashen's cheeks grew warm with embarrassment. "I am nothing, and nobody. Why should anyone want to meet me?"

"I do not know." The other woman frowned, and then cleared her face. "Nevertheless, I am instructed that you be presented to them in as fine a fashion as I can devise. Be sure to take your jewels, the ones set with sapphires. Especially the necklace. I will send Ayfare with you, as your maid."

Ashen nodded. "Thank you, Lady Marcala, for all your help."

"Don't forget your table manners," the other admonished, then turned away, dismissing Ashen.

Ashen wanted to assure Marcala that there was nothing untoward about her relationship with Harous, but did not know how to go about it. She reached out one hand, but stopped herself before she could touch the other woman's forearm. She felt certain that Marcala might slap her gesture away—or worse. This woman had never been her friend, nor would she ever be. Ashen had to accept that fact. This new coldness told her that Marcala was now, inexplicably, her enemy.

A surprising number of people made up the entourage. Ashen initially rode in a carriage, surrounded by the boxes filled with her belongings, but the poor springs and jouncing ride prompted her quickly to mount a horse instead. She couldn't help thinking that here it seemed a noble's worth was rated by how many servants and retainers were necessary for only a short journey. Zazar, by contrast, had made do very well with just Kazi. To Ashen's mild surprise, she saw Obern riding toward the back, in the company of some of Count Harous's guard. But then, she thought, since we are both in the awkward position of being not quite a guest but more than a prisoner, it seems reasonable that he should come, too. She occasionally dropped back to ride with him, pleased to see that he continued to mend well.

It was a pleasant journey at a leisurely pace to the city. Ashen's troubles diminished for a while and her heart beat faster as they actually passed through the low town. She spurred her horse to catch up with Harous. They went through the city gate and past a spectacular building—one of the lesser fanes, Harous told her. Then they approached the great castle; even as they drew near it resembled an elaborate creation by a talented pastry chef.

"Who lives in the tall towers?" she asked Harous. She craned her neck so that she was almost in danger of falling off her mount.

Harous reached out one arm to steady her. "Nobody actually lives there. They once were used as watch-towers. From the highest one, you can see almost from one end of Rendel to the other."

Ashen found that easy to believe. As they rode through the city, she felt that she could never have imagined these fine buildings. Surely this must be how the ruins in the Bog had once looked when they were new and fair and proud.

"Where is your house?" she asked Harous.

"Just here."

The little entourage drew up at the doorway to an exceptionally fine structure, a small fortification in itself, located at the base of the ramp that led up to the castle. It was fitting, Ashen thought, that the one who guards the city at Cragden Keep would also guard the entrance to where the mighty ones resided. She looked at Harous with new respect.

"Later I will take you into the castle. There is the Great Fane of the Glowing within the walls, and the courtyard where stand the Four Trees."

"What trees?"

"Those that symbolize the four Great Houses of Rendel— Oak, Yew, Ash, and Rowan."

Suddenly Ashen remembered the moment when Zazar had traced the sparkling outlines of certain leaves and how she, Ashen, had correctly identified them without ever having seen them before. Could these be the same? The sources from which Zazar had drawn?

"Yes," she told Harous. "I would like to see all of that. Will we go tomorrow?"

Harous laughed. "No," he said. "But soon. I promise. First the banquet, where you will meet the nobles. Then I will show you whatever you want to see."

"When? When is this banquet?"

"Tomorrow at midday. This afternoon and evening, you must rest so that you will be at your most beautiful."

Then she fell silent, as she always did when Harous—or anyone else—commented on her appearance. Unbidden, the question came to mind as to whether she would react that way if Obern noticed how she looked. Then she pushed the thought away.

Within an hour, she was established in the guest rooms of Harous's residence, and Ayfare had put all her things to rights. It was almost as if she had lived here all her life. She thought about disobeying Harous and slipping out so that she could explore as she willed, but the Count had stationed guards at every gate. She had to satisfy her curiosity with taking the walkway atop the walls, from which she could see much, but not nearly all that she wanted to.

Soon enough, the appointed hour for the grand feast arrived. Ayfare had worked diligently over Ashen's appearance, not satisfied until every detail was just so, bathing her and washing her hair until it shone like new gold. Even Ashen, slightly weary before, had to agree that she looked nearly as impressive as her surroundings. In the image that looked back at her from the long wall mirror, she could find scarcely a trace of the Bog-blossom that Harous had netted and taken from that soaked land to the south. As a final touch, she fastened the sapphire earrings, and Ayfare clasped the necklace about her neck, where it rested at just the correct, fashionable length to set off the neckline of the blue dress. She touched her neck, wrists, and the rise of her bosom with the perfume made from the blue flowers, enjoying the scent.

Then, alone, as Harous had unaccountably commanded her, she nervously descended the stairway and entered the Hall.

Seven men already sat at a long table, Harous among them. A single small table, with chair, had been placed in front, where the occupant could see each of the seven men and be seen by them. Even before seating herself, Ashen felt like a specimen on display. She turned wary, suspicious, and almost didn't hear all the names as Harous indicated each man in turn. Edgard, deputy for Erft of the House of Rowan; Gattor of Bilth; Royance of

Grattenbor; Valk of Mimon; Jakar of Vacaster; Liffen of Lerkland—the names swam in her head, and she put them together with the faces only with difficulty.

Almost immediately, the men, with the exception of Harous, began asking her questions. Who was she? Where had she come from? How had she been reared? By whom? How had she been spared the fate of Outlanders in the Bog? Instinctively, she answered with caution, relating only enough to satisfy the questioner. Once, as she spoke in answer, she thought about Marcala's admonition to watch her table manners. There was no chance of disgracing herself or her host; as each sumptuous course came and went, Ashen found herself too busy answering the never-ending flood of questions from these rather awesome and harsh-featured men. Her appetite had vanished entirely and she only toyed with her food.

It didn't help any that she realized early that some of these stern-faced lords questioning her so relentlessly did so with more than a trace of hostility. Why? Some of her inner turmoil was now strengthened by anger—they didn't even know her, after all! However, she continued to answer very circumspectly, weighing every reply as she spoke never more than what was necessary.

Harous interrupted the relentless stream of questions with one more, kindly put. "Please tell my friends about how and under what circumstances you met the man from the sea. This man," he said, turning to the other men, "is here with me. I will send for him presently."

Relaxing a little, Ashen gladly told the full tale of her meeting with Obern—how she had seen him fall and how she had helped him. "It was a chance meeting only, my lords," she said. "I know very little of him, except that he seems a good man."

The stout man, the one with the sleepy eyes—Gattor—roused himself at this point. "What is that ornament you wear about your neck?" he asked.

"It is a gift from Count Harous," Ashen replied. "He said it was a badge of my House. Beyond that, I know not what it might represent."

Gattor laughed, looking sideways down the table at Harous. "Sly to the end, aren't you?" he said. "Well, such caution has always proved productive in the past, and so now as well." With that, he levered his thick body out of his chair, came around the table, and bowed low before Ashen. "My compliments, dear lady." Then he left, with no other word, not even to his host.

One by one, the rest of the men—all but Harous and the silver-haired one, Royance—did likewise, to Ashen's complete and utter bewilderment; they seemed suddenly to have lost all interest in her and in the matters they had been so eager to learn of.

When they had taken their leave, Harous turned to Royance. "I think it is time to bring Obern to you, my lord," he said. He signaled one of the guards, and presently Obern came into the Hall. "Have you eaten?" Harous asked courteously.

"Yes, I have. With your men." One eyebrow raised, Obern looked over the remains of the feast—a goose roasted in its feathers, a small boar basted with honey-sauce as it cooked, various pastries and pies.

"Nevertheless, fill a platter and join us while you tell us your tale. As I recall, you made petition to me, but there was no time then, a circumstance for which I apologize. Now there is time."

"I had thought to ask only that I be allowed to go out on patrol with your men," Obern said. He cut off a generous portion of boar meat and began eating with every indication of a good appetite, if a bit awkwardly because of the sling he still wore.

"Your arm is not yet fully mended," Harous said. "You could neither ride hard nor fight."

"That will change in just a few days. Now I see that there are weightier matters occupying high-placed men, and that I may hold some part in the outcome, though I do not know what it might be."

"My men tell me that you claim to be a kind of Prince among your people," Royance said.

Harous looked at the older man in some surprise. "You have a good spy system," he said.

"To survive as long as I have, it is a necessity." He nodded at Obern. "Is this true? Are you a Prince?"

"My father is the High Chieftain of the Sea-Rovers who now live in New Vold—a place that once was called Ashenhold, so we were informed—and the keep that was deserted. I do not know if that makes me a Prince. I have always been little more than my father's backshield."

"But a person of some little consequence nonetheless," Royance said. "Thank you, Obern. Please consider yourself an honored guest not only of Count Harous, but of myself as well. My favor is not something to be taken lightly."

"And so I thank you."

There was a silence, and Obern, realizing that his part in this day's mysterious events was finished, rose from his place. He nodded, and then left the way he had come.

The two men remaining at the table sat without speaking. Royance called for another flagon of wine and sipped at it thoughtfully while he toyed with a small bunch of grapes and a slab of new cheese.

Abruptly, he set all before him aside. "I agree, Lord Harous—now that I have seen her and talked with her. You brought her here to show us all what and who she is. You saw it first, and now all the Council knows as well. Even if the summons had not come, we must go to the palace," he said. He rose in turn and held out his hand to Ashen. "Come with me, my child. There is someone that you need to meet, before it is too late."

❦

King Boroth's bedchamber was even more crowded with courtiers and hangers-on than ever. Ysa had had a small chair placed on the dais where the King's bed was located, and she sat close by, gazing at her dying husband.

For it was clear, even to the most optimistic, that the King's

Andre Norton & Sasha Miller

last moments were fast approaching. With a tinge of annoyance, Ysa noted that the Council members were not present. And then five of them came in together. But *where* was Royance? And Harous? Had Royance's loyalty turned? Without him— She refused to think of that possibility. He must be true, and only something of the utmost importance would have delayed him from Boroth's bedside at this most crucial moment. And Florian—

The thought was parent to the deed. Florian came parading in, flanked by his favorites and frivols, their demeanor anything but apt for their presence in the bedchamber of a dying man. The Prince took hold of Master Lorgan's sleeve. "How much longer will the King live?" he asked. There was a note of impatience in the Prince's tone that angered Ysa. She turned on her son.

"Hold your tongue," she said in a tone that was like a serpent striking. "Surely you can wait long enough for him to breathe his last before you climb onto a throne that is far too big for you."

The Prince opened his mouth to speak, but another small group of people entering the death chamber interrupted whatever he was going to say. He goggled at them, silent for once.

It was Royance, followed by Harous and a stranger, a girl. Royance rapped with his staff on the floor for attention. "Let all know," he said in a voice that filled the room, "that as long as our gracious Queen wears the four Rings, the ancient power that I have sworn to uphold is in force! All that I do is for her." Then he bowed to her and moved to one side.

The noise of the staff against the floor must have roused the dying King, for he suddenly sat straight up in bed, staring at the young woman now revealed. Tears filled his eyes and began running down his cheeks. Trembling, he stretched out his hands.

Ysa reach for him, gathering his hands in hers, and began to recite the litany of the Rings. But the King paid no attention. He wrested his hands away to hold out his arms as if in greeting. In a shaken voice, yet loud enough for all to hear, he addressed the girl standing with Harous and Royance.

"Daughter!" he said. And then repeated it. "Daughter. Welcome, my daughter."

"There is no daughter," Ysa said fiercely. She held up her hands. "By the power of the Rings, I swear it!" Then, to her horror, her hands trembled and fell; the Rings had suddenly become too weighty for her to bear. If what she suspected—but dare not let herself admit—was true, there was no time to lose. What the court did not witness could be denied. "Royance, clear the room. What follows must be private." She turned to try to hush the King, who still strove to speak past the gurgling death-rattle in his throat.

"Let me be!" he said more firmly than he had spoken for days. "Blood calls to blood, and there stands blood of mine—a daughter." With enormous tenderness and sweetness, he smiled at the girl.

A waft of her perfume drifted toward Ysa. She recognized it at once. The King turned his head, addressing a presence no one else in the room could see. "I understand now, Alditha, my own beloved. My daughter—" He gave a great sigh, his eyelids drooped, and he fell back against his pillows with a finality that only death could bring.

Ysa stared at him aghast, and then turned to look at the girl whom Boroth had identified as being of his blood. The crowd of courtiers had stepped back, leaving Ashen standing alone in a pool of light, her hands clasped in front of her, looking appalled at what had just transpired, and more than a little repelled by the ruined hulk who had just claimed her as daughter. She wore the Ash color—blue—such as had not been seen at court for sixteen years. No wonder Ysa had not known her for who she was; this one was of no Bog mixed-breeding, such as the ill-formed creature she had pictured in her mind! Around her neck was a necklace bearing the badge of the House of Ash, a badge that Ysa had thought never to see again. "Who—" was all that the Queen could manage to say.

"I am Ashen," the woman—actually, little more than a girl—replied, her voice shaking.

And the daughter of Alditha and Boroth was recognized at last by the Queen as she stared into the face that joined the features of her bitterest rival with those of her husband, who lay dead between them.

There was a movement among the hangers-on in the chamber, the merest hint of factions forming as she watched. Florian's lickspittles stayed close by him, naturally, but others wavered, about to make a half-step that would indicate their willingness to accept even a bastard daughter over the Prince.

As the scales finally fell from her eyes, Ysa began thinking clearly and rapidly. With Royance's cryptic words, he had given Ysa a choice, knowing how heartily she detested the Prince. Both she and Florian had enemies who would gladly begin pushing for Ashen's succession, just to rid themselves of the Queen and her son, using Ashen's double strain of royal blood as an excuse. They wouldn't care that Ashen could have no idea of how to rule the country. No, that would suit them very well, because in such a case, they would be able to seize the power that was always set loose when a dynasty fell—except for that still held by Ysa and the might of the Council, for whom this bastard offspring would be merely a figurehead. Ysa would, of course, continue as the real power behind the throne. It was a tempting possibility.

At one time, she herself had actually considered removing Florian as unfit. But to step aside for the child of her rival, and have Yew blood taken out of the succession entirely? *No!* She was the wife, now widow, of a King, and as poor timber for the position as Florian undoubtedly was, she would see to it that her son had the throne.

Without hesitation, she ended all by turning to Florian, dumbstruck for once in his life. She held out both hands so that the Rings were plain for all to see. "The King is dead," she proclaimed, her voice wavering despite her best efforts. "Long live the King!"